# SNOW ANGELS

This Large Print Book carries the
Seal of Approval of N.A.V.H.

# FERN MICHAELS

# SNOW ANGELS

# MARIE BOSTWICK, JANNA McMAHAN, AND ROSALIND NOONAN

**WHEELER PUBLISHING**

*A part of Gale, Cengage Learning*

GALE
CENGAGE Learning

Detroit • New York • San Francisco • New Haven, Conn • Waterville, Maine • London

∴ **GALE**

⁎ CENGAGE Learning˙

4/2011
3677 94 83

**LIBRARY OF CONGRESS CATALOGING-IN-PUBLICATION DATA**

Snow angels / by Fern Michaels, Marie Bostwick, Janna McMahan, Rosalind
Noonan.
    p. cm.
    ISBN-13: 978-1-4104-2022-0 (hardcover : alk. paper)
    ISBN-10: 1-4104-2022-1 (hardcover : alk. paper) 1. Christmas
stories, American. 2. Large type books. I. Michaels, Fern. Snow
angels. II. Bostwick, Marie. Presents of angels. III. McMahan,
Janna. Decorations. IV. Noonan, Rosalind. Miracle on main
street.
PS648.C45S59 2009
813'.0108334—dc22                                    2009029877

Published in 2009 by arrangement with Zebra Books, an imprint of
Kensington Publishing Corp.

Printed in the United States of America
1 2 3 4 5 6 7 13 12 11 10 09

# CONTENTS

**SNOW ANGELS** . . . . . . . . . . 7
*Fern Michaels*

**THE PRESENTS OF ANGELS** . . . . 139
*Marie Bostwick*

**DECORATIONS** . . . . . . . . . 319
*Janna McMahan*

**MIRACLE ON MAIN STREET** . . . . 467
*Rosalind Noonan*

■ ■ ■ ■

# SNOW ANGELS

# FERN MICHAELS

■ ■ ■ ■

# CHAPTER 1

*Friday, December 19, 2008*
*Eagle, Colorado*
*Interstate 70*

Grace Landry glanced in her rearview mirror to check on Ashley and Amanda, her two "dates" for the evening. She'd been delighted when their mother, Stephanie, had allowed her to take the girls to see their first live performance of *The Nutcracker* at Eagle Valley High School. Both girls were sound asleep in the backseat of her van.

They'd needed some fun and normalcy in their sad and empty lives, especially during the Christmas season. Grace's eyes teared up as she summoned the images of their frightened little faces when the local police delivered them and their mother to Hope House on Monday, four days earlier.

As a practicing psychologist, Grace had witnessed her share of abused women since receiving her doctorate nine years ago. Only five years ago, when her grandmother had left her a sizable estate, she'd started Hope House, a shelter for battered women and their children, and unveiled it to the proper authorities in Denver and the surrounding areas. It had been her hope that they would recommend her safe house to those women in need as a place to recuperate and plan for the future, and more than anything else, a place where they could feel safe. Gypsum was a small town off the beaten path, the perfect location for such a place. She'd been successful and never had any reason to question her decision. Her mother worried because Hope House was in such a remote area, but Grace assured her that was exactly what she'd been looking for when she'd bought the house and the surrounding land.

A light snow began to fall. Grace turned on the wipers, making a mental note to have chains put on her tires. With many treacherous stretches along Colorado's I-70, authorities forbade semis to pass without them. Every winter she had her mechanic install them even though they weren't required for the van. She'd rather be safe than sorry.

In the distance ahead, she noted red-and-blue flashing lights. Praying there wasn't an accident, Grace turned on the radio, locating a traffic report on one of her prepro-grammed stations. The broadcaster noted the light snow, but that was nothing unusual for this stretch of highway. Probably a broken-down motorist.

What little traffic there was slowed to a crawl as she drove toward the glaring lights. After a few minutes of creeping along, traffic came to a standstill. Grace glanced at the digital clock on her dashboard. After ten. She'd promised Stephanie she would have the girls back by eleven. At this rate, she'd be lucky to make it before midnight.

When Grace saw police officers knocking on the windows of the vehicles ahead of her, she assumed this was a random license check. Reaching across the seat for her wallet, she removed her license, awaiting her turn to prove she was a legally licensed driver.

The expected tap, and Grace pushed the button to lower the window. A gust of icy air along with wet snowflakes smacked the side of her face. Before the officer asked, she handed him her license.

"Thanks, ma'am, but this isn't a license check. We've established several roadblocks in the area. We're detouring traffic."

"Oh," Grace said, surprised by his words. A roadblock this time of night seemed odd to her. Rather than question the young officer, she listened to him as he pointed ahead.

"I hope there isn't some crazy out terrorizing the roads," she commented.

"No need to worry. We're taking care of it. If you'll take the next exit, 147 to Eby Creek Road, another officer will reroute you around the blockades. We're trying to close this area of I-70 as quickly as possible."

"Of course, officer." Grace rolled up the window and followed the taillights of the line of slow-moving vehicles in front of her. Glancing at the backseat, she smiled when she saw that Amanda and Ashley were still sleeping. Most children were very resilient. She could only hope these two were also.

Grace closely followed the other vehicles, making it look as if the slow-moving traffic were a train. The snowfall started coming down even more heavily than it had been. She adjusted the defroster to high to clear the fog on the windshield. Traveling downhill, she applied slight pressure to the brakes as she made her way off the exit ramp, stopping when she saw a group of police cars with their lights blazing.

For the second time in what was becoming a frigid night, Grace rolled down her window as another policeman approached the van. Though she was well acquainted

12

with many of Eagle's finest, Grace hadn't recognized the last officer; nor did she recognize this one.

"Where are you heading?" he asked. "We're trying to reroute everyone without creating bedlam." He smiled, but Grace saw that it was just for her benefit because it never reached his eyes. His eyes were watchful, alarmed. Grace knew the look quite well. She'd seen it hundreds of times in her line of work.

"To Gypsum," she said.

"Follow this road for the next seven miles or so. From there you'll turn left on the road leading back to I-70, then that should put you on Trail Gulch Road. The railroad track runs parallel to Trail Gulch if you're not familiar with the area."

After telling the officer she was somewhat familiar with the area, Grace repeated the correct directions before he motioned for her to move on. When she saw there were no other vehicles heading in the same direction, she felt a bit creepy being alone on such a remote stretch of highway. Hope House *was* out of the way, she reminded herself, which explained why most of the other vehicles were traveling in the opposite direction.

Amanda muttered in her sleep, and Grace

13

checked her rearview mirror again. It wouldn't be a good time for the girls to wake up. Stephanie had told her about their intense fear of the dark. Without streetlights and the usual signs advertising Big Macs and Holiday Inn Express's free breakfast, the two-lane road was totally dark, except for her headlights, which plunged forward into the night like two eerie cat eyes.

After ten minutes of slow driving, Grace checked her mileage. She'd only traveled three miles. Careful to monitor the odometer so as not to miss the upcoming left turn, she reduced her speed to fifteen miles per hour. When the van slid off the road onto the shoulder, Grace turned the wheel to the left, quickly guiding the vehicle back onto the slippery pavement. Her heart fluttered against her rib cage, and her hands were damp as she clutched the steering wheel while continuing to look for the turnoff. She checked her mileage again, surprised when she saw she'd already gone five miles. Taking a deep breath, Grace tried to focus on the road, but with the snow falling faster and heavier, it was becoming almost impossible to see more than a few feet in front of her.

Hoping to soothe her nerves, she adjusted the radio to a station playing cheerful

14

Christmas music. Grace sang along with the familiar tunes, but stopped suddenly, fearing her off-key singing might wake the girls.

Realizing she must have missed the turnoff after she'd traveled another five miles, she stopped in the center of the road, telling herself it didn't matter since she seemed to be the only one crazy enough to get lost on a back road when the weather was getting worse by the minute. Recalling the directions the police officer had given her, Grace did a three-point turn, checked her mileage, then slowly drove back in the direction she'd just come from.

Glancing from side to side as she retraced the miles and careful to watch the odometer, she still didn't see any sign of a road where she could've made a turn, left or right. Continuing to clutch the wheel and occasionally glancing back at the sleeping children, Grace kept the routine up for another fifteen minutes before concluding that there was no turnoff. The police officer must have given her the wrong directions.

Wishing she'd upgraded to a van equipped with a GPS, she remembered that her cell phone had a less sophisticated version of one. She removed it from the side pocket on her purse. Instead of the welcoming green light that usually glowed, the small screen was as black as the night in which she was desperately trying to get home in. She tried to turn the cell off and on again. Nothing happened.

Her cell-phone battery was dead.

Wasn't that one of the first rules she drummed into the women living at Hope House when she distributed the preprogrammed cell phones? *Never* allow your cell-phone battery to die because you never knew when you'd need to dial those three lifesaving numbers: nine-one-one.

But there she was, out in the middle of the night, with two little girls in her care, and no way to contact Hope House.

Deciding that the officer must have miscalculated the miles, Grace proceeded to drive down the two-lane highway, searching for an all-night gas station, anyplace where she could find a phone to call Stephanie to assure her the girls were fine. They'd been through so much, and Grace felt she was putting their safety at risk again.

After driving for what seemed like forever, it was after midnight when she pulled the van off to the side of the road. Fearing what she had to do, yet knowing it must be done, Grace leaned over the front seat and gently shook Amanda and Ashley until they were awake.

"Miss Grace," came the sleepy voice of eight-year-old Ashley. "Where's Mommy?"

Five-year-old Amanda perked up when she heard Ashley asking for their mother. "Is Mommy okay?" Grace heard the fear in their soft little voices.

"Mommy is just fine. She's at Hope House, remember?" Grace knew she was stalling while trying to come up with a plan that would have no adverse effect on the girls.

Both wide-awake, they nodded.

"But we're supposed to be home by now, aren't we?" Ashley asked.

"Yes, sweetie, we are. I seem to have made a wrong turn, and I'm lost. I'm sorry, I don't want to alarm either of you. I just need to make a call to your mother to let her know we're safe, okay?"

Her words seemed to reassure both girls. Grace removed her jacket from the seat next to her. Slipping one arm at a time into the sleeves, she was glad she'd chosen the heavy parka since she was about to venture out into Colorado's ever-dropping frigid temperatures.

"So why aren't you calling?" Amanda asked with a trace of anxiety in her high-pitched voice.

Grace admitted to herself she was not the

17

image of dependability and trustworthiness she'd presented to the girls when she'd convinced them a night away from their mother would be fun. In fact, she was just the opposite.

Reluctantly, Grace said, "I'm afraid my cell phone isn't working."

Over the top of the seat, two pairs of big brown eyes stared at her. Waiting.

"You can't leave us here by ourselves, Miss Grace! Mommy says we're never to be alone. Right, 'Manda?"

The younger girl nodded. "Yeah, Mommy says so."

Saddened at the look of distrust on their small faces, Grace leaned over the seat and brushed her hands over both the girls' heads. "Oh, girls, I would never leave you alone! What I meant to say is you'll both have to come with me. We can pretend it's a . . . treasure hunt. Whoever finds a phone first gets to pick out and decorate the Christmas tree any way she wants to. Deal?" Grace asked as she saw smiles light up their eyes.

"Deal," they said in unison.

"Then let's get your mittens, coats, and hats on. It's much colder now than it was earlier."

Grace bundled the girls up, grabbed a

bottle of water and a flashlight from the glove compartment and tucked them inside her coat pocket, then draped her purse over her shoulder so she could take both girls by the hand. It wouldn't do for her to lose contact with them. The snow was so thick, Grace could barely make out the van as they stepped away from its familiar safety.

Gazing up at the sky, Grace tried to determine which direction to head, but unlike the movies, there were no stars to guide her, nothing. She was on her own.

Deciding to walk uphill in the direction she'd been driving, she clasped both girls' mitten-clad hands in her own as they trudged through the deepening snow. Every few minutes they would stop to catch their breath. The high elevation and the effort it took to walk uphill would strain even some of the world's best athletes.

When they'd walked uphill for more than an hour, Ashley yanked her hand away from Grace and pointed to a light up ahead. "Miss Grace, look. *Look!*"

Grace's heart did a somersault. Thank God! At the top of the mountain she saw windows aglow with lights. She grabbed Ashley's hand. "I believe Miss Ashley gets to choose the tree. Come on, girls, let's hurry before —" She started to say before our luck runs out, but given the girls' past, thought better of it, and said "— they go to bed," instead.

As they trudged through the snow, their shallow breathing created swirls of fog in the cool night air. Grace wasn't sure how much longer the girls could stand the bitter cold and wind. Off to the left, Grace spied a road sign telling her they were approaching Blow Out Hill. *Great,* she thought as she pulled the girls along. She'd had a blowout all right. She'd blown the entire evening. Stephanie and the girls would never trust her again.

Heart pounding with every step, Grace rehearsed what she would say to Stephanie. She had to be out of her mind with worry by now. It was almost two in the morning. Angry at herself for her stupidity, she calmed down enough to knock loudly on the door of the biggest log home she'd ever laid eyes on.

# CHAPTER 2

Max Jorgenson jerked awake from a sound sleep when Cliff and Ice-D, his two Siberian Huskies, placed four heavy paws on his chest as he lay sprawled out on the leather sofa. When the pair saw that his eyes were open, they started barking and running around in circles.

Glancing around the great room, Max raked a hand through his hair. He'd fallen asleep again, with the lights on and the television blaring. Correcting himself, he mentally changed the words "fallen asleep" to "passed out." Who cared? He sure as hell didn't. Cliff nudged his hand with his furry nose as Max heard a soft pounding at the front door.

"What the heck?" he said as he rambled toward the front of what he referred to as his giant cabin. If there was an emergency at the resort, the management knew not to come to his retreat, knew there would be extreme consequences. He'd have someone's ass in a sling for this unwanted intrusion first thing in the morning. He peeked at the clock above the fireplace. It *was* morning already.

The muffled pounding continued. "Eddie, if that's you, you're fired!" Max yanked the heavy log door aside expecting to see Eddie, his manager at Maximum Glide, the exclusive ski resort he owned in Telluride.

What he saw left him speechless.

Taking several seconds to recover from his surprise, as was his habit when flustered, he raked both hands through his unruly brownish blond hair. "You must have the wrong house." These were the only words he could come up with as two little girls bundled in Pepto-Bismol pink jackets and matching hats and both with huge chocolate-drop eyes and their mother, their *gorgeous, green-eyed* mother, stared at him.

"We need to use your phone," Grace stated in a firm voice, then stepped to the side as both Cliff and Ice-D bumped her free hand with their muzzles.

"Yeah, 'cause our daddy —"

"Not now, Ashley," Grace interrupted.

Realizing the trio must be freezing, Max stepped aside. "Down, guys," he said to the dogs, then to his unexpected guests, "Come inside, you're letting in the cold air."

The woman took both girls by the hand and led them inside. Their faces were just a shade shy of burgundy when they stood in the bright light.

"How long have you been out in this . . . weather?" He wanted to curse but stopped himself when he glanced down at the two girls.

"There are several roadblocks in Eagle along I-70. We were directed this way, and somehow I missed the turnoff." Grace touched her purse strapped around her neck like a bayonet. "My cell-phone battery died."

"I bet your car broke down, or you ran out of gas, too," Max accused Grace.

Inching her chin up a notch, just enough not to appear too haughty, Grace answered in a firm voice, "Neither."

With a trace of sarcasm Max asked, "So you decided to take your kids out for a midnight stroll during a snowstorm?"

He could see by her expression that he'd made her angry. He hadn't meant the comment to come off as offensive, and didn't care, but really, what kind of mother dragged her children out on a night like this?

"Actually, when I couldn't find the turnoff . . . I just need to use your phone, then

23

we'll be on our way," Grace explained. "As soon as —"

He gestured with his hands, preventing further conversation. In an impatient tone, Max said, "Follow me."

"Miss Grace, can we pet the dogs?" Amanda asked when the pair of Huskies blocked their path.

Grace looked at the dogs, then their owner. She'd always been fond of animals but knew some were skittish around strangers. That didn't seem to be a problem in this case, but one never knew. She'd already put the girls at risk once tonight.

"Go ahead," Max replied to Amanda. "They're harmless."

Both girls looked to Grace for permission. "If Mr. —" She stopped, realizing she didn't know his name. "Yes, you both may pet the dogs while I make the phone call."

"Name's Max Jorgenson," he offered.

Grace looked at him oddly, then held out a slim hand. "Grace Landry." He reminded her of someone, but she couldn't place who.

Their host, if you could even call him that, was beyond handsome. With golden brown hair that hung way below his collar and robin's-egg blue eyes rimmed with long black lashes most women would die for, "sexy" didn't begin to describe him. Then

24

there was the body. Grace couldn't help but admire the broad shoulders that tapered down to a slim waist. She'd also noticed that his faded Levis clung to his rear end like a glove.

Max reached for her hand, then stopped. He'd promised himself after Kayla's death he wouldn't touch another woman. At the moment, that promise seemed irrational and stupid. He was thirty-six years old. Did he really think he could live the rest of his life without touching another woman? Without companionship? Without love? Without *sex?* It was just under two years since Kayla had died. He hadn't given women much thought before tonight. And then this . . . snow angel appeared on his doorstep. Literally.

"The phone's in the kitchen. This way," Max said gruffly.

Without bothering to see if his guest followed, Max proceeded to the kitchen. He viewed his home as they made their way to the kitchen. Thick round pine logs made up most of the walls throughout the custom-built home. In the daytime, sunlight filtered through large floor-to-ceiling windows facing the mountains, revealing blue skies, puffy white clouds, and snowcapped mountains. The designer he'd hired to decorate used deep shades of forest green, with bright splashes of candy-apple red. With the custom-made pine cabinets, splashes of red and green in framed pictures of bright red apples, and pottery in matching shades of red and green from local craftsmen, the desired effect of hominess and cheer would have been complete had there been any personal touches added. Like a shopping list stuck to the bright red refrigerator with a magnet or a tea towel draped over the sink. Maybe a few unwashed dishes in the sink. Instead, the kitchen looked like it had the day he'd moved in, something right off the pages of one of those catalogues he'd seen advertising log homes. Max couldn't remember ever making a real meal in the kitchen.

"Phone's over there," he said, pointing to an area in the kitchen comprised of a small counter, where a laptop sat upon the black marble, its screen as blank and impersonal as the rest of the space. A cordless phone was sitting next to the computer.

"Thank you," Grace said. She stared at him, willing him to step out of the kitchen and allowing her a modicum of privacy, but he didn't budge. Taking a deep breath, she quickly punched in the private number to Hope House. When nothing happened, she dialed the number again, this time hearing the requisite *beep beep beep* as she hit each number. Lifting the phone to her ear, expecting to hear a ring, instead she heard nothing. She tried the number a third time. Still nothing.

"The phone lines go down when there's snow," Max offered.

*No kidding,* she wanted to say but refrained.

"Do you have a cell phone I could use? I really need to make this call. The girls" — Grace nodded toward Ashley and Amanda, who were busy petting the dogs — "they need to . . . I just need to make a call, then we'll be on our way." She was about to explain that the girls' mother needed to know they were alive and *safe* but thought better of it.

Leaning casually against the pine-log wall, Max said, "Nope, never bothered with one. Sorry."

Grace tried the number again, but there was still no dial tone. Realizing it was fruitless to continue trying to make a call on a phone that didn't work, Grace placed it back on the base unit.

Not knowing what else to say, she hurried past the man with the familiar face to the girls, who were still playing with the lovable Huskies. She rubbed her hands together, trying to warm them. She dreaded what she was about to do, but there wasn't much choice.

"Girls, tell Mr. Jorgenson thank you for his hospitality. We have to leave. Now," she stated firmly, hoping the girls wouldn't question her.

"And just where in the hell do you think you're going?" Max asked.

Galled that he had the audacity to question her, Grace turned around to face him. "Really, Mr. Jorgenson, it's none of your business. Thank you for the use of your phone."

Turning back to the girls, Grace spoke gently to them. "Amanda, Ashley. It's time to go."

"But —"

"No buts, girls. It's time to go."

Grace took each girl by the hand. "Put your mittens on. It's still very cold out."

Thundering footsteps came from behind. "Listen, lady, I don't know what your problem is, but you can't take these kids out now! The snow is getting heavier by the minute." He pointed to the floor-to-ceiling windows that faced the mountains.

Grace realized he was right, but what other choice did she have? "We're going back to the van. I'm sure a patrol officer will find us." She realized she should be staying put. Taking the girls back out into freezing temperatures was stupid, but once they got back to the van, she'd crank up the heat. There was plenty of gas. And who knew? Maybe a patrol officer would find them. It wasn't the greatest plan, but it was all she could come up with given the circumstances.

In complete frustration, Max combed his hands through his messy hair. "Why don't you spend the night here? I've plenty of room. In the morning, I'll drive you back to your van myself."

"Please, please, Miss Grace? Let's spend the night here. We can play with the dogs. *Puhleeze?*" Amanda asked.

It would be the smartest choice. Really, it was their *only* choice. She couldn't take the girls out again in this weather. For the girls' sake, she swallowed her pride, making a snap decision. "Thank you, Mr. Jorgenson. We accept — but just for the night."

Grace turned to him. He seemed surprised she'd agreed to his offer. "That's all I'm offering."

She wanted to tell him to forget it, but there was more at stake than her pride. She had two small children to consider. "If you'll show me our room, I'll take it from there,"

Grace insisted, knowing that the invitation had cost him. Though how much, she didn't realize.

"What about some food?" He stared at the girls. "Maybe something hot to drink?" He shot Grace a questioning look.

Maybe he had a trace of manners after all. Grace turned to him. "I think we're okay, but thanks for the offer."

"I'm hungry!" Ashley said. "And thirsty. And I need to use the bathroom."

"Me too," seconded Amanda. "Really, *really* hungry!"

Grace raised a sculpted brow. "I guess I spoke too soon."

Max didn't know where this sudden urge to be hospitable came from, but when he saw the excitement on the little girls' faces, something inside him melted. What kind of man would allow a woman and her two kids to venture out into the wee hours of the morning knowing it was below freezing outside?

*Him,* he realized. Had it not been dark and cold, that's exactly what he would've done. What he really wanted to do was snatch the invitation back, find another bottle of whiskey, and go back to sleep.

Seeing the expectant looks on the little girls' faces, he blocked any further thoughts about what he should have done. This was the right thing to do. It's what Kayla would have done had she been alive.

"Bathroom's that way." He pointed to a door beneath the staircase leading upstairs.

"Thanks." Grace continued her grip on the girls, leading them to the bathroom. Once inside, she helped them remove their coats and mittens. When each had had her turn using the toilet, both girls washed their hands, loving the feel of the warm water.

"I want to take a bath, Miss Grace. I'm as cold as a frog," Amanda announced.

Grace laughed. "Just how cold is a frog?" she asked the little girl.

"Real cold. Like a Popsicle."

Ashley looked at her little sister. "Mommy would tell you to mind your manners right about now."

"She would?"

"Yeah," Ashley said. "Miss Grace, you didn't talk to our mom, did you?"

Fearing Ashley would ask this but knowing there was no way around it, she simply told her the truth.

"And first thing in the morning, Mr. Jorgenson will take us to the van," Grace finished explaining.

"I bet Mommy is scared 'cause she always wants to know exactly where we're at,"

Amanda said.

Grace felt as though she'd been punched in the gut with an extra large fist. "I know she's worried, but right now there isn't any way to let her know we're okay, so let's just concentrate on getting through the night." She sounded lame even to herself.

Both girls watched her with fear in their eyes. "What if Daddy . . ."

"He doesn't know we're here. I think it might be a good idea if we didn't talk about your daddy for the rest of the night. Are you girls okay with that?" Grace didn't want their host asking any more questions than necessary.

Both girls nodded.

"Then let's see if Mr. Jorgenson has something to drink, then we'll rest," Grace said.

With both girls following at her heels, she relaxed. They were safe for the moment and accepted her decision without question.

If she could only remember where she'd seen Mr. Jorgenson before, then maybe *she* would feel safe.

# CHAPTER 3

With the girls trailing behind her, Grace returned to the kitchen, surprised to find their host pouring boiling hot water into four red mugs. "I only have the instant stuff," he pointed out, indicating packages of instant cocoa mix next to the cups. "Milk spoils too fast."

"Thank you, Mr. Jorgenson. I appreciate your hospitality," Grace said. She opened four packs of the instant hot chocolate and added the contents to the cups of hot water. "This is just what the girls need, something to warm them up." Grace stirred the hot drinks, then called the girls to the kitchen. "Sit at the table, okay?" she suggested to the two.

"Can we give the dogs some?" Amanda asked Grace, as Ashley helped her climb onto the chair.

"Never *ever* give chocolate to dogs! Are you crazy?" Max shouted from his position in front of the sink.

Instantaneously, both girls began to cry, their little faces masks of fear and horror. Grace hurried over to them. "Shhh, it's okay. Mr. Jorgenson didn't mean to yell" — Grace shot him a death look — "did you?" Her green eyes flared like sparkling emeralds.

"Uh, no. I didn't. It's just that anyone knows not to give chocolate to a dog."

"Not everyone, Mr. Jorgenson. Especially a five- and an eight-year old." If not for the worsening weather, Grace would've left the house immediately. The last thing the girls needed was an angry man yelling at them. That was what had brought them and their mother to Hope House in the first place. Of course, there were also the beatings, but Grace truly didn't believe their host would resort to that behavior.

Grudgingly, he said, "I'm sorry, okay?"

"I'm sure you are," Grace said to him, then to the girls, "Finish your drinks."

She wanted to shout at him, tell him exactly what these two innocent children had been through in their short lives, but it wasn't his business, and she never discussed her guests' private affairs with strangers, or anyone else who wasn't a member of her inner circle.

Grace used her sleeve to dry their tears. "It's okay. Really. Let's go to our room, and I'll tell you a Christmas story." Again she eyed their host with a look that she hoped shamed him.

"What about the tree? Can I still pick out the decorations?" Ashley asked, all traces of fear gone from her big brown eyes.

"Of course. Now come on, let's get some sleep. Before you know it, morning will be here, and I want you both to get some rest. You'll need lots of energy, so you can decorate the tree."

The idea seemed to excite both girls, and for that Grace was extremely grateful. Max Jorgenson hadn't shown them where to sleep, so she took the initiative. "If you'll tell me where to find a room?"

Raking his hands through hair that Grace thought a bit on the long side, he nodded. "This way."

Taking their hands in her own, Grace followed Max up the stairs, looking at everything and anything while trying to avoid Max's rear view, plastered mere inches from her face.

A loft overlooked the downstairs. Shelves were lined with trophies, and covers of magazines were expertly framed and hung on the pine walls. In a built-in area that had special lights shining on its contents was an Olympic Gold Medal. It was then that Grace knew why she recognized Max.

"You're the skier," she stated to his back.

"Yep. That would be me," Max answered with more sarcasm than she thought necessary.

He stopped at the end of the hall to open a door and turn on the lights. "A king-size bed. That should hold the three of you. There's the bathroom." He pointed to a door at the end of the huge room. Grace canvassed the large bedroom in one sweeping glance. What she saw took her breath away.

The room was the size of the entire downstairs at Hope House. Pine furniture that matched the logs throughout the house appeared to be custom-made since each piece occupied its designated location with absolute precision. Pictures of winter scenes hung on the rounded log walls. Briefly, Grace wondered how that was possible, but the physics of picture-hanging was the least of her concerns. On the large bed in the center of the room, a navy blue, maroon, and cream-colored quilt invited her to hunker down beneath its comfort for warmth. The bath was as large and extravagant as the rest of the house. A deep tub that would hold at least six people, windows that looked out into the blue-black snowy night. Grace could only imagine the view in the daylight. Navy and cream towels hung on warming rods. No expense had been spared when the house was constructed, of that she was sure.

Not wanting to appear impressed, Grace simply said, "This is very nice. Thank you."

Ushering the girls over to the bed, she was about to help them remove their dresses when Max spoke.

"I have some flannel shirts they can wear. They're warm." Without another word, he left, returning minutes later with three red, green, and white plaid flannel shirts. The colors of Christmas. Grace was sure it wasn't intentional as there were no decorations of any kind, or anything that she'd seen to indicate that her host celebrated the holiday season. To each his own. Personally, she couldn't imagine *not* decorating.

However, touched by his suggestion, she was too startled to offer any objection. "That's very kind of you, Mr. Jorgenson."

"Max. Mr. Jorgenson was my father," he said from his position at the doorway.

Surprised once again, Grace glanced at him, then recalled his earlier hostility and wondered what had caused the sudden

37

change of heart. Probably realized he was stuck with them for the remainder of the night and was just trying to make the best of a bad situation. The man was like a faucet. Hot one minute and cold the next.

Staring at him, Grace spoke in low tones, hoping he'd take the bait. She needed some quiet time for her and the girls. They'd had enough excitement for one night. "Okay, then, Max it is."

He lingered in the doorway. Grace wanted him to leave, but something told her he had more to say before calling it a night. She continued to stare at him, while the girls each took a flannel shirt from her. "You can change in the bathroom," Grace said to the expectant girls.

"Why do they call you Miss Grace?"

Ah-ha! She wondered when he'd ask. "For some reason they took to calling me that, and it stuck. Myself, I think it's just a matter of respect. They're good girls."

Max wrapped one jeans-clad leg in front of the other, hands crossing his massive chest. "Why Miss Grace? Is there something wrong with being called 'Mother'?"

Grace smiled, knowing where he was leading and determined to take him there via the long route.

"No, I don't think there is anything wrong

with it at all. I couldn't imagine calling my own mother anything else."

He took two long strides, and suddenly he was in the room. Two feet in front of her. "Yet you won't allow your own children to address you as such?"

Grace took a deep breath, then offered a slight smile of defiance. "They're not my children." There, now he knew.

"I get it. They're your husband's," Max asked, a hint of annoyance overshadowing his handsome features.

Enjoying the verbal duel, Grace said, "I'm not married."

Max shook his head. "Look, lady, I'm tired. Either tell me what I want to know, or first thing in the morning, I'll have no choice but to contact the authorities. A lone woman out on a night like this. Two kids who don't belong to her. You tell me, what would you think if the situation were reversed?"

Grace realized he was right. She'd enjoyed toying with him for some odd reason, but to do so at the girls' expense was totally out of character for her. This man had allowed three complete strangers into his home. No matter how rude or inquisitive, it was wrong to let him think she was anyone other than herself.

Giving her a brutal, and very unfriendly stare, he raised his winged brow in question. "So?"

"I'm sorry. I shouldn't have led you to believe the girls belonged to me. They came to me, rather their mother came to me, for help. I gave them a place to stay. Tonight, I took the girls to see *The Nutcracker* at Eagle Valley High. I thought it would give them a chance to enjoy the Christmas season and offer their mom a much-needed respite. And then I encountered the roadblock on my way home. You know the rest of the story." Satisfied with her answer since she hadn't betrayed Stephanie's confidence, Grace waited for Max to say something. Anything. When several seconds passed, and he still hadn't spoken, she did.

"You look at me as though I've . . . committed a crime or something! What?" Grace asked, beyond flustered, not liking these feelings one little bit.

"I'm trying to decide if you have. Or not."

They stared at each other across the bed. His blue eyes darkened as he held her verdant gaze. Grace held his infuriating stare with an equally wicked one of her own. It was as though they were playing a game. Dueling eyes.

Max's stare wavered for a second. Watching him with a professional eye, Grace detected a glimmer of sadness behind his hard glare. Like a wave slamming against her, Grace surmised this man had known sorrow. A very deep and personal sorrow. Why hadn't she noticed it before? She didn't know. Maybe the fact that her carelessness had caused two little girls and their mother unnecessary worry? Blinded by her own stupidity. Pure and simple. There was no other explanation for her not seeing between the lines where this angry man was concerned.

Tearing her glance away from Max, Grace walked over to the bathroom and knocked on the door. "Are you girls finished in there?"

When she didn't get a reply, she knocked again. "Amanda? Ashley?"

Max was behind her now, concern etched on his face. "I have a key around here somewhere."

"I don't think the door is locked." Grace tried the knob. Sure enough, it turned in her hand. She stepped inside, fearful that something had happened to the pair. When she didn't see them, her heart skipped a beat. Then another.

"They're not in here!" she shouted to Max. "Is there a door . . . ?"

"This is the only way in or out."

"Ashley! Amanda!" Grace called. "This isn't funny."

A noise, something that sounded like a "shhh" came from the direction of the oversized tub. Grace looked at Max, who'd come up behind her. She placed a finger to her lips. He nodded. She walked over to the tub, where both girls were huddled, their arms wrapped tightly around each other.

"Amanda, Ashley," Grace stated softly as she stared down into twin sets of brown eyes.

"We got scared, Miss Grace," Ashley explained.

"It's okay, there's nothing to be afraid of," Grace coaxed.

"We're afraid of him," Amanda said, pointing a small finger at Max, who stood behind Grace.

Momentarily at a loss for words, Grace didn't know what to say. Both girls had been through so much. Max wasn't a friendly man at all; no wonder they were terrified of him.

With an air of exasperation, Max said, "Hey, I promise not to bite, okay?"

Grace thought he could've chosen his words better, could've softened his tone somewhat, but at least this was a start.

"See? Mr. Jorgenson isn't angry," Grace said, as both girls began their climb from the tub.

As innocent children often do, Amanda said the first thing that came to mind, "Then why doesn't he have a Christmas tree? You said all happy families have Christmas trees. Isn't Mr. Jorgenson happy? Does he have a family?" Amanda asked Grace.

*Good questions,* she thought, eyeing their host. "I'm afraid that's Mr. Jorgenson's personal business, sweetie. It's one of those questions that your mother wouldn't want you to ask."

"It is?" Amanda looked to her older sister for confirmation.

"I think so," Ashley said, sounding as unsure as Grace felt.

"Let's not worry about Mr. Jorgenson right now, girls. It's really, really late. At this rate we won't have much time to sleep before it'll be time to get up and go back to the van. Now, let's get you all snuggled up in this big comfy bed, and I'll tell you a Christmas story."

Both girls jumped on the bed and slid beneath the covers, eyeing Grace expectantly.

*"Once upon a time . . ."*

43

# CHAPTER 4

Max stormed out of the room before the kid could pose any more nosy questions. He hadn't missed the questioning look from the woman. *Grace.* He'd be damned before he revealed his personal life to a total stranger. It was one thing to invite them into his home; he really hadn't had a choice. It didn't mean he had to get chummy with them. Though he admitted to himself, the girls were cute and seemed well behaved. But not his problem.

Downstairs in the den, Max aimed the remote at the giant plasma television. Nothing happened. He tried again, then concluded the satellite was out. That was nothing new, especially during a snowstorm.

When he'd purchased the land at the height of his career several years ago, he'd assumed that by the time he built a vacation home, not having cable TV, satellite TV, not to mention Internet service, would be something he'd never have to worry about. Of course, he'd built his so-called vacation home a lot sooner than he'd originally planned. Blow Out Hill was still as undeveloped as it had been two years ago, when he'd moved into the giant log home.

This was supposed to be his and Kayla's, and any children they'd had, home away from home, from the mansion in Denver that he'd practically given away after Kayla's death. When he had purchased the land, he'd envisioned teaching his kids to ski on Powder Rise, the mountain, albeit a small one, behind the house. Those were dreams, and nothing more.

All his hope for the future died when Kayla, a police officer, was shot and killed in the line of duty two years earlier on Christmas Eve. No more holiday celebrations for him; it was too painful. Memories gouged him like a sharp knife, each twisting deeper, the hurt lingering like a bad odor. Friends told him his grief would lessen, the hard, brittle edges softening with time. So far they'd been wrong. There wasn't a day that he didn't think of his and Kayla's life together, what could have been. Putting his memories aside for the moment, Max hurried into the kitchen.

Searching for the transistor radio and batteries he always kept for such an occasion, he found them in the kitchen drawer next to the Viking stove. Top-of-the-line. He bought the best appliances money could buy in memory of all the times he and Kayla had spent together on Sunday mornings making breakfast and whatever else Kayla decided. Now they just sat there like a silent reminder of all he'd lost.

Putting fresh batteries in the radio, Max tuned to a local station, searching for an updated weather report. When he found the station he usually listened to, he turned the volume up. The meteorologist's static-laced report filled the kitchen, then Max heard something about roadblocks, but the rest was bleeped out. No doubt the storm at work. He made a few adjustments to the dial again, and this time the reporter's voice was loud and clear:

*"And it appears as though residents of Eagle, Colorado, and the surrounding areas will have a white Christmas after all. We're expecting more than three feet of snow before morning. A travel advisory is in effect until further notice . . ."*

Max put the four empty mugs in the dishwasher, not liking the direction his thoughts were headed. If the report was accurate, and he had no reason to believe otherwise, his "house guests" could be there for a while.

"Damn!" he cursed out loud. Max wasn't prepared for a snowstorm. Hell, he'd be lucky if there was enough food in the house for *him* to get by on for a few days, let alone two children and another adult. He could kick himself for not planning ahead. He'd been taking care of himself for a very long time now without giving a thought to another human being. The way he figured it, his lack of preparation was justified as far as he was concerned. Then he remembered the freezer in the shed. Maybe someone had remembered to fill it.

Soft footsteps startled him from his thoughts. He wasn't used to anyone in his house other than himself and the two Huskies, who were curled up on the leather sofa he'd vacated earlier.

"I just wanted to thank you again for putting us up. It was stupid of me to take the girls out on a night like this," Grace said.

Max wanted to agree, but in all fairness he couldn't. If she were telling the truth, and he had a gut feeling she was, there was nothing wrong with her taking two children to see a Christmas ballet. Rotten luck had placed her in the wrong place at the wrong time.

He looked at Grace, *really* looked at her. She was tall for a woman, a bit on the thin side. Milky white skin made him think of the clichéd term "peaches-and-cream complexion." Long black hair reached the middle of her back. Her eyes were an unusual shade of green, reminding him of the wild grass that grew alongside the mountain in the summer, their color so bold. He wondered if they were contacts, but something told him everything about this woman was real, even though she'd been evasive with information about herself. Really, he didn't blame her. She didn't know him any better than he knew her. Add to the equation she had two little girls with her, alone on a mountain with a strange man. He wouldn't be quick to offer information either if he were in her shoes.

Max waved his hand in the air. "Not a problem." It was, but he wouldn't tell her that. He figured he'd been rude enough already. Resigned to the loss of privacy for the next few days, Max decided he'd better inform Grace just how unprepared he was.

"The weather report doesn't look good." He nodded toward the radio on the countertop. "They're saying three feet of snow before daybreak."

Grace stepped into the kitchen. "I have to

get out of here at first light. Stephanie will be sick with worry!" Grace eyed the phone. "It's still not working?"

He took the phone off its stand, punched a button. "Nothing. Phone's always the first to go and the last to be repaired. People around here are more concerned with the roads."

"If they clear the roads so quickly, then my getting back to the van shouldn't be a problem," Grace stated flatly. The thought of staying under the same roof with their host for more than a night sent a shiver of alarm down her spine.

"The roads will be cleared as soon as it's safe. Eagle County is well prepared for winter storms. They'll start with the main roads first. Blow Out Hill is always last on their list."

"I take it there's no other way off the mountain?"

"Some of the local pilots keep their planes in the hangar over at Eagle County Regional Airport. They won't come out unless it's a true emergency. Life or death. Especially in this weather. So to answer your question, there is no way off the mountain other than by foot. I don't think you want to risk taking those two kids outdoors in three feet of snow. Even if this were a true emergency, I

49

wouldn't be able to contact the airport."

Contemplating her circumstances, Grace took a deep breath. As much as she hated the idea of being stuck there with a man she didn't particularly care for, she realized she had to stay put. With any luck, a police officer would run across her van and remember they'd stopped her. *Maybe,* and it was a big *maybe,* one of the officers would run her plates and remember her. Someone had to figure out who she was and contact Hope House.

She said a silent prayer that her mother had decided to spend Christmas with her this year instead of staying home in Denver. She knew she would offer comfort to Stephanie until they discovered Grace's whereabouts.

Bryce, her younger brother, was due to arrive Christmas Eve. This year would be the first time her entire family spent Christmas together at Hope House. Since its opening, Grace had always stayed at Hope House during the holidays if there were guests. She missed her mother and brother, but they both understood her need to make the women and their children feel as comfortable as possible. In some cases, a few of the women-only Christmas celebrations had been at Hope House. She prayed Stephanie would stay put until she could get word to her that the girls were fine and not in danger. Or at least not in any danger from the man that they'd been running from when they'd been brought to her doorstep by a police officer. Husband and father. It made her cringe just thinking of what the women at Hope House had gone through before they arrived. She was committed to doing whatever was humanly possible to assist them in turning their lives around. Being stuck on a mountain was simply a bump in the road compared to what they'd been through.

Lost in thought, Grace was about to sneak a quick glance at her host when everything went black.

"It never fails," Max said in the darkness. "I've got flashlights and candles somewhere in here."

Grace heard him opening and closing drawers. Rummaging through a few, he found what he was looking for when a thin beam of light illuminated the small space between them. "I've got a generator in the shed out back."

"That'll help," Grace said as she inched her way to the kitchen table.

"Yeah. I've never used it. Never had a reason to."

Grace wanted to ask what he normally did when the power went out, but she heard his heavy footsteps bounding up the stairs before she could get the words out of her mouth. Instead, she ran a hand along the countertop until she found a small box of matches beside a box of candles. She lit one, then another, placing both candles bottom side down on the counter while she searched for something to use as a holder. Searching the cabinets, she found a rock glass that would serve her purpose. Putting the candles in the glass, she headed toward the stairs to check on the girls when a gust of icy air blew in from an open door, extinguishing her light.

She heard a door slam. Grace called out into the darkness, "Max?"

When she didn't receive a response, she called again. She heard the apprehension in her voice when she spoke. "Max, is that you? I . . . never mind." Wishing she'd brought the box of matches along for such an emergency, Grace inched her way back to the kitchen. *Maybe Max hadn't heard her,* she thought as she skimmed the surface of the countertop searching for the matches. When her fingers brushed against the small box, she grabbed it like a lifeline. Striking two matches at once, she relit the candles, and was relieved when the room flickered with their soft golden light. Tucking the matches in her pocket, Grace went back in the direction of the stairs when she heard a noise. Something creaked, like hinges on a door.

"Max? I don't think this is funny."

She stopped in the center of the den, waiting for a sarcastic comeback. Getting no reply, she yelled, "Max" so loud she was sure she'd wake the girls. Feet rooted to the floor, heart rate accelerating, even though the room was chilled from the burst of cold air, Grace felt perspiration dot her forehead.

Becoming increasingly uneasy as the seconds ticked away, Grace tried another strategy. Using a stern voice usually reserved for the fearful women she dealt with, she called out, "Mr. Jorgenson? Max? If this is some kind of game, I don't want to play."

Standing still, she heard the floorboards above her creaking. No doubt her shouting had awakened the girls. Putting her anxiety aside, she carefully made her way up the unfamiliar staircase. When she reached the top, she raced to the master suite to check on Amanda and Ashley.

She remembered leaving the door open when she'd left the room earlier. Now it was closed. Maybe the gust of air from the door's opening downstairs had somehow caused it to close. Telling herself this must be what happened, she turned the knob, careful not to make too much noise in case the girls were still sleeping. Pushing the heavy log door aside, she stepped into the large bedroom.

Holding the candles in front of her as she tiptoed over to the king-size bed, Grace leaned across the wide expanse to make sure the girls were covered. When her hands continued to feel nothing but cool, smooth sheets, she knew something had gone terribly awry.

Because both girls were missing.

# CHAPTER 5

"Amanda? Ashley?" Grace called out into the darkened room. Remembering their fear of the dark, she tried another tactic, hoping to calm their fears. "The power went out. Max is fixing it now." She hoped. He didn't seem to know his way around his own home.

When she received no response, she tried again. "Girls, this is one of those times that your mother would want you to show yourselves. There's nothing to be afraid of."

Slowly, so as not to startle the girls, Grace entered the bathroom. Just as she'd expected, both girls were huddled in the tub. She lowered the candle so they could see that it was her. The damage their father's cruelty had inflicted upon them infuriated her.

"We got scared when the lights went off. Then we heard pounding on the steps. Mommy always told us to hide and cover our ears when Daddy got mad," Ashley said in her defense.

"Oh, sweetie, your daddy isn't here. The noise you heard was Max. He had to race upstairs for his warm clothes before he went outside to the shed. There's nothing to be frightened of." Grace held a hand out to assist the little girls as they climbed out of the bathtub.

"Miss Grace, could you tell us another Christmas story?" Amanda asked.

After leading them back to the bed and making sure both were warm and snug beneath the quilt, Grace eased in next to them. "Absolutely."

Ten minutes later, and a condensed version of *A Christmas Carol* minus the ghosts of Christmases past, present, and future, both girls were sound asleep. Grace quietly slid off the bed and went downstairs. Surely Max had had enough time to find the generator.

With the flame of the candle as her guide, Grace went from room to room in search of him. "Max?" she whispered loudly, but not so loud that she would wake the kids.

She searched downstairs and was about to give up when she felt a burst of cold air enter the room. "Max? Is that you?" she called.

"Yeah. I couldn't find the darned generator. I was sure Eddie put it in the shed," Max said.

When Grace heard him, relief flooded through her. "I have to admit I was getting a bit concerned."

"Why?" Max asked as he dropped a large bag on the floor.

She could've kicked herself for telling him that, but it was too late now. "You were gone a long time." Grace approached him as he entered the den.

Max slung off his worn leather jacket, tossing it on the back of the sofa, where both dogs slept peacefully. "There's a freezer out there. Loss of power won't affect it since the temp's below freezing. I figured I'd better scope out its contents since we're going to be stuck here for a while. It's stocked with everything we'll need though I haven't a clue who took the time to bother with it." Probably Eddie. The man thought of everything. He was due for a raise this month. And a paid vacation, too.

Grace eyed the large bag on the floor. "If you'll bring that to the kitchen, I'll put everything away."

"Sure," said Max gruffly, hoisting the heavy bag over his shoulder.

Grace laughed.

"You find this amusing?"

"No, not at all. You just reminded me of Santa Claus."

Max stopped in his tracks, dropped the bag and turned around to stare at her. Though the only light came from the candle, Grace saw the anger in his eyes. Cold and stark, like the harsh winter storm outside.

Between gritted teeth, he said, "Don't ever say that to me again!"

Grace had had enough. She didn't know what had happened to turn this man into such . . . a Scrooge, and she really didn't care. She was simply trying to make a joke.

"Look, Max. Whatever issues you have, they're not with me. If you can't take a little joke, you've got big problems. Might want to see someone, a professional. It could help," Grace said, then dragged the heavy bag the rest of the way to the kitchen.

"Wait! You can't talk to me like that! Who in the heck do you think you are? This is my house. You're the guest," Max ranted as he followed her to the kitchen.

"Yes I am, and you're the rudest host I've had the misfortune to encounter. If it's any consolation, I don't want to be here any more than you want me here. I'm an adult, I will make the best of it." She wanted to add, "Unlike you," but that would lower her to his level.

He raked a hand through his hair. On another man it might've been just an ordinary action. On him it was just . . . well, she wouldn't admit it to anyone, but it was rather sexy.

"Look, I don't like the holidays. Can we just leave it at that?" Max yanked the heavy bag off the floor and placed it on the counter.

Grace was right. He *was* a Scrooge! Biting her lip to keep from smiling, she announced, "What you like or don't like is no concern of mine. At daybreak, I just want to get to my van. I'm not really concerned with anything else at the moment." Of course, she was, but her concerns were none of his business. Unlike him, Grace wasn't about to voice her likes and dislikes. Certainly she wasn't going to tell Max how Christmas was her favorite time of the year and how she detested those who spoiled it for others.

She wouldn't tell him that she'd already spent days in the kitchen baking cookies, cakes, and pies for several of the soup kitchens in Denver. And she wouldn't tell him how much money she had spent on gifts for Stephanie and her girls. What kind of person didn't like Christmas? Maybe he'd had a rough time as a child. Those incidents had a way of haunting one, even as an adult. As a professional she knew that. As a woman, she couldn't imagine being with a man who didn't celebrate and enjoy the Christmas season as much as she did. Christmas was the highlight of the year for her family.

Max peered out the kitchen window. "I don't think you're going anywhere come morning. Look." He gestured at the window.

Reluctantly, Grace went over to the window and stood beside him. She couldn't help but notice the smell of winter and pine emanating from his skin. She breathed deeply, closing her eyes for a moment, wondering, then jerked her eyes open. The cold was getting to her. She glanced outside. Snowdrifts were at least three feet high. Big fluffy flakes of snow swirled through the inky night sky like miniature fairies with wings as light as a spider's web.

"I suppose a snowplow would be too much to hope for," Grace observed as she turned away from the window. Another time this might amuse her. However, with two girls whose mother was probably frantic with worry, she was anything but.

"Yep, it would be. Like I said, I'm not very prepared for this. I came here to . . ." He paused. Grace waited for him to finish, but he didn't.

"Whatever your reason, I, for one, am glad I found you," Grace added, hoping a compliment of sorts might draw him out of the black mood that seemed to hover over him.

Max removed the contents of the bag, placing them on the counter. "I'm not much of a cook other than bacon and eggs. You might want to see if there's something here you and the girls would like."

Grace was about to tell him bacon and eggs were fine with her, then thought better of it when she realized that, without power, they wouldn't be able to cook anything.

"I'm going to get the fireplaces going. There's more wood in the shed," Max said, before wandering outside again. At least he'd had the foresight to see to the wood supply. Or someone had.

She wondered if Max was incapable of taking care of his own needs. She knew his reputation on the slopes. Ski or die. She remembered Bryce telling her this during the Winter Olympics years ago. Why would she remember that now? Bryce was in high school then. Grace calculated it'd been at least twelve or fifteen years ago.

She could cook using an open fire. Searching through the food supply, she found several packages of meat. Bacon, a whole chicken, a roast, and a package of hot dogs. The latter might come in handy for a weenie-roast for the girls she thought as she proceeded to check the food supply. There were bags of frozen vegetables. Carrots, potatoes, peas, and there was even a container of frozen chicken stock. Loaves of French bread, white bread, and wheat bread. Peanut butter. Someone had known what they were doing when they'd stocked Max's freezer. In the cupboard she saw at least a dozen cans of soup, two boxes of saltines, and jars of strawberry jam and grape jelly. Max *was* prepared for a storm whether he realized it or not. Grace made fast work of storing the breads and peanut butter in a cabinet. Since it was below freezing outside, she repacked the meats and vegetables, placing them back in the bag before taking them to the front porch. She hoped there weren't any coyotes or bears in search of their next meal. If so, they were all in trouble.

Hurrying back inside, she observed Max as he placed more logs on the fire. Bright yellow flames shot up the flue, sending tiny red sparks shimmering everywhere. The woodsy smell reminded her of her father. He'd always kept a fire burning in the winter. They'd popped corn and made what her father referred to as hobo packs. Aluminum foil filled with ground meat, potatoes, and whatever vegetable they wanted. They'd toss them in the fire, then they'd finish off their campfire meal with either s'mores or toasted marshmallows. *One of Dad's burnt marshmallows would taste good,* she thought as she watched Max from a distance. She hoped he knew what he was doing. According to Bryce and those trophies and medals she'd seen upstairs, his expertise seemed strictly limited to the slopes. Briefly, she wondered what skills he brought into the bedroom.

*What is wrong with me?* she thought as she watched Max. It hadn't been that long since she'd had a date!

"Like what you see?" Max asked.

Grace was sure he referred to the roaring fire. "Yes, it's perfect. And I think it's time we went to bed. I'm beyond tired. I doubt the girls will sleep late. Kids their age never do."

"You seem to have a lot of experience with kids for a woman who doesn't have any of her own," Max observed.

Grace wasn't sure if this was an invitation to reveal more about herself or just his way of making polite conversation. Something told her she could trust him even though he'd been rude and had frightened the girls. She recalled the look of pain etched on his face. He had suffered in his life. And not just physical injuries from his profession. He'd walked through the fires of hell. Grace wasn't sure if he'd completely returned.

"Why are you looking at me like that?" Max asked.

"I'm sorry. Professional habit I guess."

"So you stare at people for a living? You an artist or what?" he inquired with a trace of humor.

Grace took a deep breath, unsure of how much she should reveal to him. While her gut told her she could trust him, she had to consider the safety of the girls and their mother before she revealed too much about herself. Not wanting to lie or reveal any details about Stephanie and the girls, Grace opted for a simple version of the truth. "I'm a counselor."

"I see. So" — he took the fire poker from its stand and pushed several logs aside before adding more — "in your professional opinion, exactly what did you see when you were staring at me?" He waved a hand in the air. "Never mind. Don't answer that. I'm sure you see what everyone else sees. A burnout who's screwed up his life and doesn't care."

Grace couldn't have been more shocked by his words. "Actually, I saw nothing like that at all." She could tell him the truth, there was no reason not to. "I see someone who's been hurt by . . . a tragedy." She paused catching his eye. "You've suffered a personal loss so . . . consuming that it's taken over the person you used to be." Grace waited for a response, a reply, anything. He perched on the hearth, shaking his head.

"Well, you're wrong, lady. I'm the man I've always been. Nothing will ever change that. Trust me. I like to drink and sleep. Nothing more." Max hesitated for a moment as though he was testing her reaction. "A real prize, huh?"

Taking a chance Grace replied, "I think you were a real prize, Max Jorgenson, at one time. Whatever happened to strip away your self-confidence, it's still there. You have to want it back."

He looked at her for several minutes, a tense silence filling the space between them.

"Yeah? Well, you're wrong. I don't ever want to be the man I was. Never." He looked down at the pine floors. "Never," he added in a low, husky voice.

Grace wanted to say, "Never say never,"

but it wasn't the right time. With this man, she wasn't so sure there would ever be a *right* time.

Putting concerns about her host's mental status on the back burner for the remainder of the night, she told him good night and went upstairs. As soon as her head hit the soft down pillow, she fell into a deep, dreamless sleep.

# CHAPTER 6

Blinding sunlight filled the bedroom, casting a burnished glow across the pine furniture. Grace sat up quickly when she realized she wasn't in her room at Hope House. Then it all came back. The roadblocks and the loss of communication with the world.

She looked at the girls next to her. They slept like babies. Careful not to wake them, she pushed her hands down on the mattress in order to ease off the bed without either child feeling the movement.

Grace used the bathroom, splashed cold water on her face, and rinsed her mouth, using mouthwash she found in the medicine cabinet. Taking a comb from her purse, she ran it through her long hair and secured it with an elastic band. Checking to make sure both Ashley and Amanda still slept, she quietly made her way downstairs to the kitchen.

She stopped at the foot of the stairs,

surprised when she saw Max in the kitchen. Grace felt a tingle trail up her spine as she observed him. He wore a fresh pair of faded jeans with a tight black T-shirt. Chest muscles pulled the fabric so taut that Grace laughingly thought how lucky his T-shirt was. She took a deep breath. He was certainly something to look at, but most skiers were. She remembered going to the slopes as a teen, then later during college breaks. All the cool guys, the ones that really knew their way around the mountains, were hot and handsome. She'd never bothered with the type simply because those she'd met were either so conceited it was pathetic, or they didn't have an intelligent thought in their heads. She figured Max Jorgenson must be a combination of both because most men living on a mountain in the middle of nowhere planned ahead. The thought hit her then; maybe Max really *didn't* care about his future.

The aromatic scent of coffee pulled her away from her musing and into the kitchen. Max poured boiling water from a pot into a European coffee press. "That smells divine," Grace said upon entering the kitchen. Surprised that he owned such a simple yet sophisticated coffee press, she waited as he pushed the press, slowly sending the dark brown liquid to the bottom of the clear carafe.

"Almost finished," Max said with a look of satisfaction on his face. He removed a small cup from the cabinet, filled it, then placed it on the counter. "I have sugar but . . . wait. Here's powdered cream," he said as he rummaged through the cabinets. "I didn't know I had this stuff."

Max dumped the powder and several spoons of sugar in his coffee. Grace smiled. She'd thought for sure he would take his java straight up.

"Thanks," she said, sipping her coffee. "Black is fine. This is good stuff."

"What? You didn't think me capable of making a decent pot of coffee?" Max said in a teasing tone. Both Huskies ran into the kitchen, barking.

"Down, boys," Max managed to say. Ice-D and Cliff hunkered beneath the kitchen table, apparently waiting for their breakfast.

"Truly, I hadn't given it much thought." She eyed the telephone. "Are the phones working yet?"

"Nope. Just checked. I did hear snowplows about an hour ago. That's a good sign."

"How so?" Grace asked, suddenly hopeful.

"Usually that means they'll head this way. I'm thinking about taking one of the snowmobiles down the mountain to check. While I'm there, I'll try to locate your van."

Grace was filled with an overwhelming desire to wrap her arms around her rude host but stopped herself just in time. "Miracles do happen!"

"You think this is a miracle?" he asked, shaking his head, his damp blond curls reaching just below the collar of his shirt.

"You said yourself it could be days before the plows head up the mountain, so I guess this is a miracle. Of sorts. I do know Stephanie, that's the girls' mother, is probably insane with worry. I wish . . . if you can't get the van here, do you think you or possibly a member of the road crew could call her just to let her know the girls are safe and that we'll be home soon."

"I'll see what I can do," Max replied.

Grace took another sip of her coffee. "I can make breakfast before you leave. I'm sure the girls will want something when they wake up. I can't believe they're still sleeping. Poor things. No doubt last night's hike tuckered them out."

Max seemed to hesitate. "Breakfast would be good. I haven't had a home-cooked meal since . . ." He paused as though he'd lost

70

his train of thought. "Forever. Breakfast sounds good. Thank you."

*Miracles of all miracles! The man said thank you.* "Better wait 'till you're finished before you thank me. It's been a while since I've cooked over an open fire. As a kid I used to love it. My dad would often cook in the fireplace during the winter. He called it 'campfire night.' Which basically meant Mom needed a break from the kitchen." The memory brought a wry, twisted smile to her face.

Max grinned. Grace realized it was the first real smile she'd seen since arriving on his doorstep. His teeth were as bright as the snowcapped mountains. "Campfire night? Never heard of that."

She explained, "Dad would take ground meat, potatoes, and whatever vegetable Mom had too much of, then he'd wrap the food in aluminum foil and toss it in the fireplace. Sometimes we'd do s'mores or popcorn for dessert. It became a family tradition of sorts. Dad built the fire, and we helped prepare the hobo packs. Maybe for lunch . . . if we're still here," Grace suggested. "Breakfast first though," she finished.

Max looked at her as though he were contemplating a private memory, his face sobering with whatever thought swirled through his head. "I'd better get out of here before the road crew decides to leave. Breakfast is highly overrated anyway. Come on, guys, let's go outside." Both dogs leapt to their feet and raced to the door.

"But I thought . . ." Grace floundered.

"Yeah, I'm sorry. Take care of your girls. I'll be back as soon as I check the roads. I'll need that phone number."

For a second Grace almost forgot she was stuck in the middle of nowhere with a man she wasn't sure she even *liked*, plus two little girls whose mother must be frantic with worry. Mentally shaking herself, she focused on the here and now.

Flustered, she looked around for something to write on. "Is there a pen and paper?"

Max retrieved a pad and pencil from the kitchen drawer and gave it to her. She scribbled out the number with Stephanie's name. As an afterthought she also added her mother's cellphone number. Who knew? They could be out looking for her right that very minute. Grace didn't want to miss her one chance to let them know they weren't in any danger. Well, the girls weren't in any immediate danger, but she could be if she didn't stop thinking about Max Jorgenson's personal life and how it might mesh with her own.

"Miss Grace! Miss Grace!" both girls called in unison as they ran down the stairs. "Can we build a snowman? Look at all the snow outside!"

Grace glanced at Max, giving him an, *Oh boy, this is where I could get into trouble* look.

"I don't know. We don't have the proper clothes, remember how cold it is. I was about to make breakfast in the fireplace. How about you two give me a hand? I bet I can find some Christmas music for us to listen to while we're cooking. How does that sound?" Grace asked, adding an extra dollop of cheer to her voice.

"Okay," Amanda said. "But I would really, *really* rather build a snowman than cook. Just so you know."

Grace burst out laughing. She was shocked when she heard Max's slight laugh. She didn't think he had it in him. Wrong again.

"I'll try to remember that, kiddo. Now why don't the pair of you run upstairs and get dressed. I'll need your help in a few minutes."

The girls raced upstairs, shrieking and laughing. Grace was thrilled to hear their childish gibberish because she knew it was a sign that they would eventually be fine despite the traumatic home life they'd only recently escaped. Kids bounced back quickly after tragedy struck. Too bad some of their lightheartedness couldn't rub off on Max. Permanently.

Out of the corner of her eye, she saw him grab her keys where she'd left them, turn, and head for the front door, allowing the dogs to come inside after a quick but brisk run.

"Be careful," she called out to his silhouette, framed in the sunlight. She watched him walk down the steps she'd used just hours ago.

Max Jorgenson was a loner, a wounded man who obviously wanted nothing more than to live his life here on this mountain in the middle of nowhere, undisturbed. So why did she feel the urge to count the minutes until he returned? Why did she feel as if a hummingbird's wings fluttered against her rib cage when she looked at him? Telling herself it was nothing more than middle-aged lust, she stepped outside and removed a slab of bacon from the bag she'd placed there earlier that morning.

Grace couldn't have predicted the last twelve hours if her life had depended on it. Reliable, steady, sure of herself, she remained coolheaded and in control of almost any situation she found herself in. Now she found her thoughts wandering and was having trouble focusing. The past few hours had been almost surreal. She'd never been in a situation where she'd felt so totally out of control. Until now. Saying a silent prayer that Max or someone would contact Stephanie, Grace returned to the kitchen to make breakfast.

Locating a radio station playing Christmas carols, she searched through the cupboards until she found a well-used iron skillet, which surprised her. Must be what he used for his bacon and eggs. Using a fork to pry the frozen bacon apart, she lined the frying pan with several slices. She found a cookie sheet and brought it over to the fireplace. Having placed the baking sheet on the logs, she waited until she could see that it was steady, then set the skillet on top. Within minutes the scent of bacon frying permeated the room. Grace realized she was hungry. "Girls," she called up the stairs, "I need your help." She didn't really, but wanted to include them hoping it would take their minds off venturing outside in the freezing cold.

"Here we are! We don't have a toothbrush, Miss Grace. Mommy tells us to brush our teeth first thing in the morning. And night-time, too. But we can't without a tooth-brush. Do you think our teeth will fall out?" Amanda asked in one giant breath.

"No, I think you'll be just fine. When we finish breakfast, we'll clean our teeth with a washcloth and baking soda if we can't find any toothpaste. That should do until we get you two home."

"No! We can't go home, Miss Grace! Mommy said Daddy might really hurt her bad next time," Ashley explained, as tears filled her brown eyes.

"Oh, honey, I meant back to Hope House." Grace steadied the skillet before standing up and taking the two girls in her arms. "Listen up. As long as you're with me, I promise you'll both be safe. Max is going to try to call your mother and tell her you're okay. As soon as I'm able to get to the van, we'll leave. Deal?" she asked.

"And we can still decorate the Christmas tree, right? Ashley says it's only five more days till Christmas. Is that true?" Amanda asked, changing the subject so fast Grace had to pause to count the number of days in her head.

"Yes, that's right. Five more days, and Santa will be here." Grace still had gifts to buy, plus a tree to decorate. She hoped to be off the mountain in time to get everything ready before Bryce arrived Christmas Eve.

Amanda started to cry hard. Giant tears spattered on her dress. She hiccoughed a few times before she could talk. "But . . . we . . . won't . . . be . . . home. How . . . will . . . Santa . . . know . . . where . . . to . . . find . . . us?"

"He'll find us, won't he, Miss Grace? Mommy says he always finds little children. Right?" Ashley asked.

Some parents didn't believe that instilling a false image of Santa was healthy. She'd seen it more than once when she was in practice. Grace was all about honesty, but in this case she couldn't come up with one reason, professional or personal, why a child shouldn't be indulged in such a fantasy. She'd believed in Santa Claus until she was twelve and remembered the disappointment when she'd learned the truth. But as her mother and father always told her, *Santa Claus is alive and well. He just moves to your heart when you're older.*

"Absolutely! He'll find you both I'm sure. Now, if I don't get some help, I'm going to burn breakfast."

She removed the skillet from the fire and took it to the kitchen. In minutes, she and the girls were seated at the table, munching on crispy bacon and soft white bread slathered with strawberry jam. With both dogs acting as guards around the table, Grace laughed, watching as Ice-D and Cliff inhaled every morsel that fell to the floor.

Grace couldn't remember the last time she'd enjoyed breakfast as much.

# CHAPTER 7

Max blasted down the mountain like a stick of dynamite. Slivers of ice zoomed past his head as he plowed through a snowbank. He couldn't put sufficient distance between himself and Grace fast enough. He wanted her out of his house. And the kids, too.

Emotions he'd put on ice long ago were starting to thaw. He knew what that meant but didn't want to acknowledge it, telling himself it was too soon. He'd felt guilty the moment he laid eyes on her. All thoughts of bachelorhood, the promises he'd made to himself would be null and void if she remained in the picture. Good thing she was just passing through.

He was halfway down Blow Out Hill when he spied Eddie's shiny black Hummer parked next to a county snowplow. Thinking there could've been an accident at Maximum Glide, he twisted the throttle to wide open and the snowmobile skyrocketed recklessly to the bottom of the hill. He braked quickly, sending a shower of freshly packed snow shooting through the air like a blaze of fireworks.

He shut the engine off, leaving the keys in the ignition. He saw Eddie talking to a group of men gathered around the Hummer. Max shook his head. The man adored his ride, never missing an opportunity to pay tribute to the vehicle's superiority over other four-wheel-drive transport.

Eddie saw him and waved. "What brings Muhammad down from the mountain in this kind of weather?"

Max gave a short laugh. "You wouldn't believe me if I told you. Everything okay at Maximum Glide?" He wanted to tell Eddie three snow angels on a mission appeared on his doorstep last night, but thought that a bit too drastic even for Eddie. "A woman broke down somewhere around here late last night. Has a couple of kids with her and needs to get word to her family that they're okay. You see any gray vans on the side of the road?"

"Place runs smooth as silk, thanks to me. Funny you should ask about the van. We" — he nodded to the group of men gathered behind him — "were just discussing whose turn it was for the next tow."

80

"Don't bother. I'm here for the van. Think it'll make it up the mountain?" Max asked, assured Eddie would know.

"It's front-wheel drive. It should. Want me to follow you in the Hummer, just in case?" he asked.

Max thought about it for a minute. "No, I think I can make it. You got your cell phone? I need to make a call."

Eddie whipped his iPhone out of his jacket pocket. "Never leave home without it."

Max took the scrap of paper from his pocket, eyeing the small, neat numbers. He could've sworn he smelled night-blooming jasmine wafting off the slip of paper. Shaking his head to clear it, he touched the numbers on the phone's silent pad. Max would never get used to technology. This reminded him of something right out of *Star Wars.*

The phone rang twice before someone answered. "Hope House. This is Juanita."

*Hope House? Juanita?*

"I'm calling for someone named Grace," he said.

"Do you want to speak to her?"

"No, no. She wanted me to call and let someone know that she and the . . . girls were okay. She got lost last night on her way home from a play. The snowstorm, she couldn't see to drive."

"Thank God!" the woman said. "Where is she now? I'll send Bryce after her. He arrived early this morning. He was so anxious to spend Christmas with her this year, he couldn't wait until Christmas Eve."

Max heard Juanita whispering to someone else. Most likely it was the girls' mother. "Hello? Who is this? Where are my children?" Another woman. The mother. Right on the money.

"I . . . Grace wanted me to call you and let you know they're safe." Why did he say that? Of course they were safe. Why wouldn't they be? "I'm on my way to get her van now. Your girls are at my house with her. They were making breakfast when I left."

"Oh, I can't thank you enough! I was sure Glenn had escaped somehow. When will you be bringing them back to Hope House?" the woman he now knew was Stephanie asked.

"She'll be there as soon as the weather permits. She just wanted me to call. My phone lines are down. She said her cell-phone battery died."

Max heard an intake of breath.

"Miss Grace would never allow her battery to die! That's one of the first things she tells us when she issues our phones. Are you sure she's all right? What did you say your name was?"

*Issues our phones? Hope House? Why did that name sound familiar to him?*

"My name is Max, and I assure you, *Miss Grace* was fine when I left her. As soon as she's able to travel, she'll be home. Tell Bryce not to be in such a hurry next time." Max hung up the phone.

"Catch." He tossed the cell phone back to Eddie.

"Easy, buddy, those things aren't cheap. What got you so riled up? You look like you've just swallowed a spoon of vinegar. No, make that a glass. What gives?"

*Bryce. What kind of name is that?*

"Nothing, just point me in the right direction so I can get the woman's van to her before *Bryce* has a . . . hissy fit."

"Well, well. I'll be a monkey's uncle! It's about time, don't you think? I do believe Mr. Jorgenson is jealous!" Eddie roared with laughter.

"Look, Eddie, cut the crap. This woman is stranded at my place with two kids. I want her out of there as soon as possible. Just tell me where her van is, and I'll be on my way."

"Don't get all whiney on me, man. Look, I'll drive you to her van. I was about to leave anyway. We've got a group of ten-year-olds on the black diamonds today. I want to stay close by, just in case."

"Thanks, Eddie." And when had ten-year-olds started skiing on black-diamond slopes? He'd been at least thirteen before he even dared to ski on such challenging terrain, but when he did, as they say, the rest is history. Three years later he was on the U.S. Ski Team preparing for Olympic tryouts. He didn't make it that year, but four years later he made Olympic history in Albertville, France, in 1992, when he won all the events in the Alpine competitions. He had five Olympic Gold Medals for his performance on the slopes. After the Olympics, he'd made millions off endorsements. He'd invested most of his earnings, so when he was ready to settle down, money hadn't been an issue.

He'd met Kayla while sitting next to her on the ski lift at Maximum Glide. She was there with a group of female police officers from all across the state. She wasn't like all the other women he'd dated, who wanted nothing more than to be seen with him in hopes their names would wind up on the front page of whatever rag made it their mission to catch "Colorado's most eligible bachelor" doing something he shouldn't.

That lifestyle got old after a while. When he met Kayla, he was older, wiser, and ready to settle down. Their marriage was nice, easygoing. Max had begged her to quit her job, but she'd refused, telling him that her father and his father were police officers. She said it was in her blood. Feeling the same way about his skiing career, even though his father hadn't expressed an interest in skiing, Max never asked her to give up her job again. If only he'd been more persistent, Kayla might still be alive. And they would've had a son or a daughter, as Kayla had just learned she was three months' pregnant the week before she was killed.

*If only. There were so many ifs.*

"That's it," Eddie said, pointing to a gray Dodge van. "I assume she gave you the keys?"

"No, she didn't. I took them this morning. Smart thinking, huh?" Max asked.

"Smart-*ass* if you ask me," Eddie said dryly.

"I didn't," Max commented.

"Want me to hang around to make sure she starts?"

"That might be a good idea," Max said, then went over to the nondescript van, inserted the key in the lock, and opened the driver's side door. He put the key in the ignition, and the van started up on the first try. "It's running," he shouted to Eddie. "Thanks, man. I owe you."

Eddie stuck his hand in the air and waved before pulling back onto the road. Max saluted him as he passed.

Thankful for the front-wheel drive, Max drove the van up the mountain in record time as the roads were all clear. More snow was expected later, but if he were lucky, Grace would be long gone before it hit.

Something about his conversation with the girls' mother struck him just then. Just exactly who was Glenn and where had he *escaped* from? Max was positive the woman had used that word.

"Escape."

Could it be possible this Glenn had *escaped* from jail or prison? And was it possible his *escape* was the reason for the roadblocks? The more Max thought about it, the more he knew he was right. He'd lived in the area most of his life. The only time he'd witnessed a roadblock was on I-70 when there was a possible avalanche threat, or bad weather closed the pass.

Stepping on the accelerator, Max wasted no time plowing up the long drive to his cabin. If he were right, and this man Glenn had escaped, Grace and those two kids could be in grave danger. How or why he knew this, he didn't know. He did know that if it was in his power to prevent another woman from dying at the hands of another human being, he would do so, no questions asked.

Racing up the steps to the cabin, Max yanked the door aside, unprepared for what greeted him.

Grace and the two girls were in the den, with Ice-D and Cliff flanking a small bearded man wearing the typical orange jail uniform. Both dogs were in attack mode, waiting for his command.

"Are you all right?" he asked Grace as he scanned the room.

She nodded, and that was when Max realized her hands were tied behind her back. Both girls were sitting next to her. Their hands weren't tied, but Max saw thick tears streaming down both of their faces. His heartbeat quadrupled at the pitiful sight.

Not allowing another second to pass, Max walked over to the man, who he assumed was Glenn and who had his back to him, and snapped his fingers. Instantly, both dogs backed off but remained alert, low, threatening growls deep in their throats.

"Don't move!" Max wrapped his hand

around the intruder's neck and shoved him against the wall toward the door. Knowing the girls were watching prevented him from smashing his fist square in the guy's face, so he opted for the next best thing.

Dragging him out the door to Grace's van, he shoved him into the passenger side. "Move a muscle, and I promise you I won't be as nice as I was in there." He nodded toward the cabin.

Glenn, a stick of a man with a receding hairline, tattoo-covered arms, and several missing teeth, held a bony arm in front of him as Max crammed his fist in his face. Blood spewed from his mouth seconds later. "Bastard," he spat out. "Those are my girls you got in that cabin! I came to get 'em! No woman's gonna take what's rightfully mine! You hear that?"

Max didn't know the story behind Glenn's claim and didn't really care. "I hear you loud and clear, you worthless piece of shit." Max ripped his belt off and used it to tie Glenn's hands behind his back. The skinny man yanked and pulled, but Max was too strong for him. He shoved him against the seat, then used the seat belt to hold him in position. "Move a muscle, and I promise it will be your last twitch." He jammed his fist into the man's nose and heard the cartilage snap.

Glenn dropped his head to his chest, wincing in pain. Before the bound man could recover from the effects of the punch, Max raced back inside the cabin, knowing he had only a few minutes before Glenn wiggled out of the seat belt.

Without saying a word, he removed the piece of extension cord with which Glenn had tied up Grace. "Stay here and don't do anything until I return."

Grace nodded, rubbing her hands. "Hurry!" She wrapped her arms around both girls, who continued to whimper and cry.

The last thing Max heard before he raced out of the cabin was Grace telling the girls that everything was going to be just fine.

She'd promised.

# CHAPTER 8

Three hours later, Max drove back to the cabin with good news for Grace and her charges.

Max entered the cabin and found Grace, along with the two girls and dogs, curled up on the sofa in the den sound asleep. And he'd thought they'd be waiting on pins and needles for his return. So much for that.

Ice-D and Cliff bolted off the sofa when they saw him. He rubbed both between the ears, then allowed them their usual licks to his face. "Okay, boys, that's enough." Max went to the kitchen. He saw that both dog bowls were full of water, and the food bowls were empty. He was about to load them up with dog food when Grace entered the kitchen.

"They both had three hot dogs apiece, plus a bowl of dog food. I don't think they're hungry."

Max stopped and shook his finger at the

pair. "You know I ought to turn you two out, make you work for your grub." Both dogs whined, and Max fluffed the space between their ears. "Go on, you two." The dogs complied, their muzzles lifted high in the air as they made their way back to the den.

"They've convinced themselves they're kings today," Grace said as she watched the dogs jump back onto the sofa, one on either side of the girls.

"They okay?" He motioned to the sleeping girls.

"As okay as they can be under the circumstances." Grace eyed the poor things to make sure they still slept. "What happened? I was sure Glenn was gone for good. Stephanie had him arrested. He was in jail the last I heard."

Max motioned for her to follow him upstairs.

"We can talk up here without waking them. Apparently, Glenn was being transported to Denver. The deputies driving him stopped in Grand Junction for a bite to eat. Thinking Glenn was as innocent and harmless as he claimed, they let him come inside to have his meal with them. He went to the men's room, and that's the last they saw of him."

"This makes no sense! How did he know where to find Amanda and Ashley? I didn't plan on any of this happening." Perplexed, Grace dropped down on a small wooden chair.

"Those roadblocks last night, they were searching for him. He had no idea he'd find his girls here. As luck or whatever you want to call it would have it, I just happen to have the only house around here for miles. He must've walked all night and wound up here, the same as you. It's a heck of a co-incidence, don't you think?"

Grace wasn't sure what to think and told him so.

"I called the number you gave me and talked to a woman by the name of Juanita. Told her you were fine and that you'd be back as soon as possible."

"Thanks so much, really. Juanita is my mother. I'm sure she and Stephanie were beside themselves with worry. Did you tell her the girls were with me and that they were okay?"

"I did."

Grace was about to ask Max if they'd said anything else, but he piped up. "Your mother said Bryce was there. Said he couldn't wait until Christmas Eve to see you."

Her eyes lit up like a Christmas tree.

"Fantastic, I can't wait to see him. It's tough to schedule visits now that we live so far apart. I can't wait to see him. It's been almost a year. I can't believe I let so much time pass. It's just that —"

"You'd better leave before it starts snowing again. We're supposed to get another two feet by nightfall. I promised your family you'd be home today," Max said, staring intently into her verdant eyes.

Grace felt a little piece of her heart break at the thought of leaving Max behind. She barely knew the man, and what she did know she wasn't sure she liked. Still, there was something about him.

She nodded. "You're right. I know the girls are excited; they want to decorate the Christmas tree. I promised them they could."

"I gathered as much," Max said.

Before he could stop himself, before he had a chance to second-guess himself, Max pulled Grace into his arms kissing her softly on the mouth. Her intake of breath, shock or desire, surprised him because instead of pulling away, she kissed him back.

"Grace." The sound of her name filled him with emotions that had been dormant for so long, their intense return stunned him.

Before either could react Max pushed her away. For a moment neither spoke. When the silence between them became too uncomfortable, Max looked at her with more than just a casual interest.

Grace looked away, then something pulled her attention back to him. She gazed into his deep blue eyes, seeing more than just the man who'd offered her a place to stay.

Hesitantly, Max smoothed the hair away from her face. "I want to say I'm sorry, but I'm not."

Grace smiled. "It's okay, really."

Max nodded. "You'd better go. The snow and all."

Neither made an attempt to move their gazes as they locked on to one another, both amazed at the sudden attraction between them.

Max spoke up, breaking the connection. "What about Bryce?"

She squinted her eyes as though he were suddenly out of focus. "What about him?"

"Never mind," Max said softly.

"Wait. Why are you asking me about Bryce? Do you know him?"

"No, and I don't want to either. Look, Grace, it was just a kiss, okay? Heat of the moment, nothing more. I've been without a woman too long. You're very attractive. I just lost control, okay?" Visions of Kayla danced before him while his heart hammered to the tune of *guilty, guilty, guilty!*

"Why you . . . jerk! What kind of . . . never mind. Give me my keys. I can't believe I even kissed you! What an idiot I am!" Grace raced down the steps as fast as her feet would move.

"Amanda, Ashley! It's time to go," she called to the pair, who were now wide-awake.

Quickly, both girls put on their jackets, shoes, and mittens.

"Can we kiss the dogs good-bye, Miss Grace?" Amanda asked.

Grace glanced at Max.

"Of course you can. They like pretty girls."

"Just like their owner," Grace muttered between gritted teeth.

Beseechingly, Max asked, "Tell me one thing before you leave."

Taking a deep breath and promising to see her own counselor as soon as she could, she rolled her eyes upward. "What?"

"Why do you keep calling your home 'Hope House'? Where is this . . . place?"

Deciding there was no point in lying or dragging this exit out any longer than was necessary, Grace turned to face him.

"Remember I told you I was a counselor?"

She waited for him to reply. He nodded.

"Actually, I'm a psychologist. Women who've been battered and abused come to Hope House. It's a safe haven. They're brought to me by local law enforcement when they need a place to stay, somewhere they can feel safe until they either face their attacker in court, divorce him, or, in some cases, leave only to go right back to the man who sent them running in the first place. This year, Stephanie and the girls, plus my own family, will be celebrating Christmas at Hope House." Grace wanted to invite him to spend Christmas Day with her even after he'd humiliated her when he made an excuse for kissing her. There was just something lonely about him. Thoughts of his spending the holiday alone dampened her holiday spirit.

"Its location is a secret," she added.

Grace watched the numerous expressions roll across his handsome face as she spoke. Curiosity, then she was sure she saw anger. Why would this make him angry? Obviously, she didn't know the man well. It didn't matter because she had a Christmas gathering waiting for her.

"Come on, girls. Let's go decorate that tree I promised you."

Excited they shouted, "Yeah! Yeah! Let's

hurry, Miss Grace, please!"

Grace gave Max one last glance before speaking. "I appreciate your hospitality, Max. Thanks again."

The girls gave kisses to the dogs, who willingly returned them with big, sloppy kisses of their own.

"Bye, Ice-D. Bye, Cliff!" they chorused, before racing out the door.

"Be safe," Max called out to Grace, then closed the door.

Suddenly the cabin seemed too big for him and the dogs. "Let's go for a run, you two. I can't remember the last time I exercised you guys. Better yet, let's go to Powder Rise, and we'll ski down the mountain."

He made quick work of gathering the dogs' boots and coats. His skis were in the shed along with everything else from his former life. Dressing the dogs wasn't easy, but necessary. They ran alongside him while he skied, and their paws had to be protected as well as possible to avoid frostbite.

Thirty minutes later, Max drove his spare snowmobile up to the top of Powder Rise. His mountain. And what would have been Kayla's mountain, their child's mountain.

Standing on top, he felt small in comparison. He stared at the miles of white and green surrounding him. Kayla hadn't enjoyed the snow that much. She probably would've been content to stay in Denver for the rest of her life. Why was he remembering that? What did it matter if Kayla hadn't liked the snow, or skiing, or anything else about it? He hadn't been all that thrilled with her chosen profession either. Couldn't understand why she wanted to put herself at risk every time she walked out the door. And he would never know, he realized.

At the top of Powder Rise, which was at best a decent blue run, Max shoved off the top, Ice-D and Cliff running on each side.

The snow made a soft swishing sound as his skis cut through it. The mountain trail narrowed to a catwalk. Large pines towered above him, an occasional gust of snow from the branches dropping in his path as he maneuvered his way side to side down the hill. Traveling at a slow and steady pace so that both dogs could keep up without becoming tired, Max realized for the first time in many long months just how lonely he was.

Yes, he had friends, but they'd stopped coming around a long time ago. They stopped coming around because he'd turned into another person after Kayla's death. Max had crawled into a cocoon of grief. He remembered the guilt he felt just for being alive. Day by day, he'd cursed Kayla for the choice she'd made. And day by day his grief had changed him, turning him into the hard, bitter man he was today. For the first time since Kayla's death, he didn't want to be that bitter, hateful man. He wanted to be the man he used to be in spite of what he'd said to Grace.

He remembered all too well the minutes that led up to the exact moment when his entire universe tilted. Max didn't like reliving the memory, but today he would. Because today he was going to put the past behind him and move forward.

*It was Christmas Eve, and Max was looking forward to spending the next week pampering his wife. Excited didn't describe what he felt when he learned they were pregnant. A child of his own. Being an only child, Max wanted at least three, if not more. Kayla said two would be her limit. He didn't care if they had just the one or a dozen. Max couldn't wait to give Kayla her Christmas gift, a brand-new fire-engine red Jeep. She'd been driving a Datsun pickup given to her by her father ever since he'd known her. He wanted her to have a vehicle that was a little more reliable, something that wouldn't break down on her all the time. She'd be angry that he'd spent so much money, but he knew she would get over* it. Heck, he had enough money to live like a king for the rest of his life.

Glancing at his watch, he noticed it was after midnight. Kayla was working the three-to-eleven shift, so he expected her anytime. For the next week she belonged to him and no one else. No work, no calls in the middle of the night to come to a crime scene. In fact, he thought they might take a trip to Denver to look at a crib, something for the baby. How he loved thinking about his child!

Damn, he was getting sappy-eyed! It was the holidays. They always did that to him. He loved the bright cheerful red and green lights that twinkled on their Colorado blue spruce, the smell of pine, clean and sharp. He'd finished his Christmas shopping. There were dozens of brightly wrapped packages beneath the tree that hadn't been there when Kayla left for work. Yes, she would be surprised. He laughed. That was an understatement.

Looking at his watch seeing that it was quarter to one, Max jumped when the phone rang.

Most likely it was Kayla calling to let him know she was going out for breakfast with a few friends from the department. She did that about once a month, and it was fine with him. She needed the time to unwind.

Max answered the phone on the third ring.

*"Max Jorgenson?" a male voice inquired.*

*"Yes, this is Max."*

*"We're sending a cruiser to pick you up. Officer Jorgenson has been involved in a shooting . . ."*

Both she and the baby died before they made it to the hospital.

# CHAPTER 9

*Sunday, December 21, 2008*
*The First Day of Winter*

Grace tied the bright red ribbon around the last package, then added a matching bow. She surveyed the mountain of gifts she'd spent the morning wrapping. This was truly going to be the best Christmas Stephanie and her girls had ever had.

She'd bought both girls the latest *American Girl* books along with a special doll of their own: a *Julie Albright* for Ashley and an *Ivy Ling* for Amanda. Both American Girl dolls were going through big changes in their home lives, too. Grace thought the girls would identify with the dolls and the stories that accompanied them. She'd purchased all the extra clothes, shoes, and ribbons that she could find for the dolls. The girls would love changing their clothes and fixing their hair.

She bought Stephanie a new ski suit and

jacket because she'd never owned a new one, saying all that she'd ever owned were secondhand castoffs. There were skis, poles, boots, hats, and gloves that promised warmth in subzero temperatures. Briefly, Grace thought of Max. Stephanie had been an avid skier before marrying Glenn. Maybe now that she was putting her life in order, she would find time to take up the sport. Max would've been an excellent instructor for her.

She barely knew the man, yet she couldn't seem to shake the image of him standing at the door when she'd left. It had been barely twenty-four hours, and here she was pining away like a lovesick teenager. Maybe a *lust*-sick teenager. It'd been a while since she'd had a real relationship. Actually, she hadn't had a real relationship since Matt, her college sweetheart, who turned out to be anything but. Oh, she'd gone on tons of dates. There was always a friend of a friend who had a cousin in town, or someone's newly divorced brother who needed a date for his annual company picnic. She liked dating but had never thought too much about marriage. She was thirty-five years old. Marriage might not be in the cards for her. That was okay because Grace was reasonably happy, loved her profession,

103

enjoyed the life she'd made for herself. More than anything, she felt like a proud parent, helping the many women who passed through Hope House. If she didn't accomplish anything else in her life, she knew she was okay with that. Opening Hope House had been her biggest dream. She'd fulfilled it, and anything extra was simply a bonus.

"Are you about to finish in there?" Juanita called out to Grace. "I have a few things I'd like to wrap."

Grace watched her mother standing in the doorway. Hope House had six available bedrooms. With Stephanie and the girls as her only "guests," just two of the other bedrooms were in use. Grace had turned the smallest bedroom into a temporary wrapping station, where she could wrap presents without being caught. She loved surprises and couldn't wait to see the look on the girls' faces Christmas morning.

"It's all yours, Mother dear," Grace said. "Promise not to peek, okay? Some of those silver-and-gold packages are yours."

"Why don't you put them under the tree?" her mother suggested.

"I am. I just wanted to wait so Amanda and Ashley could help. They're having their hair washed right now."

"That's a grand idea, darling. You certainly know how to treat those girls. Too bad you don't have any of your own."

*Oh no,* Grace thought, *the marriage talk.* Surely, her mother wasn't going to do this to her again. Not at Christmas.

"Mom, we've talked about this before. I'm not getting any younger. If a child and marriage aren't in my future, then please allow me to spoil and love those I can."

Juanita looked at her daughter, tears filling her matching green eyes. "I don't know how I raised such a wonderful and wise woman, but I did. Come here," her mother said. Grace stepped into Juanita's loving embrace.

"I just followed your lead, Mom."

"Oh, I don't know about that. I don't think I was ever brave enough to do some of the things you do, dear. Have I ever told you how proud I am of you? All the women and children you've helped throughout the years. Your father would be so proud of you."

"Stop it, or I'll get all teary-eyed and ruin my mascara," Grace said with a grin. "You know how clumsy I am when it comes to putting on makeup."

"Oh, go on. Let me get these packages wrapped before Bryce discovers what I'm doing. You know what a sneak he can be."

"I'll keep him occupied downstairs while you're wrapping. Hide them under the bed when you're finished."

"Good thinking."

Downstairs, Grace found Bryce where else but snooping into the fridge. "Is that all you do?"

"What?" He shot her his all-American smile. Bryce was as handsome as their father had been, with his coal black hair and dark eyes. He'd just completed the requirements for his Ph.D. in history, same subject as their father, who'd been a professor at the University of Colorado. Starting in January, he would tackle his first real teaching job at the same college. Seeing Bryce all grown-up would have made her father proud. He'd died of a massive heart attack when Bryce was sixteen.

"Every time I look at you, you're eating," Grace teased.

"Hey, I'm a growing boy. I haven't had real food in ages. I wish I could cook."

"Then I'll make sure to get you a cookbook for Christmas."

"Thanks, Sis. I can always count on you to be practical," Bryce said between bites of banana nut bread.

"You better save some of that for the girls.

And what's that supposed to mean?"

Bryce poured a large glass of milk, downed it, then answered, "Just that you've always been the more practical one. That's not a bad thing to be, Gracie."

Suddenly, Grace wanted to cry. Good old practical Grace. Tears shimmered in her eyes. "Think that's why no one ever . . . well, you know, fell head over heels in love with me?" Grace could ask Bryce anything, and she could count on him to tell her the truth.

"Probably. Or they never thought they were good enough. My money's on the latter." Bryce winked at her.

"You're a good brother, you know that?" Grace wrapped him in a hug. Though she was older by six years, he was twice her size, a rock of solid muscle. Years on the ski slopes had guaranteed that.

Which made her think of Max. "Remember that guy you used to go all gaga over? The Olympic skier?" Grace wasn't sure if he would remember, but she wanted to see if it was possible if Bryce knew anything about Max, other than what had been in the news during his career.

"Max Jorgenson? Darn straight I remember him. As a matter of fact, some of the guys and I are going to Maximum Glide next week. Jorgenson owns the resort. Why? You thinking of taking up skiing?"

"I might. I was just curious. I don't know if Mom mentioned it or not, but I . . . uh, spent the night at his house." Grace grinned when she saw how big Bryce's eyes got. They looked like two giant black holes.

"What do you mean, you 'spent the night at his house'?"

Grace swatted him with a kitchen towel. "Not spent the night like the way you're thinking. When I was coming home from Eagle Valley Friday night, I was detoured by the local cops. The snow was so bad I couldn't see, my cell phone wasn't charged, long story short, I wound up knocking on his door at two in the morning. Amanda and Ashley were with me."

"Maybe I was wrong when I used the word 'practical.' 'Sneaky' might be better."

"Stop it! I knew you were a big fan when you were in junior high, just thought you might want to know."

"So that's it? Did you two do . . . anything?" Bryce asked, his eyes downcast, a grin the size of Texas spreading across his face.

"Why you little shit!" Grace laughed so hard she lost her breath. Of course, that was when her mother chose to make her grand entrance.

"Grace, I haven't seen you laugh that hard since you wrote 'I love you' on all of your brother's Valentine cards."

"Oh my gosh, I did do that, didn't I?" She folded over laughing as she remembered when Bryce was in the fourth grade. He came home from school swearing he wouldn't ever return because all the girls thought he liked them. It'd been a rotten thing to do, but Grace and her mother both had told Bryce a dozen times to write out his Valentine cards for his classmates. When Grace offered to do them for him, she decided to play a joke by writing 'I love you' on all the cards for the girls in his class. He'd never let her live it down.

"Yes, and to this day Ramona Clark still has the hots for me."

"What's wrong with that?" Grace asked.

"She weighs about four hundred pounds, that's all. Nice girl, but not my type."

"What is your type, Bryce? Mother and I would love to know. Wouldn't we, Mom?" Grace asked teasingly.

"Well, I suppose this is one of those times when I need to leave the room. So I can eavesdrop."

They were all laughing when Stephanie brought the girls to the kitchen. "They're hungry again, Miss Grace. I don't know how I'll ever repay you. The food bill alone will take me years. They just might eat you out of house and home."

"Nonsense! They're growing girls. I was just telling Bryce what a pig . . . how nice it is to see someone eat all these baked goods." She winked at Stephanie.

"How about peanut butter with strawberry jam on a slice of banana nut bread?" Grace suggested.

"Yummy, Miss Grace," Amanda said.

"Yeah," Ashley added with less enthusiasm.

Grace made sandwiches for the girls while Stephanie fixed each a glass of chocolate milk. Grace would never allow anyone who came to Hope House to go hungry. Many of the women and children who passed through Hope House came to her not only helpless and beaten down. Often they were hungry as well. In many of the so-called homes, food hadn't been a priority. Grace was sure the girls hadn't had enough to eat because when they had first arrived, they were skin and bones. Though they were still on the thin side, Grace was glad to see some pink in their cheeks, and their eyes were much brighter. It still amazed her how a loving, caring touch could change one's life.

Which brought her back to her conversation with Bryce. Practical? Is that what had turned Max off after that kiss? The kiss that took her breath away. The kiss that was unlike any she'd ever experienced. The kiss that almost knocked her whole world askew. Was she a practical kisser doomed to be denied all the passion and romance she'd secretly read about in all the romance novels she hid in her room? She laughed. Love and romance of that nature was pure fiction.

"When will it be time to decorate the tree, Miss Grace?" Amanda asked when she finished her sandwich.

"As soon as your sister is finished, we'll get started." Grace smiled at the girls. When they had returned yesterday afternoon from their adventure, she'd taken them to Jingle Bells and More, one of her favorite Christmas shops in Gypsum, where she'd purchased several Dora the Explorer ornaments for Amanda and *High School Musical* ornaments that all her friends back home would love for Ashley. She'd enjoyed seeing the looks on their faces each time she said yes to their, "Can we buy this one?" The trip had cost her a bit more than she'd budgeted for, but the delight she'd seen in their eyes was worth every penny.

"I'm finished," Ashley called out loudly.

All the adults laughed.

"Then let's get started," Grace encouraged them.

Three hours later, the twelve-foot spruce sparkled with red, green, and white lights, the ornaments she'd bought for the girls, plus dozens and dozens of her own personal ornaments that she'd collected over the years. She still had the hot pink star she'd made for her mother in sixth grade.

"I think there's something missing under the tree. What do you think, Amanda? Ashley?"

The girls looked to their mother for an answer, but Stephanie just shrugged. Bryce and her mother shook their heads.

"Are you sure you don't know?" Grace inquired.

"Nope, Miss Grace we don't. We never had a tree this big before. We just had one Mommy had from when she was a little girl, but it wasn't real. It didn't smell good either," Ashley continued. "It was glass."

Grace's eyes welled with tears when she realized this was the first *real* Christmas tree the girls had ever had.

"Well, since you can't guess, I'm going to tell you." Grace smiled, wrapping one arm around each of their shoulders.

"I believe we are missing some . . . pres-

112

ents!" Grace emphasized the last word as loud as she could without scaring them.

"Presents? Real presents with sparkly wrapping paper and shiny bows?"

"Yep," Grace said.

With a questioning look, Ashley said, "But we already have our presents, Miss Grace. You bought us all these pretty ornaments."

"Oh, sweetie, those aren't your Christmas presents. Those are presents for the . . . tree. Yes, trees get presents, too," Grace improvised. Bryce gave her a high five. She *was* practical, wasn't she?

"They do? Mommy never got presents for our tree," Amanda said.

"Well, only real trees get presents because when they're cut down they leave all their . . . tree friends and family behind."

"You're pushing it, Sis," Bryce interjected.

"Yes, I suppose so. But it doesn't matter. Either way, I'm going to need the help of two little . . . elves. Ashley, Amanda, do you want to be my elves for a while?"

"Do we have to wear those shoes that curl up in the toes like the elves at the mall wear?"

Again they laughed. "All you have to do is follow me," Grace instructed, then headed toward the steps.

As the two little girls trailed behind her,

she heard Amanda whisper to her older sister, "See. I told you there really was a Santa Claus."

# CHAPTER 10

The road leading off the mountain was completely cleared of the afternoon snowfall. The forecasters had been wrong. They'd barely gotten a foot of snow. Max was glad because he didn't want to wait any longer to do what he'd decided to do as he'd skied down Powder Rise yesterday afternoon.

With both dogs securely buckled in the backseat of the fire-engine red Jeep, Max carefully drove down the mountain to his destination: Denver. He couldn't remember the last time he'd been to the city, but now was as good a time as any.

The traffic on I-70 was heavy since it was Sunday morning. Hundreds of residents of Denver and the surrounding area drove to the resorts on the weekend. With Christmas just four days away, the traffic was horrendous.

Three hours later he made it to the city. First on his list was the Hummer dealership, where he traded in the Jeep he'd bought for Kayla for a bright yellow Hummer. Eddie would love this.

Next, he drove downtown to the police station. He had already dropped the dogs off at a doggie spa for grooming, figuring by the time they were finished, he would be, too.

He was taking a chance, hoping to take advantage of his acquaintance with Kayla's former partner, Paul McCormick, who, he remembered, was a decent guy.

Luck was with him. According to the girl manning the front desk, Paul's shift had just ended. She paged him and told Max to have a seat.

"Max Jorgenson, good to see you," Paul said when he saw him. "I couldn't imagine who it was when Kathy paged me. How are you?"

"Actually, I'm doing okay. Listen, I need a favor. I hate to ask you, but it's important, and I don't know who else I can trust."

"Sure. Let's go to the break room. I can't guarantee the coffee, but it's private."

"Great," Max said.

Once they were seated, Paul poured them each a cup of coffee. Max sipped his, trying hard not to gag.

Paul got straight to the point. "So what

can I do for you?"

"Have you ever heard of a woman's shelter called Hope House?"

Paul raised his eyebrows. "Everyone in law enforcement knows about it. It's one of the best-kept secrets in Gypsum. Why? Do you know someone who needs protection?"

"No, no, nothing like that. You see . . ." This wasn't as easy as Max thought it would be. It felt like a betrayal of Kayla. "The woman who runs the place, Grace Landry. What can you tell me about her?"

"Now wait a minute, Max, Grace Landry is as good as it gets. Just ask around. Whatever beef you have with her, I'll warn you, there's a thousand guys that'll come to her defense."

"Look, Paul, I owe the woman a favor. She broke down on Blow Out Hill the other night. She had two little girls with her. I just need to find a way to contact her."

"In my day, when a lady wanted any contact from a man, she usually gave him her phone number."

"I have her number. Here." Max removed the crumpled slip of paper that Grace had written her number on from his pocket. "I want to surprise her. I don't want to call her. Can you help me or not?" Max didn't like begging, but if he had to, in this instance he would.

"Remember the old Sutton Mansion in Gypsum? It was in the paper a few years ago, something about it being on the historical register." Paul looked him squarely in the eye. "No one knows about this, Max. If word got out that it was a shelter, the women Grace works so hard to protect wouldn't stand a chance. There are a lot of angry husbands and boyfriends out there who would like nothing more than to see her shut down."

"You have my word I won't tell a soul. Thanks, Paul. I really appreciate your going out on a limb for me."

"Anytime." Paul stood, and Max clasped his outstretched hand.

"Whenever you want to go skiing, take a ride up to Maximum Glide. Ask for Eddie and tell him to give you and your family anything you want."

"Thanks, Max, I might just do that. Skiing is getting a bit pricey these days."

Max laughed. "Don't I know it. Be careful out there."

Max left the police station, picked up Ice-D and Cliff, who now smelled like strawberries and cream. There was one more stop Max needed to make on his way home.

He was going to buy a Christmas tree. He was sure the decorations were stored in the shed, along with everything else he'd packed away when he moved. Better yet, he'd buy all new decorations. He'd kept the ones Kayla had purchased packed away, but if he was going to make a fresh start, he might as well go all the way.

Three hours later, with two dogs that smelled like dessert, a fifteen-foot blue spruce strapped to the top of the Hummer, and six hundred dollars' worth of decorations, Max drove his new vehicle up the winding road heading for home.

Home. How strange it sounded to refer to his log cabin as *home.* He'd been living there for two years and never once thought of the place as anything other than a place to sleep, eat, shower, and drink. Funny, he hadn't even thought of taking a drink since Grace landed on his doorstep.

"That's a good thing, right, guys?" Max asked the two dogs.

"Woof, woof."

Max let the dogs out and unloaded the Hummer. Once inside, he put the stand together, wrestled with the tree until he got it in the stand, then filled the stand with water and the package of stuff they'd given him to help the tree stay fresh longer. Both dogs barked at the front door.

"I'm having so much fun I forgot all about you guys." Max stood aside as the two leapt through the door. Both cocked their heads to the side when they saw the giant tree in the center of the den. To prove they were still in control, both Huskies trotted over to the tree, where they lifted their hind legs and proceeded to piss all over it.

Max stared at the pair, shocked by their actions, then he started to laugh. He laughed so hard his sides hurt, and his eyes filled with tears.

"I take it you guys don't like the tree. Too bad 'cause it's staying. If you want to pee on it, be my guest, but you'd better not mess with the decorations. Or else."

"Woof! Woof!"

Max strung the multicolored lights on the tree, then one by one he carefully placed the ornaments on the branches. Ice-D and Cliff were mesmerized when he turned all the room lights off and plugged in the tree lights. The giant log cabin instantly became a home. To honor the woman who'd been his wife, he'd bought a silver star and placed it on the front of the tree where he could see it. To honor the woman who'd given him his life back, he carefully placed a crystal snow angel next to the star.

Max stepped back to admire his handiwork. He gave a long whistle as he stared at his tree. This was a time for new beginnings, a time to start fresh. Kayla would want this for him, but more important, now he wanted it for himself.

It was about time he gave old *Bryce* a run for his money.

# CHAPTER 11

*Christmas Eve, 2008*
*Ten Minutes before Midnight*

Grace had just turned off her bedroom light when she heard the doorbell ring. She dressed quickly in jeans and a T-shirt before quietly making her way downstairs. Thankful she had purchased two turkeys and a ham at the butcher shop that afternoon, she wondered how many more would join her for Christmas dinner.

Grace carefully punched in the numbers on the alarm panel before peering through a small hole at the top of the door. When she didn't see anyone, she opened her front door to see who was out there. Sometimes the women were afraid when they arrived. Grace understood this as she stepped out onto the porch in the frigid night air.

"Hello," she called. "It's okay. There's nothing to be afraid of." She waited a minute or so to see if anyone materialized from either side of the long porch that wrapped around the perimeter of the old house.

Wrapping her arms around her for warmth, she waited another minute before calling out again. "Is anyone there?" She didn't like this. Something wasn't right. Grace was about to step inside and call her contact at the police station when she heard someone call her name.

"Who's there?"

A large figure stepped out from behind the shadows of tall pine trees grouped in a corner on the side of the house. Fearing this was an angry husband or boyfriend Grace stood next to the front door with her completely charged cell phone in her hand. "I'm going to count to three. If you don't show yourself, I'm calling the police. One. Two—"

"It's me. Please don't call the police."

Grace wasn't sure what was worse; being surprised by an angry man looking to beat his wife or an idiot who didn't have any social graces.

"Max Jorgenson, what are you doing here? Furthermore, how on earth did you find me?" Grace's hands shook, and her heart beat so fast she feared it would wear out before she had a chance to calm herself.

He stepped away from the shadows. The light coming from inside the house outlined his large frame. "Can I come inside? It's cold out here, plus I'm lost."

Grace smiled, glad for the darkness. "I suppose I owe you this. Tell me you're not running from some crazed girlfriend before I let you inside," Grace joked.

He stepped onto the porch, then followed her to the kitchen.

Grace turned the kitchen lights on, pointed to a chair. "Sit."

Max obeyed.

"I'm going to make a pot of tea. I hope by the time it's ready you have a good explanation for coming all the way out here just to scare me half to death." Grace was as good as her word. She filled two mugs with tap water, nuked them for three minutes, dunked a tea bag in each one, grabbed sugar and cream from the fridge.

"Okay, tell me why you're here." She glanced at the clock on the microwave. "Do you realize it's officially Christmas? I can't wait to see . . . never mind. Just tell me why you're here. And it better be good."

Max smiled at her — a smile that actually reached his eyes. "This is probably the most outrageous thing I've ever done in my life."

"It's not, trust me. I've seen your Alpine,

downhill skiing."

Max grinned. "Pretty wild, huh?"

"Bryce appreciates it much more than I do."

Max clammed up. "Maybe coming here was a mistake. This . . . *Bryce,* I know it's none of my business, and you can tell me that, but before you do, there's something I need to say. Then if you still want me to leave, I will. No questions asked."

"That's fair enough. Say what you came to say." Grace took a deep breath trying to calm the erratic beating of her heart.

"Two years ago my wife was killed in the line of duty. She was a police officer, and she truly loved her work. She and her partner were called to the scene of a domestic dispute. The man had just beaten his wife and two-year-old daughter. When Kayla and her partner arrived at the house, the guy threatened to kill the child if they didn't back off. Kayla's partner Paul radioed in asking for a hostage negotiator. Knowing it would take time before they could get to the scene, Kayla spoke with the man, asking him to let the child go. She offered to exchange herself for the child. Apparently the deranged guy liked the idea of holding a female cop hostage. But when Kayla approached him, he must've changed his mind, something happened to scare him, I don't know, and her partner didn't either. Whatever the reason, he changed his mind. He shot Kayla twice in the chest, then put the gun in his mouth and shot himself. But at least the wife and child were safe. Paramedics got Kayla to the hospital, they even sent a patrol car to bring me to the hospital. By the time I got there, it was too late. She died, and when she died, everything in me died, too. I stopped eating, stopped socializing, I stopped everything. Then I started to drink. It never got out of hand, but it could have." Max watched her to see her reaction.

"I remember now when that was on the news. I am so sorry, Max. I don't know what to say, or what it has to do with me."

"You'll think I'm crazy when I tell you."

Grace laughed. "No more so than I do right now. Go on." She was used to listening to people. It's what she did.

"When you and the girls showed up on my doorstep the other night, I was angry. Not at you, but angry at myself. I was . . . hell, I was instantly attracted to you. I even thought of you as a snow angel." He took a sip of the tea. "I felt incredibly guilty, too. There hasn't been anyone since Kayla. I'd buried myself in my grief for so long, I think

I became comfortable with it. You and those two little girls reminded me that life is worth living. I even bought a Christmas tree with all the trimmings. Looks pretty good, too. Though the dogs didn't like it. Before I had even started with the decorating, they both pissed all over it." Max laughed loudly.

Grace smiled. "Shame on them. I remember you telling me you didn't like the holidays. Is this why?"

Max nodded. "Kayla died on Christmas Eve, two years ago. She'd just found out she was pregnant."

"Oh Max, how terrible for you! I'm so sorry."

"Yes, I was too. More than I ever imagined. That first year was hard. Then it got a little easier, and when it did, I felt so guilty that I'd plunge myself right back into that dark place just to ease the feelings of guilt that I had for being alive."

"It's called survivor's guilt and is quite common. Mother went through a period like that when my father died. She'd always been the one to catch everything from the flu to ear infections. My father never had a sick day in his life. He dropped dead of a massive heart attack while he was teaching a history class."

"I guess you never get over it, you just

learn to live with it."

"That's true. We all have our own ways of dealing with grief. There's no right or wrong way, Max. Guilt is a terrible thing for those who are left behind."

"Which brings me to the reason why I came here in the first place. Or one of them."

"I'm listening," Grace said.

"You're good at this stuff, but I suppose you already know that."

"I've done it a time or two."

"First tell me about Bryce."

Grace's eyes lit up like the tree back at the cabin. *Home,* he corrected himself, *it's home now.*

"He's absolutely wonderful. I can't imagine my life without him. We don't get to see one another as much as we used to, but we're okay with it. We talk on the phone whenever we can. Bryce isn't too good at answering his e-mail, but I'm sure once he gets settled into his new routine, he will. From what I understand, most colleges use their e-mail systems to communicate with their students. Bryce is going to teach history at the University of Colorado after the first of the year. He's very excited about his career."

"I guess I don't stand a chance. A ski bum

versus a college professor."

"Max, Bryce is my *brother*."

His eyes brightened like two blue moons. "Why didn't you tell me?"

"I guess I just assumed you knew. When Bryce was in junior high school, he was one of your biggest fans. He followed your career, watched you win all those Olympic medals. For a while, Mom and I feared he might take to the slopes instead of going to college, but he's too much of a history buff, just like my father."

"So does this mean I have a chance? A slight chance of asking you out on a date?"

Grace was so thrilled, everything around her blurred. "You can ask all you want, Max."

"But you don't have to say yes. Am I right?"

"No, you're not. Listen, there's something I want to ask you. It's a bit . . . personal, but since you drove all the way here and on Christmas Day, there's no reason not to. When you kissed me, did you really mean what you said? That it was just a kiss?"

"That's the biggest lie I've ever told in my life. I wanted to wrap you in my arms, drag you upstairs, but I couldn't. It took a lot of soul-searching for me to realize that it's okay to be happy. That's why I'm here."

"There's just one more thing," Grace asked. "Do you think I'm practical?"

"You? Practical? No way. Not in the least. Though I have to admit I don't know you very well, but I intend to."

"You're sure," Grace teased.

"One hundred percent, cross my heart. Why do you ask?"

"Bryce told me I was practical, said it could be one of the reasons I've never settled down to raise a family."

"Well, I'm going to have to tell your brother a thing or two. If you were practical, you'd be married with a houseful of kids. Where is he?"

"Actually, he's upstairs sleeping," Grace said. "Follow me. No, never mind. Wait here. I'll be right back."

Grace didn't bother knocking when she saw the light shining beneath his door. Shoving the door aside, Grace stepped into the room. Bryce was sitting up in bed, reading. "You ever heard of knocking?"

"Yes, but this is my house, remember?"

"So?"

"I have your Christmas present. It's in the kitchen."

"And it's something that can't wait until everyone else is up?"

"No, actually it can't. If you don't want it,

I can give him, I mean it, to someone who'll appreciate it."

"All right, you're not going to give me a minute's peace until I see what you've cooked up. Oh crap, Gracie, is this about that cookbook you said you were giving me? Because if it is, I'll see it soon enough."

"Bryce, march your ass downstairs to the kitchen right now. Don't ask me another question. Now go."

"Okay, okay. Women," he muttered as he slipped a T-shirt over his head.

Grace felt like a kid at Christmas. Max wanted to get to know her better. Bryce was about to get the surprise of his life. And it was going to be the best Christmas she'd ever had.

Max sat at the table sipping his tea when Bryce entered the kitchen. "Hey, Bryce, what's up?" he asked casually.

Bryce looked at Grace, then Max. "Tell me I'm not dreaming. Please."

"See?" Grace said to Max. "I told you he was your biggest fan."

# EPILOGUE

*Christmas Day, 2009*

Grace paced back and forth inside her suite. She looked at her Rolex, a gift from Max. It was almost time. She couldn't believe she'd agreed to this, but wanting to prove to everyone that she, Grace Landry, was anything but practical, when Max asked her to marry him, she agreed to his request about the location of the ceremony. And so, her wedding ceremony was about to take place on a ski slope at Maximum Glide. She smiled. She was anything but practical.

So there she was, thirty-six years old, decked out in a five-thousand-dollar *white* ski suit, waiting for Stephanie, who was now her dearest friend and also her maid of honor. Ashley, nine going on twenty, would act as lead flower girl, and, of course, Amanda would do whatever her sister told her to do.

A loud knock startled her. It was time.

"Don't you look gorgeous, all decked out in white," Stephanie remarked as she perused the white ski suit she'd chosen for Grace. Stephanie had become the manager of the sporting goods' shop at Maximum Glide. When she wasn't selling ski equipment, she acted as an instructor. Both her girls were now expert on the slopes. Max had high hopes for Ashley in the 2018 Olympics and her sister four years later.

Max had high hopes about everything. Grace couldn't be happier. Though it had only been a year since she met Max, she'd fallen in love with him the very first time he kissed her. She wouldn't have admitted it then, but now she would.

Bryce was beside himself when she told him she was marrying Max. He said it was a dream come true for him. Grace told him she was happy her dream made his dream come true, but if he thought for one minute that he was going to mooch off Max for free lessons, he'd better think again. He'd have to enroll in the classes just like everyone else.

Max was spending his time as a ski instructor at Maximum Glide. Eddie was still the manager. He and Stephanie were dating hot and heavy. Grace was sure there would be another wedding in the near future.

Glenn had been sentenced to eight years in prison, not for hurting Stephanie alone, but for escaping also. Their divorce had been final for almost eight months.

"It's time, Grace. I think this is the most exciting thing that's ever happened, don't you?"

"It is, it really is. I thought I'd never get married, and look at me now." She hugged her dear friend.

"We better go before all the lifts are taken," Stephanie teased, knowing Max had reserved a lift for the wedding party and the guests.

"Let's go." Grace grabbed her twenty-pound ski boots, her poles, and her hat and gloves. Her new "Maxie skis" were stored at the lift.

Outside, the sun shone brightly. There wasn't a cloud in the sky. The temperature was in the low twenties, but Grace didn't mind the cold. She was about to marry the sexiest man alive.

He waited for her at the top of Gracie's Way, a new trail named in her honor.

Max, Bryce, and her mother were all gathered at the top of the mountain when Grace and Stephanie jumped off the lift. She adjusted her sunglasses and skied across a small patch of ice to get to Max.

They opted for a simple ceremony, or as simple as one got considering they were going to take their vows at the top of the mountain, then ski to the bottom for the pronouncement that would unite them as husband and wife. A friend of Eddie's, who was also a justice of the peace, had agreed to marry them.

"Are you sure you want to do this?" Max asked as he bent down to kiss her.

"Get married? Are you kidding? I can't wait," Grace assured him.

"I meant are you sure you want to get married on the slopes?"

"I'm not a practical person, Max. You should know that by now. Frankly, I wouldn't have it any other way. Now, let's get this show on the slopes."

"Grace, I love you," Max whispered in her ear.

"I know you do, darling. The feeling is mutual." Grace slid around to face the justice of the peace. Stephanie stood to her right, and Eddie, the best man, stood to Max's left. Bryce and her mother stayed with Amanda and Ashley. Max had arranged for the lift to take Juanita back down the mountain.

*Everything was perfect,* Grace thought as she cleared her throat. Nothing in her life had ever been as perfect as this moment on top of a cold, snowy mountain with the sun shining down on her.

"Dearly beloved, we are gathered here on this mountain to unite Max Jorgenson and Grace Landry in holy matrimony."

After reciting the traditional wedding vows, with Grace and Max saying their "I do"s, the justice of the peace stepped aside and tucked his small black book inside his ski jacket before spinning around and directing his ski tips downhill toward the bottom of the mountain. "As planned, I will unite the couple in holy matrimony at the bottom of the mountain." Max used his poles to position himself by Grace, and once there was a reasonable distance between them, he looked at her. "Are you ready?"

Her grin was so broad it hurt. "I don't think I can wait another minute," Grace said, before shoving off. "I'll meet you at the bottom."

Bryce, Stephanie, and her girls followed behind.

With the wind at their backs, they curved and zigzagged down the mountain in near-record time. When they reached the bottom, there was a crowd gathering. "Do you know these people?" Grace whispered to Max.

"No, but apparently they know us. Look." Max pointed to several in the group who were holding signs that read CONGRATULA-TIONS MAX AND GRACE!!!

The justice of the peace cleared his throat. "By the powder, uh, I mean power vested in me by the good state of Colorado and by the fans cheering behind us, I now pronounce you man and wife. You can kiss her now, Max."

Max dropped his poles and turned to his wife, who had dropped her poles, too. Together, they slid to the ground, embracing one another. When his lips touched hers, Grace was sure the world actually tilted. His kiss was deep and passionate. Her senses were alive and tingling.

"Max?" she mumbled while they were kissing.

"Hmm?"

"The snow is going to melt if we don't stop!"

"I'm that hot?"

"Yes, Mr. Jorgenson, you are that hot. Now help your wife up, or I might break something. And if I break something, that means we'll have to cancel our honeymoon, and I really don't want to because I've never been to Hawaii, or Ireland, or Spain."

"If you put it that way, I don't have a

choice, now do I, Mrs. Jorgenson?"

"Say it again, Max."

"What?"

"Call me Mrs. Jorgenson."

"Mrs. Jorgenson, you're going to be so sick of hearing me call you that for the next two months, you just might resort to using your maiden name."

"Never, Max. Never in a million years," Grace said, as he lifted her into his arms.

"Mrs. Jorgenson?"

"Yes, Mr. Jorgenson?"

"There's something I've been wanting to say to you all day, and now seems as good a time as any."

"What would that be?"

"Merry Christmas, Grace. Merry Christmas."

"Merry Christmas, Max. I think I'm about the happiest woman alive right now."

"I love you, Grace. Always and forever."

"Oh Max, I love you, too!"

"Hey, did we order a wedding cake?"

Grace looked at Max, the love of her life and now her husband. Her life was so very rich at that moment, she wanted to burn it into her memory.

Forever and always.

■ ■ ■ ■

# THE PRESENTS OF ANGELS

## MARIE BOSTWICK

■ ■ ■ ■

# CHAPTER 1

In the fourth month of her pregnancy and thrilled by the peapod swelling in her abdomen, Kendra Erickson Loomis packed her leotards away in a drawer and bought several two-sizes-too-large sweaters to wear over black maternity tights when she was teaching at the dance studio. After enduring weeks of morning sickness, Kendra was overjoyed that she was feeling better and finally *looked* pregnant.

When Andy came home from the church that evening, Kendra made him sit down on the sofa and watch as she modeled her new maternity wear.

"What do you think?" she asked, turning in a slow circle. "Don't I look the very picture of maternal bliss?"

"You absolutely do," Andy affirmed.

Unlike Kendra, Andy had traveled down the road of parenthood once before, when fourteen-year-old Thea was born. Having

141

been through the emotional ups-and-downs of pregnancy with his first wife, the wife who had deserted them when Thea was just four, Andy knew that Kendra's pride in her thickening waistline would wane in the coming months. But right now she was happy and nothing on earth pleased Andy Loomis more than that.

"You're gorgeous," he said.

As happened so frequently now, Kendra's eyes glistened with unexpected tears. "Do you think so honestly? Or are you just saying that?"

Andy's handsome face adopted a slightly offended expression. "Kendra, are you accusing me of dishonesty?" he asked, straightening his shoulders as though to underscore the unquestionable uprightness of his character. "I'm a minister! Would I lie to you?"

"Well . . . I guess not," Kendra said. She ran her hands over her stomach, pulling the fabric of her sweater tight under her little belly to show it off.

"Oh, Andy! I'm so excited! I can't believe this is really happening! Growing up in Ohio, I had only two dreams: to be a dancer and to get married and have children. After so many years alone I'd just about given up. Falling in love, marrying you, and getting to be Thea's mom was the most wonderful thing . . ." Kendra sniffed.

"No one could ask for more than I already have and now . . . this! Andy! We're having a baby!"

"We are. In five more months. January fifteenth."

"Five months! That sounds like forever. I wonder if I can wait that long?"

"I don't see as you have much choice in the matter. Believe me, it's coming a lot faster than you think. Actually, I wanted to talk to you about that. Well, not exactly about that — about the Christmas pageant. With the baby coming so soon after Christmas, don't you think you ought to hand the directing job over to someone else?"

"Someone else? No way! How can you even suggest that? The Christmas pageant is the whole reason we met in the first place!"

What Kendra said was absolutely true.

When she came to Maple Grove three years before, it was the church Christmas pageant that brought her. At the time, she was a Radio City Music Hall Rockette, the iconic chorus line known for its intricate precision dance numbers, gorgeous costumes, and perfectly executed "eye-high" kicks. Every Christmas, for four shows a day, thousands of theatergoers lined up outside New York's Radio City Music Hall, waiting to see the Rockettes perform in the world-famous Christmas Spectacular. Kendra was a ten-year veteran of the show. If she hadn't slipped and broken her ankle during rehearsal, she might have continued on that path, living alone in New York and spending every Christmas season dancing at Radio City, and wowing the audiences who crowded the Music Hall to see the Christmas Spectacular, but never entering into the spirit of the holiday herself or even stopping to consider what Christmas was really about.

But Providence had other plans for Kendra.

After Kendra broke her ankle one of the other Rockettes, a nineteen-year-old rookie named Stacey, newly arrived from Vermont, made a few calls home and got Kendra a job directing the Maple Grove Community Church Christmas pageant.

It was supposed to be a temporary job, something to pay the bills until Kendra's foot healed and she could return to New York. She never counted on liking Maple Grove so much and she certainly never planned to fall in love with Stacey's brother, Andy, pastor of the church, but that's exactly what happened.

"You can't expect me to let someone else direct," Kendra insisted. "That show is my baby!"

Andy got up from the sofa, stood in front of his wife, and laid his hand gently on her stomach. "No, Kendra. *This* is your baby. *Our* baby. And it's going to be born just a couple of weeks after Christmas. I know how much you want to direct the pageant again and I know that no one can do it as well as you, but . . . so late in the pregnancy?

"Think, Kendra. Think about how exhausted you were last year. It took you weeks to recover. And that was before the dance studio had really started to take off. You're busier now than ever before. Nine months pregnant — how do you think you'll be able to direct the show and teach full-time at the studio?"

Kendra was silent, not wanting to concede Andy's point, but realizing that he was probably right.

Before Kendra took over as director, the audience for the annual Christmas pageant was small and getting smaller every year. But Kendra's fresh vision had breathed new life into the show, transforming it from a tired old holiday chestnut into a magical and inspiring production.

Come December twenty-third, the Maple

145

Grove Community Church Christmas Pageant was the hottest ticket for miles. People loved the pageant, but few understood how much work went into coordinating and directing such a huge production, especially with a cast that was made up entirely of local teenagers. The kids worked hard, but they were still kids. Sometimes Kendra felt more like she was herding cats than directing actors. Andy had a point. In her condition, so late in the pregnancy, could she possibly handle directing the show? Could the baby?

Andy tucked a finger under her chin and tilted Kendra's face up so she would look him in the eye. "Face it, sweetie. You're a victim of your own success."

Kendra sighed. "I guess you're right. Have I ever told you that I hate it when you're right?"

"You may have mentioned it once or twice." Andy smiled. "Cheer up. It's just for one year."

"I know."

"And just think! Before too long you'll have one more little dancer to join the chorus line."

"What makes you think the baby will grow up to be a dancer?"

"With her pedigree? Are you kidding? I

expect her to be born wearing tap shoes and tights."

"And what if it's a boy?"

Andy shrugged. "Doesn't matter. Boy or girl, the kid's born to dance. After all, this baby has Rockettes on both sides of the family tree: you, plus my sister, Stacey."

Andy grinned and laid his hand on Kendra's stomach for a moment, then rocked backward as if stunned by the strength of his unborn child's kick. "Whoa! Did you feel that? What did I tell you? Dancing already."

A smile tugged at the corners of Kendra's lips. "Andy, right now the baby is only about five inches long. You can't feel a thing in there. I only started to feel it move last week, this little gurgling shift inside me, more like gas bubbles than anything else. In fact, it probably was gas bubbles."

"Well, call it whatever you want, but I felt kicking. I'm telling you, Kendra, our baby is in there right now, doing a double-time step."

Kendra laughed. "All right. You win. I am officially cheered up."

"Good," Andy said. "That's one problem solved, now we've just got to figure out who will direct the show. That'll be harder.

"Before you took over, expectations for

the Christmas pageant were so low that I just had to find a warm body. If Stacey hadn't called from New York to say that one of her Rockette friends had broken her ankle and needed a job, I probably would have asked Marty Kemper to direct it. But now that you've raised the bar so high . . ."

Andy ran his thumb and forefinger down the ridge of his jawline, thinking. "On the other hand . . . maybe Marty wouldn't be so bad . . ."

"Marty Kemper!" Kendra shouted. "Are you out of your mind?"

Marty was a nice guy who owned an auto body shop in town and fancied himself something of an actor. And though Marty was an artist with a metalworking hammer and a spray-paint gun, taking dents out of cars was the extent of his talent. Still, that didn't stop him from trying out for and occasionally landing small parts in community theater productions where he delivered his lines with overly dramatic grimaces and gestures in a loud, slightly squeaky voice that set Kendra's teeth on edge.

"Over my dead body are you letting Marty get his hands on my production! Andy Loomis, I will deliver this baby backstage during intermission before I'll let that happen! I mean it!"

Andy laughed and held up his hands, giving way in the face of Kendra's ire. "Okay, okay. I guess Marty's just going to have to stick to hammering dents out of Subarus. But who do you think can take over for you?"

Kendra didn't hesitate before answering. "Darla Benton."

"Darla Benton? Your former arch nemesis — that Darla Benton?"

"Don't exaggerate," Kendra said dismissively. "Darla was never my arch nemesis. We just had a few artistic differences, that's all."

Andy raised his eyebrows. "A few artistic differences? Funny. That's not how I remember it."

Mrs. Benton was the widow of Jake Benton who had written the script for the original pageant and had directed it for thirty years. As far as Darla was concerned, her late husband's play, a version of the Christmas story told entirely in rhyming couplets, was absolutely perfect. She didn't want it altered by so much as a comma. So when Kendra came to Maple Grove and scrapped the entire script in favor of something she felt was more "entertaining," basically leaving out the entire story of the Nativity, Mrs. Benton was livid and determined to see Kendra fired.

And she might have succeeded had not Kendra, faced with the choice of either making up with Darla or having the show cancelled completely, added a second act that put Jake Benton's words to music and focused entirely on the real Christmas story, the Nativity. And that one decision, more than anything, accounted for the show's success.

Without the second act, Kendra's show had been exactly what she'd set out to make it — entertaining. *With* the second act the play became something much more powerful, a story that reflected the beauty, wonder, and true meaning of Christmas to everyone who saw it, Kendra included.

While sitting in the darkened church-turned-theater, watching little Thea, as a humbled and awestruck Mary, sing about the miracle of Christmas, Kendra felt an unfamiliar stirring in her soul. The flame of her faith was ignited that night and Kendra's life was changed forever.

And she wasn't the only one. The revised Christmas pageant so delighted Darla that she became Kendra's biggest supporter. Not only did she enlist the help of the Quilting Bees, the church quilt circle of which Darla was definitely the Queen Bee, to help sew beautiful costumes for the performers, but she appointed herself Kendra's assistant director. At first, Kendra hadn't been exactly thrilled at the prospect of having an eighty-year-old assistant, but Darla had proven herself energetic, helpful, and incredibly supportive. Despite their age difference, Kendra and Darla were now fast friends.

"Kendra, are you sure?" Andy asked. "Darla just celebrated her eighty-second birthday. Do you think she's up to it?"

"Absolutely. Darla's got more energy than anybody I know. She can run me into the ground most days. She understands the show. After all, she's been working alongside me for the last three years. She'll be a great director."

But Andy still wasn't convinced.

"Are you sure you don't want someone younger? Maybe we could find another Rockette who's on injured reserve. Of course," he mused, "you can't count on finding a Rockette with a broken ankle every day of the week. But maybe . . ."

Andy narrowed his eyes, feigning deep concentration. "If Stacey 'accidentally' spilled some water on the floor of the rehearsal space. You know, a thing like that might just make a girl slip and fall and then . . ."

"Andy!" Kendra slapped her husband

151

playfully on the arm. "I will not have you involving your sister in one of your nefarious schemes. There will be no new Rockettes coming to Maple Grove — especially no newer and younger Rockettes. You're just going to have to live with the one you have, even if she is old, and worn out, and simply enormous with child."

"I can live with that. Come here." Andy smiled and reached for his wife, pulling her into his embrace. "Can I tell you something, Mrs. Loomis? You're the only Rockette I'll ever want — the only woman for me, for now and forever. Got that?"

"I'm not sure. Would you mind repeating that?"

But Andy ignored her request, pulling her even closer, putting his warm lips on hers and letting the sweetness of his kisses speak for him.

# CHAPTER 2

The week before Thanksgiving, Kendra looked very different than she had twelve weeks previously. Her formerly two-sizes-too-large sweaters barely fit her now. The purple yarn stitches stretched tight to accommodate the basketball bulge of Kendra's belly, looking completely at odds with her still slender legs in their black tights.

Gazing into the studio mirror as she led her advanced beginner tap class through the last chorus of "Rock Around the Clock," Kendra decided she looked like an enormous dancing grape clinging to a withered black stem.

*Like a Fruit of the Loom commercial gone horribly wrong,* she thought as she peered into the mirror before observing that, once again, Nora Casey had turned left when the rest of the girls had turned right, bumping into Jena Lukens.

"Nora!" Jena shouted, stomping her tap

shoe. "Knock it off!"

"Sorry," Nora mumbled. Her face turned red.

"You're so clumsy!"

"Jena, that's enough of that," Kendra said, raising her voice to be heard over the clatter of the eight little pairs of feet that were still tapping out the time step. "Catch up. Both of you. Shuffle, hop, step, step, fa-lap, step. Come on, everybody. Here comes the swing step. Are you ready?"

Jena glared at Nora a moment longer before resuming the dance, pasting an insincere smile on her face, putting her arms out in front of her, and flipping her wrists up and down in perfect time to the music while her feet flawlessly tapped out the steps of the dance. With her easy grace, Jena was a sharp contrast to Nora who hesitated several moments, trying to recapture the beat before rejoining the dance. When she did she moved stiffly with her head held at a downward angle and her eyes glued to the feet of the girl in front of her, shuffling uncertainly through the steps, a heartbeat behind the rest of the girls.

Normally, Kendra would have stopped the music and had them all start again, so Nora wouldn't get into the habit of falling behind, but she just didn't have the energy. She was so tired.

It was a good thing that she'd taken Andy's advice and handed the directorship of the Christmas pageant over to Darla. The way she was feeling now, there was no way she'd have been able to get through a full rehearsal schedule and teach classes at the studio. Three months ago, she'd been filled with boundless energy and now? It was all she could do to lead the ten little tappers through "Rock Around the Clock."

Not for the first time, Kendra thought about how much had changed in the last three months.

Now she truly was enormous with child. And while she was still excited about the upcoming birth, she was worried about . . . well, almost everything. Nothing seemed as simple and clear-cut as it had been when she and Andy stood kissing in the living room, filled with love and gratitude for each other and for the new baby that would soon join their family.

It seemed to Kendra that the bigger her belly got, the more distant Andy had become. Being a pastor wasn't easy; Kendra knew that. Andy had to be a manager, diplomat, teacher, speaker, and nursemaid, as well as a spiritual guide to his flock. He had to be available to them twenty-four hours a day, seven days a week. Kendra had known from the first that being a pastor's wife meant sharing her husband with half the town and being understanding when emergencies called him away, often at the oddest hours. With the church membership growing, it was unusual for the Loomis family to go more than three nights running without the phone ringing in the middle of the night, summoning Andy to the bedside of some seriously ill church member. Sometimes, after one of these late night summonses, he was able to return home and grab a short nap before going to work, but more often than not he went directly from the hospital to the church. Kendra didn't know how he was able to function on so little sleep and, to make matters worse, recently the board of deacons had scheduled a lot of night meetings. That, in combination with the usual evening programs at the church, meant that Andy rarely ate with the family anymore.

Kendra and Thea ate their dinner together, often in silence. What had become of the sweet little girl with the blond braids and ready smile? The girl who had captured Kendra's heart three years ago? Everything changed when Thea started high school. At fourteen, Thea was in the full bloom of adolescence, giddy and silly one moment, moody and brooding the next. Kendra knew that these teenage mood swings were normal. She remembered being that way herself at that age. Even so, Kendra found it hard to understand how her relationship with Thea had changed so much and so quickly.

Having barely known a mother's love, Thea had eagerly welcomed Kendra to the family, proudly introducing Kendra to everyone she met as her mom, never using the word stepmother. That suited Kendra just fine. She loved Thea as her own child. So much so that, when she discovered she was pregnant, Kendra had been a little worried, wondering if she could ever love another child as much as she loved Thea. And as badly as she was behaving, Kendra still loved her.

But she missed the closeness and cozy talks they used to have. Now, the moment she finished eating, Thea mumbled a request to be excused and then went to her bedroom, rarely emerging until the next morning. Kendra did the dishes with only Wendell, the tawny and white cat she'd brought with her from New York, to keep her company. The greedy feline wound around her ankles while she worked, waiting for Kendra to toss a few table scraps his way. After the kitchen was clean, Kendra sat on the family room sofa with Wendell curled up beside her and watched television until bedtime, not bothering to build a fire because it seemed like a waste if there was no one to share it with.

Sometimes Andy arrived home before Kendra went to sleep, but when she tried to talk to him about his day, he would brush off her questions, saying that the last thing he wanted to talk about was work. He was still Andy, as sweet and kind as ever, solicitous of her health and the baby's, jumping up to get her a pillow if Kendra's back hurt, or to rub her legs when she got a cramp, never forgetting to ask how her day had gone, and listening dutifully while she talked. And that was just the problem. Every kindness Andy performed for her he performed dutifully . . . and distantly, as though he were going through the motions.

At bedtime, before he turned out the light, Andy would lean over and give Kendra a quick peck on the lips before rolling onto his side with his back facing her and falling into a deep and exhausted sleep while Kendra lay awake in the dark, wondering if she and Andy would ever make love again. This far into her pregnancy with her belly so big that even tying her shoelaces was a struggle,

Kendra wasn't exactly seething with wanton passions, but now more than ever, she craved her husband's affection and the reassurance of his embrace.

Andy was so busy, distracted by the growing demands of his flock. It was understandable that he had so little time for her and yet . . .

The class ended, ten little girls sat on benches in the lobby to exchange tap shoes for snow boots before heading out into the frigid Vermont winter. One by one, the girls bundled up and headed out the door to the parking lot where their parents sat waiting with their car heaters running full blast, waving good-bye to Kendra as they left and promising that they'd practice their time step every day before the next class.

Nora was the last to leave. She zipped up her jacket and headed for the door, pausing before a framed publicity photograph of Kendra in full Rockette regalia, dressed in a glittering snowflake costume.

Nora sighed as she gazed at the picture. "Kendra, was it wonderful to be a Rockette?"

"It was."

"When was this picture taken?"

"About five years ago."

Nora looked at her teacher, resting her

eyes on Kendra's bloated belly before returning to the photograph. "That was a long time ago. You sure don't look like that anymore, do you?"

Kendra stared at the young woman in the picture, with her bright smile, her legs extending from beneath the short skirt in a long, shapely line, and her stomach taut, trim, and flat as a board under the sparkly fabric of her costume.

"No. Not anymore."

"Do you think you'll look like that again," the little girl asked innocently. "I mean, after the baby?"

"I think you'd better go now, Nora. It's late. You don't want to keep your mother waiting."

# CHAPTER 3

Andy Loomis leaned back in his desk chair and rubbed his eyes, trying to ward off a headache. He'd already put in a long day and it wasn't over yet.

There was to be another meeting of the board tonight, the fourth one this month. Andy felt there was no need to call another, but Riley Roth had called the day before and very politely made the request. Considering the way things ended last time and how he'd thrown cold water on Riley's plans, Andy decided to go along with the suggestion. After all, he didn't want to extinguish Riley's enthusiasm entirely, just rein him in a little.

When he'd left for work that day, he told Kendra he was going to be late again. Her only response to this news was to shrug and say, "Okay."

In the past, she'd have given him some gas about scheduling yet another meeting that week. Now she seemed resigned, as though she'd accepted that this was the way things were and always would be. Her benign response made him feel worse than if she'd nagged him about neglecting her. At least then he could have felt defensive and gone off feeling justified that he was doing the best he could for his church and his family. Instead he drove to work feeling guilty.

The truth was, he *had* been neglecting his family. Not intentionally, but this whole business with Riley and the board of deacons had been sucking up a huge piece of his time and energy. And he couldn't even explain that to Kendra because he hadn't told her anything about it. Time was when Andy told Kendra nearly everything about his work day, but now? He just didn't think it was a good idea.

It was one thing to tell his wife about the trivial trials and foibles that were common to any church — the ongoing disagreements over what kind of music should be played on Sunday and at what tempo, the annual budget battles, the letters he received every summer from the congregant who felt that for the choir to sing without their robes was tantamount to blasphemy, or the debates about what to do with the three boys from the youth group who'd been caught trying to sneak over to the girls' cabin during the junior high retreat. But it was another thing to tell Kendra things that might make members of the church, especially people in leadership positions, appear in a bad light.

Andy had spent his whole life in the ministry. During his lifetime, Andy's father had been pastor of this same church and Andy had grown up in Maple Grove. He knew that the people of his church were basically good-hearted, well-intentioned folks, even when they didn't act like it. But, in spite of being the pastor's wife, Kendra was still young in her faith. He didn't want to share anything that might cause her to think badly of the church.

And it wasn't just that. As a newly ordained minister, during his first marriage, he'd told his wife, Sharon, absolutely every detail of what went on at the church. It had been a mistake.

For the first months of their married life, everything was fine. They were in love, excited to be working together in the ministry, and filled with expectation about the upcoming birth of their first child, even though that birth was coming a little sooner than they'd planned. Everything in their lives seemed to be going beautifully, but before long, things got tougher.

Andy was working as a youth pastor in a large congregation in Oregon. He and the senior pastor didn't see eye to eye on a number of issues and, as the differences between him and his boss widened, Andy told Sharon all about it, just as he always had. That's what had started their problems, Andy was sure.

Around the sixth month of her pregnancy, Sharon's excitement about the baby waned. She was always grumbling about the church and, more often than he should have, Andy joined in, freely adding his own complaints to hers. As the time for the birth neared, Sharon became moody and depressed. Andy was worried about her, but Sharon's doctor assured him that mood swings in pregnancy were perfectly normal and that Sharon would return to her old self after the baby was born.

It didn't happen. The girl he'd fallen in love with and married had disappeared. Sharon was good to Thea, always made sure she was clean and dressed and fed, but she didn't seem to take any delight in the baby. Andy called the doctor who said it was probably just a case of the "baby blues" and that Andy shouldn't worry too much, that it would pass; but it never did. Shortly after

Thea's fourth birthday, Sharon left, leaving a business card for a divorce lawyer and a note saying she was sorry, that she was moving to San Francisco and giving him full custody of Thea. Not too long after that Andy's parents were killed in a car accident. Andy went back to Vermont to take over his father's pulpit and raise his orphaned younger sister, Stacey. He and Thea never saw Sharon again.

It wasn't entirely his doing, Andy knew that, but he had never been able to shake the feeling that the breakup of his marriage had started when he began telling Sharon all about his problems at the church. So when Kendra had told him she was pregnant, Andy decided he wasn't going to talk about anything that could possibly upset her. He was determined not to make the same mistake twice.

But, seeing the resigned expression on her face that morning made him think he might have gone a little overboard. Maybe he'd been keeping too much from her. Now that this problem with the board seemed to be behind him, he would be more open with her.

By the time he arrived at the church that morning, he had decided that meeting or no meeting, he was going to have dinner with his family. He sent an e-mail around to everyone saying that the meeting was going to start at exactly five and end no later than six-thirty. Then, feeling good about this decision, Andy went on with his day and worked on his Sunday sermon.

Usually writing a sermon left him feeling energized but not today. By four-thirty his temples were beginning to throb and he knew it wasn't from eyestrain. Early adjournment or no, Andy simply didn't want to go to yet another board meeting.

*No,* he thought to himself, *it's not just the meeting. The truth is, I don't want to see Riley Roth.*

Riley Roth was the newest member of the church board and fairly new to Maple Grove as well. He was from North Carolina where he'd worked in the furniture business until, two years before, he'd taken a job as a marketing manager at the new chair factory that had opened on the edge of town. Riley was married. He and his wife, Dana, had twin sons.

The new factory had brought a lot of new people to town and a good number of them had joined the church, but Riley stood out among the newcomers. He threw himself into the activities of the congregation quickly and with enthusiasm. In addition to attending a couples' Sunday school class with Dana, Riley joined the Wednesday morning men's Bible study, the choir, and the finance committee. With Andy's blessing, he started a new ministry, Hands of Help, that met every other Saturday to visit the elderly and infirm to help them with chores or home repairs. It was a wonderful ministry that served not just church members, but anyone in the surrounding community who needed assistance.

When the Bells retired and moved to Florida, leaving Sally Bell's spot on the board open, a couple of the other members had suggested asking Riley to fill the vacancy. It was unusual to bring someone onto the board so soon after they'd joined the church and, at twenty-eight, Riley was much younger than the other members. But Andy had been impressed by Riley's desire to serve and thought having someone a little younger, with fresh ideas, might be a good addition to the mix. With the blessing of the board, Andy asked Riley to think and pray about joining their ranks.

Riley accepted on the spot.

Riley threw himself into his new position with eagerness. As Andy had hoped, Riley was full of energy and ideas — maybe a little too full. No matter what the service, program, or ministry, Riley had ideas about how it could be improved and almost always, those improvements revolved around the way things had been done back in North Carolina. According to Riley, absolutely everything about the church was tired, out-of-date, and inadequate. If Andy could have collected a dollar for every time Riley furrowed his brow and said, "Well, you know, back at my old church we used to . . ." they could have built a new church.

And that would have suited Riley just fine because, before long, it was clear that was exactly what Riley thought they needed to do, build a whole new church.

In 1962, the congregation had built a new education and administration wing, complete with kitchen, fellowship hall, and pastor's offices, connected to the church by a glassed-in breezeway. However, the sanctuary was original to the site. It was classic New England architecture, the kind of church that tourists stopped to take pictures of, white clapboard siding with tall, clear glass windows, topped by a soaring bell spire. Built in 1866, the church had not changed at all since its original construction. As far as Andy was concerned, the historic building was a source of pride, not concern. Yes, it was true that the recent growth in the congregation had made the pews a little more crowded, but Andy felt that was no reason to scrap such a beautiful church.

Initially, the rest of the board had agreed. They were all good New Englanders, and frugal by nature, raised on the old Yankee maxim that they should, "use it up, wear it out, make it do, or do without." Nobody was anxious to take on the expense of a new building program, not when they already had a perfectly good building.

But as the months passed and Riley continued to make pointed, persistent, and consistently unfavorable comparisons between his old church and his new church, the other board members started to wonder if he might not be right. It wasn't something that happened overnight, but early in the fall, particularly as they discussed the influx of visitors who would crowd the church to see the Christmas pageant, many of whom would like what they saw and return for Christmas services and then stay on to become full-fledged members of the church, Andy could sense a subtle shift toward Riley's viewpoint.

Denny Sugarman, who owned the biggest maple syrup farm in that part of the state, wasn't convinced. Denny hadn't said anything against the idea — he wasn't much for speaking unless he had something important to say — but Andy could see in his face that he didn't think much of Riley's big plans.

But by the time October came and leaves had turned and fallen to expose the skeletons of the trees, just about every other member of the board was thinking they ought to build a new church. And every person who held that view had very specific ideas about exactly what features and improvements a new, state-of-the-art, user-friendly church should include. That was Riley's word — user-friendly. Or rather it had been Riley's word. Now everybody was tossing it around as if they'd invented it. And, Andy noticed, everyone had a different idea of what it meant.

Some people thought that user-friendly meant adding a great big overhang to the front of the building so people could pull up to the front of the church in bad weather and unload the family under cover. Others argued that it might be even more user-friendly to recruit a team of volunteer valets to park the cars when the weather was bad. Somebody else had the idea that it was too inconvenient and old-fashioned to perform baptisms at the lake every summer and that, if they really wanted to be user-friendly, they should buy a new, indoor baptistery with a heater and chlorination system. Still another person thought that what the church really needed was a new, bigger lobby with an espresso machine and café tables.

"Something like that would help bring in the young folks and more new members, give them a place to meet after services where they can relax and get to know people."

"But we have that already," Andy argued. "We've got a perfectly good fellowship hall in the basement. The hospitality committee served coffee and cake to over two hundred people last Sunday, including more than a dozen visitors. Everyone enjoyed their cake and getting caught up with each other and meeting the new people. How would putting in an espresso machine and café tables make any difference?"

The person who'd made the original suggestion seemed stumped by that and, other than mumbling something about an espresso machine being more "user-friendly," didn't have an answer to Andy's question. But that didn't matter. Everybody still thought an espresso café would make a fine addition to the church. And just about everybody thought they needed a new sound system. In this instance, Andy was among them.

Their current soundboard was on its last legs. It blew a fuse about every three weeks. Andy thought that spending a few thousand dollars on a new soundboard, a couple of new microphones, some new acoustical tiles in the balcony made good sense and said so. Next thing he knew, Riley pulled a manila folder out of his briefcase and started passing around glossy, full-color brochures from a sound engineering consulting firm.

"These guys designed the sound system for my old church, back in North Carolina," Riley enthused while the rest of the board flipped through the brochures eagerly eyeing an array of microphones, duplicators, and monitors. "They did a great job. Put in a whole new sound system, plus rigged us up for videoconferencing, taping, and duplication. You should see it! Completely state of the art! Now we can videotape any service or program we want and record them onto DVDs so we can deliver them to the elderly or shut-ins."

"We do that already," Andy said, turning to Dean Hamilton, who, in addition to serving as a board member, chaired the church technology committee. "Dean tapes the services every Sunday morning and leaves the master in the office. On Monday, Ruth, my secretary, makes duplicates and mails them out to any people who are too ill or elderly to come to church."

"Tapes?" Riley asked skeptically. "Cassette tapes? Isn't that a little nineties?"

Dean Hamilton's gaze shifted from Andy's face to the glossy brochure with its pages and pages of new, hi-tech equipment. His eyes glittered.

"Riley has a point, Andy. Cassettes are kind of old-fashioned. I sure wouldn't mind getting some of this DVD equipment. And look at this." He pointed to a tall DVD duplicator, a shining silver column studded with all kinds of little drawers and dials.

"If we bought this we could copy sixteen DVDs at one time. And, you can even network with up to seven other units so, all told," Dean closed his eyes for a moment, doing the math in his head, "you could eventually make 112 copies all at once!"

"But Dean, we only have seven people on the list who've asked for tapes. We don't need to make 112 copies — of anything! Five of the seven shut-ins on that list are in their eighties. They don't have DVD players. Heck, most of them don't even have cable. If we mailed them a DVD, what would they do with it?"

Riley sighed and shook his head. "Pastor Andy, I don't mean to be disrespectful, but that's just the problem around here. You can't just think about serving the congregation you've got now. You should be thinking about serving the congregation you will have: the congregation you could have ten years from now if you just had a little vision."

The younger man's voice was low and earnest. "Ten years ago, my old church back in North Carolina wasn't much bigger than we are right now. But then our old pastor retired and the church called a younger man to serve. From the very first day he started changing things, making plans, plans for the church he thought we *could* be. He had a vision and it was contagious! Everybody got on board and decided to build a bigger, better church. Sure enough, within three years, they'd outgrown that building and had to buy land to build another church with a sanctuary that could seat four times as many. And don't you know? Today, that church is full, too. Six thousand people crowd that church every Sunday morning! It's a megachurch. One of the biggest and best in the state!"

Riley paused for a moment, letting his story sink in. The rest of the board was silent, a few shaking their heads in wonderment and others leaning toward Riley, anxious to hear what else he had to say. Only Denny Sugarman, sitting on a folding chair with his arms crossed over his red and green flannel shirt, seemed unimpressed.

"Again, I mean no disrespect, Andy. But I'm wondering — have you really stopped to consider what we might be on the cusp of here in Maple Grove? After all, the church is growing . . ."

Andy pressed his lips together and silently prayed for patience.

"I know that, Riley. We all know that. And no one could be more delighted about it than I am. That's why I think it would be a good idea to invest in some new sound equipment, maybe buy a second refrigerator for the kitchen. If we keep growing at the rate we have been, in a couple of years we probably will need to add some classrooms onto the education wing. But we don't need a machine that will duplicate 112 DVDs at once, and we don't need a heated and chlorinated baptistery, or an Italian espresso maker, or videoconferencing, or valet parking!"

Andy, aware that his prayer for patience

seemed to have gone unanswered, consciously lowered his voice.

"We are growing, it's true. Gone are the days when every member of this congregation can have his or her own personal pew and I thank the good Lord for that. But we are a long way from being standing-room-only on Sunday mornings. And if we do get to that point, we can always add additional services.

"To answer your question, Riley, yes. I have considered what we're on the cusp of here in Maple Grove. More importantly, I've prayed about it. We are growing and every day I pray for wisdom, strength, resources, and guidance to keep in step with that growth and to meet the needs of everyone who comes to our door. So far, I think we've done that. And if God wills it, we'll grow some more. This is His church, after all. Not my church. Not yours. God's. And He's chosen to put it in a small but growing *rural* community.

"This is Vermont, Riley. Not the hi-tech triangle. Winters here are long and harsh. The landscape is beautiful, breathtakingly so, but life here can be hard. Not many people choose to make their home in this part of the world. Although," Andy said, looking at the ring of weathered, wind-chapped faces that circled him, "the ones who do are among the hardest working, kindest hearted people in the world. But, Riley, even though we are growing, Maple Grove is still a small town. We're a community church. Not a megachurch. Unless something changes drastically in the state of Vermont, that's what we'll go on being. That's our mission. To serve this community."

Andy shrugged before sitting back in his chair. "I don't know about you, but I'm all right with that."

*It was a good speech,* Andy thought. Good enough to make everyone step back for a minute and rethink their priorities. The meeting broke up shortly after and Andy drove home feeling better than he had in a long time.

But now, sitting alone in his office and replaying the scene in his mind, Andy realized that the chance to refocus the board's priorities hadn't been the only source of his satisfaction that night. If he was honest with himself, he'd enjoyed taking the wind out of Riley Roth's sails. The younger man's subtle but continual criticism had gotten under his skin. And if he was really honest with himself, he had to admit that he just didn't like Riley, not at all.

Andy put his elbows on his desk, rested his head on his hands, and closed his eyes.

*Well, there it is, God. I don't like Riley. Not that this is news to You, but I've been doing a pretty good job of fooling myself, haven't I? The truth is, I've resented him and the other night, I got a lot of pleasure in bringing him down a peg. That was wrong of me. I'm sorry. Please forgive me.*

*And help me to forgive Riley. He's not a bad guy; just young and brash. Like I was at his age. I'm sure that senior pastor back in Oregon had to forgive me for exactly the same thing, so how can I hold this against Riley? Help me to forgive him, Lord, and to forget my wounded pride. What right do I have to take any pride in this church anyway? I meant what I said about that. This is Your church. Any good thing that happens here is Your doing, not mine. I'm just lucky enough to work for You. Help me to remember that and to love the people You've allowed me to serve, all of them, even the ones who sometimes seem so unlovable. Even Riley. Amen.*

When Andy opened his eyes his headache was gone. That didn't surprise him. He'd discovered years ago that, much of the time, a heart-to-heart with God was a pretty good aspirin substitute.

Andy looked at his watch. Quarter to five. He picked up the phone to call Kendra at the studio to tell her he'd be home for dinner, but then remembered that she had a tap class today. She wouldn't be able to hear the phone over the clatter of tap shoes. That was all right. It'd be fun to surprise her. Maybe he'd even stop and buy her some flowers on the way home.

Deciding he had just enough time to grab a cup of coffee before the meeting started, Andy put down the phone and headed down the hallway to the church kitchen, asking Ruth, his secretary, if she'd like him to bring back a cup for her.

Ruth was sitting in front of the computer, putting the finishing touches on the Sunday bulletin. Her reading glasses slipped down to the end of her nose as she peered at the clock on the wall. "It's nice of you to offer, but it's about ten minutes to the weekend and I'm heading home. Are you staying late again tonight? I didn't see anything on your schedule."

"Board meeting. Kind of a last-minute thing."

Ruth frowned. "On Friday night? You just had a meeting three days ago. Why do you need another one? Andy, you're working too hard. When's the last time you . . ."

Andy held up his hand, interrupting Ruth's stream of disapproval. "I know. I know. But this really is necessary, more of an extending of the olive branch than a meeting. I'll be out of here early, I promise. I'm going to have dinner at home."

"Well, it's a good thing," she scolded. "You can't be everything to everybody. You've got to save a little time for your family. Poor Kendra's probably forgotten what you look like. If I were you, I'd stop and pick up some flowers on your way home tonight."

"Already thought of that," Andy called over his shoulder as he left the office and headed in the direction of the kitchen.

"Good night, Andy."

"Good night, Ruth. See you on Sunday."

Andy hummed to himself as he walked down the corridor, wondering if the florist would have Kendra's favorite tulips in stock. Unlikely at this time of year, but pink roses would do. And he'd pick up a bag of those dark chocolate kisses that Thea liked so much too. It had been ages since he'd done that.

He couldn't wait to get this meeting over with and go home, couldn't wait to see his family and to surprise Kendra and Thea with his presents. He was just about to turn the corner that led to the kitchen when he heard a man's voice, Riley Roth's voice, talking to someone. Andy stopped.

"Look, I'm not saying that Andy Loomis isn't a fine, dedicated pastor. But is he the kind of leader who can take it to the next step? Does he still have that fire in his belly? This is a nice church, a growing church, but why settle for that? Why not try to make this the biggest, best church in the state of Vermont? Or even New England? Somebody has to be the best; why shouldn't it be us? We're halfway there already; why not go whole hog? All we need is the right kind of leadership, some real vision!

"Now, I know a fellow back at my old church in North Carolina, one of the assistant pastors, and he's just the sort of guy I'm talking about . . ."

# CHAPTER 4

After Nora left, Kendra was alone in the dance studio. Advanced beginners' tap was the last class of the day. People liked to keep their Friday evenings free so Kendra didn't run any classes after five on Friday.

Kendra changed into street clothes, pulling on a pair of maternity jeans over her tights, turned out the lights, and locked the door, purposely keeping her eyes away from her old Rockette photo. In the parking lot, she turned on the car to let it warm up before getting the ice scraper out of the glovebox so she could clear the windshield.

She thought about what she should make for dinner. There was a roaster and some lemons in the icebox; she could make her famous lemon-rosemary chicken, Andy's favorite. But what was the point? He wouldn't be home to eat it. He had a meeting at church. And Thea didn't care.

Standing in the frigid November air, two

teardrops seeped from the corners of Kendra's eyes and tracked down her face. The wind was blowing. Icy granules of snow stung her cheeks as she wiped the tears away with the back of her gloved hand.

By now, she was used to the emotional mood swings of pregnancy and she told herself that was all this was, that she was just being silly.

"Get a grip on yourself. Andy loves you just as much as ever," she said to the empty air. "He's just busy, that's all. Nothing has changed. Do not let your hormones get the best of you."

During the ten years she lived alone in New York without a spouse, boyfriend, roommate, or even a close girlfriend to confide in, Kendra had gotten into the habit of talking to herself, giving herself the pep talks she felt a friend or loved one would have given her if she'd had one. Since she'd come to Maple Grove and fallen in love with Andy, she'd had less need to engage in these encouraging monologues, but lately, Kendra had fallen back into her old habit.

"Look at you," she said in a scolding tone. "Standing here and feeling sorry for yourself. If you're tired of being alone, of spending every night doing the same old thing, then don't! It's the weekend. Do something fun!"

Buoyed by this sound advice, Kendra pushed the last of the snow off the windshield with a decisive sweep, got into the car, and began driving toward the high school.

That morning, Thea had informed Kendra that she had dance team practice after school. She wasn't expecting to be picked up until six but Kendra decided to surprise her and treat her to a real girls' night out.

Thanksgiving was almost two weeks away, but the stores in Maple Grove stayed open late on Friday. They could do a little early Christmas shopping and then go to dinner at Thea's favorite Chinese restaurant, Ming's. If there was time, they could go to the salon and get manicures.

Of course, even the promise of such a wonderful surprise might not be enough to lure Thea away early. As one of only two freshmen who'd made the dance team, Thea was incredibly dedicated; she never missed a practice. If Thea didn't feel she could leave early, that was all right. Kendra would be content to sit in the bleachers and watch practice. It had been a long time since she'd had a chance to see the team in action.

During her first winter in Maple Grove,

Kendra was a volunteer coach for the team. With her help, the girls had placed second at the state competition. But when she opened the studio, Kendra had to give up coaching. It would be fun to see how the routines were coming along this year.

By the time Kendra took a right turn onto the road that led to Maple Grove High, she was in a much better frame of mind. The self-pity that had plagued her only minutes before was entirely banished as she thought about the evening to come, an evening that, if everything worked out the way Kendra hoped, might help close the gap that had opened between Kendra and Thea.

It was a lot to expect from a night of shopping and chicken chow mein, Kendra realized, but you never knew; stranger things had happened. And if there was one thing Kendra had learned since becoming Thea's stepmother, it was that you could never be certain what a teenager would do. Surprising Thea like this might be the perfect way to restore their relationship. In fact, the more Kendra thought about it, the more she was convinced she was right.

She believed it right up until the moment she drove into the school parking lot, pulled up next to a white pickup truck, and saw fourteen-year-old Thea sitting in the cab of the truck with a much older boy — a boy who had his arms wrapped around Thea and was kissing her passionately.

# CHAPTER 5

Andy pulled his car into the driveway next to Kendra's, turned off the ignition, and sat there.

To say that the evening hadn't turned out as Andy had planned was an understatement. But during the drive home he'd decided two things: not to let it spoil the rest of his night and not to tell Kendra about it. He didn't want to upset her. He was upset enough for both of them.

No. Not upset. Mad. He was mad.

Who did that guy think he was? After all Andy had done for Riley, welcomed him to Maple Grove, baptized his twins, and then invited him to join the board. Where did Riley find the nerve to start a whispering campaign against him? How dare he question Andy's vision and energy, making him sound like some worn-out old workhorse of a minister, ready to be put out to pasture?

"You wanna see fire in the belly, Riley? I'll show you fire in the belly!" Andy's fingers curled into a fist and he thumped the edge of the steering wheel. "I may be twelve years older than you but I can still take you. On the worst day of my life and with one hand tied behind my back, I could squish you like a bug. Slimy little creep."

This wasn't a worst day, not even close; Andy realized that. As a minister, he was called to be there for people on their best and worst days, to walk beside them through life's joys and tragedies. He was the one who sat at their bedsides, and preached at their gravesides, who held the hand of the widow and wiped the tears of the orphan. Andy knew what tragedy looked like and that, comparatively, this business with Riley wasn't that big a deal. But even so, he felt betrayed.

Andy had gone into the ministry because he wanted to serve the people of God and, by extension, God himself. Growing up watching his father minister in this very town, Andy understood what he was getting into. He knew he would work long days for little appreciation and less money, but that was all right. He had peace with God and the satisfaction of knowing that he was putting his time and life to good and useful purpose. That was worth more than a pay-check.

Andy didn't expect to be patted on the back for his efforts and he knew that, every now and then, he and the members of his church would have disagreements. They were a family, after all, and people in families don't always see eye to eye. But in all his years in the ministry, no one had ever doubted his drive or his ability to lead.

"Really, where does he get the nerve? Twenty-eight years old, never been to seminary or spent a day in the pulpit, and suddenly he knows everything there is to know about running a church? What's up with this guy?"

Andy thumped the steering wheel again.

Well, this wasn't a problem he was going to be able to work out tonight. Besides, he had other things to do than sit here fuming. The car was freezing. He'd better go inside.

He picked up the bag of candy and bouquet of flowers from off the passenger seat and got out of the car, taking big strides across the yard and leaving a trail of footprints in the freshly fallen snow. He kicked the snow off his boots before going in and pasted a smile on his face, eager to salvage the rest of the day and enjoy a nice, quiet evening with his family.

He opened the door, hung his coat on the rack, and sniffed the air but smelled nothing.

*That's funny. Kendra usually has dinner ready by now.*

Andy walked through the family room toward the kitchen. Thea met him coming out, bumped into him in fact, but didn't speak to him. Instead, she spun around and yelled through the half-open door. "I don't care what you think! You're not my mother, so quit trying to act like you are!"

Andy stood still for a moment, confused, feeling as if he'd walked into the middle of the movie. "Hey, hey, hey. Thea. What's wrong?"

Thea pointed an accusatory finger toward the kitchen. "It's her! Kendra! She's trying to ruin my life! I don't need her to tell me what to do. It's none of her business anyway."

"Wait a minute . . . Thea . . ." Andy laid his hand on her shoulder. "Why don't you just calm down for a minute? Come back in the kitchen and we'll talk."

Thea wrenched her body sideways, pulling away from Andy's grasp. "I didn't do anything. If you want to talk, talk to her! Why did you have to marry her anyway? We were fine on our own. I never asked for another mother. I don't need another mother!" Thea turned toward the kitchen again, shouting this last, before storming down the hall to her bedroom and slamming the door.

*So much for a nice, quiet evening with the family.*

Flowers and candy still clutched in his hand, Andy pushed the kitchen door open. "Kendra? Honey? Where are you? I brought you flowers."

Andy walked through the breakfast room to the kitchen where he found Kendra sitting cross-legged on the floor with her back against the refrigerator, weeping.

# CHAPTER 6

Darla took a sip from her coffee cup and looked at Kendra doubtfully. "Are you comfortable in that chair?"

Sugar Sugarman laughed. "At seven months' pregnant, she's not comfortable in *any* chair."

Sugar was one to know. She and Denny had been married for forty-three years and had five children and nine grandchildren. Sugar had a very large and maternal heart. When Kendra first arrived in Maple Grove she'd boarded with Sugar and Denny, who treated her just like a daughter. Kendra felt the same way about them. With her own mother so far away in Ohio, Kendra was glad to have Sugar to talk to. Not only was she wise, she was absolutely trustworthy. And the same was true of Darla.

Kendra had quickly realized that when you're the pastor's wife, lots of people expect you never to grumble or gossip or even *think* about grumbling or gossiping. Kendra tried to refrain, but she was human. Like everyone else, she needed to vent every now and then. That was why she looked forward to her coffee dates with Sugar and Darla. They got together at Well Grounded, Maple Grove's newly opened espresso bar, every Tuesday morning. Kendra could be sure that whatever was said at Well Grounded, stayed at Well Grounded.

"Sugar's right," Kendra said. "It's like trying to sit with a ten-pound cannonball in your lap."

Darla, who'd never had children, nodded sympathetically. "Yes, I suppose so."

"But this is nothing." Sugar nodded her head in the direction of Kendra's pregnant belly. "You should have seen me when I had the twins. It was not pretty. By the time I got into my seventh month, I had only one maternity dress that fit — an enormous fuchsia number designed by Omar the Tentmaker. And the only thing I could get my feet into was a pair of pink chenille house slippers. Denny had to put them on for me every morning because I couldn't bend over far enough to do it myself." Sugar grinned. "Oh, I was a picture. Compared to me when I was in her condition, Kendra looks like a supermodel."

"Well, I sure don't feel like one." Kendra sighed and rested her cup on the shelf of her stomach. "It's not the baby. I'm happy about the baby. I mean . . . It's just . . . everything. Andy's been home late every night this week. We barely see each other these days. I know he's busy. With the holidays coming there's so much to do at the church, but I can't help but feel that something's wrong between us."

"Have you talked to him about it?" Darla asked.

"How can I? Of course, that little scene with Thea didn't help. He came home for dinner to find his daughter screaming and slamming doors and his wife collapsed on the kitchen floor sobbing her eyes out. I haven't been married a real long time, but I have to believe this is not the kind of thing that makes a husband want to come home more often."

Sugar twitched her shoulders, seeing Kendra's point. "So, how is the Thea situation, anyway?"

"Not good," Kendra replied. "She's furious at us. Make that at me. Andy's the one who grounded her, but for some reason she's decided that I am the cause of all her problems. But what else could we do? Josh Randall is a senior! She's got no business dating a boy his age. And she lied to us about it! She told me that she was staying late for dance team practice when she was planning to meet Josh all along." Kendra shook her head sorrowfully. "I think that hurts more than anything else."

"Don't take it so hard. Thea wouldn't be the first teenage girl who got caught lying about meeting a boy. It's a complicated age."

Sugar blew on her coffee to cool it down. None of those fancy espresso drinks for Sugar, thank you. She liked her coffee with nothing in it except a teaspoon of maple syrup tapped from trees on the Sugarman's own farm — and always kept a "nip," a tiny two-ounce bottle of syrup, in her purse for just that purpose.

"Personally, you couldn't pay me to be fourteen again."

"Well, you could me," Darla huffed. "My knees hurt. My back hurts. And I can't go up a flight of stairs without my heart beating like a bass drum. A little adolescent angst would be a small price to pay to have my old body back. Just tell me where I sign up. But, my griping isn't helping you, Kendra. Sugar's right. Thea's just acting the way teenage girls do."

"She said she doesn't want me for her

mother anymore. She said I'm ruining her life."

"And you are," Darla said. "Thank heaven for that! Thea's not thinking straight at the moment. If she were running her life the way she'd like to, she could end up with all kinds of problems. And getting her heart broken could be the least of them."

Kendra shook her head as she shifted in her chair, trying to find a position that didn't make her back hurt. "Oh, no. Thea wouldn't do anything stupid. At least . . . I don't think she would. Then again, how would I know? Until I met Thea I hadn't spent any time with children. I was always working too hard for that. Up until now we'd gotten along so well that I just figured I was a natural-born mother. Now I'm not so sure. About anything. I mean . . . if I don't know how to be a good mother to Thea, what's to say I'll be a good mother to this baby?"

Sugar put her coffee cup down on the table and looked straight into Kendra's eyes. "First of all, you *are* being a good mother to Thea. A good mother knows when to say no. Right now, that's just what Thea needs. It might not make you too popular with her, but, as I always told my kids, I didn't become a parent because I needed more friends."

"Why did you become a parent?"

"As I recall, mostly because I kept falling asleep." Sugar's eyes twinkled. Kendra and Darla laughed.

"No, I became a parent because Denny and I love children. But loving a child means you give them what they need. That's not always the same as giving them what they want. Honestly, Kendra, I think your maternal instincts are spot on. You're a terrific mother to Thea and when this baby is born, you'll keep on being a terrific mother."

"You think so?"

"I know so," Sugar said confidently.

"So do I," Darla added and then glanced at her watch.

"Look at the time! I'm sorry, girls, but I've got to leave early today. The Quilting Bees are meeting over at the church. You can't believe how many alterations we have to do on the costumes for the pageant! I was up until midnight letting down the hem on the Mary costume. Thea's certainly grown since last Christmas. Next year, I think we just ought to cast according to who fits the costume. It'd be a real timesaver."

"I feel bad about dumping all this work for the pageant in your lap," Kendra said.

Darla dismissed this with a wave of her

hand. "Don't be silly. I'm having the time of my life. I am a little tired from all these late nights, but it's not so bad. Keeps me out of trouble. Besides, you already did the hard part when you rewrote the script. All I have to do is implement your plans."

"Oh, don't give me that. New script or old, I know exactly how much work goes into putting that pageant together. You must be working your fingers to the bone. Would you like me to come over to the church and give you a hand?" Kendra started to get up from her chair. "I may not be in any condition to direct but I can still hem a costume."

Darla put her hand on Kendra's shoulder and pushed her gently back down into her chair. "Thank you, but, no. You stay right here with Sugar and finish your tea. The Bees and I have everything under control. If you're looking for something to do, think about what you'll serve for Thanksgiving dinner. You say you haven't had a chance to sit down with Andy and talk? Well, here's your chance. He won't be working on Thanksgiving."

"That's true, but neither will I. Well, I'm bringing a pie for dessert, but Sugar will be doing all the heavy lifting. We always have Thanksgiving with Denny and Sugar. Come to think of it, aren't you coming too?" Kendra turned to look at Sugar whose gaze rested fixedly on Darla's face. "Didn't you tell me just last week that Darla was coming to dinner."

"Change of plans," Darla said quickly. "My sister called from Massachusetts. She wants me to take the train to Boston and have dinner with them. I haven't seen her in months so I said I would."

"Oh."

Sugar scratched the side of her nose. "Well . . . yes . . . umm . . . actually Denny and I've had a change of plans, too. Joey, our oldest, called from Montpelier. They'd like us to go there for the holiday. He and Marta just bought that new house and they want to have Thanksgiving at their place. Kind of a housewarming. That's it. A housewarming. He's got his heart set on it. Didn't I mention that? I thought sure I called you last Thursday to let you know." Sugar squirmed in her seat and glanced quickly at Kendra before shifting her gaze to Darla who nodded encouragingly.

Kendra put down her cup and crossed her arms over her chest. "You don't have other plans for Thanksgiving. You're just making that up so Andy and I will have to spend the day together. You're both terrible liars, do you know that?"

"I'm sure I don't know what you're talking about." Darla sniffed. "But even if it were true, there are worse things to be terrible at than lying. Kendra, until he died, Jake and I were very happily married. Oh, we had our moments, every couple does, but for fifty years we got on very well. There's not many can say that. And the key to it all was communication."

Sugar agreed. "She's right, Kendra. Andy's not a mind reader. If you don't talk to him, how's he supposed to know what you're feeling?"

Kendra pressed her lips together, thinking. "You're right. I know you're right. There's this part of me that feels bad for bothering him, adding one more thing to a plate that's already heaped up with stuff. But . . ." She frowned. "There's another part of me that's mad because I want him to *know* that something's wrong. How can he not know? If something were wrong with him, I'd know."

"I thought you said you did think something was wrong with him?" Sugar said.

"I do."

"Well? What is it?"

Kendra smiled. Shrugged. "I don't know. Hmmm. Maybe I'm not quite as clairvoyant as I think I am."

"Could be. So you're going to talk to him?"

"Yes. And although I know it will simply crush you and Denny, I don't think we'll be able to join you for Thanksgiving dinner this year."

"What a shame," Sugar said with a grin.

Darla looped her pocketbook over her arm and started putting on her gloves. "Well, I'm glad that's settled. Now, if you'll excuse me, I've got to get over to the church. I'll see you both after the holiday."

She waved and headed for the door.

Kendra picked up her cup and started to take a sip but stopped with the cup halfway to her lips. She turned to Sugar, a slightly panicked look on her face. "I just remembered something. I've never cooked a turkey in my life."

"Never? Kendra, you're thirty-two years old. In thirty-two years, you've never cooked a turkey? Not one?"

Kendra shook her head. "No. I came to New York when I was nineteen and three weeks later I was a Rockette. For ten years, I spent every Thanksgiving Day high-kicking my way through the Macy's parade. Thanksgiving dinner was a turkey sandwich and a cup of coffee. Ever since I moved to Maple Grove, I've eaten Thanksgiving at your house. And I have to tell you, that's what's got me worried. You're a great cook, Sugar. Better than my mother, but don't tell her I said that."

"Mum's the word. And thank you. That's the nicest thing anybody's said to me in a while."

"You're welcome but really, this is a problem. You're a tough act to follow, especially for a woman who thinks turkey refers to a play that flopped. What am I going to do?"

Sugar reached across the table and patted Kendra's arm reassuringly. "First, you're going to finish your tea. Then, you're going to come over to the farm. We'll pull out my old recipe file. Really, Kendra, there's nothing all that complicated about making a turkey; just think of it as a big chicken. Besides, Thanksgiving is all about the side dishes anyway. You just need some good recipes and I've got the best."

Sugar put her cup to her lips and tipped it up to get the last drops of coffee before putting the cup back onto the table with a decisive thump and wiping her lips with a paper napkin.

"Now finish your tea and let's go. Grandmother Sugarman's apple walnut stuffing recipe awaits!"

# CHAPTER 7

Kendra decided that going to the grocery store on the day before Thanksgiving was definitely something to be avoided in the future.

Even though she drove to the market first thing after dropping a still silent and morose Thea off at school, the store parking lot was full of cars. She circled the lot several times before finding an empty spot. Once inside, she discovered that there were no available shopping carts, so she lurked around the checkout counter until she could nab a cart from a customer who'd already finished shipping.

Finding everything on her list took more than an hour and she spent another half hour in the checkout line, not getting back to the house until after ten. The grocery bags were heavy and she had a hard time getting the door open with both her arms full, but even so, Kendra had a smile on her face.

The idea of making her first real Thanksgiving dinner was a little daunting, but she was excited, too. Armed with a half dozen of Sugar Sugarman's best and most secret traditional family recipes, she felt she had a pretty good chance of making a meal that Andy and Thea would enjoy and remember.

Their first family Thanksgiving together, just the three of them. And next year it would be the four of them, and in the years after that? Well, who knew? One way or another, Kendra felt like she was starting a family tradition of her own.

Kendra started unloading the grocery bags, leaving the cans and boxes on the countertop and stowing the vegetables and other perishables in the refrigerator. She put the frozen turkey on the counter and eyed it doubtfully. At just under fourteen pounds, the bird seemed enormous to Kendra, but Sugar had assured her that it was the perfect size, big enough to feed the family and with enough left over for making sandwiches, casseroles, and soup later in the week.

"My feeling," Sugar said, "is it's just as much work to roast a big bird as a small one, so you might as well cook one that'll give you plenty of leftovers. Saves work in the long run."

Sugar had been cooking holiday turkeys for about forty years, so Kendra supposed she knew what she was talking about, but still . . .

Kendra filled the sink with cold water and put the turkey in it. Sugar had assured her that by immersing it completely in cold water for seven hours, changing the water every half hour or so, the turkey would be completely thawed in time for the holiday.

After putting the bird in the sink, Kendra stood back and looked at the pile of food sitting on the countertop, mentally going over her plan of attack.

"Let's see. We're having turkey, Grandma Sugarman's apple walnut stuffing, sweet and white potatoes au gratin, Sugar's squash medley with almonds and maple syrup, green beans almandine, homemade cranberry orange relish, rolls, and, as a change from the usual pumpkin, a maple nut mousse pie for dessert . . . Good Lord! Why did I let myself be talked into this? That's enough to feed an army! How will I ever get all this cooking done before dinnertime tomorrow?

"Okay, Kendra, take a deep breath. Don't panic. You can do this. You've just got to make as much ahead of time as you can. It won't be that bad. You can peel the potatoes and the squash now, then assemble the gratin and the squash medley so they'll be ready to cook tomorrow. The stuffing and green beans will have to wait, but you can make the pie today. In fact, you probably ought to do that first; thank heaven for that ready-made chocolate crust. Then, while that's baking, you can make the relish on the stovetop.

"And," she said to herself, taking the bag of freshly baked rolls she'd picked up at the local artisan bakeshop and stowing them in the breadbox, "we just won't tell Sugar that I put the kibosh on the idea of baking up a batch of her great aunt Sylvia's maple potato rolls. There's just so much I can do between now and tomorrow and when the going gets tough, sometimes the tough have to lower their standards.

"All right," she said in a firm, confident voice. "You can do this. There's just one problem. What are we going to eat tonight?"

What with all that food in the house, it seemed a little silly to bring in more, but Kendra decided that Chinese takeout was the most logical solution to the problem. If Kendra called in the order, maybe Andy would drive over to Ming's and pick it up on his way home.

Kendra went to the phone to call Andy and noticed that the message light was blinking. She'd been so busy she hadn't noticed.

With so much to do before tomorrow, the last thing she wanted to hear was that her husband was going to be home late — yet again. Kendra sighed and punched in the voice mail code, hoping it wasn't Andy; that would be awful.

It wasn't Andy. But it was awful.

As Kendra listened, she heard a mechanical beep and then a woman's voice.

"Andy? It's Sharon. Hi. I . . . well . . . Wow. When I heard your voice on the message it just . . . Well, it's just so weird to be talking to you after all these years."

Kendra heard a second voice, a tinny, unintelligible noise in the background making some kind of announcement. After a pause the woman continued.

"Listen, they're calling my flight so I have to run. I don't know if Thea told you, but my flight lands at Burlington around eight. You don't need to pick me up. I'll have a rental car. I'll be staying at the Toll Bridge Inn. Thea didn't say what time dinner starts, so if you could just leave a message at the inn and let me know? Thanks. I . . . I'm really looking forward to seeing you. And

Thea. I wish I'd . . ."

There was a long pause.

"I shouldn't have waited so long, that's all. And it should have been me getting in contact with Thea, not the other way around. It's just that, after so many years, I . . . I really didn't know what to say. Anyway. I can't wait to see you. Oh, and Kendra too. It was really nice of her to say I could come for Thanksgiving and . . ."

More undecipherable background noise interrupted her.

"Okay, they're calling my flight again. Sounds like they mean it this time. Gotta run. See you all tomorrow. Bye."

There was a click. Kendra stood in the kitchen with the receiver still held to her ear, listening to empty air.

# CHAPTER 8

Denny reached across the table, picked up a pitcher and poured a stream of syrup over his waffle, filling each crispy square with sweet amber liquid, giving himself time to consider Andy's response to his question.

"So, that's your plan? Say nothing?"

"Yep." Andy tore the top off a packet of sugar and poured it into his coffee cup. "Best thing to do is let it lie."

Denny nodded as he sawed his waffle into bite-size squares. "I see. So you're going to pretend you were never in that hallway, never heard a word Riley said?"

"Confronting him would only stir up trouble," Andy said.

Denny drew his eyebrows together into a bushy line. "The board supports you, Andy. You know that, don't you? Sure, they've gotten a little carried away over the idea of building a new church, but that'll pass. You're doing a great job. Nobody is looking to replace you."

"Riley is."

"Oh, him," Denny said dismissively before spearing two waffle squares onto his fork and taking a bite. "You don't need to worry about him," he said through a mouth full of waffles and syrup.

"Maybe. But . . . what if he's right?"

"What do you mean?"

"I've been here for almost ten years now, pastoring this church as best I know how, which is basically the same way my dad did it for the thirty years before that. We've added some new programs, changed the music some, added a few guitars to the mix, but by and large," Andy shrugged, "this church is pretty much the way it was when I was a kid."

"And what's wrong with that?"

"I'm just saying that . . . well . . . maybe Riley is right. At first, I was mad, seriously mad at him. But then I started thinking; he could be right. I accepted this pulpit because that's where God was calling me, but maybe God is calling somebody else now, somebody with a different outlook, a different vision. Maple Grove is my home. I love it here, but I don't want to stay if my doing so is going to hinder the church from reaching everyone it possibly can."

Denny put down his fork. "Andy, what are you talking about? This church is growing . . . what is it? Something like 23 percent in the last three years?"

"About that," Andy said with a nod, though he knew the actual percentage was just a hair over 25.

"Twenty-three percent. In three years. Andy, how many churches in this part of the state, not new, start-up congregations but old established churches, are seeing that kind of growth?" He stabbed two squares of waffle with his fork and, before Andy could respond, answered his own question.

"None. That's how many. Not one."

"But you'd expect that. The furniture factory brought a lot of new people into town."

"Not that many."

"Yes, but the Christmas pageant has helped, too. A lot of people come see it, have a good time, decide to visit regular church services, like what they see, and stay. That's Kendra's doing."

Denny nodded. "Some of it, yes. Kendra has done a lot toward getting them in the door, but you're the one who takes over after that and, as you said, they like what they see so they stay, and you're the one . . ."

Andy shook his head, "Hold on, Denny. I'm just the guy who's up there preaching.

There's a whole lot more to the church than that."

"That's true. I was talking to that new couple who started coming regularly a couple of months back, the Rumsfields."

"Oh, yeah. I know the Rumsfields. George and Annie. Nice couple. Sweet kids. Natasha's in fourth grade and Emily's in third."

"Right. And that's why they came at first — because of the girls. George had never been a churchgoer, but thought he ought to set a good example for his children. Now he comes for himself because he likes the people, how we take care of each other, and how everybody made them feel welcome. Most of all, he said he likes your messages because you preach so plain. There's no guilt, just that feeling of God reaching out in love."

Andy ducked his head. "You know me, Denny. I've only really got one sermon in my back pocket, same one I learned in Sunday school when I was four years old: 'Jesus Loves Me, This I Know.' My personal theology sort of begins and ends right there."

"Well, that may be, but it seems to be enough for George. He says that, for the first time, he's started to think of God as more than just a distant idea, but as real and caring, a God who understands and wants to be present in his life."

Andy was smiling now. "That's great to hear." He reached into his shirt pocket, pulled out a little black notebook, and scribbled a note to himself. "I'll have to give George a call. See if I can meet him for a cup of coffee."

"You and your coffee," Denny said, and snaked the last bite of waffle through the remaining pool of syrup. "Don't you ever eat?"

"I had breakfast before I left the house, about five hours ago."

"At five A.M.? And you're not hungry again?"

Andy shook his head.

"Well, good for you. Wish I could say the same. Anyway, Andy, my point is this; we've got a good, healthy church here. A growing one. And whether it's because of the new factory or the pageant or the people or the preaching or some combination of all that — it's working. And my feeling is: if it ain't broke, don't fix it." The waffles gone, Denny took a big gulp of coffee to wash them down. "This church doesn't need a new pastor, Andy. We've already got the best pastor in New England — you."

Andy grinned. "You trying to get me to

pick up the tab? Can't do it, buddy."

The older man held up his hand. "Yeah, don't go brushing me off like that. I've been your friend for ten years and before that, I was your dad's friend. We met in this diner for breakfast after Wednesday morning Bible study for almost thirty years, just like you and I do now. Except when your dad and I got together, he actually ate something." Denny grinned and swiped a paper napkin across his lips before crumpling it and tossing it onto his now empty plate.

"Dad always said that you were his best friend and one of the smartest, wisest men he knew."

"Any wisdom I got I probably picked up from your dad. He was a good man, Andy. And a good pastor. So are you. If you don't know that by now then somebody ought to tell you. Don't argue with me about it, just say thank you."

"Thank you, Denny."

"You're welcome. Say, how's Kendra? Just two more months 'till the baby comes, right? How's she feeling?"

"Actually, it's just about seven more weeks now. She's fine. I mean, physically she's fine, but she's been pretty emotional lately."

"Well, that's to be expected, you know. Hormones and all. Sugar was just the same with ours. Once, when she was carrying Bill, I came in looking forward to supper after spending the whole day in the sugaring shed, boiling down sap for syrup, and found her sitting in front of the TV crying her eyes out over a macadamia nut commercial."

Denny chuckled at the memory. "She just sat there sobbing and there wasn't one thing I could do or say to make her feel better. I never did get to eat that night."

"There's some of that," Andy said. "She was a mess after that scene with Thea. Thea was pretty awful to her. Kendra would have been upset no matter what; being pregnant just exacerbated the situation."

Andy sighed and wrapped his hands tighter around his coffee cup. "And it's not just the baby. I've been gone so much. You know how crazy things get at the church this time of year. So much going on. And then there's this whole thing with Riley."

"Kendra's a good woman, sensible, but she's human. Naturally, she's going to be upset when she hears that somebody is gunning for you."

"Yeah," Andy said sheepishly, "that would probably be true, if I'd told her about Riley. I haven't."

"What?" Denny shook his head in disbelief. "Andy, when you sit down to counsel engaged couples and talk to them about the keys to a successful marriage, what's the first thing you tell them?"

"I know. I know," Andy said. "Honest and frequent communication. Believe me, I know. I just thought that . . . in this case . . . in this situation, it would be better not to talk to her about what's been bothering me. You know, when Sharon left, I always thought it was because . . ."

Denny interrupted. "Andy, Sharon didn't leave because you told her too much about what was going on at the church. Sharon left because . . . well, because she did. A woman doesn't walk out on her marriage and four-year-old child because she's upset that her husband has a tough boss and told her about it."

"I realize that. I mean, it took me a while, but . . . Anyway, I'd decided to go home, bring her some flowers, and have a nice dinner with the family and then just sit and talk to Kendra, tell her about what's been going on. But, wouldn't you know it? Thea picked that same night to have her little meltdown, which is a whole different subject. Denny, one of these days you've got to sit down and tell me how you survived raising five teenagers." Andy sighed.

"Anyway, when I walked in the house,

Kendra was a mess. She was sitting on the kitchen floor and crying her eyes out. I just stood there, holding a bouquet of roses in my hand and feeling like an idiot."

"But you talked to her later, after she calmed down."

"Sort of . . . not really."

Denny shot Andy a look.

"I know! I know! You don't have to say anything. Things have been crazy since that night, but I'm going to talk to her. I already decided. Over the Thanksgiving holiday, I'm going to make some time to sit down with Kendra and have a good long talk. I promise."

"Well, you'd better, buddy." Denny growled. "Andy, for such a smart guy, you can really do some dumb things."

"You only just realized that?"

Andy twitched a little, feeling the ringer go off on his cell phone.

"Hang on a minute, will you, Denny? You know, I liked it better when Maple Grove didn't have a cell tower. Swore I'd never get one of these things, but with the baby coming I thought I'd better." Andy dug the phone out of his pocket and looked at the screen.

"It's Kendra. I should take this."

He flipped open the phone.

"Hi, babe. What's up?"

Denny picked up the check the waitress had left on the table, looked at it, and got his wallet out. But he stopped short when he glanced up and saw the look on Andy's face.

"Kendra, that can't be right. Are you sure? Tonight? She's coming tonight? Okay. Yes. I'll be right home." Andy pressed a button to end the call and slipped the phone back into his pocket.

"What is it?" Denny asked, worried. "Is the baby coming?"

Andy got to his feet, left some money on the table, and started heading toward the door. "No. Not the baby. Sharon."

# CHAPTER 9

"A year?" Thea asked, her eyes wide with admiration. "They actually paid you to just hang out and write poetry in Scotland for a whole year?"

Sharon smiled and when she did, the bronzed skin around her eyes drew together like folds in an origami fan, simultaneously exotic and balanced. Even her wrinkles seemed to suit her, at least, that's what Kendra thought.

Sharon was eight years Kendra's senior, but age had not diminished her beauty. Her salt-and-pepper hair was short and spiky, standing up or out at odd angles as if Sharon possessed some inner current of energy that could not be contained within her body and so it spilled out through every hair on her head and into the atmosphere around her. Her eyes were deep blue, wide and wondering, just like Thea's, and fringed with long, black lashes that needed no mascara and topped with full, evenly arching brows that showed no signs of tweezing. Sharon's beauty was truly natural and seemingly effortless. Only her clothing, the soft, twisted cream and gray yarns of her hand-knit sweater, perfectly accented by the rich eggplant-colored scarf wrapped carelessly around her neck and the hammered silver earrings that dangled from her ears, showed that she ever gave more than momentary consideration to her appearance. And yet, she was lovely.

Even with all she had to do to prepare the meal, Kendra had taken extra time deciding what to wear, finally settling on gray maternity slacks with a long black sweater, paying special attention to her makeup and jewelry, and even squeezing her feet into a pair of black patent leather heels she hadn't worn for months. But in spite of all this, sitting across from Sharon at the Thanksgiving table, Kendra felt like a dull, apologetic little wren perched next to a stately and honey-voiced snowy owl.

Sharon's eyes twinkled, further charming the already charmed Thea. "Well, an artist-in-residence is expected to give a few classes and lectures, public readings, that sort of thing, so I did a *little* more than 'hang out and write poetry.' " Sharon's eyes grew serious. She leaned toward her daughter as though sharing some important secret. "But not *much* more."

Sharon laughed and Thea joined in. Kendra and Andy smiled politely and continued eating.

"During the summer, I was only required to give one reading. The rest of the time was devoted to writing. I rented a flat in a wonderful little village, Buckie, on the Moray Firth. The flat was tiny and tidy with a sweet little garden in back and a marvelous view of the sea in the front. Such a perfect solitude. And when I tired of my own company, there were plenty of nearby villages to explore and people to talk to. One Saturday, I went to Elgin for the car boot sale . . ."

Thea interrupted, intrigued by the foreign-sounding phrase. "Car boot sale?"

"It's like a flea market. All kinds of vendors selling everything you can imagine. Some trash and some treasure. That's how I met Bruce and Margaret Cormac. They owned the used-book stall. Such a darling couple. We got to be very good friends. Bruce gave me this lovely old book full of Robert Burns poems. I'd read Burns before, of course, but somehow opening that book, seeing those same familiar verses printed on those yellowed pages and realizing how much those words had spoken to people over the centuries . . ." Sharon stopped short.

"I'm sorry, I don't mean to keep going on and on about this."

Kendra swallowed quickly and cleared her throat. "Oh, no. Not at all. It's very interesting. So is that why you decided to call your poetry collection *A Walk With Robbie?*"

"No. I just write what I write and leave the rest of it to the editor. She particularly liked that poem and thought it would also make a good title for the collection."

"And that's the book that won all the awards?" Thea asked eagerly.

"Just one," Sharon said modestly, "the Lightflower prize. It's been nominated for a few others but . . . we'll see."

Kendra glanced at Andy, wishing he'd say something. "That must be very gratifying," Kendra said, "having your work recognized with a national award."

Sharon smiled sincerely. "It is. I mean, a person doesn't become a poet because they crave recognition. Even the most celebrated names in modern poetry are virtually unknown to the general public, but it is nice to know that some people appreciate my work. Still, at the end of the day, it's the art itself that matters, not the recognition," Sharon said, turning her fork to the side and slicing the triangle tip off her pie prior to eating it. "You're an artist, Kendra. You know what I'm talking about."

"Kendra's just a dancer, not an artist," Thea said, giving Kendra a dismissive glance before turning back to Sharon with eyes full of adoration. "Not like you."

Kendra took a sip of water, trying to pretend she hadn't been hurt by Thea's comment, a comment that stung all the more because it was exactly what Kendra had been thinking herself.

Andy looked up from his plate. "Thea!"

Sharon jumped in, gently correcting her. "You're wrong, Thea. Kendra is an artist every bit as much as I am. Artists are keen observers, people who see and feel things in a different way than most, and use their special gifts — whether it be painting, or writing, or dancing — to help others understand the world more deeply."

For the tenth time that day, Sharon had gotten them past an awkward moment and, also for the tenth time, Kendra secretly wished she could dislike her, but she couldn't. Ever since she'd met Andy and heard the story of how Sharon had so abruptly left her child and marriage, Kendra had imagined the woman must be the worst kind of thoughtless, self-absorbed monster, but she wasn't. Not that an awkward hour sitting around the Loomis dinner table had given Kendra special insight into exactly what had motivated Sharon to abandon her daughter all those years before, but it wasn't out of narcissism, Kendra was certain of that.

"Anyway," Sharon continued, "I'm not sure that it's me that should have gotten that prize. If anything, the credit should go to Scotland. The scenery, the history, the people! It was inspiring! I've never written so well or so easily. Every person I saw on the street, every bird that sang, every ancient stone and ruin seemed replete with meaning and narrative. All I had to do was pick up my pen and copy down the stories — adding a few commas so people would know it was poetry, of course."

*How does she do that?* Kendra asked herself. *How is she able to work words like "replete" and "narrative" into a sentence and make them sound as natural as any other word?*

"It sounds beautiful," Thea said dreamily.

"It is. I plan to go back as soon as I can. The only thing I didn't love about Scotland was the food. They don't seem to hold vegetables in quite the esteem they deserve. Speaking of which," she said, turning to Kendra. "That was an amazing meal. Everything was just delicious! I particularly enjoyed the squash. What did you put in it?"

"Maple syrup. Rosemary. A few other things. I can copy down the recipe if you'd like."

"Would you?"

"Sure."

Sharon took another bite of her pie and then looked at her wristwatch. "This has been so nice. Thank you so much for having me. I don't want to eat and run but I'm a little tired. I was so excited about seeing Thea today that I could hardly sleep."

"You just got here! Don't leave yet!"

"You heard her, Thea," Andy said. "She's tired and needs to get some rest."

"Your dad's right," Sharon agreed. "But, I tell you what. You've got the day off from school tomorrow. What say I pick you up and we can go do some Christmas shopping and then I'll take you out to eat."

Thea's face lit up. "Chinese food?"

"Sure. Whatever you want."

"And after that, let's go and get manicures!"

Sharon laughed, splayed out her long,

225

elegant fingers and looked at her fingernails — smooth, ivory ovals without a hint of polish. "Well, that'd be a first for me but, sure! It'll be fun. We'll have a real girls' night out. I mean . . ." she glanced at Andy and then at Kendra. "If that's all right with the two of you. I don't want to impose on your plans."

"We don't have any plans," Thea assured her quickly before turning to her father. "I can go, can't I? Please, Dad."

Technically, Thea was grounded until Monday. That was the punishment Andy had meted out to her for the incident with Josh Randall and for speaking to Kendra so rudely and for lying to them. But Sharon's unexpected arrival had complicated things.

Neither Andy nor Kendra had been anxious to include her in their Thanksgiving plans. For a brief moment, Andy had considered telling Sharon that she wasn't welcome at dinner, but Kendra had talked him out of it. She wasn't exactly thrilled about this, especially because Thea had made the invitation without consulting either of them, but now that Sharon was here, Kendra didn't see as they had any choice but to invite her to dinner and to try to act as normal as possible.

If that's what Thea wanted, could they

really deny her the right to see her mother? Perhaps. After all, Sharon had relinquished custody over Thea years before, and who was to say that she might not try to reclaim it now? If they tried to prevent Thea from seeing her, Sharon might do exactly that. It was a tense situation, but Kendra had felt they had no choice but to make Sharon as welcome as possible. In the end, Andy had agreed. After all, it would only be for a little while. And there was something else too; hurt as Kendra was by Thea's behavior in the last few weeks, she was truly happy to see Thea so happy. Kendra knew that in spite of her grown-up looks and adolescent affectations, a part of Thea was still an abandoned four-year-old, wondering if her mother had left because of something she'd done wrong. Maybe Sharon's visit could help heal some of that pain. And if that caused Andy and Kendra some tension and anxiety, it was a price worth paying.

And it was only for a few days. Then Sharon would fly back to San Francisco and they could all go on with their lives.

"Come on, Dad. Please?" Thea pleaded.

Andy looked at Kendra who gave him a quick nod. "All right. That'll be fine."

Sharon smiled. "Are you sure? Really? I don't want to get in the way of your plans.

If tomorrow's not convenient, we can do it another day. I'm going to be around for a while."

The baby kicked, hard, catching Kendra by surprise. She jumped a bit and instinctively put her hand on her stomach. "You are?"

Sharon frowned and looked at her daughter. "Thea, didn't you tell them?"

Thea shook her head nervously.

"I have an offer to teach at the college. Actually, since the Lightflower prize was announced I've had a few offers. This wouldn't have been my first choice. I'd pretty much made up my mind to say no, but when Thea found my Facebook page and got in touch, I decided to reconsider.

"I'll be at the Toll Bridge until Monday, but after that I'm moving into a furnished cottage I found online. Not in Maple Grove, but close. Over in Keswick. I've rented it until the first of the year; just to give myself time to see if I want to stay in Vermont or not.

"And," she said, reaching out and caressing Thea's cheek, "To give me a chance to spend time with Thea and, of course, to see her play Mary in the famous Maple Grove Christmas pageant."

Thea squealed. "You're going to come to

the pageant! Do you mean it?"

"Absolutely! Wild horses couldn't keep me away."

Thea let out a whoop, jumped up from her place at the table and threw her arms around her mother.

Andy gripped the end of the table and opened his mouth as though to say something. Kendra shook her head, warning him not to speak rashly.

The telephone rang.

Even on a holiday, ignoring the phone wasn't an option in the Loomis household; too many people in Maple Grove depended on Andy. Even so, he let it sound off a couple of times before taking his napkin off his lap and pushing back his chair.

"Excuse me. I have to answer that."

# CHAPTER 10

One of the nurses, an older woman with red hair and rimless glasses, greeted Andy by his first name. Everybody on the hospital staff knew him; in addition to emergency visits like these, he had scheduled rounds of visitations every Monday and Thursday.

"Hi, Muriel. Where is she?"

"Still in emergency. The doctor's with her. The Sugarmans are in the waiting room. They were the ones who called the ambulance."

"Is she going to make it?"

"I don't know anything, Andy. They just brought her in a little while ago. Doctor Bates is on duty. I'll make sure he knows you're here."

"Okay. Thanks."

They walked down the empty corridor, following the signs that pointed to the emergency room. Kendra shivered. Andy put his arm around her shoulders. "Cold?"

Kendra shook her head. "No. Scared." Her eyes filled with tears. "She's eighty-two. She's lived a good, long life. I know that, Andy, but . . . I just don't want her to go yet. Maybe it's selfish, but I need her. It doesn't matter that she's fifty years older than I am, Darla's my best friend. I don't want her to die."

"I know. Neither do I."

Inside the waiting room, Denny was on his feet, pacing. Sugar was sitting on a dark green sofa, clutching a handkerchief in her hands and looking very pale. They looked up when Andy and Kendra entered the room.

"We got here as fast as we could," Andy said going to Denny and clasping his hand. Kendra sat down next to Sugar.

"We just arrived ourselves. I called you from the car."

Sugar blinked and looked around the room, as though searching for something. "Where's Thea?"

"Home," Kendra said. "Sharon was still at the house when you called. She'll stay with Thea until we get back. Don't worry. Now, tell us. What happened?"

Sugar sighed. "We'd just finished eating. Denny was in the kitchen, wrapping up leftovers, and Darla and I were clearing the table. I was carrying a couple of serving bowls and Darla was following me, bringing in the dirty plates. I heard a crash and a thud. I turned around and there was Darla, laid out on the dining room floor." Sugar stopped, unable to go on.

Denny finished the story. "We dialed nine-one-one. It seemed like hours before the ambulance came, but I know it couldn't have been more than five minutes. They gave her some oxygen and loaded her into the ambulance. We followed in the truck. The doctors are working on her, but nobody's been out to see us yet."

"So, you don't know what's wrong?" Andy asked.

"Heart? Stroke? I don't know."

Sugar started to cry. "I shouldn't have let her carry those heavy plates. I should have done it myself."

Kendra took her hand. "Sugar, don't. Don't cry. It wasn't your fault."

Denny crossed the room and sat down next to Sugar. "There now," he soothed. "Kendra's right, honey. This isn't your fault."

"No," Kendra said grimly. "It's mine. I shouldn't have insisted that Darla take over as pageant director. Andy warned me that it was too much for a woman her age. I should have listened . . ."

Andy pulled up a chair and reached out to grip Kendra's hand. "That's enough of that, Kendra. And you too, Sugar. You're both beautiful, powerful women, but neither of you has that kind of power. Darla is a tough cookie, as energetic as many women half her age. And she loves helping people. There was no way either of you could have anticipated or prevented this. 'To everything there is a season, a time for every purpose under heaven. A time to be born and a time to die; a time to plant, and a time to pluck up what is planted.' The span of Darla's life is God's business. Not ours. We'll leave it in His hands."

And sitting together in the empty waiting room, the four of them bowed their heads and joined their hands, committing their friend to the healing touch of the Great Physician.

# CHAPTER 11

Kendra clutched the rails of the hospital bed and leaned closer. "Are you comfortable?" she asked anxiously. "Is there anything I can do for you?"

"Yes. You can get me the heck out of here," Darla croaked. "I hate hospitals. They're full of sick people."

Muriel took her eyes off her watch, released her hold on Darla's wrist, and made a note on her chart. "Not bad, Mrs. Benton. How are you feeling this morning? Better?"

"Well, if I am, it's no credit to you people. Doctor Bates said I should rest, but how can I? People keep coming in here every two minutes to bother me. They woke me up three times to take my temperature last night. Three times! For heaven's sake! I had a heart attack, not the flu. Why does everybody keep taking my temperature?"

"I'm going to take that as a yes. Anyone who's got the energy to complain like that

234

*must* be feeling better." Muriel winked at Kendra. "Don't stay too long now, Mrs. Loomis. Like the doctor said, she needs her rest. I'll be back later to take your temperature."

"Undoubtedly waking me up so you can do it," Darla harrumphed.

"If need be."

"Thanks, Muriel," Kendra said as the nurse headed to the door. "Darla's just upset. Don't mind her."

"I don't. Mrs. Benton and I go way back; don't we, Mrs. B.? I took piano lessons from Mr. Benton when I was a little girl. Went to their house every Saturday morning. Mrs. Benton always answered the door. She was just about as glad to see me then as she is now. Nice to see she's feeling like her old self again." The nurse smiled and left to tend to other patients.

"It's true," Darla said. "Jake gave her lessons for about six years. It's a good thing she went into nursing. She wasn't much of a pianist."

Kendra smiled. "You *are* feeling better, aren't you?"

"Yes. Better than I did, anyway. But I'm still tired. And frustrated. I don't like being here. And I really don't like the idea that I've left you in the lurch with the pageant.

I'm sorry." Darla reached out her hand and rested it on top of Kendra's. "As soon as I'm out of here . . ."

"As soon as you're out of here, you're going to listen to Doctor Bates and focus all your energy on getting better. Cardiac rehabilitation is about to be your full-time job. You let me worry about the pageant."

"But," the old woman protested, "how can you manage it? You've got so much on your plate already. The baby. Running the dance studio. Hospital visits to cranky old ladies with bad tickers. And, on top of that, you've got family problems of your own: Andy and Thea. Not to mention this business with Sharon."

Kendra rested her hand protectively on her stomach. "Don't worry about the baby. I just saw the obstetrician and everything is fine. And, actually, having Sharon here has turned out to be a godsend."

Darla drew her brows together in a doubtful expression.

"It's true," Kendra insisted. "We've got it all worked out. She will take Thea to school every morning so I can get a little extra sleep. And then she'll pick her up in the afternoon, make sure she gets something to eat, and drop her off at rehearsal. That way I can go straight from the dance studio to the church. I had to rearrange my class schedule, but it'll work. I wasn't exactly thrilled when I found out Sharon was thinking of moving to Vermont, but under the circumstances, it's turned out to be a good thing. There's no way I could do this without her."

"I suppose," Darla said grudgingly. "But are you sure it's a good idea to have Thea spend so much time with Sharon?"

"Of course, it is." Kendra replied. "After all, she's Thea's mother, isn't she?"

# CHAPTER 12

"When oh when am I ever going to learn?" Kendra asked herself as she stomped on the parking brake and pulled the key out of the ignition.

Moving to Vermont with its calmer, more measured approach to life had definitely changed Kendra for the better. She wasn't the same frantic, frustrated, and impatient woman she'd been three years before. But there was one area where Kendra's growing maturity had yet to take root.

The second she got behind the wheel of a car, Kendra's inner New Yorker reemerged. She attacked the country lanes and state highways of Maple Grove with the same aggression she'd have used to navigate the Westside highway during the Friday night rush hour. But, since the roads of Maple Grove were normally devoid of congestion (here a Ford F150 pickup and three turkeys constituted a traffic jam), she did so at about four times the speed she could have achieved in New York, which was about two times the speed limit on most Maple Grove roads.

In the three weeks since Kendra had taken over the pageant directorship, things had gotten even worse. It seemed like she was always late these days and the later she was, the faster she drove. Thankfully, living in a small town where everyone knew she was the pastor's wife meant that the police tended to cut her some slack, but even so, getting pulled over and scolded by the local trooper took time which, of course, made her even later than she'd been to begin with. And today, Officer Lee had been especially stern with her.

"I'm not kidding, Kendra," he said as he tore the paper off the pad and handed it to her through the open car window. "This is absolutely your last warning. Next time I'm going to have to issue a real ticket. Slow down! I mean it this time."

"You're right, Jim. I'm sorry."

"It's dangerous! Besides, how does it look for the minister's wife to be forever getting pulled over for speeding? Not good. That's how."

Kendra nodded. "I know. I'll slow down. I promise."

"Okay," he said, though Kendra could see that he wasn't convinced. "How's the pageant coming along? Is my boy giving you any trouble?"

"Jimmy? Oh, no. He's a great kid."

The Lee boy, Jim Junior, was playing Santa Claus. It was a big part and an important one. In the first act he was the jolly old elf himself, overseeing and commenting upon the impromptu "talent show" among the workshop toys as they competed to see which of them deserved the title of Most Important Part of Christmas. And in the second act, he had to switch gears to become the wise and reverent St. Nicholas who narrates the Nativity story, making the toys, and the audience, understand that the meaning of Christmas begins and ends at the manger. It took real maturity to pull it off and, though he was only fifteen, Jimmy Lee was the right young man for the job.

"Jimmy's quiet but he works hard. When the rest of the cast gets a little too goofy or wound up, he's the one who can get them to settle down and refocus. All the kids respect him." Kendra smiled. "Guess he's like his old man that way, huh?"

"Don't go trying to butter me up," Jim said with a grin. "Next time I pull you over, you're getting a ticket. A real one."

"I hear you, officer. But seriously, Jimmy's a real good kid. You should be proud."

"Thanks. That's nice to hear. Now, where are you off to?"

"The dry cleaners. We've got dress rehearsal today and nobody remembered to pick up the costumes from the cleaners." Kendra looked at her watch. "I've got to be at the church with the costumes in twenty-eight minutes."

"Well, you're going to be late," Jim said unsympathetically. "Deal with it, Kendra. And stick to the speed limit."

"I will."

Kendra kept her word; she had to. She got stuck behind a school bus that seemed to stop and unload dawdling third-graders at every corner and driveway between the dance studio and the dry cleaner. Kendra knew it was her own fault. If she hadn't been speeding, Jim Lee wouldn't have pulled her over and she'd have been on the road ahead of the bus.

The parking lot and sidewalks were slick with winter ice and snow, so Kendra took her time walking. Not that she'd have been able to speed her pace even if she'd wanted to. Now in the final month of her pregnancy, the baby slowed Kendra's steps and made her unwieldy, but, surprisingly, this didn't bother her as much as it had a few weeks before. Recently, Kendra's anxiety about motherhood and marriage had been surely but steadily replaced with a sense of peace, a quiet assurance that whatever strength and wisdom she needed to deal with the upcoming challenges of parenting would be provided at the moment she needed it.

It wasn't that life had suddenly changed for the better. Andy's schedule was as crowded as it had ever been and Kendra's was just as bad. Andy had finally sat down with Kendra and told her about the problems he was having with Riley and the board. It was a relief for Kendra to realize that Andy's emotional distance over the last weeks had nothing to do with their relationship. But that relief gave way to feelings of indignation that someone at the church would even think of questioning her husband's leadership, even if — as Andy had explained in tones that Kendra felt were far too forgiving and magnanimous — that someone was just young and overeager, but basically good at heart.

"Good at heart! Are you kidding? Andy, you're too good to be true. I know you're a minister but . . . isn't there a limit to what ministers have to put up with?"

"Nope," he said with a wink. "There's that

whole part about having to forgive your brother seventy times seven."

"But . . ." Kendra sputtered. "In this case, I mean . . . isn't there some kind of loophole?"

"Afraid not. And you've got to promise me that, no matter what, you'll treat Riley and his family just as you always have, with kindness."

"But!"

"I mean it. This isn't the first controversy I've had to deal with since I was ordained and it won't be the last. Churches are like families, from time to time we have arguments and disagreements, but we have to work together and forgive each other, no matter what. If we didn't, we'd be torn apart from the inside out."

If this line of reasoning had to be applied to anyone besides her husband, Kendra would have accepted it readily, but Andy *was* her husband. She loved him and in the battle between love and logic, love usually triumphs.

"Andy, how can you just sit back and put up with this? After all you've done for Riley, for the whole church, how can you tolerate all this whining and complaining?"

Andy laughed. "Oh that's easy. I just remember all that God has done for me, including tolerating all *my* whining and complaining."

Kendra was worried about Andy and frustrated that she could do so little to help him beyond listening and praying. But Andy assured her that was exactly the kind of help he needed and so she did both wholeheartedly, grateful that they were communicating again.

There were so many challenges to face and Kendra was glad that she didn't have to face them alone.

Thea was no longer overtly rude to Kendra, but their relationship was far from what it had been, Sharon having replaced Kendra in the teenager's affections. Darla was out of the hospital, but faced a long road to recovery. And, on top of everything else, the baby had shifted into a position that made Kendra's back ache constantly, making it hard to sleep. Even so, Kendra was in a far better frame of mind than she had been just three weeks previously. It wasn't that the situation had changed all that much, but Kendra had.

When she'd come to faith three years before, Kendra had begun the habit of rising early and starting her day with a few quiet minutes with God. Sometimes she read the Bible, sometimes she wrote in her journal. Sometimes she sat and made a mental list of all the things she was grateful for. Sometimes she paced the floor and poured out her complaints and frustrations. Other times she opened her mind and heart and quietly waited for guidance. But no matter what the agenda, Kendra faithfully kept her daily appointment with God, growing in faith, finding peace.

But during the first trimester of her pregnancy, when she felt so exhausted that it was everything she could do to stay awake past eight o'clock, Kendra had started hitting the snooze button on her alarm in the mornings, sleeping through her prayer time. It had gotten to be a habit and so, even though her flagging energies were recharged later in the pregnancy, Kendra rarely made time for God. When she did, it tended to be a hurried affair in which she muttered a quick prayer, all the while thinking of all the things she needed to accomplish that day, following it up with a laundry list of problems that she thought God ought to fix, along with a list of suggestions as to exactly how He might go about doing that.

In short, Kendra's previously intimate relationship with God had regressed to the point where Kendra treated the Divine as some sort of celestial Santa Claus, whose sole purpose was to fill her spiritual stocking magically with all the toys she demanded.

However, Sharon's arrival changed that. She'd volunteered to swing by the house and take Thea to school in the mornings so Kendra would have an extra hour to rest before beginning her busy day. But the pain in her lower back made it impossible for her to sleep in. Instead, she resumed her old schedule, beginning her day with real, heartfelt prayer and meditation. She was so glad she did.

This one simple change had made a palpable and immediate difference in Kendra's outlook and attitude, giving her a new perspective and helping her respond to difficulties and setbacks calmly and thoughtfully. Which was a good thing because as she walked down the icy sidewalk toward the dry cleaners and peered into the storefront window of Ming's Chinese restaurant, Kendra's difficulties were about to increase exponentially.

Thea was sitting in one of the booths near the window picking at a plate of fried rice. Kendra couldn't see his face because he bent his head low, nuzzling Thea's neck while the girl giggled and pretended to push him away, but she knew that the boy sitting so close with his arm draped over Thea's shoulder like a creeping vine clinging to a wall was Josh Randall.

Sharon was nowhere to be seen.

# CHAPTER 13

Thea was in her bedroom with the door closed. When Kendra walked down the hall she could hear the furious staccato tapping of Thea's fingers on the computer keyboard as she poured out her woes and indignation to her online friends.

Undoubtedly she was telling everyone within cyber earshot what terrible, unreasonable, hopelessly old-fashioned parents she had, heaping an extra helping of burning coals on the head of Kendra in her role as wicked stepmother. Well, at least she wasn't sobbing anymore. During the ride from the restaurant to the church, Thea had said some ugly and utterly unfair things to her. Even so, Kendra hated to hear Thea cry.

Sharon and Andy were sitting in the family room on opposite sides of the coffee table, Andy on the sofa and Sharon in an easy chair, neither of them looking in the least easy. The tension in the room was thick. Kendra hesitated at the door for a moment, wondering if she ought to let them work this out without her, but Andy saw her and motioned for her to come sit next to him. He wasted no time in getting to the point.

"Sharon, you *knew* we'd forbidden Thea to see Josh. When you dropped her off at the restaurant, did you know he was going meet her there?"

"Yes. But it's not like I was dropping her off to meet him at some sleazy motel. They were in a restaurant, for heaven's sake! There were all kinds of people around and I was just down the street at the library. I'd have been back in another fifteen minutes. If Kendra hadn't walked by on her way to the dry cleaner, no one would ever have known about it. What was the harm? She's a young girl and she wants to date a young man. It's perfectly natural. And I think . . ."

"You think! *You* think!" Andy's face went red. "No. I don't think so. I don't think you were thinking at all. I'm not even going to try to discuss what sort of thinking goes on in the mind of a woman who encourages and helps a girl lie to her parents. That's a whole different discussion. But I am absolutely certain you weren't thinking, because if you were you'd have realized that Thea is fourteen years old. Fourteen! She's got no business dating a boy that age."

Sharon clenched her jaw. "I know how old she is, Andy. Better than you do, I think. Thea isn't a child anymore. She's a young woman and mature for her age, ready to test her wings. But if you insist on treating her like a child she's going to end up resenting you for . . ."

"Then so be it, Sharon! Because I do insist on treating her like a child, like *my* child! And that means protecting her! Even if that makes her resent me. That's my job as a father, Sharon! To protect her and guide her until she's old enough and wise enough to take care of herself!"

Andy took a deep breath, trying to regain his composure before going on.

"Yes, for fourteen, Thea *is* mature — except, of course, on the days when she's not. She hasn't the slightest idea what she wants out of life. This week she read a book about Jane Goodall and decided she wants to move to the rain forest and save gorillas. Last week she was going to be a network news anchor. And next week, it'll be something else. She still sleeps with a teddy bear, for heaven's sake! She's only fourteen!"

Sharon rolled her eyes. "Yes, I know that,

Andy. I was there when she was born, remember? I can do the math."

"I do remember that. Vaguely. I also remember that you didn't stick around for long afterward."

"Andy." Kendra laid her hand on his arm, reminding him to stay calm.

"Is that what this is about, Andy? You? Are you trying to hold Thea back as a way of getting back at me for leaving?"

"No!" Andy spat. "This is not about me or you. It's about Thea. It's about being a parent, about watching out for her best interests, about knowing when to say yes and when to say no, even if saying no makes her angry!

"Don't you get it? Josh Randall is eighteen years old. He can drive and vote and in a few months he'll be heading off to college. Word around town is he's applying to schools in Florida and California, anywhere warm. Doesn't sound like he's planning on coming back to Vermont anytime soon. I don't know exactly why Josh would want to date a little girl, a freshman barely out of braces, but as a father and a man, I've got some ideas."

"You haven't changed a bit, Andy. Always trying to control everybody. Don't you think Thea is mature enough to . . ."

251

"No, I don't! Because she's not! All Thea knows is that an older, good-looking guy with a cool truck and a smooth line is interested in her and she thinks that's the same as being in love. There is no way, no way in the world that this thing with Josh is going to end well. The *least* terrible thing that will happen to Thea is she'll have her heart broken. And when that happens, Kendra and I will be the ones who are left to pick up the pieces. Where will you be?"

Sharon was quiet for a moment. "All right, I deserved that. I walked out and left you holding the bag. I know that. And after what I did and how I did it . . ." Sharon ducked her head, shamefaced. "Well, it was good of you to even let me in the door. You too, Kendra. I know this can't be easy for you."

Kendra nodded. There was no point in denying what they both knew to be true. "I just want what's best for Thea."

"Me too," Sharon said. "That's why I'm here. I know I've failed Thea before, but . . . in a way, I was trying to do what was right for her. That's why I was able to leave, because I knew that Andy would be able to give Thea all the things I couldn't. I left her, but I didn't leave her alone. Because I knew she'd have you, Andy."

Sharon's voice cracked as she swallowed

back tears. "You're a good man, Andy. You always were. And a good father. I'm sorry . . . I . . ."

Sharon opened and closed her hands as if trying to catch hold of something in the air, but the words she needed, the phrases that could explain everything were beyond the reach of even a poet. "Well . . . I'm just sorry."

Andy was quiet for a moment. "I let all that go a long time ago. Like I said, this isn't about you or me. I'm only concerned for Thea."

"So am I, Andy!" Sharon's eyes pleaded her sincerity. "That's why I'm here now. All those years ago I wasn't ready to be a mother, but things are different now. I want to be part of Thea's life. I'm ready this time. If I wasn't I wouldn't be here."

Her gaze shifted from Andy's face to Kendra's and back again. "Believe me. If I thought my being here would hurt Thea, I'd leave tomorrow."

Kendra looked at Sharon. She was still beautiful, still stylish and exotic, better traveled and better educated than Kendra was or probably ever would be. But Kendra no longer felt intimidated or threatened by this woman whom Andy had once loved. Sharon's pleading eyes, the way her arms and shoulders arced forward, in an instinctive posture to protect a tender and a lonely heart, touched Kendra. She felt bad for her, sorry for all that she'd missed out on, but that didn't change who mattered in this situation — Thea.

"I would never hurt Thea," Sharon said, and then, realizing it was too late to say that she added, "not intentionally. I know I can't make up for the past, but Thea is my daughter, too. I've got a right to see her and to play a role in my child's life." Sharon shifted in her seat, rising up and straightening her shoulders and setting her jaw, shoring up her defenses before lobbing the next grenade.

"I've decided. I'm going to accept the Vermont position."

Andy looked at her, his face a blank. "Well . . . that's your right. You're entitled to live anywhere you want."

"Thanks. I know."

"You don't have to get defensive, Sharon. I won't pretend I'm overjoyed about this, but it is what it is. All I ask is that, for Thea's sake, we present a united front, lay out some ground rules so Thea won't be confused or start playing us against each other."

"Such as?"

"Don't help her go around us or lie to us.

If we make a rule for Thea then I expect you to help us enforce it. In short, no more dropping her off for clandestine meetings with Josh Randall."

Sharon thought about this for a moment, then got to her feet and put on her coat. "All right. Agreed. But that doesn't mean I'm going to tell her she shouldn't have feelings for the boy. No matter what you say, I still think Thea is old enough and wise enough to decide that for herself and I'm not going to discourage her."

"Sharon, come on. Be reasonable. Thea is still a child. She's too young and inexperienced to understand what . . ."

"No, Andy! No! Just because you're her father that doesn't entitle you to decide who Thea can and cannot love. You ought to give your daughter a little more credit for common sense and show at least a little respect for her feelings. You ought to trust her. Like I do."

And before Andy could say anything else Sharon left, letting a cold blast of winter air come in through the open door. Andy closed it behind her and turned around to face Kendra.

"Well, gee . . . that was fun, wasn't it? We should really invite her over more often."

But Kendra was in no mood to joke. She

reached out and touched her husband's arm, tipping her head toward the hallway where Thea stood watching them with a stormy, resentful expression on her face.

Andy sighed, worn out by the dramas of the day, and held out a hand to his daughter. "Thea, sweetheart. I know you're upset, but come sit down and let's talk."

"No! I'm not going to listen to you. Mom's right. You don't trust me. She's the only one who trusts me, the only one who understands me. You can tell me what to do, but you can't tell me what to think. Or who to love. Josh loves me! He said so! You just don't understand. Nobody understands me!"

Tears began streaming down Thea's face, her cheeks blotched pink and red with emotion. Kendra moved toward her.

"Thea. Oh, Thea, don't cry. Dad isn't trying to hurt you, really. He's just trying to protect you."

"No, he's not! He's trying to run my life. And so are you! You're not my mother! You don't have the right to tell me what to do."

Andy jumped in, his voice stern. "Thea, that's enough of that. You're not allowed to speak to Kendra that way."

"I'll talk any way I want to! You can't tell me how to talk! You can't . . ."

"Thea! Go to your room!"

Thea stopped, shocked by the commanding tone and volume of her father's usually gentle voice.

"You heard what I said, Thea. Go to your room. Do it now!"

Thea turned, breaking into a fresh wave of weeping, and ran down the hallway to her bedroom, slamming the door behind her so they would know exactly how she felt about them.

Kendra looked at Andy uncertainly. "Should I go in there? Try to talk to her?"

"No. Let her stew for a while. She'll calm down."

Andy walked over and flopped down on the sofa, exhausted, and patted the cushion next to him. "Come here. Take a load off."

Kendra sat down. Andy reached down and hooked his arm under Kendra's knees, turning her body so Kendra's legs were draped across his lap. Andy put his arm around her shoulders. Kendra leaned toward him resting her head on his broad chest.

Kendra laid her hand on the rounded alp of her stomach. The baby moved inside her swimming toward it, balling up under the comforting warmth of her hand.

"Andy? Do you think I'll be a good mother?"

"I think you *are* a good mother."

"I mean for our baby. Do you think I'll be a good mother to our baby?"

"Yes."

"And when our baby is a teenager, do you think it'll slam doors and say hateful things to us?"

"Yes."

Kendra sighed and snuggled closer to her husband. "I was afraid you'd say that."

# CHAPTER 14

"All right!" Kendra clapped her hands, applauding after the Raggedy Ann dancers made their last clumsy turn and then flopped onto the floor in splits, as their dance and the first act came to an end. "Very nice! Good energy everybody!"

The actors, dressed in their first act costumes, gathered at the edge of the stage.

"Really, gang. That was just great. I'm proud of you. The act ran a little long so I'm not going to do notes right now. Be here fifteen minutes early tomorrow and I'll run through them before the curtain, okay?" Kendra looked at her watch.

"I don't want to keep you any later than ten o'clock tonight. It's a big day tomorrow, show day. You need your rest. We're going to run the second act all the way through, no stops, and then you can go home. And go to sleep!" Kendra raised her eyebrows meaningfully and the kids laughed, knowing what she was about to say. "I'm not kidding! Get into your beds and turn out the lights. No staying up until three in the morning talking to each other online, do you hear me? Good."

She clapped her hands and rubbed them together. "All right, then. Stagehands, load in the manger set. Actors, get changed into your second act costumes. You've got twelve minutes. Go!"

Kendra made a shooing motion and the elves, ice skaters, Raggedy Anns, toy soldiers, and teddy bears scurried backstage to begin their transformation to innkeepers, shepherds, angels, and wise men. Kendra pointed to Connie, the stage manager, a tall willowy girl wearing black jeans, a T-shirt, and headset.

"Connie, can you have somebody get a ladder and take those green gels out of lamps fourteen and sixteen? Last rehearsal, the three wise men looked like they were getting over a bad case of seasickness."

"I'm on it, Kendra."

Kendra rubbed her eyes. She needed to sit down and rest for a few minutes, but noticed that Jimmy Lee was standing a few feet away with a serious look on his face.

"Hey, Jimmy. Everything okay?"

"Yeah . . . ummm . . ." He was dressed in

the Santa costume he wore for both acts but his expression was far from jolly. In fact, the eyes that peered out from underneath the bushy false eyebrows were worried.

Kendra put her hand on his arm. "Is something wrong, Jimmy?"

"Well . . . I was just wondering . . . is Thea still seeing Josh Randall?"

"No. Her dad and I put a stop to that. She's too young to be dating a senior."

Jimmy looked relieved. "Okay. Good."

"Why do you ask?" Kendra waited for a response, but the boy hesitated, reluctant to say more. "Jimmy, what's going on? You can tell me. Is Thea in some kind of trouble?"

He shook his head. "No, nothing like that. I know that she's been really mad at you lately."

"You think?" Kendra asked with a wry smile, recalling the silent treatment she'd been subjected to over the last week.

Jimmy smiled. "Don't be too mad at Thea. She's just kind of confused right now."

"I know. She's been a pain lately, but she's my daughter and I love her."

"Yeah. Thea's really a great girl . . ." The boy's eyes took on a wistful expression and Kendra smiled, recognizing a case of puppy love when she saw it.

"But Josh . . ." Jimmy pressed his lips

261

together, disgusted. "That guy is bad news. And some of the things I've been hearing around school . . ."

"What kind of things?"

Jimmy blushed, the apples of his heavily made-up cheeks turning an even brighter shade of cherry red. "Well. Nothing I'm going to repeat to the minister's wife, but let's just say that Josh has a big mouth. I don't think there's anything to it, but I just wanted to warn you to keep Thea away from him. I don't want her to get hurt."

"Thanks, Jimmy. I appreciate that. You're a good friend."

"Oh . . . well . . ." He ducked his head, not sure what to say to that.

"You'd better get backstage. I'm calling the act in five minutes."

"Okay," he said. "Kendra? Please don't tell Thea I said anything to you. She'd be really mad if she knew I had. Promise?"

"I promise," she assured him. "It'll be our secret."


Kendra was exhausted. Her back hurt, her feet hurt, even her hands hurt. Her fingers were swollen like pink and white sausages. The last three weeks had stretched her to the limit, but she was pleased that the pageant had come together so well.

The kids always worked incredibly hard on the show but it seemed to Kendra that this year, they had taken it up a notch. Tomorrow was the big day and they were as ready as they'd ever be. Which was a good thing. The way she was feeling, Kendra knew she'd have to use every ounce of her remaining energy to get through the next twenty-four hours. After that she planned on sleeping for about fifteen hours straight, waking up just in time to open presents and then head over to the Sugarmans for Christmas dinner.

Turning out of the church parking lot after rehearsal, Kendra tried to stifle a yawn. "Long day," she said to Thea who was staring out the passenger side window into the dark and snowy night. "But, I think we're ready. Don't you?"

Thea shrugged noncommittally. "Guess so. It was okay."

Kendra smiled to herself. Thea hadn't exactly thrown open the floodgates of communication, but it had been a week since Thea had spoken five words to her all at one time. It was a start.

"Well, I thought you did a good job tonight," Kendra said and meant it. Angry as Thea had been over the last weeks, she hadn't let it stand in the way of giving the best performance she could. Thea took the pageant very seriously. She truly wanted the people in the audience to rejoice in the miracle of Christmas.

"Thanks."

Kendra drove in silence for a moment, not wanting to push Thea. "Isn't that Jimmy Lee just the nicest guy?"

"Jimmy? Sure. He's nice."

"I think he likes you."

Thea puffed dismissively. "Jimmy's a kid."

"He's a sophomore. A year older than you."

Thea was quiet, letting the subject drop before switching to another.

"Kendra? I . . . I know I've been a big pain lately." Kendra couldn't disagree with this so she didn't say anything. "I'm sorry I've been so mean to you. I've just been really confused, you know? I'm not saying that I think you and Dad were right to say I couldn't see Josh anymore."

"Okay. Fair enough."

"But I shouldn't have been so awful to you. That wasn't fair. I know you and Dad always want what's best for me. Even when you're wrong."

"We love you, Thea. You know that."

"I know. I mean, you must love me to have put up with all my garbage the last few weeks, right?" Thea turned to Kendra and, for the first time in weeks, she smiled. "I think that maybe, with the new baby coming, I was worried that you and Dad wouldn't care about me anymore . . ."

"Oh, Thea . . . Thea, sweetheart." Kendra reached across the seat and grabbed her daughter's gloved hand in her own. "That's not going to happen. You are so special to us. Do you know something? When I first got pregnant, I was worried because I couldn't imagine that I would ever be able to love the new baby the way I do you."

"Really?"

"Really. But in the last few months I've realized that parents have magical hearts with an infinite capacity for love. I haven't ever seen the baby, don't even know if it's a boy or girl . . ."

"I hope it's a girl," Thea interrupted.

"But whatever it is, I already love this baby with my whole heart. Just exactly the way I love you and always will. Maybe that's why God created parenthood, so regular people could understand how God loves all of us with His whole heart, no matter what. I can't say that I've loved the way you've treated me the last few weeks, but I've never stopped loving you."

"I'm sorry, Kendra."

"I know you are. I forgive you. Don't worry about it anymore."

"Well, I just wanted you to know. I really do love you, but . . . I love my mom too. And I've been thinking that maybe, for a while, I might want to live with her."

Kendra clutched the steering wheel more tightly and fought to keep her face blank.

"Not forever!" Thea rushed to assure her. "And not because Dad won't let me see Josh anymore. I'm still mad about that, but I'm not using Mom as a way of punishing you and Dad. I just . . . I want to know her better. And I want her to know me. You know? She's my mom."

Kendra nodded slowly. She did know. She thought she did. Kendra loved her baby sight unseen. In spite of all she had done and not done over the years, Thea loved her mother and wanted to be loved in return. Kendra understood that. There are no perfect mothers just as there are no perfect children, but the bonds between them are powerful.

Kendra turned to look at the girl's hopeful, innocent face and the love that coursed through her could not have been stronger had Thea been a child of her own body.

"You want me to talk to Dad?"

Thea bit her lip. "Would you? I don't want

to hurt his feelings, I just . . ."

"I know," said Kendra.

# CHAPTER 15

It was still dark outside, barely past five when the telephone rang, but Andy was already awake.

He always rose early to spend a quiet half hour in prayer, craving that small oasis of peace at the beginning of every hectic day. But today he'd risen long before the alarm sounded. After Kendra had told him that Thea wanted to live with Sharon, Andy couldn't sleep. Finally, around three, he'd given up on it, gone into the kitchen to drink coffee, think, and pray about what he should do. Two hours later he was just as confused and hurt as ever.

So it was almost a relief when the ring of the telephone split the predawn silence. Such an early call could only mean that some member of his flock needed him. Tired of turning in helpless circles as he walked around and around his own burdens, he was ready to return to more familiar ground and help someone else shoulder theirs.

"Hello. This is Reverend Loomis."

"Andy? It's Sharon."

"Sharon? It's early. Are you all right? Is something wrong?"

"No. Nothing like that. It's good news. Well, actually it's good and bad news. But it's good news for me. I got a call last night, very late or I'd have called before. I didn't want to wake you."

"What is it?"

"I got a call from Scotland — from the university. Two of their lecturers were driving back from an academic conference and were in a terrible accident. One of them, a poetry professor, was badly injured. They say he'll survive, but is facing months of rehabilitation."

"That's terrible."

"I know. That's the bad news but . . . well, I know this sounds terrible but it's good news for me. The head of the department called to ask if I would be willing to come back and take over the poetry classes."

"When?"

"Now. Classes start on January third. I've only got a few days to get to Scotland, find a place to live, and get up to speed on the course syllabus. I called the airline right away, but with all the holiday traffic, the only flight they could get me leaves this morning . . ."

A flush of anger coursed through him. He couldn't believe she was going to do this to Thea, not again.

"Sharon, you can't leave, not today. The pageant is today. You promised Thea you'd be there. You promised. She's counting on you."

"I know, I know. And I feel terrible about it, but I've called every airline and this is the only flight available. If there was any other way . . . This is an amazing opportunity, Andy. I just can't pass it up. Explain it to Thea. She'll understand, coming from you."

"Coming from me?" Andy shouted. "From me? Are you serious? You're not even going to come over and tell her good-bye?"

"I can't, Andy. I'm already at the airport in Burlington right now, waiting for a flight to New York. My New York to Aberdeen flight leaves in five hours. If there had been any other way . . ."

Sharon's voice cracked and Andy knew she was crying. "I'm sorry . . ."

Andy was livid. She had done it again. Part of him couldn't believe it, but he knew it was true and that nothing he could do or say would change her mind.

"Andy . . . I . . . are you still there?"

"Yes. I'm still here."

"Tell Thea I'll write to her from Scotland. Maybe she can come and visit me. Maybe this summer. Tell her that, will you? Tell her I'm sorry. Tell her I love her. Andy?"

"I'll tell her."

Sharon sniffed. "Okay. Thanks. I have to go."

She hung up the phone. Andy stood with the receiver to his ear, listening to the dial tone, wondering how much longer it would take for the sun to rise and rouse his daughter from sleep, and what he would say to her when it did.

Andy heard a soft *whoosh whoosh,* a shuffling sound of fluffy slippers on carpet, and looked up to see Kendra standing in the doorway, his bathrobe cinched over the rounded expanse of her belly, yawning.

"Honey, who was that? Is something wrong?"

# CHAPTER 16

It was past ten when Kendra, who was just putting a batch of apple cinnamon muffins in the oven, heard the sound of water running through pipes. Andy was emptying the dishwasher, sorting the silverware into piles and putting them away.

"The shower's running. Thea's awake."

Andy sighed. "She thinks Sharon is coming to pick her up. They were going to do some last minute Christmas shopping and have lunch before Thea had to be at the church. I guess we'd better go in and talk to her."

"Wait until the muffins are done. I'm going to make some peppermint hot chocolate, too."

"Comfort food?"

"It couldn't hurt. Hot chocolate always makes me think things are going to get better. They sure couldn't get worse."

But Kendra was wrong.

272

As they approached the door to Thea's room, Kendra carrying a plate of warm muffins slathered with butter, Andy following behind carrying a tray with three cups of steaming hot chocolate, they heard Thea crying.

Kendra turned to look at Andy.

"She can't have heard anything," he said. "Sharon's on a plane to Scotland right now. And even if the flight was delayed, the phone hasn't rung and Sharon doesn't have a laptop so she couldn't have sent an e-mail. Could she?"

"I don't know. Maybe she found a computer at the airport?"

Kendra knocked on the door. "Thea? Are you all right? We brought your breakfast. Can we come in?"

Thea choked out a sob. "No! Go away!"

Andy stepped in front of Kendra. "Thea, it's Dad. I'm coming in." He opened the door.

Thea lay sprawled across the bed, crying into her pillow. Sensing something was amiss, Wendell had pushed aside the company of stuffed animals that Thea kept piled on the bed and curled himself into a ball near her head, trying to comfort her with the warmth of his presence. Thea's laptop computer sat open at the end of the bed.

The power indicator light blinked green to black and back to green.

"Thea?"

Thea's long hair hung in wet ropes down her back, still damp from the shower. She pushed herself up from her prone position and looked up; her eyes were red and her cheeks were flushed.

"Daddy!"

She held out her arms. Andy put the tray on the dresser and came to her side, holding his little girl.

"What is it, baby? What's wrong?" Thea didn't say anything, just collapsed onto his shoulders and sobbed.

Kendra put the plate of muffins down on Thea's dresser next to the silver frame that held the family picture they'd had taken the Christmas before. A few minutes before, Thea had been calmly taking a shower, like she did every morning, now, she was sobbing. Something had triggered Thea's distress but what? The computer?

Kendra picked up Thea's laptop and read the words on the screen, a transcript of an online conversation between two cyber buddies named HownDawg and LatinPopStar. Somebody had seen it, copied it, and forwarded it to Thea.

LATINPOPSTAR: Heard the Rev said MissT couldn't see you anymore. Looks like you lost the bet, dude. You owe me 50 bucks. Pay up.

HOWNDAWG: Not so fast. I've got 'till the pageant. She's going to be with her mom tomorrow. Mom's not as strait-laced as the Rev and wants to be popular, cool. Thinks she should be MissT's BFF, not her mom. All I gotta do is talk Mom into letting me and MissT have lunch alone, then we sneak out the back door of the Chinese place and into the truck and that'll be that.

LATINPOPSTAR: No way, dude! Even if you do get her in the truck, how you gonna get her to give it up?

HOWNDAWG: She's all over the Dawg. All I have to do is get her alone, away from the Rev and the stepmom. Get ready to fork over 50. That was the bet. Before the curtain goes up on the pageant, the Dawg will take the V out of the Virgin Mary. LOL. Dude, it's a done thing. I'm gonna hit that. No prob.

Kendra's lip curled in disgust and she slammed the laptop closed. "That scuzzball. How could he?"

"How could who? What did it say, Kendra?"

Andy reached toward the computer, but Thea grabbed his wrist to stop him.

"No! I don't want you to read it. I'm so embarrassed. Oh, Daddy. I'm so sorry. I'm so, so sorry! You were right all along. I should have listened to you. I was so stupid!" she cried and buried her head in her father's shoulder again.

# CHAPTER 17

After they talked to Thea, calmed her down, and then told her about Sharon, and then calmed her down all over again, Andy did what any father would do. He got in his car and went out looking for Josh Randall.

Though Thea wouldn't let him read the actual text that some anonymous friend of Josh's had posted on his blog, she had, her cheeks flaming from shame, told him the gist of the teenage Casanova's plan. Armed with this information, it didn't take Andy long to locate the boy.

Downtown Maple Grove was busy, the stores crowded with last minute shoppers, but Andy spotted Josh's white pickup truck right where he figured it would be, in the parking lot near Ming's Chinese restaurant. He was standing on the sidewalk outside the restaurant entrance, scanning the faces of the people who were scurrying past with shopping bags, looking for Thea. He looked

277

surprised to see Andy striding toward him, but tried to act casual.

"Hello, Reverend Loomis. Nice to see you. How's everything at the . . ."

Andy didn't give him a chance to finish.

He grabbed him by the lapels of his jacket, lifting him until there was a bare inch of space between Josh's toes and the snowy sidewalk. The boy's frightened face was even with his own and Josh had a clear view of exactly the level of fury he'd raised in the soul of this usually mild-mannered man. Josh gulped and started to say something. Andy took an even tighter hold on his jacket and then shoved him backward as hard as he could, sending the boy sprawling into a nearby snowbank.

"Dude! What's wrong with you? Are you crazy? You can't hit me; you're a minister!"

"Oh yeah?" Andy sneered. "I'm also a father. And when somebody deliberately sets out to hurt my little girl, it makes me crazy. Insane, even. So get on your feet, boy. Because I'm going to knock you into next week."

Andy bent his knees, taking a boxer's stance, and drew back his big fist. Wide-eyed and visibly shaken, Josh stayed put.

"No? You're not going to get up? That may be the first smart thing you've done in your life. Good move. You stay down there. And stay away from my daughter. Like you say, I'm a minister. I'm not supposed to go around pounding the stuffing out of the local youth, even if they are vermin. So you stay put, because if you get up, if you ever bother my daughter again, or spread around one more filthy lie about her, minister or no, I won't be responsible for what happens to you next. You got that? Dawg?"

Josh didn't say anything, just nodded his head.

Breathing hard, Andy slowly lowered his fist and then spit onto the snow, aiming and hitting a spot just a few inches from where Josh lay. "Glad we understand each other."

A clutch of shoppers had gathered nearby, including a few teenagers from the high school, to watch the spectacle.

"Excuse me," Andy said as he turned and headed down the sidewalk toward the parking lot, leaving the boy cowering in the snowbank and drawing the openmouthed stares of the kids.

As he approached the dry cleaners, the door opened. Riley Roth stepped out, almost bumping into him.

"Andy! Nice to see you," Riley said cheerfully before seeing the scowl on the minister's face and then looking down the sidewalk where Josh was struggling to get up from the snow.

"Do you need a hand there, son?"

Riley made a move toward Josh. Andy put up an arm to stop him, then spun around, and pointed at Josh. "Do not get up from that spot," he said in a low and menacing voice. "Do you hear me? Do — Not — Move!"

"Yes, sir." Josh let his feet slide out from under him and flopped backward into the snow again. One of the girls standing nearby giggled and the rest of the teenagers joined in before stepping over Josh's legs and going into Ming's. Josh closed his eyes, but didn't move.

Riley looked confused. "What's going on, Andy? You okay?"

"Fine," Andy said coldly. "Never better. Why do you ask?"

"Well . . . I . . ." he glanced uneasily at Josh. "Never mind.

"Listen, I'm glad I bumped into you. I'd like to call another meeting. We really should continue our discussions about the new building program. And there are a few other things I'd like to talk about as well. Some new business."

"No."

Riley raised his eyebrows, surprised by the

definitive nature of this refusal. "I know it's close to Christmas, but I was thinking that we could get together this afternoon. Before the pageant . . ."

"No," Andy repeated firmly. "I am not going to call another meeting about the building program. I've sat through all the meetings I intend to on that subject. There are a lot of things the church can and should spend its time and money on — spreading the gospel, feeding the hungry, visiting the lonely, battling injustice, and," he said, tilting his head toward the inert Josh, "reaching out to the morally bankrupt youth of our town. But we do not need a heated baptistery, a latte bar in the lobby, or a sound system to rival Carnegie Hall's, or a new building. No more meetings, Riley. Not about that."

The tips of Riley's ears turned red and he sputtered, "Now, wait a minute, Andy . . ."

"No," Andy said evenly. "You wait a minute, Riley. For three months, I've stood back and let you steer the agenda of the board, wasting everyone's time talking about trivialities that have nothing to do with the mission of this church. I shouldn't have. I've also turned a blind eye and a deaf ear, ignoring your underhanded attempts to oust me from the pulpit and bring in somebody who'd go along with your plan to tear down the historic church that has ably served the needs of this community for more than 140 years. That was a mistake too, a lack of leadership on my part. But I've learned my lesson. So no, Riley. I'm not going to call a meeting about the building program because there isn't going to be any building program. Not on my watch, not until we need one.

"Now if that makes you question my leadership or my vision," Andy said with a single nod of his head, "that's your right and I respect it. What I do not respect is that you've been going around behind my back, spreading gossip and dissent among the church body. That is not how we do things, Riley. Not in Maple Grove."

Riley shifted from one foot to another, stung by the rebuke, but not disputing it.

Andy went on. "If you want to bring forth a motion to have me replaced, I'll put it on the agenda for the next scheduled meeting, not before. But unless and until the congregation should ask me to step aside, I am the leader of the Maple Grove Community Church. And I'm done letting you or anyone else to distract me from my job to serve the people of this community."

He was quiet for a moment, giving Riley

space to voice any disagreement. When none came, Andy looked at his watch. "I'm glad I bumped into you too, Riley. Now, if you don't mind, I've got to go over to the church. I told Kendra I'd help set up extra chairs for the pageant. You're coming, aren't you?"

"Yes," Riley said uncomfortably.

"Good," Andy said evenly. "I'd hate for you to miss it. See you at church, Riley."

# CHAPTER 18

Kendra frowned as she stared at her clipboard, checking items off the list. "And you changed those green gels on lamps fourteen and sixteen?"

Connie adjusted her headset to a more comfortable position. "I replaced them with medium amber. The wise men will now look tan, not seasick."

"Good. And is the . . ."

"Yes," the stage manager replied patiently. "The sound check is done. No more feedback on the stage left microphone. We ran the light cues before you got here, twice. I reminded Joey to take the spot off Santa during Mary's solo. The props are all in place. I checked them myself . . ."

"Good, good." Kendra nodded nervously and then waddled over to a large, brightly painted cube on stage right. "And what about the Jack-in-the-Box door? Cameron's entrance was late. He said the door was stuck. If he doesn't pop out of there on his cue we lose the laugh. He's got to explode out of this thing."

"Cameron is a big liar. He missed his entrance because he was in there eating cheese puffs instead of listening for his cue. He had a whole stash of snacks in there. But don't worry, I hid them all in the prop closet. And," she said, lifting and lowering the lid of the box a few times, "I oiled the box hinges personally. See?"

"All right. Great." Kendra stood in the middle of the stage, staring out at the rows of empty seats, and bit her lip thoughtfully.

"It's almost seven," Connie reminded her.

Kendra took a deep breath and let it out. "Okay. Yes. I guess we're as ready as we'll ever be. Open the doors."

Connie grinned and turned to address two stagehands. "Laura, tell the ushers they can open the house. Kyle, go to the dressing rooms and call the act — curtain in thirty minutes. Don't worry, Kendra. I'll take it from here. You just sit back and enjoy the show."

For most people in Maple Grove, December twenty-third and the annual church Christmas pageant, marked the beginning of the Christmas holiday. People who wanted to make sure they had the best seats had started lining up in the lobby around five. By the time Kendra finally gave the okay to let the ushers open the doors, the lobby was packed. People streamed down the aisles of the church like water pouring through the floodgates of a dam. But anxious as they were to find good seats, there was no pushing or shoving among the crowd, just an atmosphere of cheery anticipation and the hum of excited conversations, occasionally pierced by shouted greetings or the laughter of people who spotted friends, family, and neighbors in the crowd. Kendra heard her own name being called.

"Kendra? Honey! Look who's here!" Andy waved to her from the back of the church. Kendra squinted to see past the bright stage lights, her face splitting into a grin when she saw Darla Benton on Andy's arm. Kendra waved back and made her way down the aisle.

"Darla!" Kendra leaned down to give her a hug but, with her bulging stomach in the way, it ended up being more of an enthusiastic pat. "How are you feeling?"

"Better than you, I suspect." The old woman clucked her tongue disapprovingly. "Shouldn't you be sitting down?"

Kendra waved her hand dismissively. "I'm

fine. A little tired, that's all. Everything has gone just great, though it will be a relief to have this over and done with. What about you? Do you feel as good as you look? Because you look fabulous!"

"Actually, I feel better than I have in a long while. I've lost six pounds since the heart attack."

Kendra laughed and rested her hand on her stomach. "Really? Well, I think I found them for you. Want them back?"

"No, thanks just the same." Darla looked around the fast-filling church. "I guess I'd better find a place to sit or there won't be any left."

"Don't worry about that," Andy said. "Director's privilege. Kendra and I have five seats saved near the front, two for us, two for the Sugarmans, and one for you. We hoped you'd be well enough to make it."

"Well, heaven help anyone who'd have tried to stop me!"

Kendra started to lead the way toward their seats but halfway down the aisle she was met by Connie. The normally cool and collected stage manager looked a little ruffled.

"Excuse me. Kendra? We've got a problem."

"What is it?"

"It's Thea. She won't get in her costume. She's crying and she says she's not going on."

"What!"

Connie started to explain, but Kendra held up a hand to interrupt.

"Never mind. You go backstage and get ready. I'll talk to Thea. Andy? Would you show Darla to our seats? I'll be back soon. Hopefully before the show starts."

"Don't worry about me," Darla said and released her hold on Andy's arm "I can seat myself. You two go talk to Thea."

Hustled isn't a word that can generally be applied to a woman entering the ninth month of pregnancy, but as best as she could, Kendra hustled up the aisle of the church, steering through the people who were coming from the opposite direction. Andy followed her, smiling and nodding to the people who were entering, but trying to avoid any lengthy conversations. Once they'd made their way out of the sanctuary and into the corridor that led to the cloakrooms that doubled as dressing rooms during the pageant, Andy fell into step beside his wife.

"I don't understand," Andy said. "You said she seemed all right when you drove over here. Between Sharon's leaving and this Josh business, I know this hasn't been the best day of Thea's life, but we talked it all through this morning and she seemed all right. Why would she suddenly fall apart twenty minutes before the show is supposed to start?"

Winded, Kendra stopped for a moment. "Can we slow down a little, sweetie? I need to catch my breath."

"Are you all right?" he asked nervously. "Is it the baby?"

Kendra took in a couple of deep breaths and laughed. "Don't I wish! I saw the doctor yesterday. Looks like I'm going to go the full three weeks until my due date. I'm okay, just enormous and out of shape. Just give me a minute.

"Your problem," Kendra continued, "is you've never been a teenage girl. They can go from elation to despair and back again in the blink of an eye. And it isn't like Thea doesn't have some real reasons to be upset. Sharon, Josh, a new baby coming, preshow jitters." Kendra ticked the list off her fingers. "Plus the fact that her father, a formerly pacifistic man of the cloth, hunted down her former boyfriend and beat him up with half the student body of Maple Grove High there to witness the scene."

"I did not beat him up," Andy said defensively. "I just pushed him into the snow and *threatened* to beat him up. Not one of my finer moments, I'll admit, but there's a big difference. I'm only human. What father worth his salt wouldn't have done the same? And I did not push him down in front of half the high school. It was only a handful of kids, four or five. Six at the most."

"Well, I'm sure half the student body has heard of it by now and by tomorrow morning, so will the rest. Maybe that's what she's worried about," Kendra said. "That once the word gets round about what a tough customer her father is, no boy will ever ask her out again."

"Good. Fine with me."

"Andy!" She laughed.

"I mean it. The problem with you is you've never been a teenage boy. You don't know what filthy, disgusting creatures they are. Ruled entirely by their . . ."

"Yeah, I get the picture." She laughed. "But they can't all be like that. You weren't like that."

"Don't be so sure," Andy said and raised his eyebrows comically. "The smartest thing we could do is send Thea off to a convent in the mountains until she's thirty."

"But we're not Catholic."

"We'll convert. And after my little run in with Riley," Andy said in a more serious tone, "we may have to."

"Oh, Andy," Kendra murmured sympathetically. "Don't be so hard on yourself. You were right to confront Riley. He's been distracting the board from its real purpose for months. You've been more than patient with him."

Andy sighed. "Maybe too patient. Riley's not a bad guy at heart. I don't want to embarrass him and I don't want to lose him. He's pushy, but he does have some good ideas. This is as much my fault as his. If I had dealt with this sooner then maybe there wouldn't have had to *be* a confrontation in the first place."

"You know," Kendra said gently, "you ought to take some of your own advice — remember that you're only human. Maybe you didn't handle this as well as you might have, but you will next time. And if Riley is the man you think he is, then the two of you will be able to put this behind you and work together. Don't you think?"

Andy nodded. "You're right."

"Well," Kendra said with a smile as she and Andy started walking again, "I'm glad we worked that out. Now we just have to figure out how to get our daughter to come out of her dressing room. After that, we'll tackle peace in the Middle East."

"Okay. But first, what are we going to say to Thea that we didn't already say this morning?"

"Nothing. We're just going to say it all again — with feeling." Kendra again ticked the list off on her fingers. "We love her and we always will. Sharon does too, in her way. The new baby won't change how we feel about her. She might have made some mistakes, but who hasn't? Josh is a huge jerk and everyone in school knows that. This too shall pass. The sun will come out tomorrow. The show must go on. And the only thing we have to fear is fear itself. That sort of thing."

"And if that doesn't work?"

"Then we retreat to our fail-safe position; we threaten to dock her allowance. Ready?"

"Ready."

They rounded the corner that led to the dressing rooms and saw Thea walking toward the stage entrance, dressed in her Mary costume, and carrying a bouquet of pink sweetheart roses as she walked hand-in-hand with Santa Claus as played by Jimmy Lee. Her eyes looked a little red but, other than that, Thea showed no signs of distress. In fact, she was beaming.

"Hi, Daddy! Hi, Kendra! Did you come back to wish me luck?"

Kendra looked at Andy who said, "Uh. Yeah. Sure. Break a leg, sweetheart."

"Thanks, Daddy." She threw her arms around his neck and kissed him on the cheek. "Daddy? A bunch of the kids are going out for ice cream after the show and Jimmy wants to take me. Can I go?"

Andy frowned and Jimmy rushed to quell his concerns.

"I'll have her home by eleven. My mom is going to drive us."

Andy looked at Kendra, who smiled her assent. "All right. Eleven o'clock. Not one second later."

"Yes, sir!" Jimmy grinned. "Eleven o' clock. I promise."

The door that led to the stage opened. Connie peered out. "There you are! Come on, guys! Onstage. We're five minutes to curtain."

Thea handed her roses to Kendra. "Could you take these home and put them in water for me?" Without waiting for an answer she lifted the skirt of her costume and scurried through the stage door with Jimmy right behind.

Andy looked at Kendra. "I don't understand. What just happened here?"

293

"I told you. Elation to despair and back again in less time than it takes two concerned parents to come to the rescue."

Kendra took her husband's arm. "Come on. Let's go watch the show."

# Chapter 19

The sound of applause still ringing in her ears, Kendra let out a deep, satisfied sigh.

Andy turned his gaze from the road and looked at her, worried. "Are you all right? Is it the baby?"

"No," Kendra said with exasperation. "Are you going to be like this for the next three weeks? Calm down. I was just sighing with contentment — and relief. The pageant went really well, don't you think? I mean, other than Cameron popping out of the box late. Did you see him? There was a big orange ring around his mouth. Cheese puffs. He must have found a key to the prop closet. But, other than that, it went off without a hitch. Thea was great. I was so proud of her."

"Well, I'm proud of you," Andy said. "I think it was the best pageant we've ever had."

"Aw, shucks. You're just saying that." Kendra tipped her head and batted her eye-lashes. "Say it again."

"It was the best pageant we ever had. I mean it, sweetheart. You did an amazing job. Everybody thought so. People were lined up six-deep to congratulate you. It was like fighting off the paparazzi just trying to get you from the lobby to the car. For a minute I thought I was going to have to pick you up and carry you."

Kendra smiled and rubbed the top of her stomach. "It's a good thing you didn't. You'd have had to go to the hospital before me."

Keeping one hand on the wheel, Andy reached across the seat and rested his hand on hers. "I'm glad we've got a little more time to wait yet. Now that the show is over we can relax, kick back, and enjoy a nice quiet Christmas."

"As soon as you finish preaching the sunrise Christmas service," Kendra said with a yawn.

"Oh, I don't mind. Actually, that's my favorite part of Christmas. And how great is it that Thea is going out with Jimmy Lee tonight?" Andy enthused.

"How great is it?" Shooting him a con-fused look, Kendra said, "I thought you said that we should send Thea to a convent, far from the reach of all teenage boys."

"Jimmy seems okay. And he looked pretty nervous when he was talking to us. He's probably heard about how I knocked the tar out of Josh."

Kendra slapped her husband playfully on the arm. "Knocked the tar out of him? Wait a minute. Weren't you the guy who insisted that you *hadn't* laid a hand on Josh?"

Andy nodded. "Yeah. But I'm starting to think that this is one rumor worth spreading: 'Don't even look at Thea Loomis with lust in your heart. Her dad's an animal.' " Andy grinned. "I like it. Has a nice ring to it."

Kendra laughed. "You're not fooling anybody. You're the sweetest man on earth and everybody in Maple Grove knows it. So why are you so happy that Thea went out with Jimmy tonight?"

"One, because it made Thea happy and two, because it gives us a whole hour and a half to ourselves. I've got a bottle of sparkling cider in the refrigerator and a sprig of mistletoe hanging in the doorway. As soon as we get to the house, I'm going to plug in the Christmas tree, and put my 'Christmas with Perry Como' album on the stereo so we can snuggle up on the sofa to have ourselves a merry little Christmas."

Kendra made a face. "You had me right up to the Perry Como part. How about we just build a nice fire in the fireplace instead? Maybe listen to the crackle of the logs while you rub my feet. They're killing me."

"Okay. I'm a little disappointed that Perry's out of the picture, but I'll get over it. The main thing is that we'll have the house all to ourselves! We'd better take advantage of it while we can. In three more weeks, we probably won't have the chance to spend an evening alone for twenty years."

Kendra winced.

"I know. I know," Andy said sympathetically. "But that's the truth of it, honey. Once the baby is born it'll be about five years before we get a full night's sleep and about ten more before . . ."

"Ow!" Kendra lurched forward and clamped her hand on the base of her stomach. "Andy, turn the car around. It's the baby. I think we'd better go to the hospital."

"Really? Are you sure?"

Kendra screwed her eyes shut and groaned.

"Okay. Right. Sounds like you're sure."

He hit the brakes in front of the nearest driveway, backed out so the car was facing the opposite direction, and hit the gas. The car fishtailed slightly on the snowy pavement.

"Andy!" Kendra shouted.

"Sorry, honey. Sorry. You're right. Plenty of time. I'll slow down a little."

"No! Don't slow down! Drive faster!"

And he did, speeding down the county road toward the hospital, completely oblivious to the squad car that was parked in the Dunkin' Donuts lot — at least until he heard the sirens and saw the strobe of flashing lights in his rearview mirror.

Jim Lee got out of the squad car and approached the driver's side door, shaking his head. Andy rolled down his window.

"Pastor, I'm surprised at you," Jim said. "I'm used to this sort of thing from Kendra, but you should know better."

"Ahh!" Kendra cried out, clutched at her stomach again, and puffed her cheeks in and out, blowing like a billows, a technique her obstetrician had told her would take the edge off labor pains.

Jim's eyes widened. "Oh my gosh! Is it time?"

"Looks like it," Andy said as Kendra let out another groan.

"Oh my gosh! I'm sorry, Pastor. If I'd realized . . . is there anything I can do? Police escort to the hospital?"

"That's all right, Jim. It's just a couple

more miles." Andy turned the key in the ignition. "On second thought, there is one thing. Thea and Jimmy went out for ice cream after the pageant. Marilyn drove them. Can you get word to them, let Thea know what's going on?"

"Sure, sure. I'll call Marilyn on the cell. Thea can stay over at our place tonight."

"Thanks."

"Andy, let me give you that police escort anyway." Jim beamed. "Always wanted to do that."

"Oh for heaven's sake!" Kendra shouted. "Would you both just quit talking and get me to the hospital! I want pain medication and I want it now!"

"Oh yeah," Jim said. "She's definitely in labor. Follow me, Pastor."

# CHAPTER 20

"Honey?" Not wanting to startle her if she was sleeping, Andy tapped softly on the door to Kendra's hospital room. "I'm back. And I brought you a visitor."

Andy peeped around the edge of the door and then, seeing Kendra was awake, pushed it open a little wider so Thea could see, too.

Slowly, Kendra shifted herself higher on the pillow, careful not to jostle the slumbering bundle beside her, and smiled. "Come in," she said softly. "Meet your sister."

Wide-eyed, Thea approached Kendra's bed and stared at the little face that peeped out from the nest of pink flannel. "She's so tiny," Thea whispered.

"Well, she came a little earlier than planned, but she still weighs six pounds. Big enough so she'll be able to come home when I do. I'm just sorry we won't be home for Christmas. I tried to talk the doc into releasing me in time, but she said no way."

"That's all right. We'll just have Christmas here," Thea said gamely, and then looked down and cooed, "Won't we, Baby?"

"Would you like to hold her?" Thea looked up, her eyes a little uncertain.

"It's okay," Kendra assured her. "She's not as fragile as she looks. After all, she's a Loomis. Made of tough stuff, just like her big sister."

With Kendra's encouragement, Thea picked up the baby, leaning down to scoop her into her arms and holding her close as she settled into a chair next to Kendra's bed.

"Hello, little girl," Thea whispered. "I'm your sister. We're going to have a lot of adventures together. I'm going to teach you how to build snowmen, and climb trees, and walk in high heels. And when you're old enough, I'll give you valuable advice about boys and dating. For openers, avoid boys who call themselves by their nicknames."

The baby stirred at the sound of a new voice, wiggling inside her pink blanket, then opened her blue eyes briefly to rest on Thea's face before yawning and closing them again.

"She looked at me!" Thea said with surprise.

"Guess she recognizes good advice when

she hears it," Kendra said.

"What are you going to call her?"

"We haven't decided yet. We were hoping you might have some ideas."

"Really?" Thea looked at Kendra, then at Andy, who was busying himself unloading a bag filled with Kendra's toiletries, things he'd picked up at the house before going to the Lees to collect Thea. "You're going to let me name her?"

"Not quite," Andy said. "We've got veto power. Cassandra is out. Nothing too precious or too weird. Moon Unit Loomis, that sort of thing."

"How about Amelia," said Thea. "Or Emily. Or . . . wait! I've got it! She was born on Christmas Eve so how about something Christmassy? Angela, or Noella, or Ivy? No, wait! How about Holly? That's pretty, don't you think?"

"Holly," Kendra mused. "That is nice. Let's think about it for a little while, but Holly is definitely in the running."

"Speaking of Christmas," Andy said pulling a wrapped box out of the bag. "I've got a little something here. Baby's first Christmas present. Would you like to open it for her, Mommy?"

He handed the box to Kendra who ripped off the paper and opened the lid.

"Oh, Andy! These are adorable!" Kendra exclaimed as she lifted the gift from the box, a tiny pair of pink tap shoes, studded with rhinestones and tied with a pink satin ribbon.

"Aw! They're so cute!" Thea agreed. "Where did you find them, Dad?"

Andy smiled, pleased by their reaction. "Online. I ordered them a while ago. I told you before; with her pedigree, Holly is destined to dance. I figured she ought to be properly outfitted from the first."

Kendra placed both little shoes in the palm of her hand and giggled. "But what if Holly had been a Harry?"

"I ordered another pair, just in case, in a very manly shade of black. I was going to send them back, but now I'm thinking I'll hold onto them, just in case. Who knows? We might have a boy. Maybe next year?"

Kendra shot him a look.

"Right," Andy said. "Bad timing. We can talk about that later."

"Much later."

Thea shifted the baby in her arms, moving her to a more comfortable position, and sighed.

"What's wrong?" Kendra asked. "Are your arms tired? Do you want me to take her now?"

"No, she's fine here. I just . . . well, I feel bad that I don't have a present for you. Guess I've been kind of wrapped up in myself lately. Sorry.

"Hey! I've got an idea," Thea said, brightly. "How about ten hours of free babysitting? That's kind of a present for everybody."

Kendra reached out and touched the girl's cheek. "That's sweet of you, Thea. Thank you. But you don't have to give me a present unless you want to. I've already gotten so many."

Thea looked around the bare hospital room, undecorated except for a small vase of roses, the bouquet Thea had asked Kendra to take home the night before. "The flowers?"

"No," Kendra said. "They're lovely, but those are yours. You should take them home with you. I'm talking about a much bigger, much better gift. Three years ago, when I fell in love with Daddy, I fell in love with you too. I never thought I'd be lucky enough to have any children and now I've got two! You're my present, Thea. You and your sister. Children are the greatest gift of all, the presents the angels bring. I love you, Thea."

Thea bit her lower lip. Her eyes glistened.

"I love you too, Mom."

There was another knock and before Kendra finished saying, "Come in," the door opened.

Denny and Sugar Sugarman came in, carrying boxes of presents and a plate of cookies. Darla followed behind, grinning and holding a bouquet of red and white chrysanthemums tied with a red and green ribbon and, trailing behind her, carrying a tiny potted evergreen decorated with little red ribbons and gold balls, came Riley Roth, looking a bit sheepish. The room was immediately filled with the sound of congratulations and laughter and cooing voices as everyone admired the baby.

Darla leaned over the little one, stuck out a tentative finger, and grinned from ear to ear when the baby grabbed onto her gnarled digit with a tiny hand. "She's beautiful," Darla whispered. "What are you going to call her?"

"We've been trying out Holly. She doesn't seem to object, so I think that might be it," Kendra said, looking up at Andy who nodded his agreement.

"Beautiful name. Very appropriate," Darla declared.

Riley cleared his throat. "Congratulations," he said as he handed the tiny Christmas tree to Andy. "You must be so happy. What a great Christmas surprise."

"Thank you," Andy said sincerely. "Surprise is the operative word. We're thrilled, but I wouldn't have minded if Holly had waited a couple more days before making her entrance, at least until after I'd preached the Christmas service. I don't like the idea of leaving Kendra here alone on Christmas morning."

"Oh, that's all right," Kendra said, trying but not quite succeeding in masking her disappointment. "I hate the idea of missing Christmas services but it can't be helped."

Denny narrowed his eyes and stroked his beard thoughtfully. "Well, now, I don't know about that. Riley, does the factory still have that big tent — the one they used for the warehouse sale?"

"Yes," Riley said slowly. "Why do you . . . Oh! Yeah! I get it! Absolutely!"

Denny grinned, showing deep dimples in his cheeks. "Great!"

He turned to address the others. "Andy, ladies, if you'll excuse us, Riley and I have some arrangements to make. Riley? Do you have a phone?"

"Sure."

"Good," he said, putting his arm around the younger man's shoulders as they left the hospital room. "I need you to make a few calls . . ."

At around ten o'clock on Christmas Eve night it began to snow, leaving three inches of fluffy powder on the ground before the snow clouds drifted east and the skies cleared. Christmas morning dawned bright and clear and the mercury stood at twenty-eight which, in Vermont in December, is practically a heat wave. It was a perfect day to try out the new sleds, skis, snowshoes, and snowboards that many people found under their Christmas trees that morning. But before they did so, a goodly portion of the residents of Maple Grove had something else to attend to.

Upon exiting Kendra's room, Denny went to see the hospital administrator and got permission to carry out the plan. That obtained, Riley called the other members of the board who, after a unanimous vote of approval, immediately sprung into action.

Joe St. John activated the church phone tree, making sure every single member of the congregation was informed of the change in plans. Gary Wilson, who owned a construction business, brought in a snow-plow and a construction crew armed with shovels to clear the hospital parking lot of snow and ice. Nancy Metzger and her husband, Bill, loaded their horse trailer with bales of hay to serve as makeshift pews. Dean Hamilton brought a portable microphone and amplifier, the one his son, Drew, used for his garage band, and snaking a long trail of extension cords from the hospital to the parking lot, set up a rudimentary sound system. Riley, with the help of his wife, Dana, as well as Brian McCarthy, Sam Daniels, and Joan Kilty, went to the furniture factory and loaded up one of the delivery trucks with the giant tent and an assortment of plush recliners, still wrapped in plastic, to serve as seating for the elderly and infirm. Sugar Sugarman went to the church and got the choir robes, collection plates, and altar implements they'd need for the service. Darla Benton called the Quilting Bees, rallying her troops to make enough hot chocolate, coffee, and muffins to feed everyone after the service. Everybody helped set up the tent. Before the snow began falling, everything was ready.

And so the next morning, the members of and visitors to the Maple Grove Community Church bundled up against the morning chill, drove to the hospital, and filed into a tent to celebrate Christmas together. Joining them were scores of doctors, nurses, lab technicians, janitors, cafeteria workers, families of hospital patients, and some of the patients themselves, including Kendra and Baby Holly, who was wrapped up in a veritable mountain of blankets topped off by the woolly, hand-knit cap that had been Darla's present to the baby girl.

With his beaming family looking on, Andy Loomis stepped to the front and wished everyone a very Merry Christmas before opening the Bible to read the story of the first Christmas, an event that had occurred in a place even smaller and of less consequence than Maple Grove, that had come a little sooner than two young parents had planned on, that had been met with plans as hastily improvised, perhaps more so, than the service of worship that Denny, Riley, and the rest of the church leaders had organized in the previous hours.

But none of that mattered. The joy that permeated that chilly tent and the goodwill that warmed the hearts of everyone who attended was as plentiful and genuine as if they'd been celebrating the birth of the Holy Child in a cathedral overlooking the majestic skyline of a powerful city instead of in a tent overlooking the snowy parking lot of a rural hospital.

After the prayers were prayed, and the carols sung, and the congregation blessed and sent forth, they gathered in the back of the tent to partake of the refreshments supplied by the Quilting Bees, smiling and chatting as they warmed their hands around steaming cups of hot chocolate and coffee.

Thea steered the wheelchair holding Kendra and Baby Holly over to the corner of the tent where Andy was standing.

"I'm going to take them back inside," she informed her father. "It's not that cold in here, but I don't think we should have the baby around all these people for very long. Too many germs."

Kendra looked up at Thea's grave face. "You heard Nurse Thea," she said to her husband. "I guess we'd better go back inside."

"Good idea," Andy said. "I'll be up as soon as I've finished here. Get some rest. Sugar is going to bring over a Christmas dinner this afternoon." He planted a kiss on Kendra's cheek and then on Thea's. "I'll see you in a little while."

Thea steered the wheelchair to a ramp that led from the tent directly into the hospital. Riley Roth walked up behind Andy and tapped him on the shoulder.

"Andy? Do you have a minute? There's

something I wanted to say to you."

"Sure, Riley. What is it?"

"I . . . well, I want to tell you that I'm sorry and to ask for your forgiveness. I was out of line, Andy, completely out of line. I love this church and I'm grateful for your leadership. That's the reason I started coming in the first place, because you're such a genuine, caring leader and that example spills over onto the rest of the congregation. I've never been part of such a loving church community and that's the truth." He glanced down at his feet, embarrassed.

"I was so excited to be asked onto the board. Especially considering my age, it's such an honor. I was worried that I wouldn't have much to offer, but I really wanted to help and . . . well . . . I guess I wanted to prove myself to everyone which, now that I hear myself say it out loud, sounds pretty stupid. And I was — stupid, I mean. And a complete . . . Well, there are words to describe me and my behavior that you don't repeat to your minister. I was all of them. I'm sorry."

Andy nodded. "Riley, I accept your apology."

"Thank you, Andy. I'll write my letter of resignation from the board and have it on your desk by Monday morning."

Andy frowned. "Why? Don't you want to serve on the board anymore?"

"Well," Riley sputtered, "under the circumstances I figured that . . . I mean . . . don't you want me to resign?"

"Naw." Andy shrugged. "Why would I? You have some good ideas. You were the one who came up with the Hands of Help ministry. That's the kind of thing we should be doing more of. Just promise me you'll stay away from things involving food service, electronics, and demolition crews and we'll get on just fine, all right?"

"All right! Absolutely!" Riley grinned and looked around the crowded tent.

"I can't imagine what I was thinking, supposing I knew more about running a church than you did. I mean, look at all these people! There are even more people here than there were at the pageant. All these hospital workers and patients! Why, if not for this, a lot of these people probably wouldn't be able to celebrate Christmas at all."

"True," said Andy.

"And look at their faces! They don't care that they're meeting in a tent, that there's no heat or lights or organ accompaniment. They don't care that the microphone made your voice sound like you were talking through the bottom of a tin can. They just wanted to be here, to be together. To hear a message of hope, to know that peace is possible, and that goodwill and faith are real. Why didn't I see it before? This is Christmas, isn't it, Andy? This is what matters!"

Andy grinned and raised his coffee cup to toast the younger man.

"Merry Christmas, Riley."

"Merry Christmas, Andy."

Dear Reading Friend,

I hope you enjoyed your trip to Maple Grove. Those of you who read my first Maple Grove story, "A High Kicking Christmas," in the holiday anthology COMFORT AND JOY, already know that I'm a big fan of all things Vermont, especially Vermont maple syrup, an ingredient that finds its way into many of my favorite family recipes.

That's why I'm offering my Reading Friends a few of the recipes included in "The Presents of Angels," including Grandma Sugarman's Apple Walnut Stuffing, White and Sweet Potato Au Gratin, Maple Almond Squash Medley, and Maple Mousse Pie, along with a few of my best tips for delicious and low-stress holiday cooking.

To get them, just go to my Web site, www .mariebostwick.com, click on the box on the left that says, "Become a Reading Friend . . ." and fill in the registration information, which I never share with anyone. As a registered Reading Friend, you'll have access to the "For Reading Friends" area where you can download the recipes, and have access to other goodies including a free quilt pattern, automatic entry in my monthly Readers' contests, the opportunity to receive my quarterly e-newsletter, and more!

If you don't have access to a computer and would like the recipes, drop me a note. Please send your request and *a self-addressed stamped business-sized envelope* to:

Marie Bostwick
PO Box 488
Thomaston, CT 06787

I hope you'll be on the lookout for my other books, especially the books in my Cobbled Court series: A SINGLE THREAD and A THREAD OF TRUTH. Set in the fictional village of New Bern, Connecticut, *New York Times* bestselling author Susan Wiggs described A SINGLE THREAD as a book "filled with wit and wisdom," and advises readers to "sit back and enjoy this big-hearted novel and then pass it on to your best girlfriend." I hope you'll do exactly that!

Thank you for joining me on this armchair journey to Maple Grove. I hope you enjoyed the trip as much as I did. May your holidays be filled with joy!

Blessings,
Marie Bostwick

■ ■ ■ ■

# DECORATIONS

# JANNA MCMAHAN

■ ■ ■ ■

# CHAPTER 1

When you're an ordinary person, you don't expect extraordinary things to happen to you. Of course, if you're an ordinary person, what you consider extraordinary may be tame by other people's standards. If anyone had ever said to me, "Michelle Duncan, your life is about to change in a big way," I most likely would have freaked out. I like safe. I like knowing what's going to happen next. Drama is definitely not my thing.

But changes can sneak up on you. They can come in such incremental ways that you're not really aware things are changing at all. Or changes can come on hard and strong and knock you silly. That's what has happened to me in the last year. My life went from run-of-the-mill to bizarre in no time at all.

When I say I'm ordinary you might think I'm being modest, but I'm not. My life decisions have never been monumental or exciting or strange. Take for instance my marriage. I married Randy Duncan after dating only a few months. It wasn't like love at first sight or anything earth-shattering like that.

We met when my car slid off the road during one of Asheville's famous fat-flaked snowstorms. My little car didn't have much traction. I should have had my dad put chains on my tires, but I'd been in a hurry to get to work. When I started to slide I remembered to tap my brakes like you're supposed to do, but that didn't help at all. So everything I'd ever learned about driving in slick snow flew right out of my head and I locked up my brakes and in a second I'd veered off the road.

My Toyota bumped up against the guardrail, then raked along until there was no more metal holding me on the road. I could see the end coming, literally. When my car groaned to a stop just short of a nosedive off the mountainside I had my eyes closed and my foot smashing the brake so hard my leg was quivering. The engine turned over and died and I just sat there with cold creeping into the car, my breath swirling in rapid curls. I don't know how long I sat there before a knock on the window startled me. I hadn't even heard the truck pull up. I must have been in a sort of shock.

I snapped to and cranked the window down.

"Are you okay?" the guy asked. He was hunched over with his hands shoved into his jacket pockets. His face was down close to my window and the wind whipped his shaggy white blond hair.

"Uh, yeah. I think so."

"You sure? You want to get out and shake it off?"

I stepped out and sort of patted myself and looked around as if I'd just lost my keys rather than had a near-death experience.

"You got close to the edge," he said. "Look, if you're okay, then I'll pull you out." He motioned to a big red truck behind us. "Why don't you get in before you freeze?"

I sat in the cab with my hands up to the heater's vent while he hooked a clunky chain up to my bumper. The winch squealed as it cinched the slack and then smoothly pulled my little car off the soggy shoulder and back onto the road. I got out and shuffled to where he stood.

"You've got to be more careful," he said. "Where you headed?"

"To work. At Mountaintop Mulch."

"That's not too far. Want to follow me?"

An odd sense of gratitude swept over me. I can't explain it exactly. Maybe I have a thing about being rescued, I don't know, but Randy was so nice and he had such sparkly blue eyes and a cute crooked grin.

"What?" he said as if he had no idea what I was thinking, but now I know that he was thinking the same thing.

"Nothing," I said and before spring thaw we were walking down the aisle.

# CHAPTER 2

It was a short aisle, just a stroll between two rows of folding chairs in my parents' backyard and we were one. We went on our honeymoon to Gatlinburg where we tried out skydiving in one of those big padded cylinder rooms with an enormous fan in the floor. I've always been athletic. Played softball in high school. Ran track. But it was hard for me to balance myself against that enormous updraft. I kept flipping off and slamming into the sides, which made Randy laugh more than I thought he should have.

We saw a couple of country music shows, but nobody important. We couldn't get tickets to see Dolly. We stayed in a ski chalet, but it was late spring by then and the Smoky Mountains were a fierce green. We drank dark sour wine and made love every single day. Sometimes we did it twice in one day because we both knew we wouldn't be getting it nearly as much once we moved in with my parents.

After the honeymoon we lived with them under the agreement that it was just temporary. We'd sneak out and do it in the truck like we were teenagers. Lying there against each other on the bench seat, the windows all fogged, we'd dream about our future. Randy would say how he'd always wanted a log cabin. So we went to the company that sold those log cabin kits and picked out a floor plan. A month later a semi pulled up and unloaded our building materials. I had a hard time imagining how that pile of logs could be a house, it just looked like a stack of Lincoln Logs I had when I was a kid.

It was unusually dry that year and the water around us was running so low that the rafting businesses that fed off local rivers were practically shut down. Randy paid a bunch of his kayaking buddies to help with construction and they threw our house up in a summer of weekends. It took a while to get it plumbed and the electricity running, but we were in before Thanksgiving.

Our new house was on property Randy inherited from an uncle. It wasn't a great piece of property since it snugged right up to a straight section in the highway. It was a dangerous spot where cars zoomed around lumber trucks they'd been stuck behind for miles on the twisting mountain roads. This was probably the reason nobody else in the family stepped up to claim the lot, but Randy and I were glad to have it. Randy made us a half-circle drive so we would never have to back out into traffic.

So we settled into our new house and life became comfortable and routine. Randy liked to spend weekends with his white-water buddies. They were mostly local boys who lived in dormitories provided by the outfitters along the rivers that snaked through the Blue Ridge Mountains. These fellows slept in bunk beds and ate in mess halls and lived to take Boy Scouts, middle-aged women, and overly-stressed business executives down the Chattooga or Ocohee or French Broad. Randy had done it himself a number of times to pick up a little extra money, but mostly he waited for the week-ends when he and his friends could slide their colorful kayaks into the river and just play.

Early on Randy took me camping with him. I always loved to see the crew carrying their boats down to the river's edge, the tops of their neoprene wetsuits flopping down around their waists in the cooler months, their shoes squeaking with their steps. They looked like a bunch of aliens that landed in the middle of all that nature in their bright puffy life vests.

Their kayaks were scarred from rough encounters with rocks. They were so fearless that it made my heart stop. They'd plunge over waterfalls into recirculating pools and peal out into eddies to rest. They played in the rapids, surfing the waves, leaning upriver to press their boats against the current.

Randy took me rafting a couple of times, but that's not the sort of thing I find relaxing and fun. To be honest, I was scared to death. What I liked to do was hang out in the woods, so I'd spend the weekends in camp while Randy boated. I'd read novels and wait all day until I knew they were getting near Bull Sluice at the end of their run.

At Bull Sluice, the river narrowed and forced itself between giant boulders. The falls dropped twenty feet, down two shelves before crashing into a churning, foamy mess. It was one of the most dangerous holes on the river and every year somebody lost their life there. A crowd always gathered to watch the action at Bull Sluice and onlookers kept ready with rescue ropes coiled in nylon bags to throw to luckless people who got tossed out of their boats. As they threw the bags, the rope would trail out and settle into the river, washing into frantic grasps.

When Randy and his friends had had enough time to make it down the river I'd pack up and take my book to a spot on the boulders where I could keep an eye upriver for them. The rocks were always warm from the sun, even in the fall. Girlfriends and wives sunned, their hair twisted up in alligator clips, their glasses flashing. I had a hot orange bikini that Randy liked. I'd squeeze lemon juice into my hair to streak it blond and rub baby oil on my legs.

When Randy's group appeared around a bend I'd hold my breath until they had whooped their way over Bull Sluice. Sometimes they would port their boats up over the boulders and go down again. Kayakers are crazy.

Once Randy was over the falls he'd pull his boat on shore and come sit next to me to warm up. The mountain-fed river was cold, even in summer. Randy would pop open a beer from our cooler and watch other boats come down. Instead of a farmer's tan, Randy kept a boater's tan, his ropey arms dark and smooth, while his legs stayed pale from being hidden under his boat's skirt. He'd try to sun his legs, but they

329

would never achieve the golden brown of his face and arms.

So that was our life most weekends. During the week I worked for Mountaintop Mulch. I'd had that job since I graduated from Western Carolina. I earned a degree in English, but I never wanted to leave my hometown of Black Knob, so I went back to school for basic accounting and over the years I got promoted up to office manager. While I wasn't the general manager, I should have been. I could work about any aspect of the business.

It was a fun job in a lot of ways. It was dirty some days, but I liked being outside. I didn't have to worry about my appearance. Lots of days I'd go in without makeup. I'd wear jeans, hiking boots, and a ball cap with my ponytail sprouting from the back, T-shirts in summer and down jackets the rest of the year. Some days I'd travel around to different mills to gauge the quality of their raw material, the bark stripped off lumber. I'd coordinate transportation to our processing plant where truckloads of bark would be screened for debris, washed, and processed into a consistent chip size. It would then be bagged and sold through our retail store or I'd ship wholesale loads to other dealers, golf courses, landscape contractors, and developers.

Most people never think of where their landscaping materials originate, but we put a lot of thought into making an attractive, quality product. Over the years, we developed chips that wouldn't wash away with heavy rain and we produced mulch in a variety of colors. Mulch was important and I knew the sales pitch by heart — erosion control, weed suppression, root system protection, moisture retention. Landscaping would be in dire straights without mulch to smooth out the edges, add depth to design, and protect precious plants.

But Mountaintop Mulch was family-owned and even though I felt I was key to the business, I knew I'd climbed as high up that ladder as I could. I wasn't all that ambitious anyway and with Randy's good job, we were fat and happy. Randy worked for Duke Power putting in lines for new construction in summer and repairing damaged lines hit by ice storms in the winter months. Between the two of us we made decent money and we didn't want for much, that was, except a baby.

It has always been hard for me to accept that I can't have children. I had endometriosis in my early twenties. The doctor said I was cured, that I should have no problem getting pregnant, but in our fifteen-year marriage Randy and I never used birth control, yet we hadn't had the slightest opportunity for hope. Randy never expressed it, but I know he blamed me, as if I somehow had control over this part of our lives.

Maybe if we'd had children we wouldn't have grown apart like we did. But after a decade of trying for a family, sex became less fun and more work than we wanted. I must admit that it was painful for me emotionally since I couldn't ever do it without hoping that I would get pregnant. People gave us all sorts of advice. Try not to think about. Just relax everybody said, and it will happen. But I couldn't relax.

We got used to it just being the two of us and we fell into our ordinary routine of work, dinner, television. Randy boated and hunted and fished. I stopped going to the river with him and instead I stayed home and read and gardened. I made jam. I redecorated our master bedroom.

I'd always been content with my simple life. I was into easy, which was probably one reason Randy appealed to me. With Randy, you always knew what you were going to get. Or at least that's what I thought.

But then my father crumbled out of a church pew with a heart attack. That's when

my comfortable life suddenly turned complicated and Randy showed his true colors.

# CHAPTER 3

A few weeks after my father's death I was at my mother's house helping her plant annuals when she stopped with her trowel in midair. At first I thought she was listening to the wren family chirping on the fence. Then I thought she was admiring the bright blue sky. I could see her mind traveling.

"Mom," I said. "Mom, what are you thinking about?"

She turned to me with a contented smile and said merrily, "Michelle, honey, run inside and tell your father to come look at our flowers. He really loves marigolds."

She started back to turning dark dirt as though the matter were settled. On my knees, moist ground seeping into my jeans, I wondered at my mother. Had she misspoke or was she confused?

"Go on," she said and hummed to herself. I turned to look at the backdoor, nearly convincing myself that my father would

come walking out with a glass of tea.

That started my early morning calls to her on my way to work. At first she was up and moving around, but after a few weeks I could tell that she was just waking to my call. She still seemed fine when we spoke, but her housekeeping started to slip, which I took as a sure sign of depression. She began to leave piles of newspapers strewn in the corner by the lounge chair, not even bothering to bind them with string and collect them in the recycling bin as she'd always insisted my father do. I found less and less in her kitchen cabinets and the refrigerator grew smelly with food I'd brought her weeks before.

"Mom, what do you do all day?" I asked her as I threw away curdled milk and rotted lettuce.

"Oh, I watch *Oprah* and I do a little piecework on my quilt and . . . oh, I don't know. I sleep a lot now. I'm just so tired all the time."

She did seem lethargic. And increasingly strange. Like the time I pulled up to the house to see her flower garden bursting with color. Curious I walked over to see how this miracle of horticulture happened overnight and found that my mother had taken every plastic and silk flower she owned, a substantial amount, and shoved them into the ground in her failing fall garden. When I asked her about it she had no recollection of having done it, but she said it didn't matter, that they were just gathering dust anyway.

Another day I found her sitting in the shed with my father's small toolbox balanced on her lap. She was wearing only a slip, its shiny cream fabric smeared with mud. Her feet were bare and dirty. Her hair was messed as though she'd just gotten out of bed and wandered into the shed.

"Mom?" I said gently to her. "Mom, what are you doing sitting in the shed?" She never acknowledged me. She only stared out of the small grimy window with a forlorn look that made panic rush my chest and my eyes fill with tears. I went into the house to get shoes, a cloth and a pan of warm water to wash my mother's feet.

I tried to talk to Randy about my mother's situation, but he had no advice. He'd never been in a caregiving position and his first and only idea was to put her in a nursing home. But nursing homes to me were for people in much more need than my mother. She could still cook herself a small meal. It was remembering to turn off the stove that was the danger for her. She could bathe, but she could also easily find herself sitting in cold water, shivering, unsure how long she had been there.

I worried that perhaps my mother had more problems than just depression and loneliness, but things seemed stable until the day a neighbor called me at work.

"Edwina is wandering around outside in her nightclothes," Mrs. Smith said. "I think you need to come see about her."

I had just closed a big shipment deal with a real estate developer and was filling out the paperwork when the call came. By the time I got to her place my mother was sitting at the kitchen table with the neighbor drinking tea and laughing over something that had happened twenty years ago.

"Mom, how are you?" I asked.

"Oh, pooh. How am I? I'm perfectly fine," she said. She tucked a loose strand of gray behind her ear and crossed her legs as if she were at high tea, her baggy pajama bottoms flopping down around her muddy house shoes. The neighbor shrugged and raised her eyebrows at me.

Within the week the neighbor called again to say that my mother was wading in the creek behind her house and this time she was totally naked. As I drove over there I allowed the word dementia to finally become a part of my vocabulary. I had not used that word, nor the word Alzheimer's, as long as I could. I couldn't avoid taking her to the doctor any longer.

My parents had gone to Dr. Johnson for thirty years and he was himself so old that I wondered if his faculties were intact. But when he spoke his eyes were clear and his wit sharp. He told me he'd long suspected this would develop, that my father had come to him with some concerns over Mother's behavior before he died. Dr. Johnson drew her blood and told me that I should start considering how I intended to care for her.

"She won't be able to live by herself forever," he said.

When had this happened? My father had known this was going on and yet he hadn't told me anything. My parents were always leaving out bits of information so they wouldn't worry me. It would have been so much easier to have my levelheaded father around to help me make decisions, but I was on my own. An only-child with a failing mother. What a lonely feeling.

My mother was so agitated by the doctor's visit that he suggested I take her home with me. I packed her suitcase and the neighbor agreed to watch her ornery old cat. Our guest room was at the top of our stairs with a view into the woods behind our house.

"Look, Mom. You can see my birdbath from here," I said. I couldn't tell if she'd heard me or not since she didn't move from her spot on the end of the bed. Her attention would leave for a while and then return unpredictably. She was always pleasant, one thing the doctor had asked me about. He'd said as long as she remained docile that he wouldn't recommend medication.

I pulled out a drawer and arranged her clothes inside. "Just let me know if you need anything."

When I came downstairs Randy was sitting in his chair watching the news. He followed me into the kitchen and poured himself another cup of coffee.

"So what's wrong with your mom?" he asked.

I looked out behind our house where gray clouds played against mountains bruised purple in the dying light.

"Dementia," I said and lowered my face into my hands and sobbed. Randy took me into his arms and gave me a soft squeeze before he let me go.

"So what's the plan?" he asked.

I shrugged. "I don't know. I don't have a plan."

"How long is she staying here?"

I was shaken by the directness of his question.

"Well, I don't know, Randy. Does it matter? We lived with Mom and Dad for six months when we were first married. Don't you think you could return the favor and let her stay here a while until I can figure out what to do?"

"Yeah. Sure. I didn't mean anything by it." He pulled a thin smile for my benefit, but I had the feeling that Randy had no intention of permitting for long-term care of any sort.

# CHAPTER 4

I took a week off from work to be with my mother and to figure out exactly what would be best for her. At first all she did was watch television. I quickly noticed that she forgot to eat, which was one reason she had been dropping weight.

"Mom?" I asked her. "Why don't you come downstairs and help me make supper?"

Always agreeable, she shuffled into the kitchen and dutifully peeled potatoes like she had done ten thousand times before. I watched to see if she was functional and she remembered to stir the green beans and check on the roast. I decided then that she needed a job and cooking was something she could almost do on automatic, at least with someone around in case her mind wandered. Randy always loved her cooking, so I thought this would be a way for her to contribute something he would appreciate.

I arranged for a young woman to come stay at the house with my mother while I went to work. I knew this was a temporary fix since she was actively looking for a job after being laid off, but I had to take what I could get. I bought groceries for the week and instructed the help to assist my mother in making dinner each night. Soon I was coming home to warm meals and we were having dinner as a family.

That worked well to bring us together during the week, but on the weekends I usually took care of my mother alone, since Randy had started spending more time kayaking with his friends. Nearly every Friday afternoon I watched my husband pull out of our drive with his boat strapped down in the bed of his truck, fishing poles dangling silver lures. During evenings of the work week, Randy stayed with my mother while I went to the grocery and ran errands, but the weekends were mine alone. He didn't have the patience to deal with her unusual behavior and he said it made him sad how she sat and looked out the window at nothing.

Once he realized she was missing and found her wandering the woods. Another time I came home to see him carrying her back into the house in her sodden nightgown. He put her to bed upstairs and then came downstairs with a look that said he had been pushed far enough.

"Michelle, you've got to find somewhere to put her. She was out near the highway. She was almost roadkill!" He fought tears. I wondered if they were tears of frustration or compassion. "We can't take care of her much longer."

"I'm doing everything I can, Randy. Just be patient. We can't jump ahead on the waiting list."

My research into long-term care revealed a strange new world. There were nursing homes for residents incapable of "self-care" as the professionals put it. Then there were assisted-living facilities where residents functioned at their own levels. The care in assisted living ranged from couples in small apartments who still kept cars and social dates, to those less mobile, yet still functional when it came to basic needs like laundry. The director at Black Knob's only assisted-care facility told me that residents who weren't a danger could have full kitchens, although they were always welcome in the dining hall. My mother, with her bright smile and her moments of clarity, didn't need to live with more severe cases of disability. She seemed too functional for a traditional nursing home.

I was feeling good about her options when reality set in. There was a waiting list of nearly a year for assisted living and those vacancies only opened when someone died or moved into a total-care facility. And worse, unlike a nursing home, where Dr. Johnson could write an admission and Medicare would help, assisted living wasn't covered. My parents had pinched pennies their entire lives, had never gone on vacations, never had hobbies. They had let life pass them by so they could save for this. Now it was time to turn my accounting skills to the task of sorting out my mother's finances and seeing what options would be open to us.

I wasn't being completely honest with Randy. What I hadn't told him was that Dr. Johnson had offered to help move my mother up on the list for the nursing home. I just didn't want to see her there. I wanted her in a more homelike atmosphere, a place where we could both still feel like we were at home.

The tipping point came with Randy on a Saturday morning when I was at the grocery. Randy went to get the mail and one of our neighbors pulled into our drive to talk. Randy said he wasn't out of the house more than twenty minutes, but when he opened the kitchen door short flames ran across the floor in a line to the sink. My mother stood frozen in the middle of the room, her nightgown terrifyingly close to the flames. Randy grabbed a throw rug and beat the fire out on the floor. In the sink he saw the smoking skillet with charred strips of meat. Mother had been frying bacon and when it caught fire, her instincts made her move the skillet to the sink. But she had strewn flaming grease across the floor on her way. Luckily, she hadn't been burned.

When I pulled into the drive Randy was loading out.

"Hey," I said as I pulled a bag of groceries out of the backseat. "I thought you weren't going boating this weekend."

He slammed things into his truck.

"What's the matter?" I asked, then I thought of my mother. "Is something wrong?"

"Why don't you go inside and see?" he snapped.

A burnt stench washed over me when I stepped into our kitchen. Randy had cleaned up the grease, but our floor had melted slightly in a line where the flames had touched it. My mother was sitting at our table as if she had been waiting for me to come home for days.

"I'm so sorry. I don't know what happened," she said. I was stunned by the clarity of her thoughts. "I just panicked."

"Are you okay?" I asked.

"I'm fine, but I can't remember." Tears filled her eyes. "Oh, Michelle, what's happening to me?"

I gathered her in my arms. "It's okay, Mom. As long as you're not hurt we can take care of everything else."

She nodded her head and dabbed at her eyes with a wad of tissue.

"Randy's *so* mad. You need to go talk to him," she said.

"But, Mom . . ."

"No. Don't worry about me. Go talk to him before he leaves."

When I got back outside Randy was slamming the back cab door and climbing into his truck. I walked up to the driver's window and put my hands on the sill.

"Is she okay?" he asked, gripping the steering wheel.

"Yes. Thank God. She seems fine. But she's worried about you."

"Michelle, I can't take this. When you get her situated we'll talk. I'm not coming back until she's settled somewhere else."

"Come back? What do you mean? Where are you going?"

"I don't know. I'll find somewhere to light for a while."

"You're leaving me here with this mess? This charred kitchen and Mom to take care of by myself?"

"It's the only way I'm going to get you to do something with her. She can't live with us from now on."

"I know that. I'm trying to find something."

He cranked the engine and sat there staring out at nothing.

"Randy, please don't do this. Don't leave me."

Those big blue eyes were torn, I could see that.

"I'm sorry," was all he said.

He pulled out of the drive. I figured he would go shack up with some of his friends at one of the outfitters. His cell phone didn't work that far out, but he'd call eventually after he cooled off. At least that was what had always happened when we'd fought before.

# CHAPTER 5

When Randy didn't come home on Monday I went through his things. Most of his boating and fishing equipment was gone, but that wasn't unusual. What I hadn't expected was that Randy took most of his clothes, toiletries, even towels. He didn't plan on coming back for a while.

Even though I knew that his cell wouldn't have reception if he was down by a river, I left him a message.

"Randy, I'm sorry about all this. Please come home. We can work it out."

But really. Was he forcing me to make a decision between him and my mother? There was no way I could walk away from my mother, so in a way, it gave him all the power.

I waited for his call. And I ate a gallon of ice cream. All week I waited while I watched reruns of *Friends* and *CSI* with my mother, who never looked away from the television although I could tell she wasn't following the storylines.

Of course, when it rains it pours and my daytime help informed me that she'd finally found a job and she gave her two weeks' notice. I had accumulated vacation, so I called off of work and decided to drive into Asheville.

Black Knob is a small community about forty-five minutes from Asheville. I went into town on occasion for a music festival or to eat in a Mexican restaurant since we didn't have one. It had occurred to me that there would be other elder-care facilities in Asheville, but I had rejected that notion earlier because of the hour and a half round-trip through the mountains. I just didn't want my mother that far away from me because it would limit my ability to visit her.

But desperate times made me search out options and Asheville was the only other place I could look. While there were at least a half dozen elder-care places in town, I found one on the Internet that called itself an adult day care, a concept I didn't know much about. On further reading, it seemed that it was like a day care for kids where they play games and have activities and snacks. It sounded intriguing since there was an open-door policy and no commitment or contracts to sign. I liked the idea of a drop-in as needed situation and called to make an appointment.

Asheville is a terraced city that wraps the side of a mountain. On approach it looks industrial until you get downtown and see the Art Deco architecture and the galleries and coffee shops. There seems always to be a group of hippies with dreadlocks and droopy handwoven bags playing guitars on the streets, patchouli wafting around them. Asheville attracts tourists, particularly in the fall when people come for the change of seasons where the mountains are a crazy quilt of colors. Asheville autumns are astounding.

I drove past the giant obelisk downtown and turned right to thread my way past a section of restaurants and wine shops toward the hospital. Beside the hospital I found Asheville's Adult Day Care and pulled into the parking lot. I had talked lightly of where we were headed on our drive and my mother seemed okay with the concept. Always agreeable, I sometimes worried she would never tell me if she were unhappy or mistreated.

"They play bingo and cards and watch movies and other things, Mom. You might like it."

I could tell she was a little apprehensive when we arrived, but she willingly followed me inside. Asheville Adult Day Care was painted strong blues and greens and was in no way childish, which was what I had expected. The walls were lined with serene photographs of local waterfalls and vistas that the residents might recognize. My mother was immediately enamored of a white Persian cat sunning on a windowsill.

I was a little disturbed to find that a number of the day care customers were wheelchair-bound young people, not the older folks I had expected. When the director saw my expression she said, "We have a number of multiple sclerosis and brain injury clients. They're really lovely people. Let's see if your mother is interested in playing bingo."

Much to my surprise Mother took a place at a table next to a white-haired woman with an abundance of costume jewelry and they began to talk as if they were old friends. Someone passed her a bingo card. She gathered a handful of bingo chips, then her smile found me and she made a little waving motion that meant for me to go on about my business for the day. Her new friend pointed, directing attention to the bingo caller.

The director laid a warm hand on my arm and said, "Just leave her here for a couple of hours. Go out and have lunch. Take a little time for yourself. She'll be fine and if not, I'll call your mobile and we'll decide what to do from there."

I thought I'd be anxious to leave my mother, but the truth was that I was flooded with relief. As I walked out to the car I felt a lift to my heart. Just this smallest amount of help was so appreciated.

I slid behind the wheel, but didn't turn the key. I watched my mother inside the giant bay window, oblivious to my gaze. I was glad to clear my mind, if only for a few hours.

I drove farther down the road toward the entrance to Biltmore. When I was a girl I'd taken a number of school trips to this grand castle and I was always awed that anyone could live such an opulent life. I could recall many statistics about this crown jewel of Asheville. The largest and single most visited tourist attraction for hundreds of miles, Biltmore House had been a country home of the Vanderbilts at the turn of the last century. Still in the family, the 250-room French Renaissance château included an eight thousand acre estate with a winery, sculpture gardens, and a magnificent hot-house. I could vividly remember the fire-places large enough to stand in upright and the bowling alley in the basement.

One day I would tour Biltmore again, but this was not the day. I sighed as I drove past the grand estate's entrance and turned into Biltmore Village, an upscale shopping area, also built by the Vanderbilts as support for the estate and to generate the local economy. What had once been furriers and coopers and bakeries were now women's clothing stores, art galleries, and restaurants. I parked in front of the Country Corner Café and went inside. I was seated on a glassed-in patio at a large window where I could watch shoppers who seemed already to be hoarding treasures for the holidays even though the trees were still a fierce green with the end of summer.

People strolled with shopping bags dangling from the crooks of their arms. Unlike downtown, where the crowd could be more eclectic and scruffy, this group was groomed, perhaps retired with the time and money to enjoy themselves. What would it be like to be one of those women who were taken care of? Those women of diamond rings and BMWs.

I ordered a glass of white wine and studied the menu which offered everything from country caviar (apparently made with black-eyed peas) and gazpacho to cheese soufflé and blackened tuna steak salad. I opted for the tuna and sat back to watch the shoppers. A table of people in the corner laughed loudly and their happiness bounced off the glass ceiling and rained down on me. I smiled and looked their way and one of the men at the table caught my gaze and returned my smile. I felt my face warm and I quickly turned away. I suddenly remembered my clothes, jeans and a loose red sweater. My hair was pulled back into a messy bun. I was *sans* jewelry except for my wedding ring. I certainly hadn't thought I'd be eating in such a swanky restaurant when I had dressed for the day. I felt all wrong and it took the rest of my meal and a second glass of wine before I shook the feeling of being out of place.

Outside again, I breathed a little better. I decided to walk off my meal with a stroll around the village. After all, this was the first real time I'd had to myself for months. I had forgotten how much I liked Asheville. Randy never wanted to come into town, never cared about going to the museum or the Bele Chere Festival. As I ducked in and out of shops I noticed a number of HELP WANTED signs on doors. I certainly wasn't dressed nicely enough to ask for a job application at one of the women's clothing stores, nor would I have had the clothing to work there anyway. But then I saw the Christmas shop, Season's Greetings. The shop was housed in a cottage; twinkle lights entwined the railings on its white front porch. More lights winked from every window. Holiday music called from some unseen place under the eaves.

The HELP WANTED sign wasn't large, but I noticed it on the entrance door peeking from behind a massive wreath. On impulse I went in thinking that my red sweater might seem appropriate here. I pushed open the door and jingle bells rang out, making me think of Santa's sleigh. A bored teenager behind the cash register showed no interest in helping anyone. I walked around the store feeling slightly claustrophobic. There was barely a pathway carved between the massive Christmas trees that dominated every room. Most rooms had a fireplace with mantels decorated with candles and garland. Whole walls were given over to ornament displays. The scent of evergreen became cloying after a while, but I didn't mind. I loved the Christmas store.

Around every corner was something that brought the tug of a warm familiar feeling.

Ornaments and things that I loved as a child. A ballerina I had wanted to be. A gingerbread man who was always her savior. The rocking horse they used to ride away. I loved that rocking horse. I touched the small animal's face and remembered my mother and gifts piled up four-feet high around the Christmas tree.

I approached the bored teenager. "Excuse me?" I said. "I see on the door that you're looking for help. What type of position is available?"

"I dunno," the girl said. "Let me get the manager."

A short, pleasantly round woman with a mass of teased hair and makeup to rival a televangelist's wife came from behind a curtain. "Hi. I'm CeCe. Can I help you?" she asked. Her red jingle bell earrings bobbed when she spoke.

"I saw your sign and well . . . I was just wondering what type of help you are looking for. Anything on weekends?"

"We need an assistant manager. That's some weekend work, but we'd need that person around a lot during the week too. You know Christmas is almost upon us." The way she said it, you knew she was happy in her work.

"Well, I can't during the week. I have a

job. I was just . . . I don't know . . . drawn to your shop."

"I know. Isn't it wonderful? Christmas every day." Her smile was genuine. "Here. Just take an application." She reached behind the counter and came out with one. "Go on. Take it. You never know."

I took the application and thanked her. Before I left I bought the tiny wooden rocking horse with a wreath around his neck. The smell of evergreen swirled from the cute shopping bag on my way to pick up my mother.

Inside the facility I spied her in a corner with her newfound friend. They were both heads down, working a puzzle.

"Hey, Ms. Duncan," the director greeted me.

"Michelle, please."

"Well, Michelle, your mother seems to have had a wonderful day."

"I was surprised you didn't call."

"Oh, no. She's been happy all day. She did have a few moments when her mind drifted some, but she came right back and everything was fine."

"Thank you so much. She looks great."

"Why don't you go on over and speak with her?"

My mother was happy to see me, but she

357

seemed a little disappointed when I asked her to gather her sweater and purse.

In the car, she waved to her friend, who raised a hand in reply.

"You seem like you like it," I said as I drove out of the parking lot.

"It's fine, sweetheart. Much better than I thought it would be." She paused and looked out the window as we passed through town. "Although, the cupcakes were a little dry."

I smiled. My mother was back.

I found the Interstate and we left Asheville behind.

Shadows fall early in the mountains and a cloak of calm descends on the valleys in early evening. My road to home was nearly dark as I turned into my drive.

"Would you be interested in going back?"

She took the longest time to answer and I worried that she hadn't really enjoyed herself.

"Mom? Did you hear me?"

"What? I'm sorry. Did you ask me something?"

"I asked if you enjoyed it enough that you'd be willing to go back again."

"Of course," she said and sighed. "It was the most fun I've had in a long time."

# CHAPTER 6

I pulled up my sloping drive and parked. I helped my mother from the car and we entered through the porch door. I tried to avoid coming in through the garage now with Randy gone. The garage was his domain and it somehow seemed wrong for me to intrude.

Inside she brushed off my attempts to help.

"My mind may be going, but my legs still work just fine," she said and headed upstairs.

*At least she still has a sense of humor,* I thought.

In the kitchen, I flung my purse on the counter and opened the refrigerator. I found the orange juice carton and was reaching into a cabinet for a glass when I saw the note on the table. I could tell it was Randy's scratchy handwriting before I even picked it up.

Dear Michelle,

I came home today to talk to you, but you're not here. I'm sorry I'm not a big enough man to wait around to tell you this in person.

I've been thinking about us a lot and I've decided I'm not coming home. I want a divorce. You know we haven't been in love for a long time and I don't want to spend the rest of my life with you and have both of us regretting it.

I don't mean to hurt you. You've been a good wife.

Randy

I sank into a chair. My hand trembled as I reread the note. "Haven't been in love for a long time"? What did he mean? How long had he felt that way and why hadn't he said anything? Didn't he know that people worked out their problems? They went to marriage counseling and talked to their preacher. Nobody just walked out on a marriage without some sort of warning, without trying to fix things.

My parents had had their problems. I heard more than one heated discussion in our house over the years, but they always seemed to work things out. There had been the overly quiet dinners and the days we didn't do things as a family because of a spat, but everything eventually turned out okay.

I was going to be divorced.

I flung open the door to the garage and there I saw all of Randy's stuff growing like chunky moss from the unfinished walls. He'd hammered nails into the joists to hang tools and fishing rods and camping equipment. Weed-whackers, gas cans, coolers, and tools were jam-packed along the walls. I grabbed a handful of the first thing I could reach and ripped. A tent came tumbling down onto the floor. Pinions pinged against the concrete and scattered. I crunched my foot through the fragile wall of an ice bucket. I pushed the button to open the garage and cranked the riding mower. It sputtered to life and I backed it out and up to the trailer on his johnboat. That stupid boat had taken my spot in the garage long enough. I was going to clean house — to pile all his stuff in the front yard and set it on fire with gas like I'd seen a woman do in a movie. I hooked the johnboat up to the yard tractor and put her in gear, but the mower lurched and stalled. I tried again and again, but I couldn't get the damn thing to cooperate. The battery made a feeble whir, but the engine refused to turn over.

"Damn it!" I screamed. "Damn it! Damn it!" I kicked at the metal wheel wells until a pain shot up my leg.

That's when I laid my head over on the steering wheel and cried. Plump tears popped onto the dusty gearshift between my legs. Most of my tears fell on the big N and the irony wasn't lost on me. I'd been in neutral for a long time. Safe. Expected. That's what I was like. A neutral kind of person. Maybe that's what had finally run Randy off. Maybe I bored him. Maybe he had found somebody else who wasn't quite so boring.

I had snot running, so I climbed off the mower and headed into the house. Inside I dug in my purse for the tissues I always kept in a side pocket. As I raised the crinkled tissue to my nose I noticed another bit of paper peeking from an outside pocket. I pulled the paper out. It was the job application from Season's Greetings. I grabbed a pen from my kitchen desk and sat down. I hadn't filled out a job application since I graduated college fifteen years before, but something told me that this was going to be a new start for me. I couldn't very well keep my regular job if I had to take care of my mother all the time. If she didn't get into a nursing home soon, I was going to be in a pickle with nobody to help me. Maybe this was what I had needed — a good kick in the butt to get me going down a different path.

I spent the next hour carefully filling out the job application and when I finished I realized that my penmanship was beautiful and my qualifications exceeded the job description that had been attached. It was a full-time position with pay equal to what I was making at the mulch company. If they hired me, I could drop Mom off in the morning at adult day care and pick her up in the afternoon. Season's Greetings could fix some of my immediate problems. It was a plan.

I called Randy's cell phone number and in a calm voice I left this message:

Randy, this is Michelle. I found your note. If you want a divorce then you can have one. Go ahead and hire a lawyer and draw up the papers. I want the house. I think that's only fair since you're the one who wants out. Oh, and we need to work out a time when you can come clean your stuff out of my house. I want to be able to park in my own garage.

Relief rushed over me when I pushed the

mobile button that ended my connection with Randy.

# CHAPTER 7

A month went by and I heard nothing from Randy. Two weeks after my meltdown in the garage, I became the assistant manager at Season's Greetings. CeCe practically begged me to take the job when she found out that I had bookkeeping skills. In only a few weeks I had gotten the employees more motivated and had reorganized the stockroom. I still didn't feel comfortable decorating displays, but I was getting there, experimenting with designs, ordering unusual things from our supply catalogs.

CeCe insisted I had good taste, that I could be a decorator. But I had always leaned toward a country style that I knew wasn't hip or artsy or something designers appreciated. I came to realize that the country part of me was just because I'd been living in a log cabin my entire adult life. Having logs for walls sort of limited the types of decorating you could do and Randy's taste had run to mounted dead animals and the occasional print of a barn or a river. He'd liked his comfortable lounge chair and the country kitchen table set we'd inherited from his parents. I'd never really had the chance to find out what my own style was. I had been thinking that if I did get the house in the divorce that I would sell it and move into Asheville. Living in town had appeal and I realized that I enjoyed being around people who were into the arts, people who liked to socialize and eat out and go to community events.

But I was still responsible for my mother and even though I saw a lot of interesting things going on in Asheville I wasn't able to connect with any of the fun. I was also in limbo about Randy. I tried to put the fact that I hadn't received divorce papers out of my mind. I bounced back and forth between being really enthusiastic about my new life and wishing I could see Randy again. I still had feelings for him and I found it hard to believe that he could just wipe away all our history, just dismiss all those feelings he had for me. I wasn't sure that I wanted him back, but I did need some closure and without seeing Randy face to face it seemed impossible.

I knew that if I contacted a lawyer and

drew up papers that he would be forced to make contact with me. But something kept me from being the one to make the first move toward divorce. Something in me felt that if he hadn't taken up with another woman that we could put our lives back together again. But then the next day I'd be indignant and resolve to end his bullshit and move on with my life.

I would be lying if I said I didn't miss him. At night, his soft snores were now replaced with the rumble of lumber trucks on the road. I still couldn't bring myself to sleep in the middle of the bed, although I'd read in a magazine that it was therapeutic to spread out. Life was lonely without Randy sitting at the table with his cup of coffee and his newspaper in the morning. It wasn't that we ever had in-depth discussions about the current day's events or religion or politics, but there was a void without the rustle of the paper and his man noises.

Some mornings I would reach into the medicine cabinet and take out his razor and look at the little bits of beard he'd left behind. I'd smell his cologne and look at his dress shoes on the floor in our closet, waiting, like me. Once I went into the garage and retrieved a garbage bag I'd filled with his clothes and I'd thrown into the johnboat. I opened the bag and smelled his Randy smell.

My mother had seen my melancholy a few times, but stayed quiet on the subject of Randy. She respected my privacy and didn't offer up her opinion on my situation during our drives into Asheville. Instead we both preferred to look forward to our days in town. My mother and I had slipped into our new routines. I'd drop her at the adult day care where the social scene was surprisingly active. She'd been getting attention from an older gentleman and never one to shy away from a man's attention, my mother began to be more concerned with her appearance.

"Why, Miss Edwina, don't you look fine today," the director would purr when she arrived after a trip to the salon. "Is that a new scarf you're wearing?"

"Oh, this thing? I've had it for years," Mother would say.

I was so relieved that she was having a good time. Most days I couldn't wait to drop her off so I could get on to work. Christmas season for retailers started with the fall festival and the influx of color-seeking tourists.

This day I was apprehensive. CeCe was going to Atlanta on a buying trip and I was in charge for the first time. The outdoor displays tended to sell the fastest and it was my job to see that new displays were up and ready for the weekend. I'd come to really love the teenage girl who had been there the first day I came in. Her name was Renee. She was a skinny little thing with droopy hair and unfortunately one of those nose rings that made her look like she was trying too hard to be something she's not. I'd complimented her appearance a couple of times and she perked up and became helpful.

On this day, CeCe was packing and giving me last minute instructions on what needed to happen that day. It was a Friday and I had to make the front lawn display, do the time cards and place an order. Since we were close to Christmas we had boxes of merchandise delivered every day and I had to reconcile the box content with our orders. We didn't open until ten and with so much to do I had intended to wait until the afternoon to do the front display, but as soon as I came in CeCe pulled me and Renee out on the front lawn and started making suggestions.

"Now, honey, I don't want to tell you what to do, but experience has shown me a couple of things that work and a couple of things that don't." I was listening intently when a beat-up blue van pulled across the street and a tall man with a head full of curly brown hair and a goatee started to unload from the back. CeCe's words faded in my ears as I watched this guy pull sculptures from the van and carry them into the art gallery across the road.

"Oh, hey, are you listening to me?" CeCe said.

"She's watching that dude in the van," Renee said. "He's hot."

"I am not."

"Yes, you are," Renee said.

CeCe ceased to talk and we three stood silent as he returned to the van. The gallery owner, who had followed him out, propped the gallery door open and then came to help.

"My, he *is* a nice-looking fellow," CeCe said. "In a rugged sort of way."

"I like manly men," Renee said. "Hey, Michelle, go on over there."

"What? No way. I'm still married."

"So?" CeCe said. "I agree with Renee. What that missing husband of yours doesn't know won't hurt him."

"I'm *not* going over there."

The guy came back out and unloaded again. I wondered if he was the artist. The sculptures were wall hangings and garden art. They were metal branches with spiky pinecones, sprays of leaves, and vines.

We moved to the swing on the porch and watched him. He never looked our way. Once his van was unloaded the gallery owner handed him what appeared to be a check. They shook hands and then he got into the van and drove away.

"So," CeCe said. "If I didn't have to leave for Atlanta right now I'd take a little break and stroll on over to that gallery and find out who that artist is."

"He might just be the delivery guy," Renee observed. "Which would be fine, because, you know, I dig the FedEx guy."

"Well, it would be good to know," CeCe said. "Because after all, Michelle, it's important we use local artists."

Both of them looked at me like cats with mouthfuls of feathers.

"I'm not going over there. I don't want to know who he is."

"Whatever," Renee said and rolled her eyes.

But by midafternoon I found my thoughts drifting across the street. When we had a slowdown in traffic I told Renee that I was going to step out for a while. She gave me a knowing grin as she waited on a customer.

The art gallery was called Handmade and

inside was a perfect hushed world. The smell was heavenly — leather and spices and evergreen. Textiles and quilts hung the walls. Hundreds of forms of pottery were mixed in with hand-hewed cutlery, blown glass, and woven pillows. There was so much beautiful jewelry that it made me gasp. And there, among the most unusual furniture I had ever seen were some of the sculptures the mystery man had carried into the gallery.

I ran my hand over the coppery surface of one of the sculptures and felt the smooth-ness of the metal.

"Isn't it beautiful?" The man who had helped carry in the sculptures appeared. "He's our most popular sculptor."

"It's wonderful," I said. I wanted to touch the shiny leaves again, but suddenly, I felt as if I shouldn't.

"I'm Gray. The gallery manager. I've seen you across the way. I think we're neighbors now." He offered his hand, so soft. He was tall, slender, and immaculate. Gray was most definitely gay.

"Oh, hi. I'm Michelle. I'm the new assistant manager over at Season's Greetings." I asked casually, "Who is this artist?"

"Baxter Brown. His work sells really well, especially during the holidays. He'll bring us more work every couple of weeks until Christmas."

"It's really lovely."

"Um, yes," Gray said.

A sales assistant touched Gray on the arm and he leaned over so she could whisper in his ear. "If you'll excuse me," he said. "I have to attend to something. It was nice to meet you."

I looked around for a while and bought myself a beautiful pair of pearl earrings. I bought my mother a new scarf woven with glistening fibers in pink that would match her soft complexion. I was on my way out, enjoying the adrenaline rush of a nice purchase when I saw Season's Greetings was packed. I dashed across the road. As I clattered through the entrance I saw relief wash over Renee.

"I'm so sorry," I said as I slid behind the counter.

"Well?" Renee said as she rang up a customer.

"Well what?"

"Did you find out who he is?"

"That wasn't why I went over there."

"Right."

"Well, if you must know, I did find out his name. It's Baxter and the gallery manager said his work is some of the most popular the gallery carries."

"This is bad," she said as she wrapped a delicate glittery ornament in tissue.

"What's bad?" I asked as I handed her a box.

"Now that you know his name you won't be able to stop thinking about him."

# CHAPTER 8

Renee was right. I did have a hard time shaking thoughts of Baxter Brown. Who was he really? Was he one of those elusive artists who lived in the mountains and only came down to deliver his goods? Was he married with a house full of children, barefoot little imps who climbed trees and made their own artwork from their father's scraps of metal? Or was he a member of one of the hippie communes that flourished in the mountains, one of the tambourine-and-guitar crew that had little use for modern conveniences like television and health insurance?

CeCe, Renee, and I spent slow times coming up with these and dozens more scenarios to explain our mystery sculptor. I had never thought about anyone I didn't know as much as I thought about Baxter Brown. I wasn't exactly sure what drew me to him, but I thought it had something to do with the way he moved. He had a smoothness almost like an animal. He was strong and sure and masculine and I'd dreamed about him, although I had not admitted that to my coworkers.

We all kept a wary eye out for the arrival of the beat-up van, but I was the one who happened to be outside, stringing lights in one of our fir trees, when the vehicle slid into a space in front of Handmade. I stepped behind the tree so he wouldn't see me. Like before he got out and began to unload his art. I was frozen there, sprays of evergreen tickling my nose as I watched him through the limbs.

He went inside and I realized I'd been holding my breath.

"Good God." I jumped at CeCe's smoky voice. "How do you expect him to ever notice you if you hide behind a tree?"

"I don't expect him to notice me. I can't go flirting with him. I'm still married."

"That, my dear, seems like a technicality at this point. How long has it been since you've seen your husband?" she whispered loudly behind me.

"Months. But if I want a clean divorce I can't be seen carousing."

"Who said anything about carousing? You could just start out by talking to him."

"No."

"Oh, you're pathetic."

Nothing like this had ever happened to me at the mulch company. I never had crazy friends before and I knew that if Baxter came out and CeCe was still there that she would march over to his van and introduce herself. Then she would make a big deal out of introducing me, which would then spoil the moment. Surely he would know that we had been spying on him.

"Okay. I'll talk to him, but you have to go back inside."

"You're going to do it?" She raised a thin, painted eyebrow at me.

"Yes. I'll do it. Now just go inside."

She nodded with satisfaction and returned to the cottage. I was left with a sinking feeling I hadn't had since elementary school when we used to have friends pass notes to boys with little boxes that read: I like you. Do you like me? Check yes or no.

Waiting for that checkmark was agony.

Just like now.

The gallery door opened and Gray came out with Baxter, a complication I hadn't expected. I went to stringing lights again, stuffing them in randomly as I watched Baxter out of the corner of my eye.

Then something miraculous happened. Gray called my name.

"Michelle? Michelle, come on over here. I'd like you to meet someone."

I turned as though startled at my name. It wasn't much of an acting job since I was truly discombobulated. I walked over to where they stood at the gaping backdoors of the van.

"Baxter, I'd like you to meet my new neighbor across the street. This is Michelle. She's the assistant manager over at Season's Greetings."

"Hi. I'm Baxter." He extended his calloused hand and his grip radiated heat.

"Nice to meet you." As we shook hands I heard a merry little tinkle and realized with horror that I was wearing a pair of our jingle bell earrings.

"Michelle is quite the admirer of your work," Gray said.

"Is that so?" His goatee pulled into a smile. Laugh lines surrounded hazel eyes like the fallen leaves of December.

Silence.

Gray interjected. "Yes. Well, Baxter, why don't I run inside and get you your check. I won't be a minute." As he turned to go Gray gave me a look that said everything. I could have kissed him.

"I do like your work," I said.

"Really, which pieces?"

378

"Oh, the coppery ones with all the leaves. And the pinecone pieces too. They're lovely."

"Thanks. Those are a lot of work. I can't make nearly as many of them as I would like. They're complicated and take time."

"Oh."

We stood there, it was awkward for a while.

"So, you work over at the Christmas shop?"

"Yeah, I'm new."

"Oh."

"Just learning the ropes." God, that sounded dumb.

He nodded and then slammed the doors on the van.

"Well, I, um," I stammered. "I'd better get back. It was really nice to meet you."

"Yeah. Me too. Nice to meet you," he said.

As I walked back to the cottage my head said, *Dummy.* How dumb could I sound? I pushed against the giant door wreath and made the jingle bells dance when I slammed the door behind me.

"Oh, my God. Oh, my God. What did he say?" Renee was on me as soon as I came through the door.

"Nothing. I don't want to talk about it."

"What? You have to tell us. What did you

say to each other?" CeCe was now in my face too.

"Nothing. We didn't say anything much. Really. Just hi. How ya doin'? Nice day. Yadda. Yadda."

Both women looked dejected.

"That was definitely a bad idea," I said. "If you need me I'll be in the break room looking for a knife to slit my wrists."

# CHAPTER 9

As the holiday season moved into full swing things got crazy.

The jangling phone and flow of customers kept us in a constant state of flux. We'd take orders for finished trees that customers selected from our Web site. They would call in, order the tree and give us their address so we could deliver and install the evergreen. It never occurred to me that people would pay a thousand dollars or more for a tree. Randy always cut our tree from the woods behind our house. He'd lop off a few limbs to make it balance and we'd spend the day unwrapping our ornaments from wads of newspaper. We used the same decorations each year and there was comfort in that. In my life, a Christmas tree had never been anything but free.

But people with money apparently don't like to do things that take up their valuable time. We frequently worked with property management companies to get inside second homes and vacation rentals to install trees and decorate these houses and condos before the wealthy arrived with their families. It was a treat to see how different places could be. There were those that screamed decorator. These houses were devoid of personal touches and seemed simply to be a showplace, like a display from the floor of any furniture shop. Other places were filled with original art, family photographs, and unusual items collected from travels. These were the houses I liked the best.

I thought working at Season's Greetings was just going to be selling ornaments and garland. How wrong I was.

"Michelle," CeCe said. "We have a truck delivering to Biltmore. I need you to meet that delivery on the grounds, reconcile the inventory manifest, and oversee the installation."

"For Christmas at Biltmore?" I was stunned.

"Right. There's a loading dock on the lower level around back where they bring in all the supplies. Ask at the gate and they'll direct you to the service road. Once you check the inventory you'll need to find Miriam from the curatorial department. She's in charge of the trees at Biltmore this year."

"How many trees are we doing for them?"

"They have more than a hundred trees in all, but we're just responsible for three. Here's the instructions and photos. The theme this year has something to do with all the countries the Vanderbilts visited. No fake trees, only live trees that they should already have up. You just have to follow the directions and get them decorated." She removed color images from one of her files and handed them to me. "It's pretty straightforward. Just jump through any hoop they give you. They're our best customer. Anything Biltmore wants, Biltmore gets."

The papers shook in my hand. My feelings must have been apparent because CeCe said, "Go on. You'll do great. They have a crew of people to help with the installation. They're all professionals and they take instruction well. Don't worry, honey. You'll do fine. Here's Miriam's cell number."

I programmed the mobile number into my phone with trembling fingers.

A few hours later I got a call that the delivery truck was on its way, so I drove across the road to the main gate at Biltmore House.

"I'm with Season's Greetings. Here to

decorate," I told the fellow in the gatehouse.

He checked his chart and smiled. "You know where the loading dock is?"

Sunlight filtered through the woodlands, making lacy patterns on the country lane that led to the main house. The drive up to the estate is three miles through forests of azaleas, oaks, and evergreen. Glimpses of rills and ponds came in and out of view along the way. Natives all knew that original Biltmore property formed the nucleus of the Pisgah National Forest.

Thoughts of the national forest made me think about Randy and where he was hiding out in the woods and I was instantly unhappy.

*Damn you, Randy,* I thought as I drove. How could he stay away so long? Something in me had thought he would have come back by now. But it was slowly becoming apparent that he might not return. I'd been telling myself each morning that sometimes you just have to let go.

Like leaving the mulch factory for my new job. Letting go of that security had been hard, but instead of dealing with lumberjacks and loads of crunched-up bark, I was heading to Biltmore to decorate for Christmas. Quite a change. Quite an improvement.

Around a curve, Biltmore came into view poised at the end of a manicured nineteenth-century lawn with reflecting pools and drippy angels. I followed a service entrance road through colorful landscaping around to the back of the house. At the loading dock I was met by Miriam, a petite, blond cheerleader sort of gal. She struck me as one of those overachiever sorority girls who lived for the next party or event. I was greeted while she scrolled her handheld for the proper information.

"Your first tree is Books of the World. Library. Know where that is?"

"Are you serious? I get to put a tree in the library?"

"Somebody's gotta do it."

It was apparent that some of the Biltmore glitter had fluttered under her feet in the past few days.

"Sure. I love the library. It's my favorite room in the house."

"Well." She smiled. "Today's your lucky day. I'm too busy to hover. Just do your thing and don't pull out any books or the curator'll have a fit. He uses white curatorial gloves for every volume. Call me if you need me." She was off.

I called the delivery truck and found that it was still an hour out, so I decided to take a look around. I went up and through the building, my instinctual memory of the house's floor plan still useful. It was early and guests were just arriving. No holiday crowds to fight yet, only a few hundred people scattered around and most of those appeared to be decorating or cleaning.

I made my way from downstairs up to the grand entranceway. On my left the marble staircase spiraled out of sight. To my right, the Winter Garden was bathed in strips of light that fell through the vaulted glass ceiling. Where usually the incoming sun bathed palms and ficus, this day giant Christmas trees rose in spectacular sparkling gold.

Past the Winter Garden and left was the Tapestry Gallery, a long hall filled with masculine furniture, walls covered in tapestries, and a large fireplace that was repeated in some form in every room in the house. I thought of the wonderful parties that had happened here. The cocktails and designer dresses and games out on the lawn. To my right I looked through arched doorways to the loggia and past to distant hills where bright patches of orange and red still hung on against a backdrop of skeletal gray. Verdant evergreen still punctuated spots.

At the end of the Tapestry Gallery opened double doors to George Vanderbilt's library where thousands of volumes filled two floors of mahogany bookcases scaled by the use of sliding library ladders on both levels. At the far end of the library, in an area roped off by stanchions, was a massive bare blue spruce. It was going to be an enormous job. Just getting the lights around the thing would be a chore, then there was the garland and the ornaments. I hesitated, then stepped over the rope.

"Wow," I whispered to myself.

I was startled to hear the rustle of branches. A man backed out from behind the tree. "Yeah, it's a big one all right." I knew before I raised my eyes. My heart expanded.

"Oh," Baxter said. His hazel eyes snapped when he recognized me.

I stood there, my words also lost.

"Hello again," he said. "Are you here to decorate?"

I forced myself to find my voice. "This is apparently one of my trees."

"Well, yes." He leaned back in order to illustrate how high the tree reached. "I hope you have help."

I laughed. "I'm supposed to have a crew."

"Well, then . . ."

"Still, I've never done an enormous tree like this before. I imagine the ornaments will be super-sized to have any impact on it. I have no idea where to start. I mean I guess I start at the top and work my way down. The decorations are books. I mean the chart says the theme of this tree is books about traveling. That sounds interesting, don't you think?" I suddenly realized I was rambling and stopped. "So, what are you doing here?"

"I made some new tree stands. A few years back they asked if I could develop a stand for these extra large trees. I just delivered a few more this morning."

"So you're a welder too. That would make sense."

"If it's metal I can shape it."

We both stood there nodding our heads in agreement.

"So, um, I'm sorry. I don't mean to keep you from your job," he said.

"No. I'm actually waiting for the delivery truck with my ornaments."

He scratched the back of his neck in a way that indicated he was thinking. "Okay, then, I've got to go. Got another job."

I panicked. The last time I had walked away. This time he was doing the walking. In my head I had a dozen witty things to say to make him stay, but I couldn't force one of them from my mouth. "Okay, sure. I'll see you later," I mumbled. I turned to study the enormous tree. Baxter's steps were so soft on the marble that there was no indication of when he left the room.

Suddenly I heard him draw breath and I twisted around to see that he was standing in the doorway. He blurted out, "Are you married?"

I bit my lip.

"I'm sorry," he stammered. "I didn't mean to be so blunt, but well . . . anyway, are you? Married? I mean, I saw the ring the first day, but now you don't have it on and well . . . ?"

It was my turn to stammer. "Well, um, technically yes, I am married."

"Technically in what way?"

"Technically I haven't seen him since August when he told me he wanted a divorce."

"Oh, man. I'm sorry. I didn't mean to . . ."

"Oh, no really. I'm practically over it." That didn't sound right. "I mean I've accepted it and I don't really dwell on it. I'm moving on."

"I see."

"So I would be . . . you know . . . open to invitations . . ."

"Well, good." He ran fingers through his thick hair and his curls popped back into place like memory wire. "Okay. So I installed a wall sculpture for a new seafood restaurant in town and they're having a soft opening on Friday night. Any chance you would go with me?"

"A soft opening?"

"Yeah, like a party for family and friends to make sure everything runs right before they open it up to the public."

"So a private party at a new restaurant?"

"Yeah, that's right. It's called Ridgeview."

"That sounds like fun. I'd love to."

"Awesome. It's business casual. Nothing extreme."

"Okay."

"Where can I pick you up?"

"I have to work on Friday. Why don't you just meet me at Season's Greetings?"

"Seven?"

"Seven."

He smiled and my heart fluttered. His slight steps blended into the echoes that came from the Tapestry Gallery. People were approaching and a tour guide led an awestruck group into the library. Their eyes widened at all the books, the massive carved desk with reading lights, the masculine furniture, and gaping fireplace.

My mobile rang and the guide gave me the evil eye. I noted the number as my delivery truck and mouthed, "Sorry," to her on my way out. I had to force myself to walk calmly downstairs in case I should happen to run into Baxter Brown again.

# CHAPTER 10

The Biltmore installation took the entire week and I never worked so hard. There was hefting and decorating and decision-making and disaster management. My adrenaline never left me and by the time Friday rolled around, I was ready for a little fun.

I took my mother to spend the night with her old neighbor, Mrs. Smith, who welcomed her with open arms and a warm pot of tea. I'd spent the day agonizing over what exactly business casual meant and finally just decided to wear a black jersey dress I had left over from a wedding. It was your basic little black tea-length wraparound. I added the new scarf I'd bought my mother and my dangling pearl earrings.

My hair had lost its lemon juice streaks. I'd picked up a package of hair color six months ago and never used it. This day I washed away my few stray grays. All my hair came out a soft, wavy brown that I twisted up in a smooth way I envisioned as classy. As I watched myself put on makeup I thought about what I was getting ready to do. I was, in essence, cheating on my husband. And I was doing it in a public way. Not that anybody Randy hung around with would be at this fancy restaurant party, but still, it was possible that this wasn't the smartest thing I'd ever chosen to do. I certainly hadn't told my mother I was going on a date.

One reason I hadn't shared that little bit of information is that I truly didn't know a thing about Baxter Brown. He seemed like the most normal person in the world, but something told me that he was very special in some way. The air just seemed more clear when he was around.

CeCe had agreed to move my work schedule around so I could take Friday off. I arrived there an hour before he was to pick me up, so he would think that I had been working all day. Baxter made the jingle bells dance at exactly seven. He wore a jacket with elbow patches that would have looked silly on anyone but a professor, and him. His lanky frame made the tweedy jacket work. We drove downtown in his green Prius. That changed my perception of him some.

The night was cool and as we walked up a hill to the front door of Ridgeview restaurant, he put his arm around me and pulled me into him. It was an odd sensation, another man's strong touch, his warmth against me. Inside we shed ourselves at the coat check. Baxter bumped knuckles with a number of men at the restaurant's door, introducing me to everyone, all of whom I immediately forgot.

"Our table's in the back." He pulled me through the crowd behind him. There was a relaxed, loose quality to his body language as he maneuvered the throng. He nodded a lot. People spoke to him, raised their glasses. He introduced me to everyone. It suddenly all started making sense. He was a local artist and many of the people were interested in his work. He'd told me he had three pieces in the restaurant.

We arrived at a round red booth in the corner. On the white tablecloth sat a small table tent sign that read RESERVED. Behind the bank seats hung a massive sculpture of a large fish with scales so defined and individually hammered that they glistened. The detail was intense.

"You did that?"

"You like it?" His smile contained assurance. He was pleased with his work.

"My God. That's fabulous."

"Thank you."

"Really. It's so pretty. I mean, I don't know the right words to describe art, but really it is just so pretty. I love it."

He motioned for me to slide onto the banquette.

"This is our table?"

"Yeah. What do you like to drink?"

Beer seemed inappropriate so I ordered a cosmo. I'd had a couple of those before and they were like drinking candy. The waiter had no more than left our table when Gray arrived. He slid into the booth beside Baxter.

"People are loving your work. I think I've made two sales already. You're going to have to get that blowtorch and hammer going this weekend," Gray said. To me he said, "Glad you could join us, Michelle."

I looked up to see the young curator from Biltmore walking toward our table. "Hey, Gray. Hey, Baxter," she said. "Scoot over."

The guys went to move in my direction and she said, "No. I mean Michelle. You scoot. Can I sit by you?"

I slid farther into the booth next to Baxter.

"So," Miriam said. "You two know each other?"

Baxter nodded. "Michelle, I take it you met my little sister today." He motioned toward her.

I smiled. Sister. How unlike him she appeared.

"She was all excited about getting to work in the library today," Miriam said to her compact mirror as she checked her lipstick. "What are you, a bibliophile?" She smiled, sparkly and white, lips scarlet.

"English major."

"Art history," she said. "Another hopeless romantic."

Baxter laughed at that. "Anybody who thinks they can make a living from any kind of art is a hopeless romantic if you ask me."

"Oh pooh," she said. "Michelle, your trees are perfect. You did a terrific job."

"That's a compliment coming from Miss Perfection herself," Baxter said with a little edge. Their eyes met and I could see they were friends.

The party grew in intensity. I'd never been to such a loud event that didn't involve a keg and a field. Just when the party was beginning to wear thin for me, Baxter leaned over and said, "I've had enough. How about you? Ready to go?"

"You read my mind."

He wasted no time in making his exit.

"Oh, no. Where are you going so early?" Miriam asked as she sloshed a green drink out of a martini glass.

He shrugged. "Love you. See you later."

They pecked each others' cheeks. We left, Baxter shaking hands and patting backs along the way. It had turned cold and once again he encircled me with one arm as we walked. Inside the car he cranked up the heat.

"You know a lot of people," I said.

"You think? It's a small town. Everybody knows everybody."

"I was surprised that Miriam's your sister."

"There's a bunch of us Browns. Hang around Asheville long enough and you'll meet everybody eventually. Our parents moved us here in high school. What about you?"

"Born and raised in Black Knob."

Back at the store's parking lot he walked me to my car.

"It was amazing," I said. "I haven't had that much fun in a long time."

"You're a cheap date."

"I try."

His expression turned thoughtful.

"What's wrong?"

"I'm sorry you wouldn't let me drive you home."

"Next time."

"Okay. Next time."

I let him hang for a moment. "It was a strange first date. Finding out that you're some local artist rock star."

"Look. You don't know me well yet."

*Yet.*

"That thing tonight. That's not me. I'm a very private person. I live in my studio out in the woods and I work all the time and I listen to classic rock really loud and do guy things."

"Have you ever been married?" Cosmos ruin decorum.

"Uh. Yeah. Almost." He grimaced. "Almost, but no. I still regret missing out on that, but things happen. You know."

"Yeah, I know."

He put his hand on my car door as though to open it and then he stood there, close. A moment for me to consider him. I held my breath as he slowly spread his fingers up the back of my neck, into my hair. He pulled me into him and my mind went somewhere else as he pressed his lips to mine.

Heat spread from my heart down my arms to my fingertips. I could think of nothing but his warm, soft lips. I realized my dream

398

state only when he pulled away.

"I'll call you tomorrow," he whispered.

"Okay," I said weakly.

My wet lips tingled with cold.

He opened my door. "Better get in before you freeze."

I did as I was told, but I wasn't in danger of freezing.

I was burning with desire.

# CHAPTER 11

As the Christmas season picked up I saw my new love interest at least once a week. It seemed like everyone called him Bax and soon it was falling easily from my own tongue. We were both absolutely slammed with holiday work and were so exhausted most nights that we didn't have official dates. He'd drop off his work at Handmade and we'd grab lunch or if it was afternoon we'd grab an early dinner. It was on one of these later occasions that Bax met my mother.

"Should I call you Miss Edwina?" he asked, a note of mischief about him.

My mother rolled her eyes at him and then to me she said, "He's cute."

Later, after we'd dropped her off at her friend's house, Bax came home with me. It was one of the most natural things I've ever done. It was never discussed. We just went to my house and got directly into bed.

We didn't even try to act as if we wanted a glass of wine. We came in the front door and Bax looked around and said, "I never pictured you living here."

I willed him to turn around and grab me. And like he'd read my thoughts his attention shifted and when his hands were in my hair I lost all sense of time and place.

I'd put out candles earlier. I had wine. The seduction was on. When we made it to the bedroom and clothes started to fall, I was amazed by how easily I shed my inhabitions too. I had wanted him for months and I was going to allow myself this pleasure without guilt or reservations or shame.

His breath was hot against my neck and then down over me. His kisses soft, yet firm as if his lips were on the most delicate china. I shivered and thrill bumps covered me.

"Ooh," he whispered when he saw my skin's reaction. He put his body all over mine in ways I'd never known. He was insistent and strong and focused on me. It felt amazing in all the right ways.

The next morning, as I sipped my coffee, I leaned against the bathroom doorframe and watched Bax shave. After he left I went into the bathroom and found his razor on the sink and his shirt hanging on the back of the bathroom door. I decided to leave them there for when I came home that night.

I also decided then that I was going to file for divorce.

I waited until the next weekend to bring up the idea.

We were on our way up the mountain behind Asheville to his house and studio. I'd helped him shop for his family's New Year's party, which they always held on the first Saturday after the holiday.

Bax's house rambled up the mountainside, three floors staggered, the bottom one a garage studio. He'd inherited the place from his grandparents twenty years ago and had been adding on to it all this time in what he called "my homage to Frank Lloyd Wright." I loved his studio. There was a tang to the air, a metal influence that I loved — the propane and the solder smell of a man's work.

We got out of the car, each of us lugging hemp grocery sacks.

"Let's go in through the studio," he said, indicating that the recent snow would make his outside slate walk slick. Inside the garage studio it wasn't much warmer. Strewn about were all shapes of metal — copper, aluminum, steel, wrought iron.

"It's always so cold in here," I complained.

"Don't you freeze working in the winter?"

"Nah. I love it cold. When I get to working and have things fired up it gets hot in here."

"What are you working on now?"

"I've been sketching ideas. Take a look at these."

He pulled a black portfolio from behind a cabinet and spread its contents on a drawing table. "What do you think?"

The elaborate drawings showed ideas totally different than either his tree limbs or his fish. They were abstract and not something I had been that exposed to.

"They're wild I know," he said.

"But I like them. Would you ever do something as little as a tree ornament?"

He stood a moment looking at his sketches, thinking. "I don't know. Maybe. I'd have to see what I could come up with. You think there's a market for that?" He slid his artwork back into the portfolio and picked up the grocery sacks. "Come on. Let's go cook."

From the kitchen window above his sink a high ridge severed sky from land in a jagged line. During the few times that I had been to Bax's before I'd gotten lost in that view. It was so beautiful that I frequently let my thoughts wander from my assigned cooking task.

"Why don't you just sit here, have a glass of wine, and look at my mountain?"

"I'm sorry."

"No. Really. What's on your mind tonight?"

I shrugged. "I'm a little nervous about meeting your family."

"Don't sweat it. They're gonna love you. What are you worried about?"

"I'm not divorced yet. What if they ask me if I've ever been married?"

"They won't ask you that. Has Miriam asked you that?"

"No. But I have decided to go ahead and file. Do you know any divorce lawyers?"

He nodded. "We can find you somebody. Do you know where he is so he can be served papers?"

"No."

"Does he have a best friend who would know where he is?"

"Not if he doesn't want to be found."

"So just where do you think he is?"

"There are a couple of places he could be hanging out. I guess I could have him served at work."

"That's a plan."

Bax dumped out gourmet eggplant dip into a bowl while I arranged soft, smelly cheeses on a tray. An hour later the table was filled with wine bottles, the air was filled with music, and the house was filled with Bax's crazy family, the most liberal group of people I had ever met. Once the New Year's party got into swing there were twelve of us in all. Bax's parents and his mother's mother, Grammy. Two brothers and their wives each brought a tween girl apiece, planned that way they said. Miriam brought a bug-eyed dog who appeared to be the most loved family member of all. It had taken awhile to get Grammy into the house and eventually Bax and one of his brothers had put the tiny woman in a chair and carried her inside as if she were as light as a feather.

The conversations started immediately — politics, international and domestic — topped the agenda. They discussed the economy, the war in Iraq, the future of the country. Then it was wine and food, a long discussion on art and furniture design. I sat in awe as two different conversations raged at each end of the table, neither of which I would even chance to interject into.

"Michelle?" I started at my name in a lull in the conversation.

"You're an English major," Baxter said. "Tell us, what do you think makes someone a Southern writer?"

All eyes were upon me and I felt a little trickle of sweat form along my hairline. I took another drink of wine to stall, but I'd had enough that wine was no longer my friend.

"Well," I needed to sound well informed. "There's the simple school of thought that a Southern story has to be set in the South or the characters have to be quirky Southern people, but I don't agree."

"Why so?" Miriam asked. "You know what Flannery O'Connor said, 'Whenever I am asked why Southern writers particularly have a penchant for writing about freaks, I say it is because we are still able to recognize one.' "

Laughter exploded around the table and everyone clinked their wineglasses.

"Hey," Baxter said. "Let Michelle answer the question."

Everyone politely settled down and turned their attention to me again. I swallowed and formulated my statement.

"That's truly one of the great quotes about writing, but I think Southern lit is more than characters. I think that a Southern story is about rhythm and a certain sensibility that reflects our strong history of oral storytelling. We write like we talk to a certain extent. There is a lyrical quality to the prose. Then, of course, there are reoccurring themes like the love of land, a strong connection to family, a rejection of outside influence."

"Well put!" Baxter's father bellowed and slapped his hand on the table. "I agree!"

As if the matter were settled, talk turned to music, then Bluegrass music. I was relieved to be off the hook. I knew there was no way I could make that level of contribution on any other subject. I wondered if Baxter had included me because he knew I'd have an opinion on the topic of literature and a little flash of gratefulness stirred in me.

As if he had read my thoughts Bax winked at me. Then he rose and walked to the cabinet that housed his sound system and music library. He pulled out an impressive Bluegrass collection and all the men gathered around the stereo.

"Lord, here we go with the Bluegrass again," Trudy said. Bax's mom Trudy was a hippie in the finer sense of the word. She embraced a wide worldview, but she chose very little of it for herself. Her clothing was subdued and comfortable, her jewelry handmade and cheap. Her hair was uncolored and gray streaks ran through it and swirled around where she had knotted it in the back. Like her husband, Mort, she was tall and lean and healthy in a carefree sort of way. Bax's father had a long white bread, round wire-rimmed glasses, and a loud opinion on everything. He cursed insistently, was an outrageous flirt, and a complete delight.

"We women ignore them when they get to debating Bluegrass," Trudy said. "Grab your wine and come with me." On the way outside she stopped to remove two blankets from a trunk by the door.

I followed her to a screened porch where she plopped into one of three rocking chairs. "I love this view," she said. "We always loved living here."

"Why'd you move?" I asked as I took one of the blankets she offered. We wrapped ourselves up and began to rock.

She looked at me sort of funny and then she said, "We wanted Bax, our oldest, to have it."

"It's so big for one person."

"Well," she hesitated and then said, "Grammy couldn't climb the stairs. We needed a place that was all one story."

"Oh. I understand that. I have a mother I'm taking care of too."

"It can be quite the responsibility to care

for a parent. Do you have help?"

"I'm using an adult day care when I work. My mother has friends she can stay with on occasions like tonight. I think I'll start driving her over to her sister's in Knoxville some weekends. Eventually she'll need more care, but right now things are manageable."

The New Year's party went on into the evening. Grammy dozed on and off and the tween girls who had disappeared into a back room reappeared to be fed again. Everyone had another go at the food and wine and then said their good nights with bear hugs. They picked their way down the icy drive to their vehicles, their laughter fading into the dark.

"Well," Bax said. "That went well."

"I love your family. They're so strange."

He laughed. "Strange in a good way?"

"Oh yes. They're so interesting. My family is just so normal. Just so ordinary."

I was washing dishes, sliding his handmade plates in and out of warm soapy water with care. It seemed that everything he owned was made by someone he knew. No store-bought, mass-reproduced thing for Bax. Even his spoons and forks were some he had forged himself, with stems and leaves for handles. Everything in his life seemed to have life, some extra detail or effort that raised it above the norm, from his wooden salad bowls to his handmade soaps.

"Hey," I said as I washed. "Can I ask you something?"

"Sure. What?"

"I don't mean to pry or anything, but why did you get to inherit this big house all to yourself when both your brothers have families?"

He stopped drying dishes and said, "It wasn't supposed to be just me."

I stopped washing and waited for him to explain.

"Remember I told you that I almost got married?"

"Uh-huh."

"Okay. So that's why I got this house. I was getting married. We were going to have a family. We wanted four kids, so this was perfect for us. Grammy needed a one story. It was all working out."

"So, what happened?"

He hesitated. Picked up a glass and considered it.

"She was killed."

"Oh, no."

"Car accident. About three weeks before the wedding."

How awful for him. How awful for me.

"Were you . . ." I mumbled.

"No. No. I wasn't involved. It was just a freak one-car accident."

"I'm so sorry."

"It was a long time ago."

"How long?"

"About fifteen years ago. I was young and in love. I'm okay about it now. Life goes on. Look, anyway," he said readjusting his stance and starting to dry dishes again. "I tried to get both my brothers to take the old home place when they got married, but they were happy where they were. So, I just started pouring all my energy and money into this house. It's the art project of my life."

"Fifteen years and you never found anybody else you wanted to marry?"

He shrugged. "I've had girlfriends, you know. But nobody who was really the one."

Later, as we lay in bed, our skin pressed together, our hearts slowed into a resting rhythm, I watched our reflection in the window against the star-filled sky. We were on our sides. His arm draped my waist. We looked at peace, but my mind wouldn't rest.

The notion that Bax was still in love with his dead fiancée rubbed my brain. How could I ever compete with the perfect dead love? Nobody had been able to so far.

Four kids? That wasn't going to happen

411

either. My heart dropped.

I stared at my image, faint like a ghost in the glass.

*Enjoy this,* I told myself. *It won't last forever.*

# CHAPTER 12

Randy showed up again in the spring. I'd hired an attorney and put the divorce into process. The papers had been served to him at work. It only took a week to get Randy's response. He came again when I wasn't home and this time he didn't have to leave a note. When I opened the door I thought I had been robbed.

Furniture was overturned and scattered around. Dishes were smashed on the kitchen floor. I picked my way through the mess assessing the damage. I quickly registered that the television and stereo were untouched and I knew immediately it was Randy.

In the bedroom, the sheets were shredded and in the middle of that mess was a pile of all the things Bax had left in the house — a razor, a shirt, a pair of shoes, a magazine, a toothbrush — all things that had spelled out to my husband that I had moved on. Randy had even gotten Bax's beer out of the refrigerator and poured it all over the mattress and tossed the cans on top of the pile. And in the middle of the pile, ripped in two and soaked in beer were the divorce papers.

I was slightly astonished by the level of anger in his act. I wasn't sure he would even care since he'd been gone nine months without a word. I was suddenly mad. How dare he come into my home and wreck it because he was suddenly jealous of my new life.

The message light on the answering machine was blinking green so I pushed the button knowing in my heart that it was Randy. His voice came on, distant. He was on his cell.

"Michelle," he said. "You made me do it. I just lost my mind. I came home and found that other guy's stuff. Who the hell is *he?* I want to talk to you. We're not divorced yet and I want to talk about this. You can't just go off and hook up with some other guy. I got the divorce . . ." His voice faded and then came back. "I wanted to talk. I'm sorry. I don't know what came over me. I shouldn't have done it, but damn it, Michelle, I love you. You know that don't you? I love you and I want to come home. Call me when you get this message. I'll pick up.

Call me."

Had he gone upstairs and seen that my mother was no longer living with me? Only the week before my mother had moved into a nice facility in Asheville. So now that she was gone he suddenly wanted to come home. It seemed Randy hadn't been quite as unhappy as he thought.

And why would he think pouring beer on my bed would make me want him back? But then he was thinking of the other Michelle. The old Michelle who would have somehow found it romantic that a man would be moved to violence by thoughts of me with another.

But that old Michelle had no dreams of any other life. The new Michelle had seen a few things in the last few months. I gathered the sheets with all of Bax's stuff and carried them to the washing machine. I pressed towels down onto the mattress, threw them in the wash too. As the machine whirred I stood by it just wondering if Bax was truly interested in me or if I was going to be only the latest woman whose heart he broke in his own kind way.

And Randy wanted to come home. It wasn't as though he had ever been mean. He'd always been a lot of fun and he definitely had a sense of humor to go along with his outbursts of juvenile behavior. He had his good points and he wasn't bad in the sack either, but that, of course, had cooled off a lot in the past few years.

Most likely Randy had never sincerely wanted to leave. Most likely he only wanted my mother to leave. When he saw her stuff gone, he was ready to come back. Bax's things put a kink in his new plan.

Bax had a way of affecting my life now, usually positively. When a spot came open for my mother in Asheville, Bax had been such a help with his van and strong arms and patience. He made the move much easier than I had thought it could be.

Now I was in the process of painting and repairing so I could put her house on the market. One more thing Randy hadn't been around to help me handle. Bax had offered his assistance, but I didn't want to take advantage, so I'd hired a crew of local boys to make a few improvements.

I decided to try Randy's mobile number, but I couldn't remember it. I found my purse that I'd dropped to the floor in the kitchen, dug my cell out, and pushed the button for my soon-to-be ex.

The number rang once.

"Michelle?"

"Randy. You son-of-a-bitch."

"Michelle, don't freak out on me now. I'm coming home so we can talk."

"No, you're not. I don't want you to come home. All I want is for you to sign those divorce papers. I'll have my lawyer serve you another set."

"Michelle, just hear me out. I promise I won't waste five minutes of your time if you let me come home and talk to you. Just hear what I've got to say."

"You can't come home to live. You're not welcome here."

"Okay. Fine. But just listen to me anyway."

"Okay. Fine."

"I'll be there in twenty minutes."

While I waited for my husband to arrive I decided I wanted a beer and didn't realize my mistake until I opened the refrigerator.

*Damn him,* I thought.

About fifteen minutes later, after I'd made a bourbon and coke, I sat down on the front porch to wait. Randy didn't disappoint, but came barreling up into the drive, jumped out and was on the porch before I could raise my glass to my lips.

"Michelle, you can't divorce me," he said.

"A little late for that, Randy."

"Look. I know I've been a jerk, but just listen to me. I want to try again. We've been together a long time. I like our life together."

"Really? What about it do you like?"

His sudden bewilderment was humorous. "What?"

"What exactly do you like about our life together?"

"Well, um, let's see . . . I like sleeping with you."

"Sure."

"I don't mean sex. I mean I like sleeping with you and listening to you breathing and I like how your hair spreads out across the pillow and you look like an angel when you sleep."

Now I was bewildered.

"And I like that you're the sort of person who likes to have dinner every night. I grew up that way and that's how you hold a family together, even if the family is only the two of us."

I was really surprised. Who was this man on my porch who had suddenly found two beautiful things to say about our life together? Apparently wonderful things for which his appreciation went unexpressed all our years together.

"What else?" I demanded.

He postured. "Um, okay. I *love* that you know so much about me."

"Apparently there's a lot of stuff about you that I don't know."

"Nothing. You know me inside and out."

I laughed and looked away.

"Who's the guy?" His voice was darker.

I hesitated. I knew he'd ask.

"He's just somebody I met at work."

"Where do you work now? I called Mountaintop and they said you hadn't been there for like five months or something."

"In Asheville at a Christmas store."

"No way. He works at a Christmas store?"

"No."

"I thought you said you met him at work."

"I did."

"Shit. Fine. So what's up? Are you dating or just shacking up?"

"Dating."

I knew it wasn't in my best interest to admit this to him, but he could have easily found out on his own and I wanted to see the expression on his face.

"He stays here?"

"Only a few times."

"Do you love him?"

"That's not the question."

"What is the question?"

"The question is . . . do I love you?"

"Well?"

"Yes. I do."

"I knew it."

"But it's a two-part question."

"What's the second part?"

"Do I love our life together?"

"And you're going to say that you don't love our life together."

"That's right. And your five minutes are up."

I could see the disappointment, and then the anger boil up inside of him. Randy always had a hard time concealing his strong emotions.

"I won't sign those papers until you have a real discussion with me. I want to go to counseling."

That made me laugh again.

"Are you kidding? You abandoned me for nine months. That's solid grounds for divorce no questions asked, really. Just sign the papers."

"Do they say you get the house?"

"You haven't read them?"

"*No. I haven't read them.* What do they say?"

"They say you take your stuff and I take my stuff and the house. We split the money in the savings and our CDs."

"And why should I give you the house?"

"Because you should."

"Okay. Look. Let's go out to dinner and have a talk about this. If you still want a divorce after we go out then I'll sign the papers and you can have the house."

"So you think you can charm me out of divorce in one date? Fine. You're on."

"Good. It's a date then."

"Your five minutes are definitely up."

"I'll pick you up at seven on Friday."

"What if I have plans on Friday?"

"Well? Do you?"

Actually I did usually have a date with Bax on Friday, but he would think nothing of it if I told him I had another obligation.

"I'll change something around," I said. "Pick me up at seven. I don't want to stay out late."

"Okay." Randy walked back to the truck, got in and drove away. He checked me in the rearview when he got to the end of our drive, then turned onto the highway and rumbled out of sight.

# CHAPTER 13

I wondered all week if I should tell Bax about my dinner date with Randy on Friday, but I decided that sharing more of my own personal drama was not how to keep Bax interested. Bax was a low-key sort of guy who liked harmony and adult behavior. I couldn't envision Bax or any member of his family ever losing control, even in matters of the heart.

I must admit that a part of me was still moved by Randy's insistence that he wanted me back. It's not like you can commit more than fifteen years to being with somebody and then suddenly walk away and not have any feelings for that person. It's not like he'd cheated on me or beat me up or spent every last dime we had drinking or gambling. Randy was a decent guy in his own way and he did deserve to have one meal with me where I sat and listened to what had actually driven him out of my life.

He picked me up at seven and I was dressed to please him. I had taken some time getting ready, trying to make myself as attractive as I could without looking as though I were trying. Randy took me to the next little town over to a restaurant that had been built out on the side of an old country store. It had rustic plank flooring and checkered tablecloths topped with candles in wine bottles. It was one of the places rich people vacationing in the mountains liked to go, a place they would call quaint. The restaurant served fabulous country food with some Italian and stir-fry thrown in. They didn't have a liquor license, so you had to bring your own bottle of wine. Randy pulled our bottle from a brown paper bag, a Chianti, which made me smile that he'd made the effort to remember the wine I liked.

Randy had asked that we be seated in a corner with a nice view. I knew he wanted to charm me with this restaurant and his wine selection. Did he think I would buy into this charade, as if this was going to be our new life together? Dates and wine on Friday nights instead of television by myself while he was off boating?

After we had given our order, Randy said, "Look, Michelle, I don't want to beat around the bush. I know I need to apologize to you and I do, with all my heart. I'm sorry for leaving. I'm sorry for hurting you. I'm sorry for being so selfish. Will you accept my apology?"

Anger flared in me. "Just like that? You say you're sorry and then everything's fine?"

"No. I don't expect everything to be fine, but I do want to try to start setting things right."

"And how's that? What's setting things right mean to you? Does that mean you get to come back home?"

"Yes."

"What's the matter? Getting a little tired of sleeping in the dorms with all the other stinky guys?"

He smiled at that. "I've stayed other places too. I've been at Mom and Dad's a while. I've surfed some couches."

So he'd been staying with his parents, driving an hour round-trip from outside of Gatlinburg to work.

"So what? Now that you've had your little vacation from me you're ready to come home?"

"I was ready a long time ago, but I was afraid you wouldn't take me back."

"Or you just realized that my mother has moved out and now that you don't have to help me with her anymore you're ready to resume your old lifestyle."

I hit a nerve with that one. He leaned back in his chair and took a long drink of wine.

"I understand your anger," he finally said. "It was a shitty thing to do."

I didn't answer, but just sat there, staring in turn at him and out the window. Our food came and we spent a while just eating and not talking. That was how we'd spent most of our meals together. Often in restaurants I'd look around at other couples and they would be doing the same thing, concentrating on eating and not even looking at each other, particularly those you could tell had been together a while.

And then there would be the couples to envy, those people who seemed to really be enjoying each other's company, people for whom the meal seemed to be more about the companionship and less about the food. I had always wanted to be one of those women who could share a meal with her man and have it be a way to connect.

But maybe some couples had said everything they had to say. Maybe some men take their comfort in just being together and they don't feel the need to prattle on about things as people do when they are in the beginning stages of a relationship. This had been the most Randy and I had talked to each other over dinner in years, but every time I went out with Bax it was one interesting conversation after another. I wondered if Bax and I were together on a permanent basis if the conversation would ever wane.

We finished our meal without confrontation and polished off the bottle of wine. We didn't order dessert, but agreed that coffee would be good. While we waited for our coffee Randy tried again.

"So, Michelle," he said. "Is there anything that I can do to make this up to you?" He looked so sad. Except for his big blue pleading eyes, he seemed more rugged than before, although I couldn't decide why. Maybe it was just my imagination. Or maybe I was simply seeing him for the first time, just a rough old guy with a really big heart. I was getting used to a little polish in a man. When I was at Bax's house I was treated like a guest, not like I was expected to cook and clean up and do everything. But was Bax a reality for me? Did we even have a chance since his ideal family was so very different than the reality I could provide?

I'd spent a lot of time thinking about Randy and Bax, weighing the pros and cons of each relationship. Each man had definite marks in his pro column, but Randy's negative column was much more complete. But was that fair? If I had spent the last fifteen years or so learning all of Bax's bad habits and dealing with his issues, would his con column be full too? Dating isn't reality. Dating is a farce, with everybody involved playacting what life should be. Seeing somebody new was about creating a perfect world, not one you could really live in each and every day.

And was there even the slightest possibility that Bax and I would be together even a year from now? Our relationship had lasted much longer than I had expected. I knew I wasn't the type of woman his family wanted for him. Although they had done their best to make me feel welcome, I knew they needed someone who could participate in their political discussions and select a good wine that wasn't Chianti. They wanted someone for Bax who could contribute children to the family equation.

Randy and I were cut from the same cloth. Problem was, Randy was willing to continue to be the same person he had always been. He just wanted to pick up where we left off. On the other hand, I wasn't quite sure what I wanted. The pull of the familiar was strong, but I was stronger. It would be easy to step right back into our life. We could go on like nothing had ever happened if I could only let go. But I wouldn't let myself fall back into that morass of mediocrity. There was nothing wrong with our old life; I just wanted something more interesting now.

Still, I loved Randy. I'd never stopped loving him. I knew this as I watched him sip his coffee while he waited for my reply. Was there anything he could do to make this up to me? Only if he could be somebody else.

"Let's talk about this in the truck. I'm ready to go home," I said.

Randy paid the bill and we were almost home before he broke the silence.

"So, what do you think?"

I sighed. "Randy, I think if you moved back in that we'd have some nice make-up sex for a few months. I think you'd go out of your way to make things up to me for a while and then everything would go right back to the way it was before."

"And you were unhappy before?"

"I don't know that unhappy is the right word. Bored is more like it. But I didn't realize at the time that I was bored. I thought I was just lazy somehow, that I didn't have any interest in anything out of the ordinary, but I've found out that's not true. I'm interested in a lot of things."

"Yeah, like what?"

"Oh, I don't know. Art. I like art. I'd never really thought about it before, but there's all sorts of art out there that I never knew existed."

"I noticed you got some new stuff in the house."

Neither one of us said what we were thinking. That he hadn't chosen any of the new artwork to destroy on his last visit. We pulled up my driveway and Randy cut the engine.

"You've changed. I can see that," he said.

"I know."

"I still love you. Don't you love me anymore?"

"Randy, I don't think it's a matter of love. I think it's more about compatibility."

"Compatibility?"

"Right. Like people who enjoy each other's company. People who like spending time together, talking and sharing things and being a couple."

"Is that what you think you have with that other guy? What's his name?"

"It doesn't matter about his name. What does matter is that I'm not the same person anymore. I need more." I got out of the truck and started up my front steps.

"Wait." Randy followed me up. "Wait."

I shook off his touch. "No, Randy. You said if I gave you tonight you'd sign the papers. I did my part. Now do yours." I was suddenly so sad. This was it. My last official time with my husband. I stopped and reached up to touch his face. "It'll be all right, Randy. You'll find somebody else."

"I don't want anybody else," he said and before I could react he had me pressed against our front door. At first I thought he was going to hurt me, then I saw the look in his eyes. He bent to kiss me. I could have fought him, but instead I chose to let him kiss me. At first it was awkward and his lips seemed foreign. I didn't return his kiss, only endured his advances, but then my thoughts drifted to another time, in a steamy truck, our bodies fitted together in a sweaty embrace. I kissed him back. I wanted him to remember this for a long time. To want me more than he had ever wanted me. I was going to pull back and leave him hanging.

I had put my key into the lock. Randy turned the key and walked me backward into our foyer before I realized what was happening. His kisses traveled down my neck to a hollow that made me shiver. He knew all my spots, all the ways to make me give up control. I liked for a man to be in charge and when Randy ran a hand up my thigh and pulled me into him I melted into his embrace.

We never made it to the bedroom. Randy pushed up my skirt and yanked down my panties so fast that I didn't have time to protest. He was in me and he was hard, as hard as he had been in our youth when our attraction was strong. He left me suddenly and the longing was painful, but he was quickly on me with his mouth and then I just let him do what he wanted.

My mind said no, but my body said yes.

I couldn't fight it. I wanted it too.

# CHAPTER 14

Randy left right after our unexpected encounter.

"Think about this," he'd said.

I was surprised when he didn't try to stay the night, but in a turn of reverse psychology I surmised that he was trying the same tactic on me that I had thought to try on him. He was trying to leave me wanting more.

I immediately took a shower and crawled into bed. I had the beginning of a nagging wine headache and the shameful feeling that in the morning I was going to be very sorry I had let it happen.

But the next morning the sun was shining and birds were singing and everything seemed right with the world. I had a date with the guys painting my mother's house and I intended to spend the entire day working out my frustrations by stripping wallpaper from the dining room. I had ideas for the little house, ideas that I'd gathered from my visits to vacation homes, from work, even from Biltmore. I could reinvent my mother's house and make it attractive enough that some rich person would be willing to pay a pretty penny for it.

I was hitting the wall hard, sending showers of old paper and slivers of Sheetrock down into my hair when my cell rang.

Randy. *Damn.*

I let his call go unanswered.

I planned on calling the attorney and having another set of divorce papers served to him on Monday. He had to know that I was serious.

The morning's sunshine suddenly gave way to a cloud bank that settled low over the mountaintops. The painters had not been fooled by the early sunshine and had been painting inside all day in anticipation of the rain.

It came in straight sheets for ten minutes then tapered off to a soft drumming against the copper roof of my mother's house. Its rhythm soothed my mind and my thoughts wandered to Bax and where he was. He'd offered to help, but I had told him that I had plenty of help. He said what about for the company?

Bax wasn't a bored guy, so if he was willing to spend a Saturday afternoon scrubbing wallpaper then he had some serious intentions.

When I heard his footfalls against my mother's maple floors my heart swelled. He walked up behind me and put his hands on my waist and bent into my neck. He stood that way for the longest time and I reached up to place my hand along his face.

"Did you see him?" he asked.

"Yes. How did you know?"

"I suspected as much. It's okay. How'd it turn out?"

"I don't love him."

"Great."

I knew I could tell Bax as little or as much as I wanted about what happened. I decided on conservative disclosure.

The rain was a buffer against too much conversation, and it was more a time to scrape in meditation. I'd watched Bax work often and I was always drawn to his arms, their ropey solid nature made me weak. But his hands were the most amazing parts of him. He could make something beautiful out of anything. He would take the most ordinary piece of metal and shape it into a beautiful, spectacular thing. His endless imagination enthralled me. He scraped with a solid advance and in no time the room was done.

"What now?" he asked.

"The bathroom?"

"Show me the way."

So we spent the afternoon scraping paper, then that night at my house, eating pizza and watching a romantic comedy. There was an ease with Bax that hadn't been there before, a willingness to be totally relaxed. The rain came steadily down for days and we stayed in with no thoughts of time.

Then on the last day Randy knocked on the front door and shot our little piece of heaven all to hell.

# CHAPTER 15

You can't reason with a drunk.

And certainly not a drunk Randy.

He rang the doorbell and waited instead of barging in, so I had no way of knowing in advance that he was wasted. It was Sunday night, not his usual night to drink.

"Is he here?" was the first thing he said as he stepped through the door. Water dripped from him, the brim of his ball hat, the hem of his coat, even his fingertips.

"Randy, don't."

"Is he? Is he here?"

"Don't be a jackass."

"I'll repeat myself. Is. He. Here."

"I'm here," Bax said. "You must be Randy."

Bax walked up to where we stood there for a second. He extended his hand and Randy just looked at it.

"Are you fucking insane, man? You think I'm going to shake your hand?"

"It was worth a try," Bax said.

"Dude, you need to clear out right now. Don't get involved in this thing with Michelle and me. You don't need all that trouble, do you?"

"Looks like we've got different ideas on what should go down here."

"Yeah. So let me tell you what my take on this thing is . . ."

I cut him off. "Randy, stop it. I mean it. Stop it. You're going to make me cry. Go outside. I want to talk to you."

"No. I want to talk to Mr. All Reasonable Man over there."

"At this point there's no way I could leave her alone with you, so you see, no matter what goes down, I'm not leaving this house tonight."

Randy hesitated, looked at his challenger a second too long and I jumped.

"Outside, Randy. Right now."

His swagger had wilted some as he walked to the porch. I could tell he'd reconsidered his options when he saw Bax's size and temperament.

On the porch he turned away from me as though he was ready to cry. I let him pull himself together and when he turned around he was angry again.

"So that's Mr. Perfect in there?"

"He's not perfect. But he is a nice person and he doesn't deserve to be threatened by you."

"God. You're always so logical, so matter of fact about everything it makes me want to puke."

"Well, it looks like you may not be too far from that."

"I'm pissed. This is my house. You're shacking up with some guy in *my* house. How am I supposed to deal with that?"

"You should have thought about that before you decided to abandon me."

He shook his head and water droplets pinged down onto his shoulder. "Didn't Friday night mean nothing to you? Hey!" he yelled toward the front door, which I had closed gently behind me. "Hey, did she tell you she was with me on Friday?"

"He knows."

"Like hell he does. Does he know everything? Does he know how you . . ."

"Randy, stop it. There's one of two ways to do this. Either you get the house or I get the house. I'm exhausted with you, so whatever at this point. Just sign the papers and I'll clear out, okay? I want to move to Asheville anyway."

"Asheville? Since when do you want to move to Asheville?"

"Since I made friends there. Since I got a job there. My mother's even there, so you see, really, there's no reason for you not to have the house. Can we make a fair settlement for it?"

"No! No!" He stomped down the stairs.

"No!" he yelled from the soggy yard.

"Hell no," he said before he got into his truck and gunned the engine.

I wanted to return his voice, to yell, "But you promised!" But what good would it have done?

He drove away and Bax came outside.

"You okay?" he said as he laid a hand on my shoulder. I turned my face into Bax's shoulder and he wrapped me in his arms.

I nodded, choking back tears. I was okay, but Randy's displays, no matter how juvenile, were tugging at my heart. Why else would I have agreed to give him the house? Was I really that desperate to be rid of him or was I beginning to feel a little sorry for him?

# CHAPTER 16

The front doors to Laurel Gardens whispered wide at my arrival. The lobby was filled with downy-haired women in ice-cream-colored blouses and a couple of bald fellows in cardigans. They played cards and a few were enjoying cocktails. Some sat flipping through magazines, while others watched birds gathered at a massive birdhouse outside the bay window. It was practically a commercial for the place. All heads turned in my direction as I walked past.

My mother's apartment was upstairs since she was still mobile. But the staff's assessment of my mother's level of independence fell short of what I had anticipated. While it hurt me to know that my mother was fading more, it had helped in the financial department for her to need care that I couldn't provide. Dr. Johnson had helped and she had qualified for assistance.

I knocked lightly on her door, but heard

no reply.

I pushed the door open and there was my mother's thin frame silhouetted in the window, a hand held poised as if to speak. I watched her for a moment, but her hand never moved.

"Hey, Mom?" I stepped into the room cautiously so I wouldn't startle her.

"Mom?"

She slowly turned her vacant stare to me. A questioning expression made her thin lips quiver before recognition tickled her face. She lowered her hand and stood with both her arms limp at her sides. It took her a moment to find my name.

"Michelle."

"Look, Mom. I brought you some flowers," I said.

"You can't eat flowers."

"I'll just put them in a vase for you. How about that?"

"They're trying to poison me in here."

That made me stop and look at her thin frame. Did she truly believe that they were trying to poison her? Had she stopped eating? I had been so absorbed in my love life and in selling her house that I hadn't been thinking of her.

"Are you hungry?" I asked her.

They wouldn't let her cook for herself.

They had turned off her stove and taken away the microwave.

She turned back to the window and said, "No, dear, I'm not hungry at all. The food in here is really good."

My shoulders fell in relief. She'd been having more frequent moments of slippage. I arranged the flowers and set them in the middle of her small dinette table.

"There," I pronounced, realizing I was speaking to her as if she were a child. "Isn't that pretty?"

Her mind had wandered back to wherever she had been when I came into the room. I settled back against a pillow on the sofa. She was at the window for the longest time, not moving at all. She gave no indication that she even knew I was in the room.

"Mom?" I said, but she didn't respond. "Mom, I've got myself into a bad situation."

No response.

"I'm in love with a guy. A guy who can't love me back. He needs things out of life I can never give him." I sighed and tears burned hot and aching against the inside of my eyes. I hung my head and let them fall.

"And Randy," I continued. "He's coming around again. Telling me he loves me. And I still love him. I do. But I'm not sure that I was ever *in* love with him. He's just such a burden. In some ways. Not in all ways. I mean, he's not bad. But when Bax breaks up with me then I'll be all alone. I've never been alone. I've always had somebody."

No response.

"I mean, the last two weeks with you in here, Mom, it's the first time I've ever lived on my own. I went directly from living with you and Daddy to living with Randy to living with you again. I'm not even sure if I'm capable of being by myself."

I put my face into my hands and openly sobbed.

My mother's soft touch brought me out of my tearful trance.

"Mom."

She sat down beside me on the couch and patted my hand much like she used to do when I was young.

"Are you in love?"

I sniffled and nodded.

"Which one is it?"

"Baxter."

"Does he make you happy?"

I nodded again and tears trickled out.

"Does he love you?"

"I don't know. I think he does, but he hasn't said it. His actions say yes. But maybe we're just too different and he knows it. Maybe he knows it can't work out."

"Why won't it work out?"

"Because he wants a family and his parents want him to have a family and I'm not, well, I'm not as educated or cultured as his people. And . . . and . . ."

"Those are some big things," my mother said and leaned back as if she were thinking the most deep thoughts.

Just when I thought I had lost her again she spoke.

"Are you scared?"

"Yes."

"Of being alone?"

"Yes."

Silence for a while, then she took a deep breath and said, "Pick love."

"What?"

"Safety's an illusion." I looked directly into her worried eyes. "Don't look back when you're a little old lady and say you wished you'd gone after love."

"But what if he doesn't love me? The woman he really loved died in a car accident. How can I ever compete with that?"

"You can't. Don't try."

I put my head in my mother's lap and cried until I was exhausted.

# CHAPTER 17

The new divorce papers that gave Randy the house were ready that next Wednesday and I'd left a message on his phone that I had them and wanted to talk. I didn't want him served by some stranger again and I didn't want to show up unannounced if I could help it. I truly believed he would eventually give in and be reasonable.

"I'll take you," Bax said. "I don't want you going alone."

"I don't think so. It'll only make him mad."

"No. I'll sit in the car if you like, but I'm taking you."

So that was that.

The drive down to the Chattooga in South Carolina was what I imagined heaven must be. Instead of clouds, heaven for me would be mountaintops rolling into the distance, a glimpse of waterfall down a mountainside, forest so dense you couldn't walk through it. But it was always a challenge to enjoy the beauty of the drive when one wrong move could send you off the thin winding road and over a cliff. So I was glad that Bax drove and I could pretend I was enjoying the view when really I was pressing down a big ball of dread in my throat. Instead of taking in the distant mountains, I was trying to wrap my mind around the fact that I was on my way to serve divorce papers to my estranged husband while my new boyfriend waited in his little hybrid car.

We got off the artery road and cut through land with little human influence to an even smaller vein that led down to a wide creek where an outfitting company sprouted. The woods were a fierce green from all the rain, still dripping and muffled in that way that soaked up sound. I knew the river would be running high. Some of the braver boaters would be out today, but the outfitters wouldn't take novices down on such a day. The outfitters' headquarters was surrounded with random dusty vehicles with boat racks. The musty funk of a hundred sour life vests wafted at me as I went into the sparse plank cabin. I was right. No tourists were out today.

"Hey," I said to Joe. I'd known Joe for almost as long as I'd known my husband.

"Shit," he said.

"Where is he?"

"Bull Sluice."

I got back in the car and we pulled silently away. Bax had said he would stay in the car if I wanted him to, but I knew how far away from the car I would have to walk to get to Bull Sluice. That meant if things did go wrong, Bax wouldn't be around to help me. I gave directions when necessary and we didn't speak otherwise. We parked and walked a narrow path through thick forest. At places we climbed down by roots as land fell away. And there he was, standing sentry on the edge of a boulder surveying the new lay of the water. The river was loud, snarling by, spray drifting downstream with the white churn.

I walked all the way up behind Randy. Like magic he sensed me and turned.

"Whoa," he said.

"I called. I told you I was coming." I had to speak loudly.

"I know."

"So, let's go somewhere and talk."

"Man, do you have to do this here?" He looked at a couple of his friends who were crouched down on the boulders trying to act as though they were surveying the water and not watching us.

"Yeah. Apparently I do."

"You brought him?"

"I gave you the house."

"What?"

"The house. You can have it. It's all in here. All you have to do is sign."

"I don't care about the house."

"Randy, don't do this. Just sign the papers and we can get on with it."

He got right in my face and said, "No."

"You're just trying to torture me. Just sign it."

Bax walked up behind me and Randy took a defensive stance.

I would never have expected what happened next. Bax held up his hand in a gesture of peace, but Randy didn't see it that way. So he punched him. Right in the face. Bax was stunned for a second, then he pulled me behind him and stepped up and belted Randy right in the stomach. Fists flew and the next thing I knew Randy was standing staring into the mist and Bax was gone.

"Oh, my God! Oh, my God!" I ran toward the edge. Bax was nowhere. "Randy!" I grabbed him. "Randy, do something!"

Bax bobbed to the frothy water's surface, but his face didn't come up and he was sucked under the water churn again.

"Get him now!" I screamed.

Randy grabbed one of the rescue ropes that were always strewn about on the rocks. He waited, anticipating where and when Bax would boil to the top again.

Bax came up, face up and spewing water.

"Hey!" Randy yelled, but Bax was so disoriented that he failed to connect. He went under again.

"Randy! Do something! You have to save him!"

"He can do it," Randy said calmly.

Bax emerged again and Randy and I shouted his name. Bax's eyes fixed on us and Randy let the rope sail across the river, upriver about five feet and in less than a second the rope had washed into Bax's hands. Randy made a motion of wrapping the rope around his arm and before Bax was sucked under I saw him emulate Randy's movements.

He came up again and the rope was around his arm and Randy, who had already walked downstream, steadily began to pull him out of the water. Down along the bank Randy scrambled until the water petered out into flat swirling eddies forty feet beyond the falls. Randy pulled Bax close to shore and Bax stumbled out, literally quaking with exhaustion and disorientation.

"Damn," he sat down on a log and hung his head.

"Are you okay?" I asked.

"Yeah. Oh, man. I thought I was dead. Wow. Wow. That was a trip," he said. He looked up at Randy. "Thanks, man. I mean it."

"Yeah. Don't mention it," Randy said, but there was no sarcasm in his voice.

I looked at Randy and remembered when he'd saved me after I'd skidded off the snowy road. How he had snatched my mother from death on the highway in front of our house. And now he'd saved Bax.

And he loved me.

He was an all-right kind of guy. It was really too bad that he wasn't going to be my husband after today.

I still had the papers clutched in my hand. I shoved them toward him. He looked at them.

"Just tell me this," Randy said. "Before I sign these I want you to tell me if you love him or not."

I held my breath, hoping that Bax hadn't heard, but I saw he was waiting for the answer as much as Randy.

"Well?" Randy said. "I'm waiting."

I stalled, but I had no choice.

"I do. I love him."

As if he were almost in pain, Randy slowly took the papers from my hand. He laid them on a flat rock, clicked the pen, and signed by the little yellow arrows.

# CHAPTER 18

I gave myself three months to find another place. Randy didn't push me. He didn't even bother to check in to see where I was in the process. I took an inventory of what I wanted from our life together. I didn't particularly want the country kitchen set or a recliner, so I quickly realized I didn't have that much to move. I decided that maybe a condo would be a good thing for me, but the condos in Asheville were pricier than I'd anticipated and I spent months trying to find a place I could afford. Even the real estate agent got frustrated with me. Bax wasn't at all helpful and one night when we were making dinner at his house I asked him if he had any suggestions.

"I mean, you know so much more about Asheville than I do. Don't you have any ideas for me?"

"Yeah," he said popping an olive in his mouth. "I have an idea. Why don't you just move in here with me?"

I could barely force my own food down I was so surprised. I just stared at him.

He went on talking around his olive in a casual way. "I mean, I've been thinking on this and you're having a hard time finding a place and . . . well . . . it's not like I'm intending on seeing anybody else. Are you?"

"No," I choked out around my mouthful of bread.

"So, anyway. What I mean to say is that I would very much like it if you moved in here with me."

He still hadn't told me that he loved me, even after my forced admission at the river that day. And now he was asking me to shack up with him. That was not the order in which I had hoped things would go.

"So," I said. "Are you saying that we're, you know, together?"

He laughed slightly. "We've been seeing each other for nearly a year. I think that's long enough to know."

*To know what? Say it.*

I wondered if I would regret it, but I said, "Okay." I nodded and tried to sound as casual as he had.

"So you'll move in with me?"

"Sure. Why not? I mean, if it doesn't work out then I can just keep on looking."

"Why wouldn't it work out?" He looked perturbed.

"Oh, I don't know. I'm just saying. It'll be a big transition for you is all. You're so used to being by yourself."

"I don't like being by myself. I never have."

So I moved into Bax's perfect home, knowing that nothing I had would make an improvement. I would only be dragging my imperfections in, showing how much less taste and style I had than he did. I knew it was dangerous, showing myself to him in a way where I could no longer mask my flaws and bad habits. I also knew that I might be ruining a perfect romance for myself as well. Maybe I wouldn't be so enamored of him if I was with him all the time. If I heard him in the bathroom in the mornings clearing his head and I smelled his dirty laundry. But I figured this was as close as I could ever expect to get to Baxter Brown. He and I both knew that I wasn't marrying material for him. I wasn't naive. I knew the day would come when I'd be on the condo search again, but until then, I could enjoy sharing his life.

So it was August when I finally got all my things moved in and set up the way I wanted. I had been careful not to bring too much, not to impose too quickly. But Bax had cleared out shelves and the medicine cabinet and linen closet. The house was so large that my things seemed to be absorbed and they didn't stand out at all in the eclectic nature of his home.

Bax kept his clothes neatly aligned and evenly spaced in his walk-in closet. He moved his clothes all to one side and gave me the other side. We got into the habit of standing in the closet talking as we picked out what we were going to wear. We were getting ready to go to the Southern High-lands Artists Guild opening night gala when Bax reached over and pulled my black wrap dress from a hanger.

"Wear this," he said. "I've always liked that dress and you never wear it."

"Oh sure," I said, happy for the attention.

Later at the show, Bax stood beside me as the director and curator read the winners. There were a number of purchase awards, which Bax explained to me meant that companies or collectors agreed in advance to pay a certain amount, say ten thousand dollars, for a piece of art from the show. After viewing the entire exhibition, these folks then selected a piece for their collection and the artist received the sale and a purchase prize ribbon.

Then there were the top awards for excellence and the last and most prestigious award was Best in Show. Bax didn't seem all that surprised when his name was called for the top award. He stepped forward and received his check and ribbon and was informed that a large bank in town had purchased his wall sculpture for their lobby, so he received a purchase prize too. Overall, it was a spectacular night for him.

We milled around the crowd for a while, many people congratulating Bax and slapping him on the back. He was his usual affable public self, the compliments rolling off of him without effect.

"Let's get out of here," he said and pulled me toward the exit.

We rode silently through the streets of downtown Asheville and then east up the mountain. I gasped as we turned in at a sign that read GROVE PARK INN.

"Oh, are we going to Grove Park?"

"I made us dinner reservations."

"Really? Oh, I've always wanted to go here. Did you know that F. Scott Fitzgerald lived here?"

"Seems I remember hearing that."

"He was apparently not the best boarder. Sort of a lush was what I read."

Grove Park Inn rose against the blue

mountains. The main building's exterior was a mottled patchwork of large random granite stones. The entrance was surrounded by wide columns of the same smooth stones that gave the main building its rustic, irregular look. Bax told me that the Grove Park Inn was nearing its one-hundredth year.

"I love it here. You know how much I admire the Arts and Crafts style," he said.

We stepped into the expansive lobby, a mountain lodge, but the furthest thing from rustic. Enormous granite fireplaces flanked the Great Hall and fires blazed even though it was the end of summer. Comfortable overstuffed chairs and leather sofas were grouped for conversation. Through the Great Hall we walked out to the Sunset Terrace where rocking chairs looked west upon the sunset and Asheville's glimmering skyline was tucked between the Blue Ridge and Smoky mountain ranges.

"We have reservations in the Sunset Terrace Restaurant," Bax said. Inside, each white tablecloth was topped with silver candleholders and more utensils than I had ever had to figure out before. Bax laughed when he saw my expression.

The maître 'd eased my chair up behind me, then unfolded my napkin and placed it on my lap. Our water glasses were filled by a waiter and the sommelier came around to ask if we would be having wine with our meal.

"Can I order?" Bax asked.

I nodded and he made a selection from the wine list. The sommelier said, "Very good, sir," then zipped away.

The pianist in the corner played "Moonlight Sonata," its sonorous sounds clearly recognizable in the quiet dining room. Other diners leaned forward around their own candle glow, whispering to each other, smiling, sipping wine.

"The view is just spectacular," I said as the last of the day's color faded from the sky. I glanced back at Bax and he was staring at me in such an odd way that I blushed. The sommelier returned with a waiter trailing behind carrying a silver bucket on a stand. The sommelier presented the wine. Bax read the label and nodded.

I was startled when the bottle popped. The sommelier told us a little about the wine, relaying that it was indeed a champagne, from the Champagne region of France.

"Thank you, but I'll pour," Bax said.

"Very good, sir," the sommelier said and backed away.

Bax said to me, "It's one of my favorites."

The wine bubbled to the tops of our glasses and came precariously close to running over. When the bubbles had settled, Bax filled them again and this time he raised his glass and said, "A toast."

I raised my glass.

"To new beginnings," he said.

I smiled. "What a wonderful thought. To new beginnings."

We clinked our glasses and drank. The champagne tickled my nose with its fizzy sweetness.

"Now," Bax said and reached into his pocket. He pulled out a small box wrapped in golden foil. A delicate red ribbon bound the cube. I couldn't help but let out a little gasp. This was the first real present Bax had given me.

"Go on. Open it," he said.

I gingerly unwrapped the red ribbon and removed the gold foil. Inside was a sturdy black box and inside that box was a black velvet jewelry box. I lifted the lid and gasped a second time.

Inside was the most wonderful gold ring I had ever seen. Six medium-size diamonds sprinkled around a hammered dome that wrapped into a ring. It was sculpture for your finger.

"Oh, my God. This is beautiful. Did you

make this?"

He smiled. "It was one of the hardest things I've ever made. Your finger is so small."

I wanted to slide the ring onto my hand, but I hesitated. What did this mean? If I put it on my ring finger then I would be assuming that he was proposing. Was he?

"Here, let me," he said and I sighed with relief.

He took the ring out and held it up. "I hope it fits," he said and took my left hand in his.

"Michelle," he said, his firey hazel eyes searching inside me. "Will you do me the honor of being my wife?"

I didn't know how to respond. I had never allowed myself the opportunity even to consider this option.

"Bax," I whispered. "Oh, Bax. Are you sure?"

He laughed. "Of course I'm sure. I love you. I don't ever want to be without you."

I couldn't believe it.

"So, what do you say?" He held the ring poised to slide onto my finger.

"I say yes! Yes! Of course, I'll marry you!"

He slid the ring on. A perfect fit.

The restaurant broke into applause and I dabbed at my eyes, my mascara smearing on the pristine linen napkin.

He grinned that sly Baxter grin as I tried to contain my happiness. Everyone in the restaurant was watching us and finally, when Bax could see that I was overcome by emotion he stood and gathered me in his arms and we walked out onto the terrace until I could get myself under control.

"If you liked this just wait until tonight," he said.

"What? Don't tell me you have another surprise. I don't think I can take any more surprises."

"I booked us a room. Just for tonight. You'll love it."

Feeling calmer and a little playful I quipped, "Well, you were pretty sure of yourself. What if I'd said no? Then you'd be stuck staying in that expensive room all by yourself."

"Oh, I don't know," he said. "I had a pretty good idea how things would turn out."

# Chapter 19

As the limousine threaded its way through the countryside, my heart ached with the sweetest longing. I had found a true love, not one that was convenient, not one that happened to be easy, but one that was chosen and one that was hard. We were different in so many ways, but we were both wounded. He had lost his first love. I had never had a child to love. He'd spent years lonely. I'd spent years in the wrong relationship.

My driver pulled up to the guard at the gate and we were allowed to enter. Across the expansive lawn, Biltmore burned with holiday lights. Christmas trees winked from the long windows, giant wreaths were heavy on the doors, poinsettias burst from the urns fronting the entrance. The car glided to a stop at the Grand Entrance and the driver came around to open my door. I touched my mother's hand.

"Mom, are you ready?"

She nodded.

A slight smile touched her lips as she took in the spectacular site.

"You go first," I said and gently helped my mother step out to the driver. The driver handed her on to Bax's father and they started up the steps. Miriam fluttered down the stairs in her silver bridesmaid's dress with the wide red sash.

She climbed into the limo beside me. "You look beautiful. Let's give your mother a chance to get in there and get seated and then we'll go in."

She held my hand in anticipation as we waited for the call.

Her mobile beeped and I heard one of Bax's brothers. "We're all ready," the tiny voice said.

Miriam clicked her phone and chirped, "Okay. We're coming in."

She turned to me with pink cheeks, her eyes so wide she seemed like the one getting married. She had organized the entire event and was determined to see it went off smoothly. "Ready?" she asked.

I nodded. "I'm ready."

A crowd had gathered at the front entrance and a smattering of applause met me when I emerged from the limousine. As I ascended the stairs, I heard a woman exclaim, "What a beautiful dress!"

I hadn't wanted the traditional white, flowing gown. After all, I had been married before. But Bax had insisted that I find a dress that made me feel like a princess. Miriam had scoured local stores, shopped online, and culled through a hundred magazines to find the perfect dress. And she had.

My gown was pale golden raw silk with seed pearls sprinkled along its sweetheart neckline. It had an empire waist and fell straight with just enough material to make a short train that trailed behind me. Miriam had pulled my unruly hair into a loose bun and attached white roses and strands of pearls. My bouquet of white roses and greenery cascaded to my knees. Miriam and I looked like Christmas decorations in our gold and silver dresses.

I glided into the Grand Entrance Hall and walked past the Winter Garden. My heels made a delightful click-click on the marble floor and the few visitors left on this holiday tour night stopped to watch me. I made a left at the Tapestry Gallery and walked along the archways that lead out to the dark loggia beyond. A night wedding had been Bax's idea and I had loved it. The doors to the library were closed, the only time I had ever seen them this way. There was a stanchion swagged with red velvet ropes outside and a gilded sign that read TEMPORARILY CLOSED FOR PRIVATE FUNCTION.

Miriam clicked her phone again and said, "We're here." Behind the door I heard a shuffling. A violin and cello began.

Miriam turned to me and held my hands. "You're my sister now."

"Thank you," I said and leaned to kiss her lightly on the cheek. "For everything."

She smiled and I saw her push back tears. She turned in front of me, straightened her shoulders and opened the heavy wooden doors wide. She turned to wink at me and then she step-paused, step-paused away.

I was there by myself only moments, but it truly seemed like hours. My mind went in a dozen directions all at once and then I knew I had to move. I hesitated. I could stand there a moment. Be unmarried for a minute more. And I did.

And then I went into that library of ten thousand beautiful books. Bax stood waiting in a black tux, an expectant smile across his handsome face. And that day, in front of a blazing Christmas tree, in a mansion in the hills of North Carolina, I married the love of my life.

And that, my friend, is extraordinary.

■ ■ ■ ■

# MIRACLE ON
# MAIN STREET

# ROSALIND NOONAN

■ ■ ■ ■

For Mike,
one of the good guys.
Truly the Finest.

# CHAPTER 1

"Snow." The white stuff starts coming down as Officer Joe Cody turns onto Main Street. It floats in the air like confetti, skittering over the hood of the patrol car. "I'd love to know what genius decided snow was festive."

"Looks like we might have a white Christmas." His partner, a baby-faced black cop so tall he seems to be folded into the vehicle, opens his window and stretches his right hand out to catch some flakes. "You can take the kids sledding, Cody. Snow angels and snowmen. All that winter wonderland stuff."

"Let's hope not. Snow snarls traffic. Screws up street parking and throws a wrench in everybody's plans." Joe shakes his head, his dark gaze never leaving the road. It's the day before Christmas and downtown Flushing, New York, is full of pedestrians, packed with cars, yellow cabs, and buses. Colored lights blink in store-fronts and giant snowflakes hang over the center of the street, neon white etched in the pearl gray sky. The streets are a swarm of vendors' carts and people, mostly shoppers and commuters streaming toward the subway station. Women with strollers and teens glad to be out of school. Joe scowls at the open window. "Would you close that? We'll be out in it soon enough."

"Sorry, Mr. Scrooge," Mack says in a fake British accent. "It's just that . . . tomorrow's Christmas and I'd really like another lump of coal for the furnace."

Mack always does that; cracks Joe up just as his temper's rising. It's one reason Joe chose to work with the rookie cop. Maurice Womack, Mack to anyone on the job, is an observant cop, but he doesn't take much seriously. And Joe knows you can't survive in this job without a sense of humor.

"Shut up." Joe fights back a grin as he inches the car down Main Street.

"Come on, now. Shake off that mood. It's Christmas Eve, Cody. You gonna be a buzz-kill straight through 'till New Year's?"

"That's the plan. When you're strapped to the nuts with bills, Christmas is a non-issue."

"Don't you 'bah, humbug' me. You got

two little kids at home who are counting on Santa Claus to deliver."

Joe pulls the car onto the sidewalk, a half-assed parking job, but that's the beauty of driving an NYPD vehicle. "We're making your stop, picking up the ring and all, so keep the theatrics to a minimum."

"God bless you, Ebenezer."

"And we're spending Christmas together?" Joe cuts the engine and swings out of the car. "How'd I get so lucky."

"Just the day tour, man. My nights are reserved for Nayasia." Mack hands him the radio and leads the way toward the jewelry store, his giant strides eating up the speckled sidewalk.

"Right. The bride-to-be." Joe straightens his jacket and forces a smile as they pass by two girls clinging to Grandma's hands — twins, from the look of them. "You sure you're ready for this? It's a big commitment."

"What's that mean?" Mack asks without breaking stride. "Don't treat me like I'm eight years old and sleeping in Batman Underoos."

Joe holds up his hands. "You said it, not me."

"Besides, commitment isn't the 'C' word it used to be. Astute men like myself know that the evolved human creature seeks a monogamous mate."

"Monogamous? I'm proud of you Mack. Some of that college rubbed off."

"Don't go changing the subject. I'm ready for this, Cody. Besides, I never hear you complain about it."

"Yeah, well, marriage suits me just fine. Got myself a great girl, beautiful smart kids. Life is good."

"Really? Then why are you so cranky lately?"

Joe winces. "I'm not cranky; just honest." It's a bald-faced lie and he knows it, but that doesn't mean he's got to spill the details to Mack. Really. Mack may be his partner, but if the two of them get any more personal, they'll have to take their story to one of those touchy-feely talk shows like *Oprah* or *Ellen.*

"You're in denial, man." Mack stabs a finger in the air, nearly poking a woman swinging through the door of Macy's. "Sorry, ma'am."

"Whatevah." She shifts her packages and darts around them.

Mack turns back to Joe. "I don't know what's eating at you, but you'd better deal with it and move on so you can enjoy some eggnog with Mrs. Claus under the tree. You know what I'm saying? You got to step up to Christmas or else you'll open your eyes tonight and find three ghouls coming at you with flashbacks and predictions that'll scare the bejeevers out of you."

"The only thing waking me up in the middle of my night is my son cutting a tooth." Joe stretches his neck, trying to get the kink out. "In fact, PJ was up again last night, two A.M."

"Poor kid."

"Poor me. I took the shift."

"Whatever, big daddy. See, that's the kind of thing I'm looking forward to. A house and a family. I'm getting a dog, too."

"Good luck with that. Sheila and I have enough trouble trying to get the kids house-broken." Joe spots the jewelry store just beyond Macy's. Thank God. "Does Nayasia know she's getting a ring?"

"It's a surprise, but I do know she wants a marquise-cut stone. She's told me enough times."

Joe touches his chin, reminded that he doesn't have a gift for his wife. Christmas Eve and he's got nothing. Sucked so dry by a mortgage that he can't scrape together a few extra dollars. You try to do the right thing, work overtime, and put a roof over the kids' heads, and still there's nothing left at the end of the day.

Mack tugs open the jeweler's door. "You coming in?"

"This is one job you need to do on your own. Besides, if I see the prices in there I might lapse into a coma or something."

Cocking one eyebrow, Mack ducks inside. Big, sentimental lug. Joe doesn't know Nayasia well, but he figures her for a lucky woman.

The dispatcher calls for a unit in Sector Adam to assist an ambulance. Joe turns the volume down on the radio and moves back toward Macy's. In front of the store he presses his back to the wall to keep an eye on the street activity. This is a good spot to soak it all up: the colors, the energy, the twinkle of Christmas. A lacy carol piped over the store's PA system mixes with staccato horns and groaning city buses. Yeah, the city makes an effort at Christmastime. Plenty of sparkle and even the surliest New Yorkers soften a bit.

But this year all reminders of the holidays are like a punch in the gut.

It's the mortgage. An albatross. Noose around his neck.

These days, money is a hot button issue between Sheila and him. Yeah, they both wanted to live in Bayside, a good neighborhood, excellent schools and all that. They bought the house this year, plunked all their savings into the skinny row house with a stone age kitchen and a driveway as a front yard. Now they are saddled with a mortgage payment that has them eating Ramen noodles.

No dinners out. No sitters. No cable. No fun. Sheila's talking about serving potato soup for Christmas dinner.

"We'll get by," Sheila always says. And then she goes and puts something on a card.

It didn't take long to max out the Visa. They were well on their way to hitting the limit on American Express when Joe called Sheila off. "If we keep spending like this, we'll never bail ourselves out," he told her.

So she agreed to give up her card. No more credit. Clothes and gifts and such would come from cash leftover after the bills were paid.

Which isn't much. Certainly not enough for the two of them to exchange gifts this year. Last time he checked, there was a twenty and a few singles in the cookie jar. So they came up with a no-gift policy between the two of them, but knowing his wife, he doesn't trust her.

He glances to the display window on his right. Three mannequins posed in a snow scene draped with fat gold ribbon. The dummy in the center wears a quilted red jacket. A thick jacket, tapered at the waist.

It's the perfect gift.

Sheila needs a jacket. How many times has he told her that, and she just shrugs it off. "I'll just be out for a second," she says. Or "I'll get by without it." And then she loads on a sweater and scarf and goes pushing PJ's stroller to the pharmacy or walking Katie to school, out there in the freezing cold.

She would love that red quilted one. Joe knows that, even though he's no shopper. Red goes well with her whiskey brown eyes and dark hair, brings out the pink in her cheeks. And that's the shame of it. He finally finds the perfect gift, something she would love and use, and he doesn't have the money to buy it.

He sets his jaw and turns away from the window display. He could work all the overtime in the world and still be broke. The store's music is nauseatingly cheerful; cherubic voices singing, "Angels we have heard on high, sweetly singing o'er the plains . . ."

Mack emerges from the jewelry store with a blue velvet box and a huge grin. "I got it."

"Great. Can we go now?"

"Wait. Aren't you going to ask me how it looks?"

"It's a diamond ring. How the hell is it supposed to look?" Joe motions Mack toward the car. "Come on, Mack. Next you'll be wanting me to try it on."

"Would you mind?"

Joe scowls. "Get the hell out of here."

"You are in one foul mood, my friend. Least you could do is be happy for me."

"I'm ecstatic. I'm just really good at hiding my emotions."

As they pass Macy's, Mack sings along with the Christmas song, a long extension of o's that ultimately forms the word "Gloria."

"Please," Joe says under his breath, "you're embarrassing yourself."

But Mack keeps singing. *"In excelsis Deo . . ."*

People are looking now, heads snapping toward the big black singing cop. Joe does not make eye contact with them; this is the sort of spectacle he can do without. "Cut it out."

Mack sighs as they venture out of range of the music. "I never did understand that song. Who's Gloria, and what does she have to do with the birth of Jesus?"

"Gloria's not a person. It's Latin for . . .

something." In eight years of Catholic school Joe learned the basics about the Nativity story, but Latin was beyond him.

Fortunately the crackle of the radio interrupts: "Nine-Charlie?"

Joe pulls the radio from his belt and clicks to speak. "This is Nine-Charlie."

"Nine-Charlie, respond to a ten twenty-one. Past burglary at the Shuka Market." The dispatcher gives the address and a call-back number. Joe knows the small grocery store just a dozen blocks away. A middle-eastern market.

Immediately Mack stops humming, the goofball expression fading from his eyes.

It's not a crime-in-progress; no need to rush. Still, you never know what you're going to find out there. Anticipation thrums in Joe's chest as they approach their patrol car.

"You ready to roll?" Mack asks.

Joe opens the cruiser door. "As ready as I'll ever be."

# CHAPTER 2

Working her way through a display of miniature sweaters that would be oh-so-cute but oh-so-impractical for PJ, Sheila Cody presses her lips together and tries to get a grip. She must restrain herself. Keep the urges at bay. Ignore the AmEx card in her jeans' pocket, the slender, shiny plastic that would be the easy answer to this shopping dilemma.

What can she get for the kids with twenty-three dollars and seventy-five cents? That's all the cash she has left to buy Christmas gifts. Damn.

The traditional Christmas Eve shopping trip with her sister is turning out to be a bust this year. There's Jennifer a few aisles away, toting around half a dozen bags of gifts and still looking to acquire more, while Sheila has politely declined every suggestion of a purchase. Jen must realize something is wrong, but since it's Christmas she doesn't want to approach a sensitive subject with Sheila. As in, why don't you get a job, Sheila? As in, why didn't you and Joe stay in that rattrap apartment instead of pouring all your money into a house?

Moving on from the little sweaters, Sheila pauses at an elaborate toy train set up in the children's department to entertain children. At this early hour there's only one sleepy preschooler running a caboose over the track while his older sister, a teen in a St. Francis Prep sweatshirt, looks on.

"Cool train," Sheila says, more to herself.

The little boy looks up at her, then back at the track as Sheila takes it all in . . . the elaborate train station. The bridge over the lake. The miniature trees and cars and houses. PJ will love this.

Well, he *would,* but he's not getting it.

Way too expensive, and besides, this set isn't for sale, though she's sure they carry it upstairs in the toy department.

Toys. She swallows over the knot in her throat. She knows her son; if there could be only one toy under the Christmas tree, it would be a toy police car, a "peeze car," as he calls it, just like Daddy's. She reaches for her back pocket; feels the hard corners of the card. The toy department upstairs would have something like that.

She turns away, takes a deep breath. No. She promised Joe. She promised herself.

There are ten gifts for the kids to unwrap under the tree. Granted, it's all crap from the Dollar Store, things like a statue of a skating bear, a bubble necklace, and a dry erase board for Katie. A ball, a foam sword, and some tub toys for PJ. It's the sort of junk she won't let them buy because it clutters the house, but faced with the prospect of a Christmas without toys, well, she went for the junk.

She lets her breath out. Okay. It's going to be fine. The kids are getting junk for Christmas, but it will be their junk. Junk that won't send Joe and her to bankruptcy court. Besides, Christmas is about more than toys and merchandise, and they might as well get that across to the kids now. They'll certainly see that when they notice there are no gifts under the tree for Mommy and Daddy. Sheila and Joe have agreed not to exchange gifts, though Sheila still feels guilty about that. Nothing for her Joe, and he works so hard all year, snapping up overtime at work and being a father to the kids whenever he's home, getting down on the floor with PJ or helping Katie with her homework.

A surge of emotion threatens to make her

all misty-eyed. Her Joe is a good guy. Well, she'll just have to show him how much she loves him in a different way. Something more . . . personal.

With new resolve she turns from the train set and heads back to the men's department, where she left her sister browsing. She skirts around a display of men's cologne — man perfume, Joe calls it — and finds Jennifer trying on a silly stocking cap from an outerwear rack.

"Isn't this great?" Holding the braids of the cap, Jen kicks out her feet and bobs back and forth, an offbeat clog dance that makes her look like a scarecrow. Thin, tall, and blond, Jen is the polar opposite of her petite, brunette sister. At times Sheila gets peeved that Jen can eat anything and not gain weight while she has to be careful, though Joe says he's always had a weakness for more "shapely" girls.

"Cute," Sheila agrees, "but it's not you. It doesn't go too well with your briefcase and cashmere coat."

"I'm not that nerdy." Jen flicks a braid toward her. "But I was thinking of it for Ian. Lots of students at Juilliard wear these hats. It's the new big thing. I see them all over campus." Jen works in the admissions office at Juilliard, a great job, except that she regrets leaving her three-year-old at day care five days a week.

"Okay." Sheila picks up a blue and gray knit cap. It is beautifully crafted, but a little dopey, a braid dangling from each earflap and a pom-pom on the top. "But Ian is three. Has this style hit preschool yet?"

"Don't be silly. Ian isn't a fashion-follower."

"I hope not. At three you should have the freedom to buck the OshKosh B'Gosh pressure."

Jen snatches a pink hat from the stack and plunks it on Sheila's head. "Oh, it's priceless. Don't you love it? It'd be so adorable on Katie, don't you think? And see how warm it is? You can get one for PJ! The kid won't get an ear infection with a hat like this on his head."

"I don't know . . ."

"Come on, Sheila. We've been here since the doors opened at seven and you've found something wrong with everything I find."

"It's not really a necessity, and I told you, Joe and I agreed to buy just the bare necessities this Christmas."

"Oh my gosh, since when is a hat nonessential? Our kids need these. Think about it, Sheila. You're going to let Katie go out in the snow without a hat? She walks to school, right? You know how the wind whistles down Fifty-third Avenue in the winter."

Sheila can see it: her little Katie tromping through a snowdrift, her downy hair tossed by the wind. Her little ears beet red from cold.

And PJ. Are his chronic ear infections brought on because he doesn't own a warm hat like this? Of course he has hats, but none of them handmade in — she checks the label — Ireland, no less. Her Irish grandmother will be so proud, but . . .

Her gaze lights on the price tag. Fifty. Fifty dollars?

She can't afford it, even though a good, responsible parent would buy these hats for her children.

But Sheila can't. She's a failure as a mother. A stay-at-home mom who can't pull together the cash for a roast for Christmas dinner or knit caps to keep her own children warm.

Tears sting her eyes, tears of disappointment and shame. She pulls the pink hat off and turns away before her sister can catch her crying.

"Sheila?" When she doesn't answer, Jen continues. "What's wrong?"

"We can't afford it." Her voice is tight, strained, and she can't face her sister. "We have a budget."

"Forget about the budget; it's Christmas."

"I can't." A sob steals Sheila's breath away. "Everyone isn't loaded like you." It's rotten to snap at Jen like that, but Sheila can't help it.

A moment later she feels a hand on her arm; her sister is turning her around. One look at Jen's face makes Sheila burst into tears, full force.

"Oh, honey . . ." Jen pulls her into her arms.

"I'm a terrible mother," Sheila sobs. "I can't afford to take care of my own kids."

"You take great care of them." Jen's voice sounds fragile, like a thin panel of glass. "I'm the bad mother, spending so much time away from Ian. I love my job but . . . maybe you can't have it all. He hates me working."

"How do you know? He's three, Jen."

"But he's sending me a clear message. Every morning when I drop him off at day care he crawls under the teacher's desk and yells for me not to leave him. Every morning. And it tears my heart out, but I button my coat and go. I just leave him there. Every day." Her voice quavers. "I'm a terrible mother."

"Me, too," Sheila sobs.

And for a moment their sobs turn to laughter, then back to sobs as the two sisters hug each other and hold on tight in the men's department of the crowded store. Two not-so-terrible mothers having a sister moment.

# CHAPTER 3

Despite the reported robbery, it's business as usual inside the Shuka, the small grocery store a few blocks from Main Street, Flushing. There is something distantly familiar and comforting to Joe about this market, something about the smell or the language spoken by the two cashiers who exchange words before one disappears to find the store's owner in the back.

"Smells good in here," Mack comments, glancing at his watch. "After this, we need to grab some breakfast. I'm starved."

"You're always hungry," Joe says. It isn't even nine A.M. and Mack wants to go on meal? Then again, something in here is making his mouth water.

Joe spots the small meat section of the market, the huge rack of meat turning against the wall of flames. Gyro. That must be it, the savory, tangy smell. His grandfather used to take him to a Greek restaurant in Astoria. World's best gyros, Grandpa said. His eyes scan the aisles of specialty groceries. Shiny mandarin oranges. Plump, sweating grapes. Sticky figs and dates. A glass case with bowls of smooth hummus and baba ghanoush, fat olives, wedges and wheels of cheese. A pastry section, where flaky triangles of honeyed baklava glisten.

"Greek food?" Joe asks the clerk, an older woman with fiery red hair and gems sewn into the neckline of her black sweater.

She shrugs. "Greek, middle-eastern. Mr. Boghosian is Armenian." Boghosian is the owner, the complainant.

"Do you know anything about the robbery?" Mack asks her.

"Only what Mr. B. says. At the end of the day, he is the only one who handles the cash. Puts it in the safe or to the bank."

"And how long you been working here, sweetheart?" Joe asks.

"Eleven years. His wife hired me back in the day, but she passed a few years ago. There's another gal who's been here longer, Lizzy, but she's not here today. She's at home baking for her family. Quite a baker. Lizzy does all the baking for the Shuka." As the woman recounts her employment history at the Shuka, Joe can't help but wonder what that shade of hair color is called. Fire ant? Flaming carrot? It sure is bright.

They are interrupted by a graying man who shuffles over as if he cannot straighten under the huge burden on his shoulders.

"Officers." He nods. "Garo Boghosian." Despite the reading glasses tipped low on his nose, the man doesn't seem so old when Joe catches his gaze. Forty, maybe fifty. One of those guys who has aged beyond his years. "Will you come with me, please?"

Joe and Mack follow him to the office, which is really just a desk and some files across from a kitchen area in the room behind the store. The wide butcher block counter and stoves probably hail from the sixties, but they are clean, "spic and span" as Joe's mother likes to say. The desk is cluttered with papers, circulars, and invoices that curl under the light of a desk lamp.

"This is what I have to show you." Mr. B. pulls the chair away from the desk, revealing a small safe tucked into the knee area. "When I left last night, it was locked up with more than fourteen hundred dollars inside. Receipts, too. As well as some private papers, my passport and such. When I returned this morning, the money was gone. Everything else is here, but the cash, the whole bundle of it, has been stolen."

Mr. B. backs away as Mack squats down

beside the desk and shines his flashlight into the kneehole. "No visible scratches. No sign of forced entry. And you say they left credit card receipts?"

"They did." Mr. B. nods. "He just went for the cash."

"He? You sound sure that the thief is male. Any chance it could have been one of those ladies outside? Someone on your payroll, maybe in need of a little extra cash for the holidays?"

"Those girls?" The scowl on the old man's face is a road map of discontent. "Impossible. For years they've worked for me, never took a penny. Not one cent. Ruth and Maro are like family." The words seem to drain him of air, and he opens his mouth with a stab of pain. "No, they are better than family. More loyal."

"I'm no forensic expert —" Mack straightens, rubbing his jaw thoughtfully — "but I got to say, this looks like an inside job, sir. No sign of force here, and though we haven't checked yet, I'm willing to bet no one messed with your locks or the gates in the front."

"Of course, it is an inside job." Boghosian pulls the lone chair against the wall, and then sinks onto it. "My son. My own son."

Joe shoots a look at Mack, who nods.

Here's where things get awkward, Joe thinks. Take off the cop hat, roll out the shrink's couch.

"Mr. Boghosian." Joe makes his stance wider and evens out the weight; chances are he'll be here a while. "Are you telling us you think you were robbed by your son?"

"*Ayo,* yes. He is the only one with the combination. The only one with a set of keys. My son Armand. Yes." He leans his face into his wide palms.

"Did you talk to him?" Mack hooks his thumbs into his gun belt as though this is all a casual conversation. "Ask him about it. Maybe he's planning to pay you back."

"Please." The older man sighs. "Don't patronize. We both know that a person looking for a loan does not steal money from a safe in the dead of night."

The guy's right. Joe nods at his partner; Counseling 101.

"Okay." Mack adjusts quickly. "So you two aren't talking? Did you have a fight or something?" When Boghosian doesn't answer, he adds, "Did he come to you and ask for the money, and you said no?" Silence. "Help me out here, Mr. Boghosian."

"Let me ask you this, officers." When he lifts his face, the gray ash of age has given way to lucid passion. "What is a father to do for a nineteen-year-old boy who wants to be a good-for-nothing bum instead of taking up the family business? Says he's going to be a musician. Going to Juilliard. A music sensation, playing his saxophone. That's what he says, but it's all a ruse. The truth is he's a bum mooching off his girlfriend. He shuns his father, sleeps all day, then spends his nights in bars and nightclubs."

Mr. B. points toward the store, where the scanner beeps, monitoring purchases. "And this store? This Shuka which I built with my own hands and blessings from God? This is where he should be, learning the family business. A good Armenian boy respects his father. A good son would be here, learning the business."

Joe nods as the big picture comes into focus. He doesn't let on that he's heard this all before, which he has. He thinks of his own son; can't imagine losing track of PJ this way. Right now it's hard to imagine his two-year-old just waking up with a dry diaper. But he can't help Mr. B. get his son back. Right now he can't do anything for this man but listen.

"He's nineteen?" Mack rubs his chin. "Law says he's old enough to be on his own. But he can't go on stealing your money. I recommend you change the combination of your safe. Change the backdoor locks. Don't give him the opportunity to do it again."

"Protect yourself," Joe adds. "That's the first thing you gotta do, Mr. B. We'll take a report, send it up to the detectives, but since there's no sign of breaking and entering . . . I gotta be honest; it won't go anywhere."

"No, no. That's not right." Mr. B. waves at Joe to stop. "You must arrest him. I will give you the address where you can find him, his girlfriend's apartment, and you must drive over there and apprehend him." He smacks one hand against the other's wrist. "Put the handcuffs on him. Take him to jail. That and only that might set him right."

"We can't do that, Mr. B." Mack is shaking his head. "We can't arrest your son unless he's formally charged."

"You don't have to arrest him." The older man leans over the desk to write the address, the strokes of his hand sure and polished. "Simply pick him up and toss him into your jail for a few hours. A few hours is all I ask. Believe me, this is the only way to get through to him. This will give him the message that what he is doing is wrong." He offers the scrap of paper to Joe. "This is where his girlfriend lives."

Not to be rude, Joe takes the address and slips it into the pocket of his uniform trousers. "Can't do it, Mr. B." His voice is apologetic. He can understand this man's frustration. "We can't lock people up that way."

"Ah, but what if you find him with illegal drugs when you go to arrest him? That you can be assured of."

"He's an addict?" Mack asks.

*Bingo.* Joe feels his gut sink. Somehow he knew they were headed that way.

"Narcotics." Mr. B. squeezes his eyes shut. "He acts like it's his own discovery, but it's opium. We had it back in my country. Poppy plants. They turn the brain to jelly."

"I'm sorry to hear that." Joe knows they've come to the end of the interview; time to get the paperwork from the car, take down some information and give the job back to Central. Nothing to be done here.

Once again, no happy ending. Just finish the job and move onto the next.

Gotta keep moving; it's Joe's motto at work. He and Mack will exchange a few words or laughs in between jobs, pushing ahead to the end of the tour when they can both peel off the Superman costume, close their lockers, and head home.

All the while pretending it's all normal.

496

All the while ignoring the hole being worn through their hearts.

# CHAPTER 4

"Did you know the world is a snowball?" Armand Boghosian follows her up the stairs to her apartment, that song is cycling through his head. "Marshmallow World."

"Would you stop?" Wendy's eyes spark with annoyance as she turns to him on the landing. Those eyes . . . He is in love with the mettle of those eyes. Her smooth skin, tiny bones, dark almond-shaped eyes. Her exotic quality. "You've been singing that song since we hit Junction Boulevard. People on the subway thought you were a lunatic."

He laughs. "It's just so true, and it's stuck in my head. The arrangement for a saxophone . . . no, it can't be done, but I hear it anyway. Yes, it works. Like up and down a hill, no really, a snowy slope. You know how the music goes? But what does it mean?"

She climbs the next flight of stairs, waits for him on the landing. "Listen, you can come in, but you can't stay. You have to get your stuff and go."

"I keep hearing the Darlene Love version, but she wasn't the first to do it. Did you know that Bing Crosby recorded it? Way before Phil Spector got a hold of it." Armand knows music. He pays attention to labels and performers and lyrics. "Do you hear it? I mean, the sax line . . ."

"I'm serious." Wendy's voice is shrill as she throws the bolt on the door. "Don't get comfortable."

Why is she so cold? Icy. Because the world is a snowball.

The walls of her apartment seem whiter than usual. Stark and bright. A marshmallow world, just like the song says. See how it grows? Now white is everywhere. Blazing white like the lights in his head. Makes him want to grab her and pull her onto the rug.

Living in sin, the two of them. Though his Armenian father would pop a vein if he knew Armand was living with a Chinese girl. Papa wants his son to marry a nice Armenian girl, a dark-eyed, mustachioed girl who would sit at home and pop out a dozen children. Armand laughs at the thought. And Armand knows that her family just tolerates him. Wendy can't seem to convince them that he isn't Iraqi.

"How can you laugh? I'm not kidding." Something in her tone snaps him back. "You know I don't want to do this. You know I love you." Her voice catches, and she presses a hand to her mouth.

He tries to pull her into his arms, but she spins away. "I love you, too."

"No, you don't." Her arms are crossed, guarding her torso. "You can't love anyone when you're addicted. That's all that matters to you. The next score. The mission."

"That's how it goes." Whenever it snows . . .

The song keeps spinning, a snowball tumbling downhill, picking up speed.

"Oh, my God, do you hear yourself? Talking a mile a minute, gibberish. You're all hopped up on speed, aren't you? Isn't that why we had to connect with your friend last night?"

"If you think I'm bad, Razz is in it deep. He's always going. Can't live without it, that's what he tells me."

"Don't make excuses. You are an addict, Armand. You." She swallows, her eyes glimmering tears. "Oh, God, this hurts so much."

"Wen, you can't break up with me. Nobody breaks up on Christmas."

"It's not Christmas yet."

He stands behind the couch, holds on. Slow down. Maybe she's right. Got to slow down. A breath.

No, that doesn't work. Still flying. He fishes in his pockets. Where's the stuff Razz sold him?

"Oh, my God! Look at you, all twitchy. You can't even talk to me. Look me in the eye."

He looks at her then. That tiny body he can lift with one arm, the heat in her eyes, the red shot through her black hair. He wants to fold her into his arms and press his lips into her neck, but when he steps forward she backs away.

"No, Armand. You have to go."

He can barely hear her for the roar of blood pulsing in his ears. "You know I'm not a bad guy. I'm kind to kids and old ladies. I give kids free saxophone lessons at the Flushing Y." His words are coming fast, faster. "I got you this really great Christmas gift." A lie. Big lie. Oh, shit. "And I'm gonna give you money for this month's rent because I just got a loan from my father."

Her eyes open slightly, as if seeing potential. "And are you paying back the money you borrowed from me last month to support your habit? Or am I just supposed to forget about that?"

"I'll pay you back. Soon. I'm going to get the money."

"No, you won't." Hope drains from her. She's crying now, tucking herself into the corner of the sofa. "Just go."

"Wendy . . ." He goes to her, leans on the arm of the couch. "Don't cry." He smoothes her fire hair, touches the gold loops in her ear.

"I can't do this anymore." She is crying into her hands.

But he can barely hear her voice for all the noise. The song, the pumping blood.

Got to slow down. Wendy's right; slow it down.

He finds Razz's plastic bag in his pocket and stares into it. Which one is the valium? He should know this by now. He fishes three out and pops them in. Too dry.

In the kitchen the fridge is hopeless. He finds a half-empty beer by the sink. Swirls warm beer in his mouth, down the hatch.

And hey, it's snowing outside. White flakes swirl beyond the grimy kitchen window.

"Did you know it's snowing? I'm not kidding." He sits beside her, tries to get her to look up. When she doesn't, he leans close, whispers in her ear: "Don't worry. I put on the brakes. Screech."

She doesn't laugh, but she'll come around.

She always does.

The world is a snowball. Yeah.

"Marshmallow World." Like the guy who wrote that song wasn't high . . .

# CHAPTER 5

A few blocks away Joe and Mack are ticketing illegal parkers on Main Street, the four-lane street that cuts through Flushing like a central artery. Generally Joe would prefer root canal to writing parkers; it irks him that the city uses cops like him to fill their coffers. But he and Mack are writing the double-parkers, people who leave their cars dead in the street, clogging traffic and blocking buses. Double-parkers are morons.

He flips to the next ticket in his memo book and starts writing a gold Caddy with stuffed animals on the dashboard. For idiots like this, there is no mercy just because it's the holidays. Hell, he should charge extra just for the poodle tchotchkes blocking the rear window. He fills in the plate number, the date, checks the boxes on the ticket form. He's tucking the copy of the ticket under the car's wiper blade when a heap of wiry white hair in a matted red cape comes whirling out of the J&J newsstand.

Mrs. Claus? No, just the Cadillac's owner, spitting mad. "What the hell are you doing, touching my car?"

One quick look at her dark-rimmed eyes and wild hair tells Joe she hasn't had the best of days. "Double-parked, ma'am."

"What, are you kidding me? I go into the store for two minutes and you bang me?" Lifting the ticket from the car, she unfurls a string of curses. She may look like Mrs. Claus, but she talks like a truck driver.

People look over. A man runs out of the card store and jumps into his vehicle a few cars ahead to avoid a ticket.

Joe steps back onto the curb without a word. Long ago he learned that some battles are a waste of words.

"This is low! You got some nerve, hitting people on Christmas Eve." The irate woman waves the ticket at him. "I should tear this up."

*Actually, you should park out of the street next time.*

"Don't walk away while I'm talking to you!"

*Screaming is more like it.*

"I hope you have a rotten Christmas!"

"Yeah, back at you," Joe mutters in a voice only Mack can hear.

Mack, who has observed the whole thing, cocks an eyebrow and slips into his proper King's English. "Are there no prisons? Are there no workhouses?"

"Shut up." Joe's in no mood. Already he's dealt with two fare-beaters, an elderly woman who couldn't find her way home, and a hopped-up kid with earrings up one side of his head singing "Marshmallow World" at the top of his lungs. The street's lined with double-parkers, illegal vendors clog the sidewalks with their faux cashmere scarves, fake designer bags, and Rolex knockoffs.

All in a day's work, but what's the point? Nothing he does makes a difference. Write the fare-beaters a fine, but that won't stop them from doing it again when backs are turned. Help the old lady get home, but she'll be lost again tomorrow. Chase off the illegal vendors and they'll be back within the hour.

As he and Mack write their way to the underpass, Joe sinks into the doldrums. How did this become his life, shoveling crap against the tide?

Speaking of crap . . . the smell of the encampment stings his nostrils as, under the trestle from the number seven train that runs overhead, a sheet of cardboard shifts

506

and Crazy Mary emerges from her hovel.

"Here comes Santy Claus!" she crows, soot darkening her cheeks. With her ill-fitting coat and watch cap, Mary looks to be in her sixties, though Joe wonders if she might be his age under all that gunk.

"What are you doing back here, Mary?" Mack scolds her.

"It's getting cold out." Joe worries about the old woman. If the forecast is right, it'll drop to below twenty tonight. "I thought we got you a ride to the Flushing shelter yesterday."

"I went, I went, but you know. Got to la-dee-dee and so and so."

"Is that right?" Joe tries to keep her talking while he checks her makeshift lean-to for other tenants.

"Oh, look! Here comes Santy Claus!" Her eyes go wide as she points to the red Santa cap worn by a young man with a briefcase. Probably an office joke, but still.

"Maybe Crazy Mary isn't so crazy after all," Mack observes.

Joe gets on his cell to call the Homeless Ride Service. "We're getting you a roof over your head for tonight, Mary."

"Well, hallelujah, but no thank you, boys. Can't leave my spot here or Santa will never find me."

"Makes sense to me," Mack mutters. "I'm telling you, Mary's more grounded than Sergeant Minovich. Making us write parkers on Christmas Eve . . ."

"Mary needs to spend the night inside." Joe shifts his phone, says he'll hold. "We'll get you somewhere warm, Mary. A nice cozy bed."

"Oh, no, no." Mary's face puckers with distaste. "Beds for lazybones. No bag a bones. Bagabond. Sagapond . . ."

Joe holds up his hand to stop her rant. "Not this place. You're gonna like it, Mary. I guarantee." His last words were drowned out by the roar of the number seven train overhead. A moment later, people begin to stream down the stairs.

Mack shifts from one foot to another, shoots Joe a look.

"Still on hold," he tells him.

"Please God, don't let them take forever. We got the precinct Christmas party at four. Sheila's bringing the kids, right?"

"Yeah, right."

They are hit by a new cloud of stink. A round man appears on the stairs, dragging a filthy athletic bag. His beady eyes glimmer as he eyes them, then checks the cardboard shanty. With a grunt he drags the sack past the two cops and into the hole.

"You can't stay here." Mack's voice thunders through the hollow space under the trestle. "Don't get too cozy in there."

Mary's eyes go wide with indignity; her arms cross as she glares into the hovel. "Like two peas in a cod!"

*Sometimes she almost makes sense,* Joe thinks.

"Sure smells like cod," Mack agrees.

"This is what my life has come to." Joe shakes his head, lets out a snicker. "I've become a sanitation engineer. We're the garbagemen of humanity. That's our job."

"Nah. That would be too easy." Mack rubs his hands together, trying to keep warm. "If it were that simple I'd have half of Flushing wrapped up in a big old Hefty bag."

# CHAPTER 6

With the stroller in one arm and Patrick Joseph in the other, Sheila clambers down the stairs of the bus and steps into an Arctic blast on Main Street. Her two sweaters are useless in this cold. She hustles over to the sidewalk where Katie has planted herself, good little soldier that she is, and struggles to unfold the stroller in the finger-nipping wind.

"Phew! That was a workout." She unfolds the stroller and motions for PJ to climb aboard. "You're soon going to have to start walking yourself, little man." Without acknowledging her, he plunks into the canvas seat and curls his legs up. "Oh, I get it. Why walk when you can ride like the Grand Pooh-Bah?"

Katie laughs. "He's not a Poopah. He's a Tigger." She hooks her little mitten onto the stroller and keeps pace as Sheila starts pushing.

When they pause at the intersection, Sheila hooks her scarf over her head for warmth while Katie looks around suspiciously. "But Daddy's precinct is there, down *that* street." She points toward Union Street.

"I know, honey, but we have to stop and pick up some food to donate." A ten-dollar bill from the cookie jar is tucked into the pocket of Sheila's jeans, and though Joe might disagree, Sheila is going to use it to teach her kids an important lesson. They need to think of others less fortunate. They need to share what they have.

"Couldn't we bring food from home?" Katie asks.

"We could, but I didn't want to lug it. Besides, I thought you would like picking something out yourself. Something a little girl would like to eat."

"Yeah, I can do that." They walk in silence, then Katie adds: "Am I going to give the girl the food today?"

"We'll put it in a basket or a box, and someone else will take the food to the poor people another day."

"I hope they take it to the girl by tomorrow. She might need it for Christmas."

"Good point." Sheila extends her finger to the small food mart ahead called the Shuka.

"We'll stop in here and get a few things. It'll only take a minute."

"Okay, Mommy."

Such a good kid, Sheila thinks. Patrick Joseph had better take a few pointers from his big sis. Sheila is so glad the kids have each other. She'd love to have more, but Joe worries about money. Yeah, she worries, too, but he doesn't have to know that.

She wheels the stroller toward the Shuka's entrance and the automatic door rolls open. "Come on, toots," she calls to Katie, who has stalled at the gumball and trinket machines lined up outside the store. The combined smells of roasting meat and garlic, clove and cinnamon remind her of her mother's kitchen. These are the smells of Christmas. For a moment Sheila is worlds away, propped on a chair at the kitchen counter so she can help roll the strudel cookies.

"Mommy, help!"

Her daughter's voice startles Sheila from her daydream. She whirls and finds Katie caught in the door, the metal bar repeatedly banging her into the wall as it tries to close.

"Oh, my God!" Rushing over, Sheila wedges her hands between the door and wall and gives the frame a shove. Immediately the door pops open, freeing Katie.

"Don't break it! Please!" someone inside the store growls.

"Oh, honey, are you okay?" Sheila hunches down, examines her daughter, then pulls her into her arms. "Scary, huh?"

"It wouldn't let go of me." Katie's words are muffled by Sheila's sweater.

"If you please, stay away from the door." The older gentleman is stern, unapologetic.

Sheila straightens and sucks in a breath, ready to defend her youngster. "Excuse me, but did you see what your door just did to this child? Oh, my God. It could have taken her head off. It kept trying to close on her. Or did you not see that? You need to get this thing fixed. You'd better report this to the manager."

"Lady, I am the owner. And I say there's no need to fix it. It's not broken." He steps up to the door, runs his hand over a scanner about four feet above the floor, and the door rolls open. "You see? It works perfectly."

"Not for her." Sheila squeezes her daughter's shoulders. "It could have crushed her."

"Pshaw! She's fine, isn't she?" He tips his chin to his chest, staring at Katie over his reading glasses. "Little girl, are you all right?"

Katie presses into Sheila's legs, a timid

lamb. "I guess so."

"You see? No harm done."

"Not exactly." Sheila stands her ground as retorts rise in her throat. *Are you crazy? That door is going to kill someone! I'm calling a lawyer! We'll sue!*

But something stops her from giving voice to those threats. Despite his officious demeanor there is something forlorn about the store owner; it's as if he is wounded inside.

"Now then . . ." He shoots a razor sharp glance toward PJ. "I'll thank you to keep that one in his buggy while you're shopping in my Shuka. No more calamities. Are we clear on that, Miss?"

Sheila hurries Katie over to the stroller and wheels it toward the produce aisle. "Don't worry, we'll keep it short."

The nerve! She hustles the kids behind a huge bin of Fujis and takes a calming breath. The man has a steel pair! She's tempted to walk out, but she can't let her temper get in the way of this teaching moment about the real meaning of Christmas: the spirit of giving.

"Mommy, he was rude," Katie offers, her eyes wide from her glimpse of adult matters.

"Yes, he was. So let's get our food and get

514

out of here. Have you thought about what you'd like to get for a donation?"

Katie crosses the aisle to a mound of chocolate covered caramel corn and pats one cellophane bag. "How about this?"

"Not nutritious enough."

Katie purses her lips. "Do we have to give her spinach?"

"No." Sheila loves that Katie imagines the recipient to be a girl like herself. "But we need something that can be stored for a long time, so canned foods are good. How about tuna? It's loaded with protein."

Katie's tiny nose wrinkles. "Like the tuna you eat? It's too smelly. And why was that man so mean?"

"Sometimes you just don't know what other people are going through. Maybe he's having a sad day."

Together they decide on mandarin oranges and garbanzo beans. As they approach the checkout counter the man steps out from behind the clerk, and Katie cowers. This time Sheila notices the bitter curl of his lips and redness around his eyes. Definitely a sad day.

As Sheila fishes out her ten-dollar bill for the cashier, PJ stirs in his stroller. *Hold still, please* . . . Sheila wills him to behave for one more minute. When she glances down, she sees that he is smiling his drooly, single-tooth grin and trying to hand his baggie full of Cheerios to the cranky man.

"Oh, PJ . . ." She reaches down to stop him, but the man is already bending down to him, smiling.

"Thank you very much, young man," he says, accepting a piece of cereal. When he looks up at Sheila, his brown eyes are warm. "Please, if you have a moment . . . you cannot leave without some of our award-winning baklava. Take some home to enjoy for your holidays. And for the children . . ." He reaches into a bin behind him and produces a shiny orange clementine. "Do you like orange?" he asks Katie.

Her lips seem buttoned shut, but she nods.

"Very good, then." He places the clementine in her hand, then ducks behind the pastry counter. Sheila feels like she's won the Lotto. The honeyed pastries will add elegance to the platter of very simple sugar cookies she's been baking for the holidays. At a time when she could never afford the ingredients for something this lavish, the baklava is truly a gift.

By the time he emerges with the small white box, Sheila is fairly choked with emotion by the man's sudden turn of disposition. Chalk it up to Christmas, she thinks.

Katie thanks the man and zips her pink parka. "We have to go give chickpeas to a little girl."

Suddenly Sheila wishes there were something she could do for him. "Merry Christmas," she says.

He just nods, watching her little family as they pass carefully out the door.

# CHAPTER 7

"Three o'clock, man. We got one more hour on patrol and then we are done with this rodeo show for endless hours of holiday, so-happy-we're-getting-married sex." Mack looks up from his memo book; chews his pen. "Did I just say that? I don't suppose it applies to old men like you."

"Yeah." Joe turns onto Sanford Avenue, liking the blur of color from blinking lights strewn over bushes and houses. "I'll just head home, pop my teeth out, and have Sheila rub my bunions. I got wicked big bunions."

"Cody, that is disgusting."

Joe is biting back a grin when the call comes over the radio.

"One-Oh-Nine-Charlie, respond to a ten fifty-four, Aided Case, possible overdose. Nineteen-year-old male."

This is the call that's going to ruin Christmas; Joe can feel it in his gut. He banks the wheel sharply to head toward the apartment house as Mack writes down the address.

"Contact is a Wendy Min, Aided's girl-friend," the dispatcher adds. "It's her apart-ment."

Joe accelerates. "Sounds to me like we just stepped in it."

Mack flicks on the lights and siren. "And I thought we were gonna make it through this shift without getting stuck."

"We still might," Joe says, though his instincts tell him otherwise. He mentally calculates different deadlines. There's the precinct Christmas party going on right now. If they can get off this job by four he can still catch the tail end. Then there's the Christmas pageant at church. Joe promised his wife he'd make it to six o'clock mass to watch Katie portray Mary in the Nativity scene. Hard to believe his little girl is going to do her first acting role, lines and every-thing.

He wants to be there for his wife and kids tonight. On the other hand, there's this nineteen-year-old male . . . God knows what the job involves, and once Joe is into it, that nineteen-year-old kid will take priority over everything.

As they get close, Mack reads off the ad-dress again.

Joe slows and squints through the windshield, trying to find the numbers on the high-rise apartment buildings just off Main Street. "But if we do get stuck, isn't it your turn to take the overtime?"

"My turn? You're always fighting me for the overtime."

"Yeah, well, I got places to be."

"And I'm supposed to get engaged tonight. What's that, chopped liver?"

"Actually, this will demonstrate to Nayasia just how unpredictable her life is going to be." Spotting the ambulance ahead, Joe punches it to the end of the block. "It's no bargain, being married to a cop."

"Speak for yourself," Mack says, nodding at the emergency van with its rear doors gaping open.

A second later Joe throws the cruiser into park and they both bail.

A young Asian girl, a petite thing with red-streaked hair and multiple piercings, sits in the back of the van inhaling oxygen from a mask.

Joe turns to the EMS worker, last name Dolinsky, though she goes by Dolly. "How's she doing, Dolly?"

"She'll be okay." Dolly moves to the side of the van, out of the girl's hearing range. Her straw blond hair, which is always styled in an imitation of Jennifer Aniston's latest, is tucked back with a pair of navy earmuffs. "She was a little shocky after seeing the boyfriend. Lost her lunch." Her gaze shifts up toward the building. "Todd is upstairs with him. He was pretty blue when we got here, but we tried CPR." She shrugs, her eyes flickering with emotion. "In the end we had to pronounce him."

Joe feels that small, radiant gem of hope harden to a cold pebble in his chest. So the kid is dead. They're all too late. He rubs his chin. Now it's just a question of identifying the body, notifying next of kin. No happy ending here.

Dolly tugs on a wild strand of hair. "We weren't sure if you guys would want to set up a crime scene."

He nods toward the girl. "It's her apartment?"

"Belongs to the girlfriend, but apparently he's been staying here. She says her parents live in the building, too. First floor."

Mack rounds the corner of the ambulance, his thumb hitched toward the girl. "You want to check upstairs first, give the girl a chance to calm down?"

"Sounds like a plan."

They enter the narrow lobby lined with small mailboxes. An old building, no elevators. Joe attacks the stairs, his daily workout.

On the third floor landing he waits for Mack and they take the hallway together. A nice building, fairly new carpeting and wallpaper, little colonial lamps lining the corridor.

The door to 3-H is cracked open, and Joe pushes in. "Todd . . . ?"

"It's about time you guys got here." Todd looks up from the computer desk where he's sitting. Fish swim across the monitor behind him, complete with a bubbling noise.

Joe looks from the paramedic to the body curled into the fetal position on the couch. He can't see the kid's face, just a mass of thick dark hair and studs lining his ear, one with a diamond.

"Nineteen? Just a kid." As he moves closer to check the body, Joe realizes that he's got ten years on this kid. What would have happened if his life had ended back at nineteen?

The things he would have missed . . . His Sheila's laugh, that tinkling sound that drains tension away. The softness of her, the gleam of her spirit. The heat of her body in his arms at night. And the kids . . . The whisper of downy hair against his face, the grooves of their little shell ears after a bath. The way they clamp onto him like little monkeys when he carries them to bed.

Ten years. Yeah, he's done some living since he was nineteen.

"What a shame." Mack glances down at the body. They've seen plenty of dead bodies, but you never get used to it. "No visible bruises or trauma. Actually, he looks pretty peaceful."

The modest studio apartment shows no sign of a struggle. In fact, it's neater than most homes Joe visits, artistic and casual. A tapestry of a Chinese dragon covers one wall, opposite windows that overlook the zigzagging buildings of Flushing. There are bookshelves and a coffee table made of brick and plank, a small computer desk with a wood chair, a table and chairs tucked in a little eating alcove.

"We'll have to ask the sergeant if he wants a crime scene," Joe says. "From my take, it doesn't seem suspicious, but then we need some background on this kid."

Mack flips open his cell phone and heads toward the door. "I'll call the sergeant."

Todd stands. "My guess is the autopsy will show a toxic level of drugs. The girlfriend saw him popping things and we found that baggy of pills on him. Looks like Oxycotin." He shoves his hands in his pockets. "I guess we're done here." The EMS crews do not transport bodies; that's the job of either the coroner's office or a funeral home. "I'll have the coroner send a wagon. You want Dolly to bring the girl up here?"

"Thanks, Todd. Merry Christmas."

Todd tips two fingers to his forehead. "Merry Christmas, Joe."

Alone in the apartment, Joe thinks about checking for ID. Although the girlfriend knew the kid, they'll need someone from the family, preferably next of kin, to identify the body.

From the inside pocket of a black North Face jacket Joe takes a brown leather wallet. It's fat with bills, at least a few hundred in cash. Seems like a lot for a guy this age to be carrying around. The license photo matches the victim, a good-looking kid. His eyes flash on the name: Armand Boghosian.

Why does that ring a bell? Boghosian. He can hear someone belting it out, accent on the second syllable. Right . . . that was the name of the guy from this morning, the owner of the Shuka.

The man who suspected his son of robbing the store safe.

Joe frowns as he looks from the license to the boy curled on the couch.

What are the chances?

# CHAPTER 8

In the Chinese language there are many words for misfortune, and since the day her parents met Armand, Wendy has heard them all: *Buxing. Xie. Daoyun. Huo.* Words that mean disaster, bad luck, and evil. Misfortune sent by the gods. Her mother had even compared her boyfriend to the splendor of a comet, considered to be an omen of bad luck in the old culture.

Mummy always warned that Armand would bring her trouble. Recently, Wendy began to worry that her mother was right, but she never thought it would come to this. Never.

Wendy hugs herself. Will she ever be able to go back to her own apartment upstairs? Will she ever be able to rid her mind of the image of him curled on her sofa, skin so pale? Cold against her fingertips.

*Oh, Armand . . . why? Did you mean to do it or was it just a really stupid mistake?* Bad luck, as Mummy always predicted.

Thank God Mummy arrived in time to usher everyone here to her parents' apartment, the home she'd grown up in. Wendy cannot return to her own place, the haunted studio upstairs, especially with Armand still there.

She looks past the police officer who is interviewing her to the dining alcove where the bald cop perches on the side of a chair, sitting that way so that his gun belt doesn't scratch her mother's furniture, no doubt. This one is a sergeant, so they call him. Upstairs in Wendy's apartment, a third cop sits with Armand, watching him, guarding him. A dignified gesture, but too late.

Both her parents rushed home from the restaurant, leaving Auntie Fang to mind the shop. Auntie Fang with her good intentions and bossy ways. With any luck the kitchen staff will still be there by dinnertime. Mummy has the kettle on for tea and coffee, and Ba slices a pineapple to share with the officers. Surreal. For now, her parents will be respectful but guarded with the police. Later . . . later she will hear about misfortune, many times over.

"So what time was it when you saw him last?" Officer Cody brings her back with his gentle voice. Something about his patient dark eyes, the space he gives her to breathe, suggests that he is a father with children of his own.

"Ten, maybe ten-thirty this morning. We spent the night together, though we were out all night. Two clubs, then this after-hours place. He was looking for this guy Razz, wouldn't stop until he found him."

"A friend?"

"His drug dealer," she says softly, hoping her parents do not hear. "He started playing around with some stuff a few months ago. Now he can't live without it." She presses a hand to her mouth, punched by her own words.

"Was he using this morning?"

She nods. "He was totally wired. Cocaine, I think. I told him to slow down . . ."

"So you left him here alone around ten this morning?"

"I had to be at work by ten-thirty to help with the lunch rush. My family owns Happy Luck Chinese. I wait tables there part-time. I'm a student at NYU."

His brows rise. "That's a very good school. Did Armand go there, too?"

"No, he was taking a break from school, but he wanted to attend Juilliard in the fall. He was applying there, trying to get an audition. He's a brilliant musician, but it's very competitive."

"Another great school. My sister-in-law works there." He turns a page in his memo book. "You said Armand was living with you. Did he have any family in the area?"

"His mother is dead. I think his father is the only family he had. I never met him, but he owns a little Armenian grocery near here . . ."

"The Shuka," Officer Cody offers without looking up.

"Yes. How did you know?"

"I've met his old man. He's going to be heartbroken."

For the first time this afternoon tears sting her eyes. It seems so intrinsically sad, a father mourning his son, especially when the son was so convinced that his father didn't care. She bites her lower lip, trying to compose herself to finish the interview.

"The last thing I said to him was that I wanted him gone when I got back from work," she confesses. "I didn't mean it. I still loved him, but I couldn't take the addiction anymore. Such a roller-coaster ride. It should have been no surprise with Armand born in the Year of the Dragon. He was irresistible and charismatic. A tremendous talent. Everything had to be on a grand scale. For him it was Juilliard or nothing."

And his destiny turned out to be nothing.

How had she fallen for him, a romantic born under the sign of the dragon? Dragons do everything on a grand scale. A grand scale performance. A grand scale passion. A grand scale addiction.

A tiny whimper ripples through her. She presses a fist to her mouth as Officer Cody stands.

"Thanks for your help, Wendy. My partner will stay upstairs with the body while I try to locate his father. I'd like Mr. Boghosian to ID his son up in your place, if that's okay. The morgue is not a good scene for anyone."

She nods, rocking forward, hugging herself as she thinks of Armand upstairs.

Take your time, she wants to say. The apartment is all yours; I'm never going back.

She cannot return. His ghost will always be there, clinging, refusing to leave because he loved her so fiercely. He didn't want to leave, and the last thing she said to him was that he had to get the hell out. But he won't go. Armand will stay.

And she will never have the courage to return to her home and face the fiery dragon.

# CHAPTER 9

Joe steps out of the patrol car and pushes through the thick, wintry air toward the Shuka. He's swimming through molasses. The snow has tapered off, giving way to an ashen sky bleeding into night. Dark sky, dark mood. Bring it on.

This is one of the worst parts of his job, the bad news. NYPD has a "Knock on door" policy. They know news this grim can't be trusted over the phone. But every cop sweats over notifications. They train you to serve the public, shoot a weapon, track suspects, and arrest perps. But there's no training for this.

In his entire career he has made three notifications, and he recalls each in vivid detail. The guy with the Yankee cap who fell to his knees in shock. The middle-aged couple who flatly denied that their daughters could be dead. The mother who ran to his police cruiser in her bathrobe and bare feet, as if she could reverse time and bring her son back to life by rushing to his side. These are moments Joe does not want to witness and yet he is forced to be a part of them, an actor in the drama.

Still, he does not prolong the agony or drama. Inside the store, the clerks direct him to the back office where Garo Boghosian is seated at his desk, working on a ledger in the pool of light from a reading lamp.

Joe is relieved that he's seated.

"Officer?" Mr. B. looks up. "Did you find my money?"

"Mr. Boghosian, I'm sorry, but I have some very bad news for you. There's a young man down the street. He died from an apparent drug overdose. We think it's your son Armand."

For a moment the older man just stares, as if he cannot comprehend this. Then a cry escapes him, the desolate gasp of a wounded man.

Joe looks down, gives the man a moment.

"My son. Oh, my boy." Mr. B. removes his reading glasses, slips them in his shirt pocket. "How can you be sure?"

"His girlfriend found him at her apartment, but we would like you to identify him. If you can come now, I'll take you there myself."

"Then we must go." He turns off the reading lamp, slips on a brown wool coat.

All eyes are on them as Boghosian stops to ask the cashier with the gemmed shirt to mind the store while he goes to his son. Sensing their hope, Joe turns toward the door and leads the way. The cashiers will know soon enough.

As he opens the cruiser door for Mr. B., Joe wonders if Sergeant Minovich has stopped by the girl's apartment yet. Chances are Minovich is going to be pissed at Joe for going out on a limb to bring in the kid's father. The standard procedure would be to let the coroner haul off the body and let next of kin ID at the morgue. Free up Joe and Mack to move on to another job.

But it's Christmas Eve and Joe can't do that to Mr. Boghosian. Bad enough he's got to identify his son; to schlep into the city morgue for them to roll your kid out of a giant file drawer . . . Naw. Joe wants to do this with as much dignity as possible, even if it means putting out extra time and effort.

"It's not far," Joe says. In the rearview mirror he sees the old man huddled in the backseat, his face pinched with pain and shock.

"Let me ask you something, officer. This boy you found, there is a chance he's not my son. He may be some other boy, and my son is somewhere else, still alive and vital."

Joe bites his bottom lip. He's seen denial before. "Anything's possible. But, Mr. Boghosian, his girlfriend says it's him. Right now I'd say we're officially 99 percent sure."

"I see." Boghosian clears his voice. "Well, if you don't mind, I will cling to that 1 percent for now."

"Fair enough."

"You know, he is my only son. Such a source of pride and joy for his mother. But since she passed, there has been only sorrow. He used to be a good boy. I don't know where it all went wrong. Like the yarn in a favorite sweater. You get a pull here, a little hole there, and suddenly your sweater is unraveling, falling apart on you."

He rubs his eyes, sighs.

"I still hope you are wrong about my son. He has a business to take over, you know. All my life I am a hard-working man. I work to build my business so that I will have something to pass on to my son. A solid family business. My shop paid for music lessons. Clarinet and saxophone lessons. And yet, despite my blood, sweat, and toil, my son did not want it. No head for business, he tells me. He wants to be a saxophone player. I have to ask you, what is the use of that? Even if you are loaded with talent, will a saxophone put bread in your mouth? A roof over your head? Will it feed your children when they are hungry?"

"Yeah, but it's not easy to play a musical instrument." Joe is glad the man is talking. Talking helps.

"Music is all well and good, but a man must provide for his family. Do you know when I started my business, I was a very young man, then, back in Armenia . . ." Mr. Boghosian launches into a story of how he made his first business deal, selling the stuffed grape leaves his mother used to make.

Listening, Joe thinks of his father, who always loves to spout stories, tales of ancient ethics from the old country — Ireland, in his case. About all the scrimping and saving, making do with a single pair of shoes and a dream.

Joe has always tried to tune his old man out, but now that he hears Mr. B. philosophize he realizes this is exactly what he's been telling Sheila these last few months. The stuff she used to come home with: a dozen empty baskets "for gifts," she said; dream-catchers from a craft show because

Katie was having nightmares; a giant hobby horse with Appaloosa hide and creepy glass eyes. Every day a new bike or scooter or a special puzzle that's supposed to turn the kids into Einsteins. And the stuff she ordered online? Forget about it. Rain boots for the kids with polka dots and dinosaurs. And that plastic desk she ordered for PJ? He'll outgrow it before he can even use it, not to mention the shipping cost for that hunk of plastic.

For some reason that stupid desk pushed him to the limit, and he snapped. Yelled at her that she had to stop throwing their money away on crap; had to focus on the basics like food on the table and a roof over their heads.

That didn't go over so well. Big fight. But in the end, Sheila heard him. She agreed to stop using the charge cards, and he agreed to start taking his lunch. A little embarrassing for a grown man to be lugging Tupperware into the precinct every day, but okay, he's willing to do his part.

Since that blowup, Sheila has been better with the shopaholic thing. Yeah, sometimes she still worries that the kids will be deprived, but deprived isn't always about money. Look at Mr. B.'s son. You can do all the right things, pay for music lessons, and work like a dog to pay the bills and still, somehow, it can all go wrong.

Whatever it is that makes kids grow up right, it's not about money. He's glad he can see that now. He clenches his jaw as he checks the man in the backseat, the man clinging to that 1 percent of hope.

Rotten odds. What a shame.

# CHAPTER 10

"Pumpkin, you've been flicking those lights on for an hour now." Sheila leans into the open patrol car parked in a garage bay, out of the cold, and reaches for her toddler son, who scoots away. The precinct cops brought the cruiser in for the family holiday party, along with a Harley-Davidson motorcycle, and a horse named Nella. Although most people have gravitated to the room across the hall with refreshments and a tree, a dozen or so diehards like PJ remain here. Other kids seem enchanted by rides on the horse or a climb onto the seat of the motorcycle, but not PJ. That kid is a police car lover, through and through.

"Patrick Joseph, why don't you clear out and give someone else a chance to drive. We can go across the way for some juice. And maybe Daddy's over there. He should be here by now."

PJ doesn't notice her; he's too engrossed

in the cruiser's lights and buttons, a lit computer screen and a steering wheel he's actually allowed to touch.

"Where in the world is your daddy?" she asks again.

This time her son looks up from the steering wheel, smiling that gummy smile. "Daddy drive peeze car," he answers.

Well, what kind of answer did she expect from a two-year-old? But really, where the hell is Joe? He should have been here an hour ago.

Moving to the hood of the car, she watches PJ through the glass as she takes out her cell phone and calls Joe for the millionth time. Once again, the call goes right to voicemail, which means he probably has his phone off. "Damn."

"Little ears here, Mom." A cop claps a hand on her shoulder and grins.

"Rick!" She turns and gives him a big hug. Rick DeFonso has been tight with Joe since they went through the police academy together. Rick and Angela have two and one on the way. "How are you?"

"Can't complain. My shift is over, but I thought that was your Katie playing in the other room. Getting big."

Sheila feels a pinch of pride. "First grade now."

"And this is the baby?"

"Not a baby anymore. PJ's two next month."

He leans into the car. "Pardon me, sir, but you should be wearing your seat belt if you're going to drive like that."

For a moment PJ ducks his head shyly, then reaches over to flick on the rack lights.

"How's Angela doing? And where are your kids?"

"They were here earlier with my sister. Angela's on bed rest."

"Oh, no! Not again."

They discuss Angela's pregnancy, their Christmas plans, the kids. Rick mentions that Joe and his partner got hung up on a job. "I heard the call come over the radio. Sounded like a fatality."

"On Christmas Eve? That's sad." And it sounds like a job that's going to detain her husband for a while. She tries to tamp down her disappointment, knowing that when other people need Joe's help, they *really* need him. Sheila checks her watch, glances toward the other room. "I guess he won't be making the party, and we have to get out of here soon. Katie's in the church Christmas pageant at six."

"Is that right?" Rick slides into the car beside PJ. "You want to go round her up?"

I'll keep an eye on Speed Racer."

Sheila thanks him and heads out. Just as she reaches the door, a siren peals. She turns back to the cruiser to see Rick roaring with laughter.

"Don't show him how to use that, Rick. He'll never stop."

Rick waves her off. "The siren is half the fun."

In the next room children scramble through a mound of boxes and wrapping paper under the tree. Apparently Santa has distributed gifts. Sheila locates Katie at a table for six with two other girls and three stuffed animals. At first she's glad to see that her daughter found some friends, but that relief gives way to agitation as Katie hoists a two-liter bottle of soda, aiming to pour.

"Katherine Bernadette Cody, what do you think you're doing?" Sheila rushes over and wrests the bottle from her.

"I got a tea set, Mom. See?" Katie lifts a tiny china saucer and cup. "We're having a tea party, except the tea is really root beer."

"Oh, no, no. You're not pouring today, my dear. You've got to wear that dress in the pageant." Sheila tips the bottle and carefully pours cups of soda for the girls. "It is a lovely tea set. So nice of Santa. I hope you thanked him, Katie. Drink up, ladies. Katie has to go. Can't be late for church."

As she caps the bottle she mentally calculates the time it will take to pack up this tea set, sticky now, and get the kids out the door. She hoped to talk her daughter out of opening the gift today so there'd be more under the tree tomorrow, but what can you do? Kids are kids. At least she can tuck PJ's gift away for tomorrow. He's been so enthralled with the real police car, he won't even notice.

An EMS worker who's been watching joins them. Dolly is one of Joe's favorite paramedics, a real pro. "I wouldn't serve those stuffed bears any more," she jokes. "They're looking a little tipsy."

"Merry Christmas, Dolly." Sheila hugs her. "How are you?"

"I'm good. Just thinking that it's been a long time since any of my kids had a tea party. They're all out of the house now. One in Boston. My son Tommy is getting married."

"Congratulations, Dolly." Sheila smiles as she begins to stack small pink china cups. "But your tea party days aren't necessarily over."

Dolly laughs. "Oh, I'm done with that."

"What about the grandkids?" Sheila suggests.

"You know, you're right. Tommy and Laura are talking about kids already. Won't be long." Dolly squeezes Katie's shoulder. "I can only hope to have one as sweet as this kid. God bless 'em. They grow up so fast."

# CHAPTER 11

Dread is a bitter taste in his mouth as Joe leads Mr. Boghosian into the apartment building just off Main Street. "It's a third floor walk-up, but we can take our time on the stairs."

"I am strong." Garo Boghosian taps two fists against his chest. "Every day I exercise. Stairs are no problem."

With a nod, Joe gestures toward the stairwell, letting the older man go first. On the third floor Joe leads the way, then asks Mr. B. to wait outside the door one moment.

Inside, Mack is sitting in the computer chair far from the kid, his body angled so that he can keep one eye on the television, the other on the door. "Hey, man." Mack stands, rubs his hands together. "You got the father?"

Joe nods toward the door. "He's waiting out in the hall. Did you reach the coroner?"

Mack's dark eyebrows arch. "They're sending a wagon. And Minovich left singing your praises. He actually liked what you did. Thought it was a good idea to go and get the kid's father."

"Wonders never cease." It's not as though Joe lives for the sergeant's approval, but it's always a relief to know that he won't be getting any flack for the way he handled a job. Joe rubs his jaw; he hates this, absolutely hates it. "Might as well get this over with."

"Okay, Mr. B." Joe opens the door wide, holds his hands up as the man steps in. "Mind if I give you a hand?" He's had people go down, big, burly guys pass out cold at the sight of a body, and he doesn't want Garo Boghosian to get hurt.

"Fine," the man says, somewhat begrudgingly, as Joe puts a hand under his elbow and leads him over to the shadowed form on the sofa.

Boghosian draws in a breath, a stab of pain. "I believe it is him."

He pushes away from Joe and leans over the still body. His fingertips graze the studs along the rim of the boy's ear. Then he stoops low to study the face, unhampered by the cold touch of death. His hands trace the boy's shirt, tugging the collar down slightly, revealing a small tattoo at the back of the neck that Joe didn't notice before. A crow? No, a dragon. Very goth.

The older man leans closer, nearly collapsing onto the body. "Yes, oh yes." Boghosian's voice cracks. "It is him."

Quickly Mack slides a chair over. The two cops help Garo onto it, making sure he's stable, though the father leans into his son. He will not break contact with the body, as if his touch alone might bring his son back.

"Oh, Armand," the man sobs, "my Armand." He touches the boy's cheeks, cups his shoulders, shakes him as if to wake him up.

Joe bites back the sting of emotion as the man rubs his boy's back, so similar to the way Joe checks on PJ when he comes home late at night and his boy is in bed. You check the rise and fall of his chest, sweep the baby hair off his forehead, press your lips close to feel for a temperature. Joe isn't sure where or when he learned to do this, but it's part of his routine, an instinct.

Mack turns away from the wailing man and shoots Joe a look that says he'll be outside. Mack has trouble handling stuff like this. Not that it's easy for anyone, but tonight Joe cannot look away. Somehow, if he witnesses this man's grief, it seems he will share in Garo Boghosian's pain and somehow lessen it.

The door closes behind Mack, and Joe widens his stance, prepared to wait it out.

The sobbing man is sitting on the edge of the sofa now, cradling the boy's body in his arms and rocking him as if he were a newborn baby. "My son, my little Armand . . ."

Joe watches, powerless to help. He stands in the shadows and waits, respectful, silent, as the man sobs into the night. Nothing Joe can do for him, nothing anyone can do unless you can roll back time and stop a kid from making a fatal mistake.

Like Superman, when he grinds the planet to a halt then spins it backward once or twice, spinning back to yesterday, two days ago. Going back in time for a do-over. A chance to save Lois Lane or Armand Boghosian or anyone whose death tears an unbearable hole through the heart.

But that's comic book crap.

Real life is waiting until a father can compose himself enough to release his dead son's body.

Yeah, real life is a lot of waiting.

# CHAPTER 12

By the time Sheila wheels the stroller up to the steps of the church, she is ready to spit nails.

In the five minutes she allowed herself to change clothes and freshen up her lipstick at home, Joe must have called. His brief message said he was stuck on overtime. No kidding!

She'd let Joe take the car to work that morning thinking he'd be home by now, but no. So she's been stuck lugging the kids out through the cold night with PJ in the stroller. Some of the sidewalks are slick with tramped-down snow, and right now it's so cold outside it brings tears to her eyes.

Or at least that's what she keeps telling herself as she swipes a sleeve over her face and wrangles the kids into the church vestibule. The velvet warm air, the scent of burning candles and incense and Murphy's Oil Soap calms her with its deep-seated tradition. The smell brings her back to a calmer place. Midnight mass with Joe. Attending mass with the student body of St. Alban's. Waiting in the pews for the class to finish confession. Spring days of Lent spent staring into the panels of colored light from the stained glass windows.

Well. No time to stare these days. She's got to get Katie down to her Sunday school class, and PJ needs his nose wiped. Actually, the kid probably needs a clean diaper, too, but she's not going to chance taking him into the bathroom if the pageant is about to start. Somebody's got to be there for Katie.

Sheila folds up the stroller, yanks out the diaper bag, and stashes the stroller behind the coatrack.

"Mommy, are we late?" Katie stretches to the tip of her toes to hang her coat on a hook.

"I think we're right on time, but we have to get downstairs and find your class." Still breathless from the cold, Sheila smoothes Katie's hair down and points her to the stairs.

Their little girl in her first role, and her own father is missing it. Such a pity. That damned job! She knows it pays the bills, and God knows the world needs cops out there, but sometimes she just hates being married to a cop.

Down in the church hall Katie finds her class, and Sheila joins her sister and brother-in-law, who have saved her two seats. PJ cries out for his cousin Ian, and the two of them swing their legs and share Cheerios.

"Where's Joe?" Jen's husband Paul turns and looks over his shoulder.

"Stuck at work again, can you believe it? He promised he'd be here for this. I swear, it's going to break Katie's little heart."

"That's too bad," Jen says sincerely.

Sheila notices that Jen and Paul are holding hands, inconspicuously. So sweet. Jen has the perfect husband. Paul is a quiet guy with a high-paying job as an actuary — not to mention regular hours.

What Sheila wouldn't give for some regular hours.

Just then her gaze goes to Ian's coat on the floor. It's casually dropped there, along with a hat — a knit stocking cap. The expensive cap Jen just bought this morning.

Sheila bites her lower lip, stung by jealousy. Not even a gift? The kid just gets a new cap for nothing? It is so not fair, but she bites her bottom lip and grabs Patrick Joseph, who squirms in her arms as the pageant begins.

The lights dim and the children's choir starts to sing, a gangly clump of innocent voices. "Away in a manger, no crib for a bed . . ."

At least the music settles PJ a bit. He pushes to the corner of Sheila's lap, to a spot where he can see, and settles in to watch.

Cold fingers of regret tug at Sheila as she watches the three wise men journey through the audience, heading toward the "star" on-stage. This is not the way Christmas is supposed to be — a mad rush, a voicemail, an empty seat beside her. Her Joe really should be here to see this.

Her throat is thick with emotion as Katie walks onstage with the boy playing Joseph, a real "knucklehead," according to Katie, but then she has a low tolerance for boys. Her freckled, heart-shaped face is radiant as they approach the manger. Joseph lowers the infant doll to the manger, losing his grip so that it tumbles awkwardly. A laugh ripples through the audience, but Katie is unfazed; she reaches down and rewraps the doll, setting it down properly.

Good girl.

Jen reaches across and gives her arm a squeeze as Sheila feels warmed by pride. Joe would get a kick out of that. She turns and, to her surprise, sees him standing in uniform at the back of the church hall. Even from a distance she can see that he's a bit misty-eyed.

He made it. Big sigh. Thank you, Lord.

# CHAPTER 13

That night as Joe reaches into PJ's crib to say good night, he flashes back to Garo Boghosian cradling his son's body in the long shadows of the apartment that evening.

With a dull ache in his chest Joe ruffles the tuft of hair on PJ's forehead, then kisses him on the cheek. "Good night, buddy."

PJ's eyes shine, circles of sleepy speculation. He doesn't answer, but when Joe pats his back the boy reaches up and pats Joe's arm in return.

The simple gesture makes Joe want to bawl like a baby, though he's not sure why. He turns his face away and cuts out of the room fast so that he isn't asked to explain tears that are unexplainable. He dives for the stairs, but Katie calls out as he passes her bedroom.

"Dad?" She folds her hands over her quilt. "I can't sleep. I keep thinking I hear Santa's sleigh outside my window."

Joe pulls his lips into a halfhearted grin. The kid has some imagination. "Don't worry. He won't come 'till after you fall asleep. You know that."

"I know, but I'm too excited to sleep." The pillow is fat beneath her head. Her cheeks are rosy pink, the pearl buttons of her nightgown iridescent in the scrim of light. Geez, she's like one of those kids with sugarplums in her head.

Her sweet anticipation scares him, knowing that one day she'll find out the truth. It's a ruse, all a big lie. He rubs his forehead, sick about the fact that his little girl was in for a huge disappointment.

"Daddy, are you okay?"

"Yeah. Just tired."

When he leans down to kiss her good night her arms snake around his neck for a hefty hug. He gives her a squeeze, growling like the old days. "Bear hug."

Her laughter covers his bad mood until he is out of the room and bounding down the stairs.

Under the jeweled lights of the tree, Sheila reigns over her Christmas kingdom. Flames dance in the little candles on the shelf. The house smells of cinnamon and clove and sugar cookies. Carols take the edge off the quiet, and his wife hums along, her dark head bent over some last-minute gifts to wrap. She loves this holiday so much.

He hates to disappoint her, but his head is in a different place right now, miles away from this cozy Christmas scene.

"Hey, honey. Take a load off and tell me what you think about this awesome car we got for PJ. Where did I hide that sucker? Hold on a sec, let me find it. Want a beer?"

"No, thanks." Right now alcohol would put him over the edge. He sinks into the leather recliner and tries to relax. He's always been able to close his locker at work and leave the job behind, and that's what he needs to do tonight. Enjoy the whole Christmas world that Sheila put together for them. Close your eyes and relax . . .

But when he closes his eyes he sees Garo Boghosian rocking the body of his son, sobbing over the curled, stiff body.

When he tries to shake it off the image morphs to Katie cradling the doll in the Christmas pageant, rocking the baby Jesus. The connection jars him, sends him flying out of the chair.

"What is wrong with you?" Sheila smirks up at him. "Did you and Mack share a Christmas toast on the way home?"

"No, no, nothing like that." He paces in front of the tree. "I'm just strung up tight, thinking about the kids. Do you ever wonder about the Santa thing, Sheila? The big fat lie we tell our kids. The way we jack them up with candy and hope around the holidays. 'Santa knows what you're thinking. He sees you when you're sleeping. Santa brings toys to good girls and boys.' We pump them all up with the Santa stories, big fat lies, then, their balloon gets popped. They fall hard and fast, figure out that it's all a parental conspiracy. Yeah, we set 'em up, then deck 'em, like a bunch of bowling pins."

"Bowling pins?" Sheila is shaking her head in disbelief. "Hello? Did you get bitten by the Grinch? I don't even know what you're talking about."

"The big lie, Shee. The whole Santa debacle, which just sets them up for more fallacies, like telling them that God listens to your prayers and takes care of you. The big lie; that's what I'm talking about."

She pushes up from the floor and straightens, her eyes dark with concern as he paces past her. "Joe, you're scaring me."

"Yeah, well, it's a scary realization that's going to hit our kids eventually. They're going to wonder what the point is. What's the point?"

"Honey —" She reaches for him but he

paces past her, her hand slips from his shoulder.

He moves away from her, lingering in the shadows by the window because he can't have her touching him when he feels this way. He's not going to let this all go, not going to soften at her touch. He's way beyond that. "The thing is, I learned an important lesson out there today. If there even is a God, he's not up there cheering anybody on. Nothing matters. Nobody can make a difference. You can get down on your knees at mass and pray to God all you want, but at the end of the day there's a kid dead out there. The homeless are still homeless and people treat each other like animals and kids OD on drugs before they even have a chance to begin their lives. And I gotta get up on Christmas morning and leave my family and go out and do it all over again." His voice catches, a tight barb in his throat.

"Aw, Joe . . ." She comes toward him, stepping carefully over the wrapping paper and bows, but he holds his arm out.

"Don't touch me, Sheila. You can't make this any better." A fury burns through him, a flash-fire of pain and resentment as he paces the living room, hating every bow and garland and snow-covered crèche in his path.

"Was that what your overtime was about? A kid died?"

He shakes his head and paces, an image of death blooming in his mind: Armand's body curled up, just as his own son tucked in a fetal position, asleep upstairs. That could be his son someday, his PJ. One bad choice and it's all over.

"Tell me about it, Joe." She steps into his path. Sheila never can let go of something. "You need to talk about it. We talk about stuff, remember? We don't hold back, and we don't go to bed mad. Those are the rules."

He glares at her, then skirts around her. "It was a nineteen-year-old kid, a drug overdose. An adult, legally, but if you saw him . . . he's a kid. But the kicker was that his old man called us in the morning to report that the son had stolen his cash. Stolen it to buy drugs, that's what he told us. The father wanted us to go after the kid. Pick him up and throw him in jail. Sort of a fake arrest like Andy Griffith used to do on TV. Scare him straight."

"Oh, man. And you told him you couldn't do it? That you'd lose your job and get sued by the ACLU?"

"Basically." He remembers filling out the complaint report with Mr. B. Filling in the captions, just another piece of paperwork to land in the detective squad's in-box upstairs in the precinct. "So we blow the father off, basically. We follow procedure, file the report. A few hours later, the kid turns up dead."

Sheila's lips press together in a slash. "How awful."

"And when the father ID'd the body . . . I'll never forget it. He lifted the kid in his arms and cradled him like a newborn baby. Rocked the body in his arms as he cried over him."

Tears glimmer in Sheila's dark eyes as she silently shakes her head.

Joe is pissed off at himself for bringing her into this, spreading the pain. He's pissed at her for prying, as usual. He's just basically pissed.

He pivots away, back to pacing the room while Sheila tries to calm him down, says he did the right thing — her usual spiel. It falls around him like melting snow. Something on top of the bookcase catches his eye; a tiny blue bubble, a turret light. He reaches up, his hand closing over metal mounted in half a cardboard box. It's a foot-long car. A toy police car.

"What the hell?" His gaze snaps over to Sheila. "What is this?"

Her jaw drops. "That's where I hid it. Man, am I glad you found that. It's for PJ, a police car. Or a peeze car, as he puts it. It was a gift for him from the precinct Christmas party, only he was so busy climbing in and out of a real patrol car that he didn't notice. So I'm wrapping it up to be his Santa gift, since we didn't really have enough stuff to put under the tree for him. A little short on toys, but I did stay on budget." She crosses toward him. "Isn't it cool? Once we plunk in batteries, the lights and sirens will actually work. I know, it'll be a little annoying, but —"

"No!" Joe cuts her off, acid rising in his throat. "No way! No son of mine is going to be a cop!" As if the car is blazing hot, he flings it across the room. It shatters an ornament at the bottom of the tree. The explosion is just a small ping compared to the fury roaring through his blood. He and Sheila both stare as the car and shards of glass land in a bed of wrapping paper.

"Joe . . ." Her tone is a mixture of surprise and conciliation. "Easy, there."

But he will not be soothed. He will not be calmed or pacified. In fact, he's tempted to pick the toy up and tear its metal doors off with his bare hands. What the hell was Sheila thinking?

If he stays one more minute he's afraid of what he might do.

So he leaves. Out the front door, into the cold night.

# CHAPTER 14

"Oh, my God." The words are half prayer, half a sigh as Sheila watches the front door close behind her husband.

Outside without a coat he's going to freeze, but she knows there's no stopping him. "What was that about?" she says aloud as she steps gingerly toward the shattered ornament.

She has never seen Joe lose his temper, certainly not with that magnitude. Usually she's the hothead of the pair. She picks up the large shards of glass by hand, then hits the rest with the Dustbuster.

She swipes her hair out of her eyes and stands before the tree, bewildered.

She didn't see this coming. She didn't know Joe was crumbling inside. How could she have missed that?

But she heard him tonight, loud and clear, and though she didn't want to admit it to him, she's scared.

This kid's tragic death has pushed Joe over the edge. Of course, the crisis had to be brewing for a long time. And now, it's come to this . . . Has he really lost faith in God? The thought of her Joe, so lost and alone, makes her feel queasy. How could he doubt God? How could he not know that God isn't just "out there" but here, there, and everywhere?

Sheila is scared, but she can't sit here feeling sorry for herself and Joe. She's got to pull off this Christmas, at least for the kids. She flashes on the lights and familiar ornaments of the tree as Bing Crosby croons "White Christmas." She loves that movie. Got to watch it every year. Joe pretends to tolerate it, but she suspects he secretly enjoys the guys' attempts to boost up their former general.

Galvanized by the crisis, Sheila wraps two more presents, starts sifting the ingredients for cinnamon crumb cake, and puts away the baklava from that nice man at the Shuka. She'd been looking forward to indulging in a piece, the phyllo dough drizzled with honey and pistachios, but her appetite has fled. Geez, she didn't even have a chance to mention the shop owner's gesture to Joe yet. She stuffs the kids' stockings with homemade Rice Krispie treats,

Matchbox cars, neon-colored toothbrushes, and candy-cane pencils.

With a deep breath she picks up the toy police car and inspects it. The steel cage of the car is solid, but an axel snapped in half, and one wheel is missing. There's no fixing it. She feels a twinge of guilt as she stashes the car into the back of a closet; she'll deal with the remnants later, but tomorrow morning PJ will have one less present to open. And really, the police car was to be his big gift. Damned if Joe didn't pick the worst time to have his meltdown.

One of the songs from "A Charlie Brown Christmas" is playing, and she feels heartened by it as she pours the batter for her crumb cake. As she slides the pan into the oven she hears the front door open, followed by a cold draft.

Joe appears in the kitchen doorway looking more composed but still frazzled.

"Feel better?"

He shakes his head no.

"Come with me." She yanks off her apron and takes him by the hand. "Sometimes it helps to remember what it's all about. You gotta focus on our priorities: the future," she whispers as she tugs him up the stairs.

First stop, Katie's room. Princess Katie. Sheila puts a fist to her mouth to suppress a giggle when she sees that her daughter is wearing her fanciest nightgown with its pearlized buttons and lace collar. Trying to impress Rudolph, no doubt.

Sheila drops a light kiss on her forehead, then hauls Joe into PJ's room, where they both lean on the crib rails and gaze down at their son, who's got one tiny foot tucked between the slats.

"Next Christmas he's going to be in a bed," Sheila says, shaking her head. "I can't believe it."

Joe touches his pudgy foot, and his feet stir slightly. "Monster boy. But they're both little angels when they're sleeping."

"Little angels who are here because of you."

The warmth drains from his face and he turns, heads back downstairs. "Don't remind me."

"Joe . . ." She bounds down the stairs behind him. "Don't be this way."

"It's not something I can help, Shee." He moves past the tree, as if trying to escape her, trying to avoid a difficult conversation. "You know I love them, which makes me feel that much worse. I brought them onto this spinning planet where there's no master planner. It's all a mess, and there's no guarantee they won't feed into the frenzy.

How do we know they won't turn into addicts or homicidal maniacs? There's no guarantee."

"What's this about a guarantee? We could all pop off tomorrow, but that doesn't mean we're allowed to give up on today."

"You give up fast when the bottom drops out." He pulls aside the lace curtain, stares past the glow of colored lights draped around the window. "When you realize there's no one in control, no God."

"Joe." She winces. "You know you don't mean that." After all those years of Catholic School and mass, the man she loves can't be losing all faith in God. "You need to go to confession or say a rosary or something. Talking like that."

He holds his arms up. "God, I wish it were that easy."

"Okay, see that? Number one, you just prayed to him. And number two, He can make your wishes come true. It's that easy when you have faith."

"Yeah, well, I don't have it. I don't have faith like you do, and it's not coming back over a string of rosary beads." He shakes his head, his dark eyes sad. "Naw, at this point, it would take a miracle to turn me around."

"Really?" She folds her arms, defiant. "Well, then, that's what I'm praying for. A miracle. If it'll take a miracle to bring you back, then I'm on it." She nods, her dark eyes penetrating. "I'm on it as of now."

The next morning, with forced cheerfulness, Sheila drags herself out of bed at six A.M. and props the kids at the table so that they can have Christmas breakfast with Dad before he has to go to work. She puts on a Christmas CD and makes warm cocoa for the kids with peppermint-stick stirrers, but PJ's eyes are still drooping and Katie is cranky.

"Why do we have to wait till Daddy gets home to open the presents?" Katie's stony gaze is fixed on her crumb cake, which she hasn't touched yet.

"Because we want to do it together, as a family," Sheila says with a sugary smile.

Katie's face puckers in a sneer as she looks from one parent to the other. "We're together now. Why don't we open them now?"

"Because Daddy has to go to work soon. But he gets off at four. We'll open them then, when we can relax together."

PJ pushes his cocoa along the table. Sheila grabs it before it spills; her fault for not using a sippy cup. He folds his arms and leans one cheek on the table, his eyes glassy.

Sheila stares down into the cocoa, annoyed with herself. Why did she think this would work at six A.M.?

"But Mommy, Daddy . . ." Katie-the-politician makes eye contact, driving her point home. "I need to open the presents now. We always open our gifts on Christmas morning. It's trajectional."

"Traditional," Sheila corrects her.

Joe's coffee mug pauses on the way to his mouth. He puts it down, shoots Sheila a pained look. "She's right . . ."

"No . . . no!" Sheila insists. "We've waited this long, what's a few hours?" She turns to her daughter, the little instigator. "There's a new tradition now. We're going to celebrate together, wherever and whenever we can be together as a family. You get it? If Daddy has to work on Christmas morning, we'll celebrate Christmas night."

Katie tugs on the lace collar of her nightgown, her face puckered with distaste. "I don't think I like the new tradition."

"Yeah, well, you'll get over it." Sheila stabs at a square of coffee cake and plops it on her plate. Nobody else is eating, and Joe still seems lost, his face pale and sallow. Maybe it's the early hour. Maybe she was foolish to try and pull together a family breakfast.

When Joe takes his keys from the hook

and kisses the kids, she follows him out to the front door. "Kids . . . they know how to push your buttons."

"They sure do." His eyelids are tight, tense, as if it's painful to keep them open. "I'll see you later."

"Okay. Hey . . ." she calls after him as he opens the door. "Merry Christmas." She steps toward him for a big hug, but he plants a kiss on her forehead and ducks out the door into the chill of Christmas morning.

"Well . . ." She folds her arms across her chest, shivering. This has the potential of being the coldest Christmas on record.

# CHAPTER 15

Main Street, Flushing, is uncharacteristically quiet and sparsely populated this morning as Joe wheels the cruiser past small shops, the lone department store, and the gaping staircase that leads down to the subway.

In the passenger seat, Mack is equally subdued. Joe shoots him a scowl. "You falling asleep on me?"

"I'm awake." Mack stretches, his knees banging the glove compartment. "Just moving in slo-mo. I don't think we slept at all last night, if you know what I mean."

"Yeah. How'd Nayasia like the ring?"

"She loved it. Hollered and screamed and stamped her feet like a crazy person. Her mother and her aunties were all grabbing me and kissing me like 'We're so happy for you!' and 'Welcome to the family!' when last week, they hated my ass." He sighs. "It was great."

"Good for you. Hard to believe you're getting married," Joe's voice is flat, lackluster.

"What's that supposed to mean?"

"Just saying. It's hard to believe."

"Yeah, well, you can start believing, Cody, because I'm ready to take the plunge. You are looking at Mr. Responsibility. Gonna get me a house and a dog and a shitload of kids."

"Good for you, Mack." Joe shakes his head. When did his American Dream go sour? He's got everything but the dog and his life has fallen flat around him.

They're about to stop for coffee when the first call of the day comes in.

"Nine-Charlie, respond to a ten twenty-one. Past burglary at the Shuka market."

"What the hell . . ." Joe recognizes the address right away — Mr. Boghosian's place.

"I know, I know, you don't like to pick up a job before you've had your first cup." Mack scribbles down the address, but Joe is already turning the cruiser around.

"Don't bother," Joe grumbles. "I remember where it is."

As he drives, Joe mulls over possible reasons Mr. Boghosian has called the police. Maybe someone broke into his safe again last night, which would mean that the burglar wasn't his son, after all. More likely

570

the older man is reaching out for help, needing someone to talk to, working through denial.

Sad, but it happens. Shit happens and people call the police. There have been plenty of times when Joe has played a therapist on jobs, but today he's in no mood for it.

Hell, the way Sheila was looking at him last night, he could probably use his own therapist.

The Shuka looks the same as it did yesterday when Joe backs the patrol car into an alley across the street and parks. "Like Yogi Berra said, 'It's déjà vu all over again.' "

Bleary-eyed, Mack squints at the market across the street. "Yeah, right. Who was Yogi Bear, anyway?"

"You're kidding me, right?"

"Okay, yeah, I know. Cartoon dude, had his own show."

Joe scowls as they cross the quiet street. "You ever hear of the New York Yankees?"

"Now you don't have to go and get all condescending about it." Mack waits as the electronic door slides open. "You know I'm not into baseball. Hoops. Basketball is my sport."

Inside the Shuka, savory smells lace the air. The sight of pastries and gyro and candied fruit remind Joe that he barely touched Sheila's crumb cake this morning, left the house before he finished his coffee.

Only one of the cashiers is on duty today — the woman with the Day-Glo red hair. Maro . . . or is it Ruth? Today she's wearing a leopard-print sweater that hugs every curve.

"Mr. Boghosian called us?" Joe nods toward the back office.

"Do you know anything about the robbery?" Mack asks her.

"Only what Mr. B. tells me." She flicks her hair from her eyes. You might mistake it for a sexy flick if she were twenty years younger. "He's very upset. Someone robbed the safe last night."

"Not again." Joe gives her a hard look, hoping she'll provide further detail, but the cashier simply nods.

"A terrible thing, to wake up and find money missing on Christmas morning." The woman shakes her head, her gaze flitting to the back of the store as her boss emerges. "Ah, Mr. B. The police have arrived."

He shuffles over, stooped but wiry. "And not a moment too soon." Mr. Boghosian's face is pinched, his tone sour, but this is not the despondent man they dropped off here last night after identifying his son's body. It's going to be a problem; Joe can feel it in his gut. Mr. B. is delusional, lost in denial.

"Officers, my safe was robbed last night. Would you like to step into the backroom? I have left everything in place in case you would like to collect evidence. Fingerprints and such."

Joe catches his partner's eye; Mack shrugs.

"Let's have a look," Mack says.

"It's in the office —" Mr. Boghosian points, but Joe is already striding down the aisle past crates of mandarin oranges and plastic containers of chocolate jellies.

"That's okay, Mr. B. I remember," Joe says.

"You must be mistaken," Mr. B. says. "I've owned this store twenty years, and I have never before invited the police into my office."

Joe rubs his forehead. It's going to be a long morning. "Yeah, okay. So why don't you show us your safe, Mr. B.?"

Nothing in the backroom has changed since the previous day when the store owner showed them the safe under the desk. When Mack squats down and shines his flashlight on the safe under the desk, Joe feels a stab of impatience. It's one thing to indulge the man for his loss; do they need to play out this charade in denial?

Joe stands back and watches as the conversation follows the same pattern from yesterday. Like a repeat of a bad TV show; it isn't any better the second time. Mr. B. assures them the "girls" in his employment would never steal from him. He insists that it's an inside job; he knows who did it.

His son.

Joe's heart sinks. This is going from bad to worse.

Mr. Boghosian launches into the same story he told them on Christmas Eve. That his son is the only one with a set of keys. That his son plans to go to Julliard, but right now wastes too much time playing his saxophone and staying out late in clubs.

It pains Joe to listen to him, like a cat clawing at his heart. And how is Mack staying so calm, listening and nodding passively, as if he's never heard this story before? Watching the two of them, it's freaky. You would never know that this older man lost a son yesterday.

When Mr. Boghosian tells the cops he wants them to arrest his son, Joe interrupts. "Excuse me, Mr. Boghosian, but do you mind if I consult with my partner a minute?"

"Of course not." The older man pushes

away from the desk and shuffles toward his shop. "Use my office. I'll go check on the girls up front."

Watching him leave, Mack shakes his head. "The girls are pushing forty, but whatever."

"That's the least of his denial." Joe keeps the rumble of his voice low; he doesn't want to be overheard. "Can you believe this guy?"

Mack shrugs. "Yeah, the son sounds like trouble."

"Are you kidding me?" Joe squints at his partner. "Bad joke, Mack."

"I'm not squirreling around. You know the son is the one who stole the cash."

"Is this some kind of sick joke?" Joe rubs his forehead, a headache coming on. Is this what happens when Mack is sleep-deprived? His partner's brain was definitely not firing on all pistons. "Think, Mack. This job is identical to the one we handled yesterday morning. Remember the result? The kid in that apartment off Main Street?"

Mack's eyes close, skepticism in his gaze. "Actually, I don't remember anything like that." He hooks his thumbs into his gun belt. "What the hell are you talking about, Cody?"

"Don't play with me, man. I'm in no mood . . ."

"Who's playing?" Mack's voice is shrill with annoyance. "I'm just trying to help this man out, get this job done, and get some coffee. You want to go to the car and get the paperwork, or should I?"

"Mack . . ." Joe lowers his voice again. "The guy's just claiming theft because he needs help. Which is understandable, since he lost his son yesterday. It's a cry for attention, but taking a report isn't going to do it."

"Wait. Just hold — hold on, there." Mack holds a hand up. "You saying this guy's son died yesterday."

"The kid in the apartment, remember?" When Mack's eyes glaze in confusion, Joe growls in frustration. "The overdose?"

"Not ringing a bell for me."

"Come on, Mack. Cut the crap." Aggravation needles his usual composure. He can't wait to get back to the precinct and shove yesterday's report into his partner's face.

"Excuse me, officers?" Garo Boghosian pokes his head in the doorway, then shuffles in. "I have an idea. My son doesn't think I know these things, but I can give you the address where he is staying. His girlfriend's apartment."

"Sounds good." Mack steps away from Joe, relieved at the interruption. "I'm going to the cruiser for paperwork. Officer Cody will take that information."

Joe mouths a sarcastic "Thanks" before Mack ducks out the backdoor of the grocery, but the older man doesn't see. Mr. B. is bent over his desk, scrawling something on a notepad.

"There." He tears off a piece of paper and hands it to Joe. "His girlfriend's address. Chances are, you will find him there today."

"Yeah, okay." A sick feeling curls his stomach as Joe takes the paper, wishing he didn't have to be a part of this horror show. Mr. Boghosian is obviously in deep denial and Mack is being an idiot. Things have gone from maudlin to bizarre.

When Mack returns with the paperwork, Joe leans back into the shadows and lets his partner take the lead. Mulling over it all, he wonders if this could all be a nightmare, a really sick dream. He shifts from foot to foot, considering. He's never had a dream with such great odors before — the smells of citrus and cinnamon and gyro wafting in from the grocery. Nah. It's no dream. Just a really twisted reality.

At last the paperwork is wrapped up and the store owner walks the cops back through his shop.

"You got a nice little shop here, Mr. Boghosian," Mack says. "We'll file this report and the detectives will let you know if they find anything."

Translation: Don't hold your breath.

Mack heads out, but Joe can't leave without trying to get through to this man; he just wants to scrape a patch of reality, to bring the man back, painful though that may be.

Joe pauses at the register, then extends his hand. "You know, everyone has regrets in life. Things we wish we could change."

Garo Boghosian clasps his hand, a surprisingly strong grip. "Sage words, officer."

"Let me ask you, Mr. B., if you could have your son back, right now, what would you say to him?"

The man clenches his jaw as he draws in a breath, his chest rising like a puffer fish. "It's not what I would say, but what I would do. I would take my money back and wash my hands of him. No son of mine shall be a thief! He is no son of mine."

Joe just nods and waits, expressionless, knowing this is not the end.

A moment later, Boghosian's face crumples in pain. His breath comes out in a gasp as his chin drops to his chest, despondent.

Joe waits as a sob breaks the air; there's

nothing he can do for this man, nothing anyone can do.

"You know the truth, officer. You know that is a lie." When Garo Boghosian lifts his head, tears shimmer in his eyes, reminding Joe of the man who had sobbed over his son's body just yesterday. The huddled man lifting his son in his arms, rocking the grown man's body as if it were as light as an infant's.

Joe nods. "I know."

"If you find my son, please bring him back to me. I will make sure he gets help. I will make sure he is placed in a very good rehabilitation hospital."

The man's words, so steeped in pain and delusion, are a knife in Joe's gut. "I'm sorry," Joe says, looking to the door, looking to escape. He's got to get out of here. Now. "I'm sorry about your son." His chest tight, he leaves the despondent man behind and escapes to the cold, fresh air.

He glares at Mack, who falls into step beside him.

"What's wrong with you, man?" Mack asks.

"What the hell were you doing in there?"

"Following procedure."

"Yeah? Since when is lying to a man about his dead son procedure?" They reach the

579

patrol car, but Joe can't get in yet. He can't sit in a tight, super-heated space and think about that man and his dead son. He can't go back to a job that has him answering after the fact and taking reports.

Joe stares down at the side of the car. "CPR. I've always hated that logo. I hate this job. Guys go into the NYPD for excitement, but really it's all a paper chase. And don't think you'll be helping anyone. Like I always say, cops in this city are the garbagemen of humanity."

"Cody, I know you're pissed off, but I don't know what you're talking about with the dead kid. We didn't sit on a body yesterday."

Joe wheels around, slams his hand on the roof of the patrol car and curses. "Like hell we didn't. Why can't you remember?"

"Because it didn't happen." Mack holds his hands up. "Hold on. I got a perfectly legitimate way to solve this. We'll go back to the precinct and pull out all the paperwork from our last tour. You can show me the forty-nine on Mr. Boghosian's son. What's his name . . . Andrew?"

"Armand." Joe fishes in his pocket for the keys, but comes back with the note Boghosian gave him — the girlfriend's address. "See this?" He hands it to Mack. "That's

the address where we found the kid yesterday."

Mack frowns at the paper. "Doesn't ring a
bell."

Still searching for the car keys, Joe reaches
into the pocket of his uniform pants and
finds another square of paper. He checks it,
the bold handwriting nearly stopping his
heart. "Okay, this is where things are getting spooky."

"What?" Mack asks as he opens the passenger door.

Joe squares his jaw, trying to absorb the
*Twilight Zone* moment. He flashes the note
at his partner. "Got this yesterday from Mr.
Boghosian."

It's an identical scrap of paper with the
same scrawled address.

# CHAPTER 16

"Katherine Bernadette Cody, put those presents down and help your mother decorate these cookies," Sheila calls from the kitchen.

Katie peeks at her mother from behind a gift wrapped in red foil, but she doesn't give up her spot under the tree.

Icing drips over Sheila's fingers as she tries to glaze a church-shaped cookie. "Don't make me give you a timeout."

"But Mom, it's Christmas morning, and you know I love to do this. I like to guess what's inside." She gives the red foil present a shake, then tries to squeeze it.

"Katie, stop! What if it's breakable?" Sheila doesn't recall what's inside, but she's losing patience. She drops the sticky knife into the bowl of icing and charges into the living room. "Come on, now. Put the present down and come into the kitchen."

"But, Mom . . ."

How many times a day does Katie say that? Sheila has a feeling she's going to hear that expression a million times before her daughter turns eighteen.

Sheila licks her knuckles, then points to the base of the tree. "Put it down, and leave the gifts alone. You've become a real Christmas nut." *Just like your mother,* Sheila thinks. Watching like a hawk, she waits while her daughter releases the package, then picks up another.

"This one's from Santa. He brought it last night." Katie hoists the large, flat box, nearly half her size. "Who's it for, Mom?"

"I don't know." Sheila recognizes the paper, a pattern of triangular gold and silver angels, but she doesn't remember wrapping the gift. "Well, that's why I don't recognize it," she says as she reads the tag. "It's for me."

"You got something from Santa, Mommy." Katie's rosebud lips curve in a smile, as if the notion of adults getting gifts strikes her as silliness.

"I guess so." Annoyance swells in her chest at the thought of Joe buying her a gift after they promised each other they wouldn't. How could he?

Then again, the writing on the tag doesn't look like Joe's. So who's it from?

As Sheila bends down to replace the gift, she notices a few others wrapped in the angel paper. "This is weird." There's one for Katie, one for Joe, and a good-sized gift for Patrick Joseph who, at the moment, is taking a blissfully long nap upstairs.

Very strange. Sheila straightens, staring down at the presents. "Where'd these gifts come from?" she says, thinking aloud.

Katie giggles. "Mommy! They're from Santa."

"Of course they are." Sheila puts her hands on her daughter's shoulders and guides her back toward the kitchen. "Now let's wash your hands so you can get to decorating. The trees and snowmen are looking pretty bare."

She's just getting Katie settled at the kitchen table with an apron and colored sugars when Joe calls.

"PJ's napping and Katie's helping me decorate cookies," she reports. "What's up with you?"

"Shee, I'm having a bizarre day."

"What's wrong, honey?"

"Remember that kid I mentioned yesterday? The one who overdosed?"

"I don't think I'll ever forget that." Their heated discussion of the previous night was not characteristic of their relationship. She'd never seen Joe storm out like that; it was the most tumultuous Christmas Eve of her life.

"Thank God you remember, because Mack is drawing a blank. The weirdest thing is going on. The kid's father called us again this morning. Only Mack says it's not the second time. He says it never happened yesterday."

"What?" Sheila sprinkles green jimmies onto a tree cookie. "Did Mack fall and hit his head or something?"

"Nah. He got engaged last night."

"Well, that could explain it. I'll bet Nayasia is thrilled."

"Sounds that way, though I don't know why. She's going to spend the rest of her life with Mack."

Some sort of comment passes from Mack — the wry kidding that always goes on between those two. Sheila moves away from Katie. "Really, honey. The kid who died yesterday . . . What's the deal with that?"

"I don't know. I'm still scratching my head."

"Is the kid still alive?"

"How could he be?"

Joe's question hangs in the space between them.

Sheila draws a cautious breath. "Joe, this

is insane. What are you going to do?"

"I don't know, Shee. Right now we're headed back to the precinct to look up yesterday's paperwork, figure out who's got this right."

"Sounds like an episode of *Lost.*"

He switches gears. "How are the kids?"

"Absolutely fine, though I got my own little mystery going here. Did you play elf last night and sneak some presents under the tree?"

A tired sigh comes over the line. "No, Shee."

"Well, that's weird, because, suddenly, there are some gifts here that . . ." She looks around to see if Katie is listening. Hard to tell. "There are some things that I didn't put there. Must be from Santa." She steps into the living room, lowers her voice. "Are you telling me the truth, Joe? One of the packages is for me. Did you buy me something?"

"We had a deal — no gifts. I kept up my end of the bargain."

"Then where did this stuff come from?" she asks.

"Did you talk to your sister?"

Jen? Sheila bites her lower lip. "That must be it. The little sneak. I've got to call her."

"That solves your mystery," Joe says flatly.

"Except that I can't find the . . ." A quick glance tells her Katie is watching. "I can't find the *thing* I threw in the closet after you broke it. The item of contention." She spells it out. "The p-o-l-i-c-e c-a-r?"

"Geez, you're challenging my verbal skills. I can't read and stay on the road at the same time." He pauses. "That toy police car?"

"Did you take it?" Suddenly she can visualize the toy in the trash out back.

"Nope." Behind his voice the radio crackles — the central dispatcher. "Shee, I gotta go."

"Okay, honey. I love you . . ." But suddenly the connection is lost, and Sheila can only hope he heard her last words.

# CHAPTER 17

The Aided Call is a welcome distraction from the surreal morning.

Auburndale House, an assisted-living facility, is a regular port-of-call in their sector. Joe and Mack are the first responders on the scene. As Joe pulls into the building's narrow driveway he spots Coral Winfield, the buttoned-down black administrator who always reminds him of a school principal.

Coral marches right up to them. "Good morning, officers. Mrs. Persichetti lost her balance and went down. I got an ambulance on the way, but she says she's not going to the hospital."

"Can't blame her for that," Mack says as they follow Coral into the building's lobby, where the woman is seated in a wheelchair, surrounded by a handful of people.

"I don't know what all the commotion is about. Flashing lights out there, and look . . . the police. Really, it's not necessary. I'm going to my son's house for Christmas dinner, that's all." Mrs. Persichetti has the gravelly voice of a lifetime smoker and the jewelry collection of a queen. From all the bling on her hands, it's a wonder she can lift them at all. She pats the blood pressure cuff on her arm, her watery blue eyes on the cops. "Officers, really, you shouldn't have come. I'm just fine. Had a little spill, is all. That's all."

Joe moves closer and leans down so that he is eye-level with the woman. "What happened, ma'am?"

"Well, you see I was trying to get something out of my bag when it caught on my coat. The clasp, right there, it got caught." Her withered hands tremble slightly as she touches the metal clasp of her purse. "You see? I paused to work it loose and it threw me off balance."

"Were you dizzy?" Joe asks.

"No, no, none of that. And I'll thank you to call off the ambulance, officer. It's Christmas Day and my son David is taking me to his house for Christmas." The man in the leather jacket she calls David looks to be in his seventies, though David's son seems hearty.

"We'll get you there, Ma," says David. "Just let the paramedics check you over, make sure you didn't break anything."

Mrs. Persichetti rolls her eyes. "I did not break anything. I would know." She frowns at her son. "Broke my hip last year. I knew it then, didn't I?"

"Your son is right, ma'am," Joe says politely. "No one wants you to spend your Christmas in the emergency room, but if you can wait a few minutes, I'd feel much better if we could have our paramedics take a look, give you the green light."

"Well." She smacks the armrests of the wheelchair. "I suppose I can wait a few minutes, but I'm moving to a real chair. The indignity of this thing, like a bicycle with no steering mechanism."

Joe straightens and smiles, feeling a certain sense of rightness in the outcome here. This is a job he can handle. He knows how to talk to people. Maybe there are still a few aspects of this job he doesn't hate.

While they wait for the ambulance, Joe keeps Mrs. Persichetti engaged in conversation. For a ninety-three year old, the woman is sharp as a tack.

The ambulance arrives with a blast of whooping siren and flashing lights. Mrs. Persichetti groans. "So much fuss." When Todd comes into the lobby carrying an emergency kit, the elderly woman extends her left arm. "Here we go again. You can take my blood pressure and fuss over me all you want, young man, but I'm not going to the hospital."

Todd crouches down beside her. "That's about the best offer I've had all day."

While Todd takes her vitals, Joe heads outside to find Dolly. Seeing Todd, Joe realized they don't need to get the paperwork back at the station; Dolly and Todd can corroborate the story on Armand Boghosian.

The rear doors of the ambulance are flung open, Dolly's dark blue legs stretching out to the pavement. She's leaning in, unlatching a backboard.

"I don't think you're going to need that," Joe tells her.

"Yeah, you got a livewire in there." Mack joins them.

"Glad to hear it." Dolly pushes the orange board back into the van. "Last job we had was a cardiac arrest. CPR in front of the whole family huddled around watching in their jammies. It wasn't pretty."

"Speaking of jobs —" Joe jumps right in. "We followed up on that kid who OD'd yesterday. Found his father to identify the body. That was a sad one."

"Yesterday." Her eyes flash on Joe intently as she reaches back, yanks a clip from her blond hair, then twists it around and clips it again. "You must be talking about last week or something, Joe. Yesterday was my day off."

No . . . it can't be. Joe feels his resolve fading fast.

Mack smacks his elbow. "See? Told ya."

"No, no." Joe steps away from his partner, rubs his elbow. "I mean Christmas Eve, Doll. You remember. The kid in the apartment off Main Street? Asian girlfriend?"

Dolly's bright eyes flicker over to Mack. "Is this some kind of joke?"

"No, I —"

"Exactly," Mack steps in on him, shutting him up with a lethal look. He's just trying to keep Joe from stepping in it deeper, but it pisses Joe off. "Just a stupid joke," Mack says.

But it's not a joke to Joe. It's a cold, hard fact that isn't matching up to reality. His world is off kilter, totally warped.

"Yeah, well, Merry Christmas to you guys," Dolly says. "But don't jump the gun. April Fools' Day is a ways off yet."

# CHAPTER 18

"Look, man, I don't know what's going on with you, but it's okay. You know?" Mack steps on the brakes, a little too hard, and he and Joe swing forward slightly. It's unusual for Mack to be driving, but Joe wants to focus; he's got a lot to think about.

"It's the holidays," Mack goes on. "People get stressed and off the frizzle and whatnot. I know how it is, man. When we get off today, you'll go home and be with your family. Kick back and forget any of this ever happened."

"Just keep driving," Joe mutters. Holding one of Garo Boghosian's notes in each hand, he tries to ignore Mack's poor driving skills so that he can piece it together. This is a bizarre situation, a mystery more puzzling than any case he's ever sent upstairs to the detectives.

No one else seems to remember the kid who died yesterday, but it happened.

He saw Armand Boghosian's dead body being rocked in his father's arms.

Damn it, he saw the kid's body.

Why doesn't anyone else remember that?

He stares at the notes in his hands, the curved swirl of Garo Boghosian's script catching his eye. Mr. Boghosian was so unaffected this morning, as if the trauma of his son's death never happened.

"Don't these notes prove anything?" Joe says aloud.

Mack beeps the siren to ease ahead of traffic on Main Street. "Okay, man, the two notes are spooky. But what's the point? Why are you trying so hard to prove that Boghosian's son is dead when everything says it's not true."

Why? Joe's heartbeat accelerates. "That's a good question. Why am I letting this make me crazy? Because maybe he's not dead. Maybe we still have time to find him alive." He flips the siren on, stuffs the notes back into his pocket and gives Mack the address of Wendy Min's apartment. "Get there, forthwith."

Adrenaline pushes him up the stairs, one flight, two . . . three. He pounds on the door of Wendy Min's apartment, identifies himself as the police, then waits.

No answer.

"What's going on?" Mack asks, catching up.

Joe lets out a breath — relief. "We're in time, I think. They probably didn't get back from the after-hours place yet." He's already striding down the hall, headed back to the stairs. "We'll wait in the car, catch the kid before he comes in downstairs."

"You mind telling me what the hell you're babbling about?" Mack calls from behind.

"We're trying to save a life." Joe's voice thunders through the stairwell.

"Something tells me your methods are not really in line with department policy."

"You got that right," Joe says as the soles of his boots clatter down another flight of stairs.

Outside the patrol car is parked a few yards from the building's front entrance, next to a fire hydrant. Close enough, Joe thinks as he slides into the passenger seat and closes the door.

Mack gets in beside him. "Okay, this is weirding me out, like you know the future or something."

"Nah, I don't. Just one kid's future." Or maybe one kid's destiny if he doesn't intervene? The scene from *A Christmas Carol* flashes in his mind, Scrooge asking the third ghost if this is a vision of what might be or what will be . . .

But the Scrooge in Joe's head is played by the cartoon version of Mr. Magoo, and if he tries to explain this to Mack, his partner's going to lose all confidence in him.

"I just have this feeling we can do something positive today," Joe says. "That maybe we can save a life."

Mack bites his lower lip, nods. "Okay, that'd be cool." He tosses his memo book on the dashboard and adjusts the driver's seat. "I'm up for that. We got the Superman costumes on; might as well be heroes."

"Yeah, I wish it was that easy."

Just ahead of them an old Dodge pulls up and double-parks.

"That's a bonehead move," Joe says. "Right in front of us."

Mack picks up his memo book. "Should I write him?"

Joe waves it off. "Let it go. There's an old lady in the back. It'd be like you were writing your grandmother."

Mack flips on the radio, tunes into a station. "All Christmas carols, all the time," he says with a grin.

"Angels we have heard on high, sweetly singing o'er the plains . . ." Mack hums along. "Here goes that Gloria song again. What the hell does she have to do with

Christmas?"

Before Joe can answer his eyes alight on a couple staggering up the street, coming from the direction of the subway. The lanky kid wearing a black North Face jacket leans heavily on the girl, a petite kid who needs to take three or four steps for every one of his. Joe flashes on that jacket, remembers searching it, finding baggies of pills in the pockets.

"That's got to be them." He pops out of the cruiser, leaves the door open as he lunges over to the doorway. Yeah, it's them. He recognizes Wendy Min's exotic almond-shaped eyes and red-streaked hair. The line of studs on Armand's ear stand out from here. Joe can barely believe he's seeing the kid with his own eyes — Armand Boghosian, walking and breathing and very much alive.

Nothing short of a miracle.

Joe is tempted to stand there gaping in awe at the amazing thing — a young life — but he's got to do something to preserve it. He plants himself between the kids and the door to the apartment house. Off to his left, Mack moves cautiously, not quite sure what's going on. Joe isn't so sure, either, except . . .

Except that he's got to stop Armand Boghosian from going up to Wendy's apartment.

The kids approach the door, Armand talking a mile a minute like a raving auctioneer. His hands flit through the air in empty gestures. His dark eyes are bloodshot and glassy.

High as a kite. Probably cocaine, Joe suspects. Maybe some prescription drugs.

Stepping into their path, he calls to them. "You two better stop right there."

Panic crosses Wendy's face. She braces, holding Armand upright as she takes in the two cops closing on either side. "Is there a problem, officers?"

Joe isn't exactly sure what he's going to do until the words slide out. "We're here for Armand. His father wants to see him. He's got a few questions about some money Armand borrowed last night."

Expecting resistance, Joe is squarely planted, his senses on alert.

But there is only defeat as Wendy glares up at her boyfriend. "Did you take that money from your father?"

"The money isn't a problem. It was all right there, a bundle of money. Rolling like a snowball. You know, how it rolls? The way the world is a snowball? See how it rolls?"

"Armand . . ." She climbs out from under his arm, presses her hands into his chest to

598

boost him up. "You're not making any sense. You told me — you promised — you swore that money wasn't stolen. Armand, how can I ever trust you?"

"You don't get it. You gotta get it." The kid is babbling, deranged. "See how it's all white? It's a sugar day, you know what I mean? You have to get out and roll along."

"Oh, my God." Wendy presses her hands to her panicked face. Her voice cracks with emotion. "I can't do this anymore. You have to go. Go and get straight. I can't help you, Armand. I thought I could, but I was wrong. I can't do it."

Armand is draped over her, a marionette in storage. She straightens and pushes him away, and he teeters back on his heels. Twitching. Unsteady.

"You're coming with us." Joe closes the space quickly, takes the kid by the shoulders. "Get down," he instructs briskly. "Down on your knees." Better to have the kid closer to the ground if he collapses, which seems likely in Armand's altered state.

Armand sinks down and, within seconds, Mack is on the kid, patting him down, snapping on cuffs, pulling small plastic bags of drugs from Armand's pockets. "What do we have here? Looks like a good amount of drugs."

"Oh, my God!" Wendy presses spidery hands to her face, pale fingertips peeking through black fingerless gloves. "What are you doing to him?"

"He's under arrest," Mack says.

"Oh, my God! Are you taking him to jail?"

"That's where you go when you get arrested," Mack tells her as he finishes patting the kid down. "You have the right to remain silent . . ."

But Joe waves him off. "Don't Mirandize him. We're not arresting him."

"We're not?" Mack squints at Joe as if he's gone crazy. "I got the cuffs on him." Police procedure prescribes that you don't put cuffs on them unless you are arresting a person. A civil liberties thing.

"That's okay. Let's get him in the car," Joe says. "I'll take the complaint for this one if it hits the fan."

"Cody, you are stark raving out of your mind today."

"And you know what? I'm starting to feel really good about it," Joe says as he and Mack help the kid to his feet and guide him to the patrol car.

"Don't hurt him!" Wendy sobs.

"He's gonna be okay," Joe tells her as Mack guides the kid's head safely under the roof of the vehicle. "We're taking him to get some help. Rehab."

"I know, I know. He's an addict, but —" She presses her fists to her eyes. "He's a really good guy. I know he needs help, but please, please don't hurt him."

"We won't." Joe opens the passenger door, anxious to get rolling. So far they've broken a few dozen procedural rules, and he wants to get the hell out of here before he can think about how it might all come crashing down on their heads. "He'll need your help when he gets out," he tells the girl.

She nods. "I'll do everything I can. He's a good guy, he just . . ."

"Yeah, I know." Joe lifts his chin, his gaze scanning the apartment building. There's that third floor window, the apartment where he spent a dark eternity twelve or so hours ago.

A lifetime ago.

Cody slides into the car to find Mack staring out through the windshield. "What the hell are we doing? Joe, we gotta either book this kid for possession or let him go right now." Mack sneaks a look in the rearview mirror and lowers his voice. "And you better hope and pray this kid doesn't sue our asses for violating his constitutional rights."

"Flushing General," Joe says. He's breaking a dozen rules and laws, but he needs to do this. He's got to get it right, at least this one time. "We're taking him to the rehab center there."

"No program's going to admit him on Christmas Day." Although Mack is in argument mode, he puts the car in gear and rolls. "Besides that, we are the police, not social workers or shrinks, and there's no law on the books that says the drug police can swoop down and throw your ass into rehab."

In the backseat, Armand is still hyped up and chattering to himself a mile a minute. Something about rolling marshmallows. The kid might need his stomach pumped.

Joe turns back to his partner. "If anyone asks, we found this kid flying high as a kite, disturbing the peace. Figured we had to get him to the hospital, make sure he's okay."

"And why didn't we call an ambulance?" Mack poses the question.

"We'll say we couldn't wait. Don't you get it? This kid in the back is Armand Boghosian, Mr. B.'s son. And I'm telling you, sure as I'm sitting here now, he OD'd yesterday. For some freaky-deaky reason, it looks like we've been given a second chance here, a chance to save this kid's life, and I, for one, am not going to sit around arguing department procedure while this kid fades out of the picture. Now are you going to get on board with this, or what?"

"I'm driving, aren't I?" There's a cool grin on Mack's face when he turns and bumps fists with Joe. "I sure hope the cheese-eaters took off for Christmas," Mack adds.

"Internal Affairs, yeah, they would be a problem. But really, do you think they're out here on Christmas morning?" Joe waves off the possibility. Right now he's got to take his chances. "Just drive."

# CHAPTER 19

"You still here?" A nurse smiles at Joe when she steps into the hospital room to check the IV drip.

"I'm just going to stay until his father gets here." Joe knows he's not obligated to wait, that Armand Boghosian is in capable hands, but he has to see this through. He needs to know that, when he walks away, Armand's father will be here for him.

So he's been standing in the shadows, using the time to pray to God for this kid. He started with a few *Our Fathers,* then switched over to a more stream-of-consciousness thing, figuring that God is probably as sick of hearing that memorized prayer as he is of saying it. And he wanted to tell God that he was grateful, thankful in an overwhelming way. Every cell in his body is ringing with peace and this new sense of power. He was part of a miracle, or, maybe just a witness to it.

*Either way, I gotta thank you, God. Thanks, and please, watch over this kid and put him on the right path. Give him a chance to do something good with his life.*

The nurse's gaze moves along the clear tubing, which Joe has been watching with an odd feeling of hope. They told him the clear bag is filled with a saline solution combined with vitamins, but it's gratifying to watch it drip into Armand's veins. Like it's infusing him with health. Getting him on the road to recovery.

Corny? Yeah. Mack would cut him to the quick if he heard Joe talking that way. Maybe it's a good thing he went off to the hospital cafeteria for two coffees.

"He should be capable of conversation soon," the nurse says. "Maybe he'll make sense this time." When they brought Armand in he was suffering some withdrawal symptoms, restless and irritable and pissed as hell that the attending physician ordered his stomach pumped — "gastric lavage" they called it. Thank God the staff had asked Joe and Mack to step out for the worst of it. When they returned, Armand had calmed down.

Now he seems to be sleeping, his mouth caked with charcoal, his dark hair damp with sweat. The kid is still a mess, but to

Joe he's a miraculous sight. Alive and breathing. Alive.

The nurse slips the blood pressure cuff over Armand's arm; it pumps and releases automatically.

"Is he sedated?" Joe asks.

"No. We don't like to give anything to a detox patient. We try not to."

"Don't talk about me like I'm not here," Armand murmurs, though his eyes are still closed. He turns his head against the pillow, and the diamond studs along his ear twinkle in the pasty fluorescent light. "I'm still miserable from having that tubing shoved inside me. My throat hurts. That doctor needs to have his license revoked."

The nurse grunts. "Dr. Cohen had to be on the safe side, Armand. You had enough drugs in your pocket to kill an elephant."

"That's ridiculous. I would never kill an elephant."

The nurse is ready to leave, but she clearly wants to get the last word. "Time to take some responsibility, Armand. We can clean you up and dry you out, but you're the one who's going to have to decide to make the change."

His only response is a groan.

"Think about it," she says curtly, then ducks out.

Joe moves closer to the bed. He's never gotten involved in a job this way, but it's too late to pull back now. "You know, you're lucky to be alive."

The kid's head lolls to the right and his dark eyes spill open. "Oh, yeah. The cop." He lets out a long breath. "You going to arrest me now?"

"I'd rather not. Me? I want to go home to Christmas dinner with my family. And you? You got some work to do. You need to get straight. Clean and sober."

Although Joe expects a fight, Armand winces, his eyes straining as though in pain. "I know that. God, I know. I really screwed up."

"It happens," Joe says. "We all make mistakes, but some of them can cost you, and I'm telling you, yours could've cost you your life." As soon as he says it, Joe worries that it sounds trite. He tries to think fast, bring the conversation back to basics. "So I hear you play the saxophone."

"Yeah, it's what I do best. Damn good sax player, for what it's worth."

"Your father said you're auditioning at Juilliard." Joe takes out his memo book and removes a card from the back.

"That's what I tell people to get them off my back. Juilliard isn't going to want a guy

607

like me, especially . . . especially after all this." He looks up at the monitors. "Am I going to have a criminal record now?"

Joe shakes his head. "You know, the cops aren't out there just to arrest people. Now and again we actually get a chance to lend a hand." He extends the card, Jennifer's card, to the kid. "My wife's sister, she works at Juilliard. Not that I can guarantee anything, but she might be able to help you get an audition. If you're as good as you say, maybe they'll give you a shot."

The kid's eyes go wide as he reads the card. "Wow, I . . . thanks. But you never even heard me play. Why would you stick your neck out?"

Joe shrugs. "It's Christmas."

He puts the card on the bed table. "I'll call her as soon as . . . when I get out of here."

"Finish the program. Give it your best shot. She'll wait 'till you're ready."

But Armand's focus has shifted past Joe, to the doorway. "Papa?"

Garo Boghosian pauses on the threshold, arms in the air, his entire being a swell of emotion. "My son. My beautiful Armand."

The young man's face crumples as tears fill his eyes. "Hey, Papa."

Stepping back, Joe takes it all in.

Garo Boghosian shuffles up to the bed and pats his son's cheek. "I have been wanting to see you, but not like this." Anger and concern flare in his eyes. "What happened to you?"

"I screwed up." Armand's voice breaks on a sob. "I'm an addict, Dad. I need help. I want to make a change, but I can't do it alone. I need help."

"I knew it." Tears fill the father's eyes as he freezes in place, as if locked in the cell of a film strip. "I knew . . . and I'm going to make sure you get what you need. There are people here who will help you, if you are willing to do the work."

In the pallid sheen of the overhead fluorescent lights, Garo Boghosian reaches for his son. Joe watches the father lift the young man's shoulders into his arms, cradling him as Armand sobs like a newborn baby.

Something deep inside Joe swells, an overwhelming feeling evoked by the scene before him. The embrace of father and son slides over the nightmarish image that has haunted him, and at once the visage of death disappears.

This is the new reality.

This is the culmination of a miracle.

# Chapter 20

"Yes, yes, Auntie," Wendy Min says in the fluent Mandarin her parents have always insisted upon. Her thoughts stray from the phone pressed to her ear. "I'll be there in a minute."

Standing at the window of her apartment, looking out at the snow swirling under the light of streetlamps, Wendy Min wants to end the call. She wishes her parents and her auntie Fang would just let her be for a few minutes.

They don't know that she saw her boyfriend dragged away this afternoon. They don't know that she dreamed of his death last night, a dream so vivid she can still feel the sting of salty tears in the back of her throat. And now . . . what will come next? So many thoughts and feelings to sort out. So many hopes and fears, dreams and worries.

It's that gray time of day, one of the shortest days of the year, when night begins to tug at the sky early, a greedy child pulling away the bedsheet. And today of all days Wendy feels all the more reluctant to let the night win. Night is the future, and anything can happen in the future. Wendy was raised to believe that you cannot avoid the destiny that comes rushing your way. The tsunami of the future. But today, she is not so sure. Today, for the first time, the storm passed over.

"What's that?" Auntie Fang's voice draws her back to the present. "Fresh peas. I'll go to the corner first and see if the market is open. Yes, Auntie. Bye-bye."

Wendy closes her phone but she does not turn away from the window, knowing he is out there. Armand is out there, somewhere, alive. Not the cold, petrified body in her dream, and not the powerful dragon of his birth sign rising up over her in fury, a swirling ghost of unrequited destiny.

He is alive. That nightmare was wrong. Her spirit dances, lifted by the knowledge.

Her gaze skitters over the urban landscape, the rooftops and jagged edges of boxy high-rise apartments blocking the gray sky.

*I know you are out there,* her mind speaks to him. *And I love you.*

The ring of her cell phone interrupts, and

she flips it open, wondering what Auntie Fang wants now. *"Wei?"*

"I love you." His voice is chalky and dry.

"Armand!" she whispers, closing her eyes so she can see him. Imagine him in a bed of crisp white sheets, a lifeline running into his arm, tethering him to the earth.

"I miss you already."

"How are you? Did the police treat you well?"

"I've been better, though the cops were real gentlemen. It's the doctor who insisted on pumping my stomach that really pissed me off."

She takes a breath infused with hope. This is almost too good to believe, that the greedy addiction might end and, somehow, its hold on Armand would be broken. For so many months she has been wishing and praying that his life could be saved; now that it seems to be happening, she is almost afraid to embrace it. "I'll visit you every day. What can I bring?"

"No visits allowed for a while. Apparently we inmates can't be trusted. But they're telling me I can call you at night. I'll call you every night."

Suddenly her throat grows thick, clogged with all the emotion and tears and worry she has kept tamped down, deep down inside. To think of Armand, safe in a place where there's a chance he'll get better . . . it's overwhelming.

"Wendy . . . you still there?"

She swipes at a tear with the back of one hand. "I'm here." Turning away from the window, she faces her shadowed apartment, which isn't quite so intimidating now that she knows that last night's horrific dream was not a prophesy. "It's just . . . I've been so worried about you."

"I know."

"What are you doing now?"

"Standing in my apartment, looking into your eyes."

"A photo?"

"No. The eyes of the dragon."

"The tapestry." His voice sounds tired now, brittle as spun candy, and she worries that she's tugging on him in the wrong way. She's not sure exactly what they do in rehab and therapy, but she doesn't want to be an obstacle to Armand's recovery. "Pretend you really are looking into my eyes," he says. "What do you see?"

She switches on a lamp and the dragon tapestry fills the room with vivid color, its swirling composition no longer menacing at all. In fact, the image now has a sense of balance that has never been apparent to her before. "I see good fortune grounded by intense power. I see someone who takes his life very seriously."

"Go on . . ."

"I see a talented, brilliant musician."

"Now you're just trying to pump me up." He sounds tired.

"Get some sleep. I have to go search out fresh vegetables for Auntie Fang's special dish. You'll call me tomorrow?"

"'Tomorrow," he says, and she marvels that a single word could hold so much promise.

# CHAPTER 21

The minute he walks through the door, Sheila knows he's back. She sees it in the way he kneels down beside Katie and helps her speculate on the contents of a gift. The old Joe drops down on all fours with PJ, pretending to be a "peeze car" so PJ can ride his back with sirens whooping. And when he pulls Sheila into his arms and lifts her off her feet for a kiss that makes her giggle like a three-year-old . . .

Oh, yeah. Joe Cody, her Joe, is back.

"You're home early." Sheila wipes her lipstick from his mouth, then rises on her toes to kiss him again. "Smudged your lipstick a little."

He grins and swipes at his face. This time his smile radiates from his eyes, and the small laugh lines warm her better than a day at the beach. "It was pretty quiet, so the sergeant let a few of us go. Needless to say, I bolted out of there in record time."

Katie is spinning in circles around them, picking up gifts and dropping them at their feet. "Time for presents!" Her toothless smile is pure jubilation.

"In a minute, Katie." Sheila holds up a hand to her daughter, turns to Joe. "I'm dying to hear about your day. Last time we talked you were headed back to the precinct to find the paperwork on that kid who overdosed. So what did you find?"

"That's a long story." Joe's eyes are mysterious . . . dark, enigmatic gems. For a second Sheila flashes on how she ever landed a man so good looking.

"No, no! Don't talk now." Katie reaches up and yanks on her dad's arms. "We have to open presents! You can't inspect me to wait all day."

"No, pumpkin, we don't *expect* you to wait all day, but Mommy wants to talk to Daddy and . . ." Suddenly aware of the glimmering tree and piles of gifts and strings of garland and lights on the windows, Sheila stops herself. It's Christmas. What was she thinking?

"Katherine Bernadette Cody." Sheila folds her arms, her voice crisp. "Are you and your brother ready to begin opening your gifts?"

"Yes!" Katie jumps in the air, hugs her, then hurries over to start tearing at paper.

While Joe goes for the camera, Sheila sinks down to the floor and lures PJ over to open his mystery gift. As he tears into the paper, the conversation with her sister replays itself in Sheila's mind. No, Jen insisted, the gifts are not from her; she still has the Codys' gifts sitting under her own tree.

PJ peels off the paper and his jaw drops, his lips a round O of awe.

The gift is his heart's desire, his favorite shiny, bright icon.

"A peeze car!"

Amazed, Sheila grabs at the toy car, but PJ maneuvers away with it and walks it over to Daddy. "See Daddy?"

"A police car? Wow!" A gracious Joe knocks on the hood and hugs his son. "You must have been really good to get that from Santa."

PJ basks in joy for a moment, then takes to the floor with his new wheels.

Sheila points to their boy and mouths to Joe: "That's the one you tossed!"

He shrugs, then points the camera at PJ and snaps a shot. A-ha! Sheila is onto him. He's playing cool because he's the one behind the mystery gifts, after all.

Meanwhile, Katie drags herself away from two Dollar Store items that she "loves" to demand that Sheila open her mystery gift, which is surprisingly heavy. The wrapping flies away, and Sheila heaves off the lid to reveal a beautiful quilted down jacket in a rich shade of ruby red.

"Oh, my gosh, it's beautiful." She jumps up to slip her arms into the cushy sleeves. It fits her to a T, and it's so warm and just her color. And Lord knows she has needed a winter jacket. Layering sweaters just isn't warding off the cold anymore, but this . . . this is elegant and smart and so warm. "I love it."

She blinks back tears and hugs herself in the coat, feeling very loved for this moment. Then she spins toward Joe and wags her finger. "And you're in big trouble, Mister. We had a no-gift policy this year."

He shrugs. "Shee, I swear, I didn't get it for you. I wanted to. I saw it in the window of Macy's, but I knew it would be too much. We had a deal."

"Then who did? Who bought this?" Sheila throws her arms up, the new jacket stretching with her. She absolutely loves it, but if Joe didn't get it for her, who did?

Sheila and Joe share in their daughter's joy as she makes her way through the other gifts, grateful for each bubblemaker and white board. PJ hasn't touched another gift since he opened the police car, but that's okay with Sheila. You can't separate a boy from his heart's desire.

In the kitchen, Sheila checks the roast — a gift from that man at the Shuka, Mr. Boghosian. His delivery boy dropped it off with a card early this afternoon — something Sheila has to ask Joe about when they have a minute to talk. Sure beats the ham-potato soup she was planning to serve. Now there'll be roast beef and mashed potatoes. Jen is making a broccoli casserole, and Joe's brother Greg from Syracuse will undoubtedly bring some nice wine.

Ladling beef broth onto the roast, Sheila smiles over how much this Christmas has come together. When she spoke to her sister earlier, they made a deal for the new year that's going to work well for everyone. Jen is going to pay Sheila to watch little Ian during the work week, and now PJ will have a playmate around while Katie is at school. It will be a joy to watch the two cousins being raised as brothers for a while, a notion that chokes Sheila up when she thinks about how close they'll become. And the money Sheila will make in the process . . . well it's all a godsend. It'll give Joe and her some breathing room. No more money arguments. No more bursting into tears in the middle of a department store.

This family, this house, this Christmas . . . they are truly blessed.

"I just realized it's our first Christmas in this house," Sheila calls. "I hope your brother can find it. Did you give him directions, Joe?"

"He's a cop. He'll find it."

Sheila pops in a Christmas CD and heads back to the living room, where Katie is modeling her mystery gift — the beautiful handmade hat with braids.

"Gorgeous and warm, just what I wanted for you." Sheila kisses the top of her daughter's head. "And that points the finger back at Jen as the gift-giver."

Then Joe opens his package, and a half dozen pair of black socks spill out.

"That's not something Jen would buy." Sheila ducks back into the kitchen for a trash bag. "Sorry, honey, but it looks like you got the booby prize. Black socks?" She covers a giggle. "Okay, then."

"But I think it's a great gift." Joe holds up a packet of dark wool as if he were inspecting gold bullion. "Reinforced toes and heels, these are perfect. I've worn through my socks for work. Got holes in the heels. My pasty white toes stick out. It's kind of embarrassing in the locker room, but I didn't want to say anything. I mean, it's no big deal. Better to have a roof over our heads than to buy new socks, right? But these . . . these socks are a very thoughtful gift."

Sheila whips gift wrap into a bag, steps around Katie, who is setting her teacups up on the dining room table, and then nearly trips over PJ as he crawls by with his car.

Inside the living room she removes her smart red jacket and sinks onto the couch beside her husband. "So I suspect Mack did it," she says.

He slips an arm around her. "How about your sister?"

"She says no. She's bringing our presents over when they come for dinner."

"Then who gave us these gifts?" Joe asks.

"I don't know, but tell me what happened to you today. Did you pull out the paperwork from yesterday to show Mack?"

"Actually, we didn't get that far." He shifts, leaning against the arm of the couch so that she can see his face. "About halfway through the morning, I realized that I was wasting my time trying to convince everyone that a kid was dead. Instead, I decided to be proactive. I went to the apartment where we'd found his body, caught him before he went in. Mack and I took him to the hospital for treatment." He seems to be rethinking it as he tells the story. "At the end of the day, the kid was alive, reunited with his father. I still can't believe it. Well, I guess I can. He's alive, Sheila."

"Because of you."

"I'd like to think so, but really, I'm just glad that he's still here."

She hikes her knees onto the couch, grabs his shoulders, and gives him a shake. "Don't you see? That was it! It's the miracle I asked for."

"Easy." He laughs, steadying her with his hands. "You know, I love the way you leap to conclusions with the smallest crumb of evidence."

"Are you kidding me?" She whacks him on the shoulder. "Jesus, Mary, and Joseph, what's it going to take to make a believer out of you, Joe Cody? You wanted to make a difference, and you did! You saved a person's life, and I don't think we can begin to know how many people that affected. And maybe, just maybe, this kid will go on to make a difference in other people's lives. Maybe you can't conceive of all the good that will come of the action you took today."

"I hope you're right. I already talked to Jen about setting up an interview for Armand at Juilliard after he's out of rehab. She thinks she can make it happen for him."

"Nothing short of a miracle." Sheila shivers in awe. She fixes her gaze on her husband, her kind, courageous Joe. "You were part of a miracle, honey. I'm so proud of you."

He leans close and kisses her, lightly at first, then with more pressure, his lips prodding hers. Stung by desire, she closes her eyes and sinks into a happy sigh. Her Joe is back . . . her own hero.

When they come up for air, he cups her face gently. "You know, it's a good thing I have a wife I can talk to. I hated dumping on you last night, ruining your Christmas Eve with a story about a nineteen-year-old dying. But if I hadn't told you about it, I'd really think I was losing it."

She squints at him. "Mack really doesn't remember?"

"No. And neither did the EMS workers who pronounced Armand dead." He shakes his head. "You know, when I saw that kid walking down the street today, it was just this huge moment. Huge. He was all strung out, but he was *alive.* That's not something you appreciate every day." He sinks back on the couch. "It's an amazing day."

"It's an amazing life." She snuggles in beside him. "And you know what? What if you aren't the only one around here who is

623

privy to miracles?" She smoothes down the red jacket beside her. "I think we had a few miracles of our own here. A police car that repairs and wraps itself. A jacket and hat we can't afford. And those sexy black socks."

"I still think we have Jen to thank for all that."

"That's not fair! I believed in your miracle. Can't you give mine a little respect?"

"Okay, Shee. Nice miracles you got there."

She smacks his knee, but doesn't object when he presses a kiss into the sensitive spot under her ear. She closes her eyes, wondering about the gifts. Maybe it was Jen.

Or maybe some things defy explanation.

Small miracles.

# ABOUT THE AUTHORS

**Fern Michaels** is the *USA Today* and *New York Times* bestselling author of *Razor Sharp, Final Justice, Collateral Damage, Up Close and Personal, Fool Me Once, Sweet Revenge, The Jury, Payback, Weekend Warriors, The Nosy Neighbor, Pretty Woman*, and dozens of other novels and novellas. There are over seventy million copies of her books in print.

Fern Michaels has built and funded several large daycare centers in her hometown, and is a passionate animal lover who has outfitted police dogs across the country with special bulletproof vests. She shares her home in South Carolina with her five dogs and a resident ghost named Mary Margaret. Visit her website at www.fernmichaels.com.

**Marie Bostwick** was born and raised in the Northwest. Since marrying the love of her life twenty-four years ago, she has never known a moment's boredom. Marie and her family have moved a score of times, living in eight U.S. states and two Mexican cities, and collecting a vast and cherished array of friends and experiences. Marie has three handsome sons and now lives with her husband in Connecticut where she writes, reads, quilts, and is active in her local church.

A Kentucky native, **Janna McMahan** now lives in Columbia, South Carolina with her husband and their daughter. Many of Janna's stories are set in the lush hills and farmland of the Bluegrass state and the swamps, beaches, and marshlands of the Lowcountry. Janna is the winner of the South Carolina Fiction Project, the Piccolo Spoleto Fiction Open, the Harriette Arnow Award from the Appalachian Writers Association, and the Fiction Prize from the Kentucky Women Writers Conference. Her short stories and non-fiction have been published in various journals and magazines including *Arts Across Kentucky, Wind, Limestone, The Nantahala Review, StorySouth, Alimentum, South Carolina Homes & Gardens, Skirt!, Appalachian Journal, Charleston,* and Knight-Ridder newspapers.

**Rosalind Noonan** is a former editor and copywriter for various book publishers. She has studied writing for screen and theater at The New School. Her first novel, *One September Morning,* was published in 2009. She currently lives in the Pacific Northwest with her husband and two children.